Catherine Cookson was born in Tyne Dock, the illegitimate daughter of a poverty-stricken woman. K~ she believed to be her older sister c¹ ce but eventually moved d married a local gramn she began writing ab people with whom she i .f birth as the background ..s.

Although originally accla...ied as a regional writer – her novel *The Round Tower* won the Winifred Holtby award for the best regional novel of 1968 – her readership soon began to spread throughout the world. Her novels have been translated into more than a dozen languages and more than 50,000,000 copies of her books have been sold in Corgi alone. Thirteen of her novels have been made into successful television dramas, and more are planned.

Catherine Cookson's many bestselling novels have established her as one of the most popular of contemporary women novelists. After receiving an OBE in 1985, Catherine Cookson was created a Dame of the British Empire in 1993. She and her husband Tom now live near Newcastle-upon-Tyne.

'Catherine Cookson's novels are about hardship, the intractability of life and of individuals, the struggle first to survive and next to make sense of one's survival. Humour, toughness, resolution and generosity are Cookson virtues, in a world which she often depicts as cold and violent. Her novels are weighted and driven by her own early experiences of illegitimacy and poverty. This is what gives them power. In the specialised world of women's popular fiction, Cookson has created her own territory'
Helen Dunmore, *The Times*

Books by Catherine Cookson

THE BONDAGE OF LOVE

Catherine Cookson

CORGI BOOKS

THE BONDAGE OF LOVE
A CORGI BOOK : 0552145335
9780552145336

Originally published in Great Britain by Bantam Press,
a division of Transworld Publishers Ltd

PRINTING HISTORY
Bantam Press edition published 1997
Corgi edition published 1998

5 7 9 10 8 6 4

Set in 11/13pt Sabon by
Phoenix Typesetting, Ilkley, West Yorkshire.

Corgi Books are published by Transworld Publishers,
61–63 Uxbridge Road, London W5 5SA,
a division of The Random House Group Ltd,
in Australia by Random House Australia (Pty) Ltd,
20 Alfred Street, Milsons Point, Sydney, NSW 2061, Australia,
in New Zealand by Random House New Zealand Ltd,
18 Poland Road, Glenfield, Auckland 10, New Zealand
and in South Africa by Random House (Pty) Ltd,
Isle of Houghton, Corner of Boundary Road & Carse O'Gowrie,
Houghton 2198, South Africa.

Printed and bound in Great Britain by Clays Ltd, St Ives PLC

To Norreen

Who, for the past sixteen years, has kept my abode bright and has lightened many a dark day with her mirth. I say, with deep regard, thank you.

PART ONE

Prologue

It had begun between Katie Bailey and Sammy Love on the day Sammy's father, Davey, was buried. It was then that Sammy, aiming to comfort Katie, told her that his father had asked him to talk to her.

Having had a private weep in his bedroom, Sammy went across to Katie's room and told her just that, that he had been bidden by his father to talk to her because she was lonely. And it was strange that Katie should be grateful to him, for, if not bitter enemies, they had been antagonists for some years, ever since Willie, Katie's younger brother, became attached to Sammy Love, a common, loud-mouthed, swearing, brash nine-year-old. The association had disrupted the family, and upset Willie's mother, Fiona.

Fiona was of the middle class and, naturally, she did not wish any of her children to associate with such as Sammy Love, an urchin from Bog's End, whose father had done time in Durham jail. But this wily youngster had proved himself of some worth when he saved Bill Bailey's life, and thereafter had been welcomed into the family circle, as, in a way, his father had.

Davey Love, a big, seemingly gormless Irishman who made everyone laugh each time he opened his mouth, had become so beloved of the family that he had been brought into their home to spend his last days. And during those days, everyone in this house had felt the better for his presence: from little Angela, Bill's and Fiona's Down's syndrome daughter; up through Mamie, their adopted daughter, who is now nine years old; Willie who is twelve; Katie fourteen and Mark sixteen; and to Mrs Vidler, Fiona's mother, who had been Bill's deadly enemy up to a short while ago, when that lady's character was definitely changed by a dramatic event; and last, but certainly not least, to Bert and Nell Ormesby. Nell, who, some years previously through her own tragedy, had become a helper and companion to Fiona, and Bert who was one of Bill's workmen. These completed the close family, and there was not one of their lives but had been touched by the big, ungainly, loud-mouthed, but wise Irishman.

On that particular day Katie definitely had needed comfort for she had been almost ostracised, at least by her stepfather Bill, for being the means of severing a close friendship between him and Rupert Medrith, a relative of Sir Charles Kingdom, the man who had helped to put Bill where he was today in the building world.

Katie had been only thirteen at the time when, in

a mad fit of jealousy after having found Rupert, for whom she had an almost adult love, naked in bed with his girlfriend in her cottage adjacent to the grounds of Bill's house, she had almost brained her with a heavy wooden bowl. It had just missed the young woman's eye. She had also left her mark on Rupert, as he had eventually turned on her by dragging her by her hair and throwing her outside on to the ash path.

From that day, Rupert had naturally cut all connection with the house. But, as he still worked as manager of a garage Bill had, the two men continued to meet.

Bill could not forgive Katie for what she had done: he had valued Rupert's friendship, for it had stemmed from Sir Charles and Lady Kingdom, and had, in a way, become stronger after Sir Charles had died.

But on the day of Davey Love's funeral, among the throng of people outside the church, Rupert had spoken to Fiona for the first time since the event, and because Katie was standing by her side, after some hesitation, he had said, 'Hello, Katie.'

Staring back at him she had answered simply, 'Hello,' and at the same time she had wondered why she had been so silly all that time ago. What had been this feeling that had driven her almost mad with jealousy? What had it been all about? Next to loving Rupert, she had loved Bill, and so his subsequent ignoring of her had thrown her into deep misery, and she rarely spoke to anyone except in monosyllables.

But on that day when they returned from the funeral, there stood Bill in the hallway of the splendid house of which he was justly proud. And he looked at her, the stepchild he had loved most of all in his adopted family, and she had looked at him and when she cried from the depths of her, 'Oh, Dad! Oh, Dad! I'm sorry. I'm sorry,' he swept her into his arms. And as Fiona and the rest of the family looked on, they all knew a great welcoming sense of relief. Life would return to normal.

It was after Katie had dashed upstairs, also to end her spate of weeping, that Sammy Love had knocked on her door, and she had looked at him as if she had never seen him before. He was two years younger than her, yet he had always seemed much older. He wasn't as tall as her and he was very thin, wiry her dad called him. That was another thing that had made her dislike him and go for him at every possible opportunity, because her dad seemed to love him. In fact, she knew he considered him not only as one of the family, now that he was to live with them, but had always thought him someone very special, even when he cursed and used four-letter words.

Then there was Willie. Willie had stuck to Sammy like a limpet all these years. He couldn't breathe without Sammy. She recalled there had been rows in the house because of Willie's determination to be friends with this boy. What was it about him that made people want to be friends with him? Perhaps it was the same quality that his father had possessed, only in a larger quantity. You couldn't say he was good-looking. She had never noticed his eyes before, except whilst they were having a slanging match, when they had looked like round black marbles. For a boy, they were large eyes and longish lashes, but his nose was over big, as was his mouth. He had what she supposed one would call a blunt face, from which his chin seemed at times to stick out.

When she had felt his hand in hers she had experienced a queer sensation. It was as if she were younger than him: he being fourteen, coming fifteen, and she only twelve coming thirteen.

On that day she knew that she would miss Mr Love. She had been able to talk to him and she had discovered he wasn't thick as everybody imagined him to be. He was funny and said things back to front, and he made you laugh, and you always seemed better for having him near. Yet, as she had looked at his son, she had thought, the mind was a stupid thing: it made you love somebody to distraction, then dislike them for having humbled you; or, as in Sammy's case, here she was beginning to like him when the only feeling she had had for him up till now had been disdain. When would one know where one was, if things like that could happen to you? But they were still holding hands as they went down the stairs. And when they both realised what the family might have to say about this apparent association, they quickly disengaged, and such was their understanding of one another now that they could openly laugh at it.

I

It was less than a month after Davey's funeral that the friendship between Katie and Sammy caused the first squall in the otherwise normal life of the household. Bill was up in the playroom having his daily half-hour with his daughter. He had picked her up and was once more extolling her progress at modelling. Nell and Bert, with their new baby, had been brought up to view his daughter's latest masterpiece. It was quite a good clay copy of a stuffed poodle the child had got in her stocking and to which she was very attached.

Bill stood at one side of the low table and pointed his finger towards his wife and said, 'Now don't tell me, Mrs B, that has come about by chance, or that somebody's helped her, because she was just sticking the bits on when I came in.'

'I never said a word.' Fiona spread out her hands as she looked at her friend Nell. 'And yes, it's a very good copy. Who's arguing with you, Mr B?' She stressed the name.

'Well,' – Bill was addressing Bert who was bouncing his 'gift from God', as he called his new son, up and down in his arms – 'she always has a query in her voice. Oh! to the devil. Come on, pet, let's downstairs. I've been in this house for over an hour and nobody's asked me if I have a mouth on me.'

'I did ask you if you wanted a cup of tea,' Nell put in now, 'but you said you wanted something stronger right away. Did you have it?'

'Yes, I had it, missis. But now I'd like a cup of tea.'

They were all laughing as they made for the nursery door; but it was pushed open before they reached it, and there stood Mark. His face looked tight and his head was bobbing as he said, 'Dad, there's ructions going on in the recreation room. As you know, my room's above that and I can't concentrate. It's Willie and Katie again, but more Willie by the sound of it. Something should be done with him, he's getting beyond it.'

'Have you looked in?'

'No, I haven't, because had I done so I would likely have used more than my tongue. I'm getting fed up with that crew. There's no peace. How d'you expect me to work?'

Bill's head drooped, Fiona turned hers to the side, but neither of them said anything. Yet, on the landing the glance they cast at each other told of their combined thoughts: there were plenty of corners in this big house that Mark could go and be on his own. But Mark had a bedroom to himself, and what was at one time a dressing room adjacent was now his study; and you couldn't expect a young man studying for exams to go and find a quiet corner, if he had a study all his own, now could you?

The commotion in the recreation room, which was at the far end of the downstairs floor, reached them as they descended into the hall. There they were met by a glee-faced Mamie, who exclaimed loudly, 'Oh, they are fighting, fighting like billy-o. And Sammy tipped Katie up and threw her on to the ground.'

'Wh . . . at!' Bill and Fiona spoke simultaneously. Then they were all hurrying along the corridor. And when they burst into the recreation room Willie was yelling, 'Why did you keep it to yourself all this time? You could tell her, why not me?'

Seemingly unaware of the visitors, Sammy replied, 'I've only recently told her. And why I didn't tell you was because I wanted to keep some things to meself. D'you understand? No, you wouldn't; you're too thick-headed. You've had it too easy, you have.'

'Here! Here! Now, look here! What's all this about?' Bill put Angela down on to the floor and, turning to Sammy, he demanded, 'What's happened? And why has he had it too easy? And what have you been keeping to yourself that he thinks he should know?'

Sammy's face was scarlet, his mouth was tight, then bitterly he said, 'I've always kept Thursday nights to meself.'

'Yes. Yes, lad, I know.' Bill's voice was meant to have a calming effect. 'You went to confession on a Thursday night, always; you still do.'

'Yes, I still do, but confession doesn't take up all Thursday night: I did something else after, which I've kept to meself.'

'Well, whatever this was, did your dad know?'

'Yes, he knew, and he said it was right: a fella should have something to himself, a space like, where you haven't to give an account of what you've been doing or whom you've been talking to.'

Bill nodded quietly now, saying, 'Yes. Yes, I understand that. Well, it's no use asking you, is it, what else you did on a Thursday night?'

'Yes, you can ask.'

'Now! Now!' Bill's voice changed. 'Don't you use that tone to me. You know me and I know you.'

Sammy's head drooped and a muttered 'Sorry,' came from his tight lips. Then looking at his stepson, Bill said, 'What's this all about, Willie?'

'Only because I was going with him.' Katie's voice was quiet, even flat, and they all stared at her in silence until she went on, 'Sammy suggested I should join a club or take up a sport of some kind, tennis or some such. And I said to him, he was the one to talk, he didn't take up anything, he didn't even like football or cricket. And it was then he told me and said I could go with him if I liked, on Thursday night.'

'Go with him? Where to, Katie?' Fiona was standing by her daughter now, and Katie looked up at her as she said, 'The Fickleworth Sport and Leisure Centre.'

Fiona glanced at Bill, whose face was stretching. He was looking at Sammy again. 'You've been going to the Fickleworth Centre?' he said.

'Aye . . . yes.'

'How long for?'

'On two years.'

Bill nodded. 'You went after you'd been to confession?'

'Yes, that's what I did.'

'What have you taken up?'

'Judo.'

'Judo!'

'That's what I said, and a bit of karate. And I thought Katie could take karate up because it's self-defence if she's attacked or anything. You never know. You do it with the flat of your hand, like this,' and he demonstrated.

'Wait a moment! You didn't . . . you threw her on her back.'

Now Sammy was bawling again, 'I was showing her what to do; and I didn't hurt her. Did I? You learn to throw at judo and learn to fall. And I helped her to fall.'

'My! My!' The two words came from the open door where Mark was standing. He was looking at Sammy and, nodding at him now, he said, 'True? You do judo?'

'Yes; yes, Mark, I do judo.'

'All right. All right. Don't get your hair out. I was just going to say, it's a good thing. There's a fella in my form, he has a black belt. Are you in the Newcastle club?'

'No, I'm not in the Newcastle club, Mark, I'm in the Fickleworth Centre.'

'But that's . . . well, that's in Bog's End.'

'It isn't in Bog's End.' It was Bill speaking now. 'It's on the south side of Bog's End, and it's a very fine place, let me tell you.'

'Nobody's arguing with you, Dad.'

'No, they're not,' Fiona put in now, 'so don't you start. Well now, may I say something?' But even as she spoke she knew how silly the question would sound. 'Why are you making all this fuss? I think it's a marvellous thing that Katie should take up a defensive sport.'

'It isn't a defensive sport; they're all cissies!'

'Now, now, now.' Bill's hand went out towards Sammy. 'Hold it! Hold it, both of you. As for you, Willie Bailey, you're an ignoramus, and so is anyone else who says that karate and judo are for cissies. Football is and cricket is. Oh yes, cricket is, compared with them. Yes, definitely. But we're not on about the merit of games, are we, Willie? It's because you've got the pip that Sammy dare ask Katie to go along to the Centre. Now, in a way, I can understand that, because he hasn't asked you.'

'I have. I did months ago. But I didn't tell him where or what. I asked him if he would like to take up fencing or such, and he laughed his head off. Another cissie game, you know, fencing. And Katie's told me she's always wanted to take up fencing.'

Bill lowered his head. Yes, Katie would. But foils would be no good to Katie if she ever got into one of her rages again; it would have to be sabres. And he knew a bit about fencing himself. He had done some a few years ago, but hadn't stuck at it. It was too complicated, your feet and all that. He looked at Sammy again and asked quietly, 'What else d'you do?'

'I took up fencing first. I still do a bit now and again. But there's always a crowd waiting their turn.' He nodded at Bill now. 'It might be near Bog's End, but it's well attended, not only by them that come from that end either. And I know three who have left the Newcastle club' – he now bounced his head towards Mark – 'and joined the fencing at the Centre.'

'It's a fine place.' Bert spoke for the first time. His child was lying quiet in his arms now, and he repeated, 'It is, it's a fine place. It's done more good for this town than anything else: it's made decent citizens out of hooligans.'

Bill now looked at Bert and said, 'You know it well? Have you done any work there?'

'Yes. Yes, Bill, I've done quite a bit of work there with young swimmers and boxing. They've got a fine ring.'

'Well! Well! Well!' Bill's head was moving from side to side; then it stopped and he looked at Sammy again and said, 'Did you say you still go to confession on a Thursday night? Well, we're hearing some confessions tonight. Let them all come here.' Again he was looking at Bert and saying, 'You know, you are a dark horse.'

'I don't see how you make that out, Bill. Where d'you think I spent all my bachelor evenings? I'm not a drinker, and some of the television I found an insult to my intelligence. I didn't waste whole evenings on that. So what did I do? I went down to the Centre and enjoyed myself: seeing hooligans off the street corner taking a pride in themselves; teaching them how to box, not to bash somebody's face in, but to give them self-confidence and to help others. The boxing helped more that way than the swimming did, because, you know, you get nothing out of swimming, apart from pleasure for yourself. I know that.'

'And it's free, I understand?'

'Yes, you understand aright, for them that can't pay. But for the likes of our friends Samuel there and Katie and such, if they can pay they are expected to. I think it's five pounds a year to join.'

'Oh, we can never reach that.' Bill was shaking his head and making an effort to put a lightness on the situation. But looking at Willie, he saw this was going to be difficult and he made the mistake of saying, 'Let Sammy show you how it's done. If he can toss Katie, he can toss you and then you might like to—'

'And I mightn't like to go, and he's not going to do it to me. If he wants to go out with her let him go, but I'm not going to be made an idiot of.' And at this he pushed past Nell, almost overbalancing Angela, and stalked from the room.

'Oh, you've done it this time, Sammy.'

'I've done nothing I'm ashamed of Mr Bill, or that I regret. I thought Katie needed . . . well, something, and that's why I told her.'

'You did right. You did right, Sammy.' Fiona

was nodding at him, and now she appealed to her daughter, 'And . . . and you would like to take up something like this, Katie?'

'Yes, Mam, I would like it very much. But I'm sorry that in a way it's caused trouble between,' – she looked at Sammy now and added – 'well, will you try to make it up with him?'

'No. Oh, no. As me da said—' Sammy's head drooped now and he didn't finish or repeat what his da had said, but the adults knew that he must have got tired at times of Willie's possessiveness and so had talked it over with his father; and the Thursday night escape from Willie's domination had to be safeguarded.

'I'll speak to him.' They all stared at Katie, this Katie who seemed so different, for there had been a constant war raging between her and Willie since they were children. After Angela had come on the scene, there had been a respite, but it had worn thin at times. It just showed you, Fiona thought, you never knew your children, not really. She could never imagine her wilful, hot-headed, stubborn Katie apologising in any way to her brother.

Some similar thoughts were going through Katie's mind as she went up the stairs and along the broad corridor to Willie's room: she hesitated for a full minute before she knocked. When there was no answer, she knocked again, louder this time, and when it was pulled open there stood her red-faced, wet-eyed brother, and he barked at her straightaway, 'What d'you want?'

'I'll tell you if you let me in.' Her answer was so

unexpected that he turned himself about and walked back into the room. She followed, closing the door quietly behind her.

She watched him go and sit before his desk that was placed below the window. He picked up one of the three books lying there and banged it down on the desk again. And then her voice came to him, saying, 'I'm sorry, Willie. I wouldn't have said I would like to go if I had thought it would cause this trouble between you. And . . . and I can tell you, he only asked me because . . . well, he's sorry for me. He's been sorry for me for the past year or so, when Dad wouldn't speak to me and I was in everybody's black books. And I was feeling terrible inside because I knew I might have killed that girl and of what it would have done, not only to me, but to the family. It did enough to us all, I know, and Sammy was just sorry for me.'

He swung round now on his chair, but his voice was low as he said, 'We've been close pals for years.'

'Yes. Yes, I know that, Willie, nobody closer. You were like brothers, and it was you who fought . . . well, that is, practically fought with Mam so that he could be invited to the house, because she would have nothing of him at first. It was only when he saved Dad from those would-be murderers that she took to him. But . . . but you stuck to him all the time. I know . . . I know how you feel.' She watched his head droop and when he muttered brokenly, 'He . . . he won't have anything to do with me now, not after this, and he'll have you.'

Her voice rose. 'He won't have me. All he's doing is taking me to this place and introducing me to the karate teacher. And I think it's a good thing to know about defence, because . . . because one or two of our girls have been followed. But anyway, if you won't be friends with him again or won't come along with us to this place, then I won't go.'

'Oh, you'll have to now. You've started this. Well, I mean, no . . . well, you didn't start this, he did. And I won't forget he's kept it to himself all this time. He should have told me.'

'Yes,' she nodded at him, 'in a way I think he should. Perhaps,' she tried to explain, 'it was because the place is so near Bog's End and he didn't want you or the family to think he was mixing with anyone down there. You see, his father was very proud, you know, when you befriended him.'

He stood up now and rubbed the end of his thumb across his mouth before he said, 'Did he hurt you when he toppled you over?'

'No. But I can tell you it was a surprise; funny, really. It wasn't being thrown on the floor, it was the way he did it. He says I shouldn't go in for that, not really. Well, not at first; ju-jitsu is better. It's odd' – she was smiling at him now – 'but he says it means "the gentle touch", or "the soft touch".'

They were now looking at each other rather sheepishly until she asked quietly, 'Will you come with us? Because I do want to take up something outside school.'

He looked to the side as if considering; then he muttered, 'I'll see. But mind,' – his head jerked round now – 'I'm not taking up any of those fool things.'

'No. No,' she quickly agreed with him. 'You can just have a look round, as I will, the first time.' There was another pause; then she said, 'Come on down.' But to this he replied quickly, 'No, I can't, not yet, Katie. Already I feel ridiculous. I'm always ridiculous, aren't I? Aren't I?' His voice had risen. 'When I think about it I know I am, or have been, for the way I've clung on to that thick-headed Irish dolt downstairs. I . . . I've put him first in everything.'

'Oh, he knows that and appreciates it. And, as I said before, if it hadn't been for you he wouldn't be here today. He's said as much.'

'He has?'

'Oh yes. Yes.' It was good to lie in someone else's defence. It sort of made one feel better with one's self. And now she went on, 'He wouldn't say it to you, but it's come out when we've been going at it hammer and tongs . . . he and I, I mean.'

Willie was shaking his head, and so she said, 'When you come down and go into the recreation-room again, all the others should be in the drawing-room. If he's not in the recreation-room, he'll come along.'

He made no reply to this but simply stared at her; and she nodded at him and smiled, then turned about and went downstairs.

Her mother was coming out of the drawing-room pushing Mamie before her and saying, 'I am not sewing spangles on that dress. It's a pretty dress, a party dress, and you're only going to a party.'

'Nancy has spangles all over hers.'

'I don't care what Nancy has, you're not having spangles. I'm not putting spangles on that dress.'

'Why?'

Fiona drew in a deep breath. She never thought there would come a time when she would dislike her adopted daughter, but over the past two years she had become a trial. Since she was small, she had always wanted her own way, but from the time she knew she had money of her own, which was in the care of her grandfather, she had become . . . well, the only word for it was obnoxious. She was an obnoxious little girl. And so Fiona looked gratefully at Katie when the answer came from her, 'Because spangles make things look cheap, miss,' she said.

'They don't! They don't! Nancy looks lovely.'

'Don't you bark at me!'

'Huh! You!' The indignant figure made for the stairs now, muttering as she went, and her mutter brought a bark from Fiona, saying, 'Don't you dare, miss, come out with your grandfather's piece again. I've told you before, if you want to go and live with your grandfather that's all right with me and everybody in this house. So get that into your head. Any time you like I'll pack your bags.'

'I wouldn't worry about her, Mam. She wants her ears boxed. I bet, if they were counted up, she's got more clothes than you, me and Angela put together.'

'You may be right there.'

In the drawing-room Bill voiced Katie's sentiments, only more strongly, when he said to Fiona, 'She wants her backside scudded, that one, and I'll be the one to do it before long, I'm telling you. There's one thing certain, she doesn't take after her mother or father. I sometimes think it's a pity she didn't go with them when the car went up.'

'Oh, Bill.'

'Never mind, oh, Bill,' – his finger was pointing at Fiona – 'you're the one that has to put up with her: keep your tongue quiet and use your hands. See if that'll make any difference.'

Nell put in now, 'Is it that Miss Nancy has got something new?'

'Spangles.'

'Spangles?'

'Yes, spangles. Apparently she's got a dress that's all spangles, and madam wants some put on her party dress.'

'Oh, that's a lovely dress. You mean the last one?'

'I suppose it's the last one; I don't know. But it's one of her party dresses. She's had three in the last year.'

'Funny that,' said Bill, nodding as if to himself. 'The old fella can send money galore for her clothes, but he's quibbling at paying her school fees. And I don't know what he'll do next year or so when she moves up, because they'll be trebled. In his last letter the old bloke asked if that kind of school was necessary, for there was good education all round these days. By the way, that family, what kind of people are they? She's been going to tea every Friday there for months now, hasn't she?'

'Yes, but you met her at the parents do; you were talking to her, remember? She said her name was Mrs Polgar, but that she was usually called Gertie.'

'Oh yes. Yes, of course, I remember. Very chatty. Smart, not bad-looking either.' He now turned slightly to the side and winked at Bert, and Bert's unexpected reply brought laughter from both Fiona and Nell, while Bill said, 'You watch it, boy. Watch it.' For what Bert said was, 'With a name like Gertie to go with the spangles she's passed on to her daughter, she should be just up your street, boss.'

'Let's get out, Bert,' Nell said hurriedly. 'We've outstayed our welcome. Be seeing you, Fiona.'

'Bye-bye, Fiona.'

Fiona nodded at Bert the while still laughing; and Bill, calling after them almost in a yell now, cried, 'And if either of you want to enter this house again, ask for an appointment.'

'Will do. Will do.' They both turned and nodded at him, their faces serious now. 'Yes, sir, we'll do that.' 'Goodbye,' added Bert now, 'and the best of the rest of the weekend to you, sir.'

When the door closed on them, Bill threw his head back and said, 'Talk about people changing; there's a change in a man if you ever saw one. He's a dark horse, you know. He's got a lot up top that I never dreamed of. I'm . . . I'm going to put him on the board.' The latter was said casually as he stooped down and lifted Angela from the rug, where she had been playing with her poodle. And, dropping on to the couch with her, he added, 'He's worth it.'

'Oh! Oh, Bill.' Fiona sat down close beside him, then put her hand on his cheek and turned his face towards her and added, 'At times, you know, I like you very much. When I don't love you, I like you. But when I love you and like you at the same time, I like you very much, Mr Bailey. Nell will be over the moon.'

'Aye, I bet she will, and he'll get the surprise of his life. Oh, he'll say he can't do it, that he's not fit for that kind of position. And my answer to that'll be, I wasn't at one time either. But look at me now.'

'Yes, look at you now. That was a wonderful piece in the paper yesterday about the houses, and from an unsolicited quarter. "*Bailey's homes will be hard to beat.*" And they went on to describe the mosaic that woman's having in her flat.'

'Huh!' He laughed now. 'She's a marler that one, she must be a millionaire; two or three times over, I would think. She's paid for half the place now and she's always urging me to hurry; she wants to get in. But I have to tell her, "No, madam, we can't hurry." As for the mosaic, she's having it brought from Italy, and two Italians to put it down. It will be all over her private hall. I nearly suggested her doing the main hall with it, too, but I didn't. Anyway, it'll be like a palace before it's finished. And I think that's what the bloke who wrote that piece saw; and it's only half done.'

'Has she got a big family?'

'I don't know anything about her family, love, but I know that she's got three dogs, two of them are as big as ponies. The third one, a little Pekingese, would go in a pint pot, and it rides on the back of one of the other Afghans. And I've got another piece of news for you.'

'Well, spill it, Mr B.'

'We're invited to the Hunt Ball.'

'Oh! Well, that isn't earth-shattering, but it's very nice.'

'Yes, it's very nice, especially when the invitation came from Mr George Ferndale.'

'Ferndale, the barrister?'

'No other, and one of the chief men in Sir Charles's trust. They are the power above the board, if you get me.'

'I get you. Did you accept?'

'I thanked him and said yes. And he said his wife would be getting in touch with us.'

'Oh, that's nice. I hope she calls.'

'So do I.' They bowed their heads politely at each other, then laughed. And musingly now, Fiona said, 'It's fantastic. You're fantastic, the things you've done.'

'You're not taking into account, Mrs B, the things I'm going to do. This pleasant lot should last for three years or so. In the meantime I'll have to look further afield because there's no more big plots left in Fellburn or on the outskirts, as far as I can gather. And I wouldn't likely ever be able to take this crew again with me, but whatever I do, dear, I must look after my lads. You see, I look upon them as family, eleven of them; I feel I've brought them up. They're all in good positions now and they thanked me in their own way, such as calling me, behind my back, "Big Bill Bawling Bailey".'

'That's a new one.' She was shaking now.

'Well, it used to be just "Bawling Bailey", but now it's Big Bill. I suppose I should take it as an honour, you know, MA, or D.Litt., like the square-heads have after their names.'

She leant forward now and slowly stroked Angela's hair away from her brow and laughing eyes as she said, 'I was just thinking yesterday of the burden our lot are on you. Well, not quite a burden, but there's four of them, including Sammy, of course. And by the look of it Mark is quite determined to go in for medicine in rather a big way, not just as an ordinary doctor; he's got the idea of being a surgeon.'

'A surgeon? Ah, I hadn't heard that bit. But then again I couldn't see him being an ordinary doctor; he would never be able to acquire the bedside manner; he would be like ours, who marches into this house, comes up to the bed and says, "What's the matter with you?"'

Fiona laughed and said, 'Yes, he does, always. But he's wonderful, nevertheless.'

'Aye. Aye. He's been wonderful about her.' Bill now outlined the shape of his daughter's face with his first finger. The mongol look wasn't prominent, but it was there, and no-one, not even Dr Pringle, was able to convince him that her mind wasn't normal, in fact was even superior to those of some children of her age and that she would grow up and develop like any other child.

Fiona was saying now, 'But he's well aware that when he leaves the Royal Grammar next year he'll have perhaps up to ten years slogging before him. And it'll have to be paid for. He says' – she now glanced at Bill – 'he'd like to do his training in London if possible, there or Edinburgh. But I've already pointed out to him that the living in London would be terribly expensive. Yes, he said, he knew and he didn't know how he was going to approach you.'

'So he told you to soften me up, eh?'

'No. No, he didn't. It wasn't like that at all. It's very rarely you see him at his desk without his head down. I found him moping and he said he was wondering what he should really do. You see there is the medical school here, and apparently a very good one, but London and Edinburgh, of course, have built up their reputations over a long period. He feels he should stay here.'

'Oh, does he? Just to save expense? Well, when you next find him moping, you can hint to him to forget about the expense. But I'll expect him to pay me back and look after me in me old age.'

She put her arm around his neck, and he said, 'Look out, woman! And stop making love to me in front of the child. She takes everything in, you know. Don't you, love?'

'Da . . . da. Mum . . . mum.'

'Yes, there you are. That's plain enough for you, isn't it, da . . . da, and mum . . . mum? You say yourself you hardly spoke a word until you were five. Anyway, that's Mark settled. Now there's only the others. The other two males are at Dame Allan's and it'll be some time before you've got to worry about them. You know, I'll always think it was another nice thing that Sammy did when he, too, had the choice between Dame Allan's and the Royal Grammar School and he picked Dame Allan's, as Willie had done, knowing there would always have been his big brother's reputation to contend with at the Royal Grammar.'

It was odd, Fiona thought, that he always found and put forward Sammy's good deeds. He rarely pointed out those of Mark or Willie. But then they rarely did the same kind of things that Sammy did, unselfish things. A tiny spark of jealousy caused her to think, he loves that boy better than he does mine. But then, she musn't forget he owed much more to Sammy than he did to either of hers. And again, Sammy was but a replica of himself as a boy and a young lad, with the quick-fire and brash tongue.

Kissing her quickly on the lips before thrusting the child onto the rug again, he said, 'I'm off into the office, but I promise you, only an hour. In the meantime, look up your posh magazines and pick on some highfalutin shop where you can go and get a dress. But not, mind,' – he was wagging his finger at her now – 'with spangles on.'

She did not speak until he had gone through the

doorway and was about to close the door, when she said quite calmly, 'Just might at that.'

For answer he turned and gave her a long look, pushed the door wider and then banged it closed. And she sat back and thought, yes, she would like to put a spangle on her dress, metaphorically speaking that is. Here she was, thirty-six years old, she was bringing up three males and three females and a man who demanded all her love, and had sworn to her and meant it when he told her what he would do if she ever looked at another man. She had this beautiful house. She had everything that any sensible woman would want, would dream of. Yet there was . . . *what*? She didn't know, only that when Rupert used to drop in they talked about different things, not about children or house-building. She couldn't remember the gist of their conversations only that they were pleasant. His presence stretched her mind; that was it.

She shuffled to the front of the couch. That indeed was it, stretching one's mind. Her life was such that her husband was doing everything for her and she was doing everything for her children, but nothing for herself. Why shouldn't she take up something? Oh dear. Oh dear. She shook her head: she could hear Bill; his roar was deafening her even now. As she said, hadn't she everything? Six kids and him, a beautiful house, a mother who had changed character, friends like Nell and Bert, she went out to dinner at posh restaurants, she had been invited to the Hunt Ball.

But that spot in her mind said, so what?

2

'Look! It's all right going in by bus, but what about coming back? It'll be dark.' Fiona was addressing Sammy, the while Katie and Willie stood looking on, both knowing the argument that Sammy was about to put forward, because they had been all over it.

And now he was saying, 'Look, Mrs B. All right, we'll go halves; you can pick us up somewhere coming back. But if you were to drive us to those doors in a car, well, I'd lose some of my friends.'

'What d'you mean, you'd lose some of your friends?'

'Just what I say, Mrs B. To them I'd become toffee-nosed.'

'Don't be silly, Sammy. I bet every one of those that go there, they've got a car. At least, their parents have.'

'Oh, that's where you're wrong, Mrs B. Every one of them hasn't got a car. And many of those that have . . . well, you wouldn't call them cars, not even bangers.'

They looked at each other, then she said quietly, 'Is it such a rough part?'

'No. It's not rough at all. Well, what I mean is, not like the middle of Bog's End. It isn't in Bog's End, it's well out of it.'

'But, as you said yourself, Sammy, the *patrons*' – she stressed the word – 'are mostly from that quarter.'

'Yes. Yes, they are.' There was an edge to his voice now and his chin came out. And on this Fiona said quickly, 'All right! All right! Don't get on your high horse, Sammy Love.' She pushed him playfully in the shoulder, and at this he doubled his fist and gave the impression he was returning her gesture as he said, 'Fair enough. We'll bus there and ride back. You know where my old school is, Mrs B, don't you? You once deigned to come and view it' – he pulled a face at her – 'and you found your son' – he thumbed towards Willie – 'waiting outside. Oh! That was a day, wasn't it, Willie?' And Willie answered, 'I'll say.'

Since the flare-up on Saturday, Willie had been very quiet, and it was only as a concession that he was accompanying them tonight; and as he had emphasised strongly, he wasn't going to fall in with any of their ideas. And at this Sammy had said, well, he could be assured that nobody there would force him because there were queues waiting to take up every sport.

As they made for the door, Fiona said to Katie, 'Keep your collar up, dear, it's cold out there. And . . . and you haven't got a scarf on.'

'I've got this roll-neck sweater on underneath,

Mam; there was no room for a scarf.' She smiled at Fiona, and Fiona said quietly, 'Be careful, dear.'

'I'll be careful, Mam. Don't worry.' Then, with a grin, she added, 'I only need one lesson then I'll be able to toss them on their backs, both at once, too.'

Amid derisive laughter she followed the boys out.

They took the bus from the crossroads, and twenty-five minutes later they alighted at Denham Road, for this particular bus did not pass the Sports Centre.

Denham Road was almost on the outskirts of Bog's End, which became apparent to Katie when she realised that demolition of houses was already in progress and others, which were inhabited, were partly boarded up. On an open piece of ground children were playing with an old car amid shrieks of laughter.

Willie had seen similar places in Bog's End some years before, when he had first made his way to Sammy's school. But this kind of dereliction was new to Katie, and she knew that Sammy was talking all the while in order to keep her attention from her surroundings.

Then, having crossed this space, quite suddenly they were walking along an ordinary street again, and this, Sammy Love pointed out, was the new council estate.

When Katie drew in a long breath, Sammy turned to her, saying, 'That's better.'

She half stopped and stared at him and said, 'You

don't always come this way then? I mean—' she jerked her head backwards.

'No; you're right, I don't always come this way. I thought I would introduce you to the other half; but you've really seen nothing as yet. Willie, here, knows a bit about it. My school and where I once lived was a good introduction. But don't worry, we won't come this way again. I only thought, if you saw for yourself how things are around here for most of the youngsters, you'd understand what a blessing the Centre is.'

Whatever impression Sammy had meant to make on Katie by introducing her to the real Bog's End, he didn't know. Had he known, there would certainly have been a bust-up between them as of yore, for she was angry. He was treating her as if she were a pampered child who had never left the protection of her own home. Well, wasn't he right? She never had really left the protection of home. And in comparison with anyone in this area she had been a pampered child before Bill Bailey, as he was then, had come on the scene, but more so since he had become her dad. Yes, she had been pampered, as had Mark and Willie. No, perhaps not Willie. He had stepped out of what her grandmother would call his class, and that at a very early age, when he had sought the friendship of her dominant companion, Sammy Love. Why was it? she was asking herself as they passed through the new council estate, some houses with well-tended gardens, others with weeds, with an old pram or some such stuck in their middle.

Why was it that Sammy always appeared older than herself? Even before he had begun to grow, as he was doing now, he had always acted as if he were years ahead of her. She sighed now as she gave herself the answer: he was the son of his father and an only child, and only children always appeared older than their years; but mostly it was because he was the son of Mr Davey Love, and that couldn't be a bad thing.

'You're not getting huffy, are you?' Sammy had bent towards her and was peering into her face. There was a grin on his own, and she answered it, 'No, of course not. I'm enjoying every minute of this walk. It's really beautiful.'

When his elbow dug into her side, she said, 'We'll take up the reason why for all this, later on, won't we?'

'Just as you say, miss, just as you say.'

'Hello, there!'

They stopped and Sammy called back, 'Hello, Jimmy.'

When the tall young man came abreast of them, he looked from one to the other; then the smile moving from his face, he addressed Sammy, saying, 'What d'you mean, coming up our street?'

'Oh, I just wanted to show them the slums, Jimmy.'

'Watch it!' The grin was back again. And now Sammy said, 'This is Mr . . . no, not Mr, it's Jimmy, Jimmy Redding. Now if either of you decide to take up fencing, he'll show you where to put your feet.'

They were walking on now and the young man,

looking at Katie, said, 'You're making for the Centre?'

'Well, where else would she be making for, coming through this dump?'

'You on your high horse again? Mind, I've warned you. You know where I'll put one of those feet of mine.'

'Like to see you try. By the way, I've only got half my introductions in. This is Katie and' – he turned – 'this is Willie, both Baileys.'

When the young man stopped, they all stopped, and he held out his hand to Katie, saying, 'Pleased to meet you,' and then to Willie, 'Same to you, Willie.' And when they walked on again the young man said to Sammy, 'Something tickling you?'

And yes, there was something tickling Sammy. It was the look on Katie's and Willie's faces when Jimmy had stopped them for the introduction and had insisted on shaking hands. He liked Jimmy, he was a fine fella. He had been a friend to him. He must tell Katie about him some time. There was a story she wouldn't believe.

The handshaking had tickled Katie, too. But it had also left an impression on Willie, for strangely he was feeling now more like his old self than he had done for days, sort of relaxed, friendly-like. It had been funny that young fella stopping and shaking hands like that in the street, and with such vigour as if he had known them before and was glad to see them again.

The council estate ended abruptly at a crossroads and it was also as if the crossroads gave onto a gateway into a different world, at least a different kind of living. For there on the far side was what looked like a park, its high iron gates wide open, and running at right angles to it on the further side of the crossroads was a terrace of high, well-built houses with small iron-grid gardens in front of them.

They were just about to obey the green light when Jimmy pulled them to a halt by whistling. It was a high, shrill whistle and it stopped a young girl as she was about to go through the park gate. And now looking down on Sammy, he said, 'It's Daisy.'

Sammy merely smiled in return, for he could have said, oh yes, it's Daisy. Daisy's never hard to spot. A blind man could pick out Daisy.

The green light gave them way again and then they were all hurrying to where the girl was waiting just beyond the gate. She was wearing a mini-miniskirt: the fashion in skirts was, you could wear them down to your ankles or up to your hips, take your choice. Daisy had definitely pointed out her choice. The skirt was a saxe-blue colour and it had the privilege of being edged with an inch-deep, red fringe which went a little way towards shading her buttocks. She was wearing a skin-tight red jumper. Around the highish neck were hanging at least three strings of beads, and from her ears dangled a pair of ear-rings with loops on the ends, studded with pieces of coloured glass.

What the original colour of her hair was she must

have long forgotten, for that which now reached her shoulders was of a pink hue. However, nearer the scalp it turned into a dark blue and her parting was indicated by a brown streak. Her face was heavily and badly made up. Whilst awaiting them she had been looking into a small mirror, the while aiming to wipe off excessive lipstick from her lower lip in order to make a clean line. She did not take her eyes from the glass to look at the three people standing watching her, until she lowered it to return it and the handkerchief to her shoulder bag. And then nonchalantly, she said, 'Had to come out in a hurry.'

Jimmy stared at her for a moment before he said, 'These are Sammy's friends, Katie and Willie Bailey.'

Her form of acknowledgement was to look first at Willie, then at Katie, a long-drawn look at Katie. Then she walked on, and they accompanied her.

It was after some minutes of silence Jimmy said, 'What was your hurry?' And for answer he got, 'Dad's playing hell, going mad. Our Lucy, and that's a right name for her an' all, second one in three years. As me ma said, the Archangel Gabriel wasn't near her this last time. Me granny says she wants some tape in her knickers.' She looked sideways at Jimmy now and laughed. 'She, me granny, thinks that lasses still wear bloomers. Me da was for taking his belt to her, our Lucy. And he would have, he was as mad as three hatters. It was only the fact that me ma slapped him in the gob with a plateful of his own dinner and sent him

43

flying that saved her. Then she had to fly an' all, me ma. The lot of them skedaddled.'

'Where did you go?' Jimmy was asking quietly now, but there was a quiver in his voice, and his eyes were bright, although he wasn't smiling.

'Where we always go, the Browns next door.'

'They must get fed up with your lot. Were the lads in?'

'Not so much of . . . your lot, Jimmy Redding. No, they weren't in. If they had been they would have had more sense than to stay in as they know what me da's like when he's playing Father Hankin and God rolled up together. Anyway,' – her head wagged now and she was yelling at the top of her voice – 'just look at your lot. You've got no room to talk. Look at your lot.'

They had stopped: Jimmy had gripped her by the shoulders and was shaking her as he said, 'I do, Daisy, I do; but stop that yelling. You don't want the whole park to know' – his voice dropped and there was a touch of laughter in it again as he said – 'that we're both as common as muck.'

When a chuckling sound came from Katie, Daisy, turning on her, snapped, 'And you, po-faced. Wipe that grin off else I'll wipe it off for you.'

'Shut your big and crude mouth, girl.'

Jimmy's words were still low, but Katie was amazed to see the effect they had on this pink-haired, common-looking firebrand.

They were through the park now, and no-one had spoken; nor, after turning sharp right, did the first sight of the Fickleworth Sport and Leisure

Centre bring forth any audible feeling from either Katie or Willie.

It was a very imposing building, or to be more correct a series of buildings, stretching away on either side from the central high point, the entrance to which was a pillared portico. Then they were passing through two electrically controlled doors into a large hall.

Motioning Katie and Willie to stay, Sammy approached what looked like an hotel reception desk; Jimmy and Daisy having decided to wait for him, sidled about the hall.

After speaking to the young man behind the desk, Sammy pointed back to Katie and Willie, and Willie said softly, 'You all right, Katie?'

'Yes. Yes, I'm all right. She's a rude piece, isn't she?'

'I'm glad you took it as you did.'

She said nothing to this. But after a moment, she said, 'Willie.' And his voice still soft, he said, 'Yes?' Then he was surprised to hear the next words, 'We've been lucky, haven't we? I mean, being brought up as we have.'

To this he could say nothing because Sammy was beckoning them towards the counter. And there the young man said, 'You . . . you want to join? And you can pay the fee?' Before either of them could answer, he smiled as he said, 'That's good. I always like to book new members in who can pay the fee. But still, it doesn't matter one way or the other.' He looked at Katie now, saying, 'What are you going in for, miss?'

'I . . . I think it might be ju-jitsu.'

'Oh, defence. Well, that's fine. And you?' He was addressing Willie and Willie wetted his lips, swallowed and said, 'Well, I . . . I only came for a look round; but I think it's going to be . . . well, very interesting. I . . . I might . . . may I leave it?'

'Leave it? Of course you can leave it. There's plenty time to make up your mind, isn't there, Sammy?' He pouted his lips in Sammy's direction, then went on, 'Six days a week. Take your choice, from nine in the morning, swimming, till ten at night when they finish boxing. There's a lot in between. Oh, yes, I'd say. And we're open on Sunday. Well, now, Sunday's a different kettle of fish. There's talks and discussions and lots of things go on on a Sunday. Anyway, here's a pamphlet. That'll tell you what you've got a choice of.' He now looked to the side towards where Jimmy was talking to Daisy. Her gaze was directed towards the floor, and the young man behind the counter remarked, 'Those two been at it again? Daisy's a pickle, isn't she? No harm in her though. No harm in her. They're a family, the Gallaghers, the whole lot of them. But there they are,' he shook his head, 'Sunday after Sunday the whole family filling the back row of the church.' He now nodded towards Katie, saying, 'Catholics?'

'No. No, we're not Catholics.'

'Well, that'll even things up a bit. Half of them that come in here are, you know. Father Hankin unloads them all on us.'

'You talk too much, Sandy.' Sammy's tone was

curt, and he motioned Katie and Willie towards where Jimmy and Daisy were standing, saying, 'Well, come along; we'll do the rounds else we'll have no time for practice.' . . .

As Katie was to say to Fiona later that night, she didn't know about Willie, but she was amazed at what she saw there. And she went on to describe the fencing room, the boxing ring that was set in a kind of small amphitheatre, the badminton rooms, the table tennis rooms, the restaurant and what Jimmy had proudly called their common room, where you could go and write a letter or sit quietly. Then there was the swimming pool, and the private baths behind; seaweed bath, salt bath. And all this was only on the ground floor. On the second floor was a marvellous roller-skating rink, and on this floor, too, was a large café where you could purchase all kinds of snacks and, twice a week, fish and chips. It being Tuesday night, and presumably a fish and chip night, the place had been crowded.

And of Daisy, she said again, 'Oh Mam, you should see Jimmy's girlfriend. No magazine could do her justice. And yet,' she had added after a thoughtful moment, 'there's something about her; I could imagine, given the chance, she would have made something of herself, because she's far from stupid. And I must tell you about the family sometime. Oh, yes, when Dad's here I must tell you about the family; at least how Daisy herself describes them.'

But before this, back at the Centre, Willie was being instructed into the art of fencing by the said

Daisy, who apparently had been fencing for the past two years, and twice a week at that, and was no mean hand with a foil. In fact, as she was now bragging, 'I'm goin' on to sabres, no matter what Mr Davies says.' She now went into a Welsh accent, '"Sabres are not for ladies, not even young lasses, sabres are menswear, so to speak. Stick to the foil and it won't let you down; but you pick up a sabre and you can do nothing with it but show yourself up."' She had added that she was glad that Jimmy wasn't of the same mind as 'Look you' Davies.

They were in the small room where all the fencing gear was kept and she was saying to him in no small voice, 'Bend your knees, further. Now put your right heel towards your left instep.'

When he got slightly fuddled keeping his knee bent and obeying the last order, she said, 'You know where your heel is, don't you? It's much smaller, but it's the next thing that sticks out after your backside.'

Willie straightened his twisted body so quickly that it almost knocked Daisy on her back. Then he leant against a rack where there were stacked a number of thick, white, padded coats and, placing two hands over his mouth, he tried to still his laughter, the while she hissed at him, 'Cool it! Else they'll hear you next door, and Jimmy's in the middle of a bout. He hates noise and such 'cos he can't hear himself instructing. Ah, come on.' She was smiling now, and in a very low voice, she said, 'You looked so funny; just me rawness as Jimmy would say. He's always on about me rawness.'

Willie straightened up from the rack and sat on a form on the opposite side of the room, and as he wiped his eyes, he said, 'How old are you?'

'On sixteen.'

'You're not, are you?'

'Yes. Yes, I am.' Her tone was definite.

'Good gracious! I wouldn't have thought it.'

'Well, how old did you think I was?'

'Oh, fourteen.'

She drew up her small frame now and her head wagged as she said, 'Let me tell you I'm often taken for nineteen.'

'No, no,' he said now, 'unless it would be in the dark.'

'What d'you mean?' She was on the defensive again.

'Well, if people heard you they might think you were nineteen, but never to look at.' He started to laugh again. 'Yes, if they heard you in the dark, definitely they would think you were nineteen.'

'You think you're funny?'

His face straight now, he said, 'No. No. I was only, well . . . well, I saw the humour of it.'

'Well, all I can say is your sense of humour's a very private thing, if only you can see what there is to laugh at in it.'

'Oh,' he was on his feet now. 'I'm saying all the wrong things. You see, I've never met anybody like you. Oh, there I go again.' He shook his head. 'Well, I mean, the only person like you I know is . . . Sammy, and we've been great friends for years.'

'You and Sammy friends?'

'Oh yes.'

Her eyes widened now and then she wagged her finger slowly at him as she said, 'His father died just recently, and he went to live with . . . is it you and her . . . your sister he lives with?'

'Yes.'

'Really?'

'Really. The whole family likes him, in fact, more than likes him.'

'Did you know his da?'

'Oh yes. Mr Love was a wonderful man.'

'Mr Love was a wonderful man? You say that?'

'Yes. Yes, I say that.'

'D'you know where they used to live? Well, they did until Sammy saved some bloke. Oh,' – her head was bobbing now – 'it was *your* da that he saved?'

'Yes.'

'And . . . and so you took him in to live with you?'

'Yes, but he had stayed at our house a lot before that.'

'And you knew Mr Love?' she said again.

And again he said, 'Yes. Yes, I knew Mr Love. We all knew Mr Love, and like the name, we loved him. And we were terribly, terribly sorry when he died. We looked after him for quite some time before he died.'

'In your house?'

'Yes, in our house.'

'He was a Catholic, a wooden one, but, nevertheless, he was a Catholic, like Sammy.'

'I know.'

'And he had been along the line and he was always punching people up.'

Willie smiled broadly at her now, saying, 'Yes, I know. It wasn't really his fault.'

'No?' It was a very large question mark to this syllable, and he repeated, 'No. It was because of circumstances in his life and the fact that he had a quick temper.' He almost added, 'As you have.' So far though, to his knowledge she had used only her tongue, but he wouldn't put it past her. On this thought he wondered what she did here besides fencing, and he said, 'Do you only fence, I mean . . . ?'

'No, I don't only fence. I do ju-jitsu.'

'No!'

'Yes.' The word was drawn out and her voice was quiet and she was smiling. Then she added, 'So . . . you . . . look . . . out.'

'I will. Thank you for warning me.' Then he added, 'Do you think Katie will take to it?'

'Well, it's up to her, on how she feels. I took to it because I wanted not only to protect myself, but also to get at those who got at me for no reason whatever. Oh, you wouldn't understand.' She shook her head. And when he said, 'No, I don't suppose I would, not yet anyway,' she became silent, the while looking at him, and then she rubbed her finger round her painted lips before she asked, 'What . . . what kind of a house have you got? Is it a big 'un?'

'Yes, biggish.'

'Has it got a garden?'

'Yes, a very big garden.'

Her neck seemed to stretch out now from her beaded collar as she said, 'And, I suppose, you've got a swimming pool, and everything that goes with it?'

He didn't answer her, but when she said, 'Well?' he said quietly, 'Would it matter to you if we had, because it doesn't matter to me, or anybody else in the house. And we have a games' room, too, with all kinds of gymnastic appliances. In a small way, of course. Not like here, but it's very handy. It's only a pity that I've never felt that way inclined. I'm not athletic at all. I play a little cricket, and I have to play rugger, as everybody else does, at school.'

'Which school d'you go to?' The question was quiet.

He seemed reluctant to say it, but he had to, 'Dame Allan's in Newcastle.'

She turned away from him now and, taking a coat from a peg, she handed it to him, saying, 'I have five brothers. I used to have six, but John went to Australia. He could have gone to a good school, but me da wouldn't let him. Even when his teacher came and explained that he was very good with maths and science and he could do better, because he had a head on him. But me da wouldn't hear of it because he was the eldest then, and there were eight of us below him; he said he had to go to work and help to bring the others up.' She now turned her head away as she ended, 'He said it was his duty to help to bring us all up.' Her voice now sounding as if she were talking to herself bitterly, she said, 'Folks must get some fun in some way out of having you in the first place, but what do they do? They expect the result to pay for it all their lives.' She turned and looked at him again. 'Parents ruin people's lives, you know. They do. I have proof of it. We all have proof of it in our bolt-hole, the Browns next door. There were three sisters to begin with; there are only two now because Janet died last year. Annie is the elder, she's in her sixties, and then there's Bella, and they both could have been married, I understand, if it hadn't been for a death-bed promise they gave their mother to see to their father. And he lived until he was nearly ninety, next door. But as rowdy as our lot are, we've become a family. I'm positive they love it when we're having a bust-up and when my da is on the rampage, because then they know we'll all swarm in there. And they bed us down, and have done over the years. And, you know, me ma's reasoning is funny, because she says they had to give their mam the death-bed promise about look-ing after their dad for the simple reason it was all written, God cuts the pattern and then He fits it in in pieces, and if they had married they would have gone away and there would have been no Browns for us to go round to, especially when we were younger and . . . and me da was running riot with the poker. Yet it was funny, he never came into the Misses Browns's, and when he met them in the street he would always touch his cap to them. Very funny. And yet not funny, because in the house he would say the most terrible things about them, and their spinsterhood, and how they could get rid of it if they would only give him a chance.'

'Here!' She pushed a jacket at him. 'Get that smarmy look off your face. I'm not holding this in front of you for you to examine the lining. Get it on.'

'But . . . but why?'

'For the simple reason, if you're wearing that and it's buttoned up to your neck and you've got a foil in your hand, it helps you to bend your knees, and to know where your heel should go.'

As he looked at her he had the strangest feeling. It was something akin to that which he felt for Sammy. In this moment he also felt he couldn't get home quickly enough to tell both his mam and dad about her, and the things she said. In a way she could almost match Mr Love.

Yet, it was strange: when he got home he didn't mention their one-sided conversation; in fact, he had little to say about Daisy Gallagher for almost a year after attending this first fencing class in the Sports Centre.

It was Katie who did the talking when they got home. She had seen a demonstration of karate and another of judo. They were different, but both were for self-defence. She was going to take up judo first, because this would teach her how to throw. Karate was supposed to be the gentler type of defence, but this required one to have very strong arms. And yet, no, she had said, as if it were she herself who had been delivering the lecture, it really depended on the swiftness and the movements of the body. You bent backwards and you brought the assailant with you. And here she had actually described what she had seen, with Sammy being a willing model on this occasion. And she had finished, 'Everybody was so nice,' only for Sammy to put in, 'Oh! Oh! Oh! What about Daisy?'

'Oh . . . yes, Daisy. I must tell you more about Daisy sometime, Mam. She's a scream. You know whom she put me in mind of?' She now turned to Sammy. 'Your father. When she opens her mouth, somehow you've got to laugh; more so when she's angry.'

'Yes, and you put your foot in it. In fact, your two feet, by laughing in the wrong places. And' – Sammy had turned to Bill – 'she called her po-face and promised to wipe the grin off her face.' And Bill, looking at Katie, said, 'The girl said that to you?'

'Yes. Yes, she did.' Katie was laughing back at him.

'And you didn't do anything?'

'No. I know when to shut up.'

As Bill looked at her, he thought, I wish, my dear, you had learned that earlier, for then Rupert would still be a visitor to the house. Since he had gone and Davey had died it seemed that they had lost half their family. And Fiona was feeling that, too, he knew. Something was worrying her; he couldn't get to the bottom of it. It had nothing to do with the child. Oh, no. She loved Angela as much as he did now, and was even more protective of her. But there was something; at times she acted as if she was lonely. But that was ridiculous; she had six of them to look after, besides himself. Of course, she did it with the help of Nell, who was also her close friend. And she was on excellent terms with her mother now. So what could be troubling her? Oh, well, perhaps he should take her out more; he would if he could spare the time. Well, he would just have to spare the time, and the Hunt Ball would be the beginning of it. As the saying went, 'There's no good in keeping a dog and barking yourself.' And he had all those dogs on the works, and two good managers, and all his own tribe were foremen. So, yes, he would give himself more leisure in the future, and that would likely straighten everything out.

3

The Hunt Ball was a great success. They were welcomed personally in the hall by George Ferndale and his wife Elsa.

George Ferndale was a keen horseman. He was also a barrister and a member of the board of the Sir Charles Kingdom trust.

Bill had found him a likeable enough man. He was built big and had a brusque manner to match his frame. He was what Bill called a no-nonsense fella. His wife, of course, was the opposite. She was what Bill would have termed a plastic-type model, nothing below the surface. To Fiona, she represented the High Church, good works and small, select dinners type. On the other hand George Ferndale saw Bill as an honest, hard-working climber, and in parts, a very rough diamond. And later on in the evening, after a very good meal, he wondered how the rough diamond had ever linked up with a woman such as this one? It wasn't only that she looked a spanker, she was definitely of the middle class, and interesting into the bargain. In looks and every other way, he thought, she could knock spots off the dames sitting round the table whom he knew practically inside out, for hardly a week passed but they met up in one or the other's house. They were a clique, he had to admit, but they all afforded him good business. Here, however, was someone, at least a pair of them, and so different in type and class that he felt he would like to know much more about them. Yes, not only her, but him.

When, during the dancing, the four of them were left at a table, he looked at her and said, 'How many children have you?'

'Six.' Fiona smiled at him. And at this Bill put in, 'You'd better explain, else you'll get a fella into a muddle.' Then looking at George Ferndale, he said, 'She's got three of her own, one of mine, and two adopted.'

'Oh, you've adopted?' It was Elsa Ferndale asking the question now. 'How brave of you.'

'Oh, there was nothing brave about it. The little girl came to us when she was three after her parents died. They were friends of Bill's. And then we adopted the young boy who saved Bill, you might have heard, from those two murderous individuals.'

'Oh yes, yes. Yes, of course, the Irishman's son,' put in George Ferndale. 'Oh yes. Well now, I know something about him. Not about the boy, although the papers were full of it at the time, yes. But the father. I was in court the day he was sent up the line. It's a wonder he didn't get life; he had practically knocked it out of his wife's lover. Hard case, wasn't he?'

'No, he wasn't a hard case.' Fiona's hand had gone on to Bill's knee and pressed it hard which, in a way, said, leave this to me. And then she went on, 'You have the wrong idea about Davey Love, I'm sorry to say, for he was a wonderful man.'

'You mean Davey Love was the father of the boy who . . . who . . . ?'

'Yes, the father of the boy who saved Bill. The same Davey Love. He was a clever man, a wise man. His temper was his only fault. Otherwise, he played the clown, one could say. He made out that he was a thick Irishman, while all the time he was a very deep and wise one. You mightn't believe it, you know' – she was smiling into the now stiff countenance of George Ferndale – 'no, you mightn't believe it, but in the main he was greatly loved by almost everyone he came in contact with.' And now her smile widened as she said, 'Except those men who would run off with his wife, and other men who had the stupidity to call him a thick Irish Paddy. Apart from that you wouldn't find a gentler man.'

'You amaze me, you know, Mrs Bailey.' He now turned to Bill. 'Is she right?'

'Every word of it, every word of it.'

'Well,' said George Ferndale, 'it's good to know I'm not too old to have surprises.'

Fiona turned to Elsa Ferndale now, saying, 'You have a son about the same age as mine, haven't you?'

'Oh, yes. Yes.' Mrs Ferndale was nodding at her.

'Roland is just turned seventeen, and he's got his first car.'

'It's his first, and if he's not careful it'll be his last.'

They all looked at George Ferndale now as, after emptying his glass of cherry brandy, he went on, 'They shouldn't be allowed on the road until they are twenty, if then. Mad, that's what they are, youngsters, when they get behind a wheel, mad.'

'Well, they're only young once.'

George Ferndale leant towards his wife, saying slowly now, 'That's a stupid thing to say, Elsa. We've all only been young once, and in my opinion this is the time to have some sense knocked into you.'

'George,' his wife's voice was slightly admonishing, 'don't you think you've had your quota for tonight?'

'Oh, woman!' He turned from her to Fiona, now asking abruptly, 'Where's your son at school? What's he going in for?'

Her voice was quiet as she said, 'He attends the Royal Grammar, but he's hoping to go to London to start on a medical career. That's if he passes his exams, of course, and they're rather stiff.'

'All exams are stiff, dreadful.'

They were all looking at Elsa Ferndale again where she sat sipping at a liqueur. 'I don't know how they expect the young to have the brains to answer all the questions that are put to them. I think some parents expect too much of their children. And you expect too much of our children,

George. I've said this to you before.'

'Yes, dear, and undoubtedly you'll say it to me again.'

Fiona had the tact not to ask which school their son attended; but Bill wasn't possessed of such reticence, and so he said, 'Where does your boy go to, Mrs Ferndale?'

'St Augustine's Academy. It's a very good school, highly thought of.'

Yes, Fiona thought, for those who can afford to pay. It was known as a crammer school. Yet she recalled Mark saying there was a boy in St Augustine's who was cramming in the same subjects as he himself was studying, and that he too wanted to study medicine.

'Would you like to dance, Mrs Bailey? I think my legs will still carry me round. I said my legs, but I won't account for my feet. So, if you find yourself suddenly on the floor, you have been warned. Your case will come up next week.' He was smiling widely at her now and she at him. And Bill watched his wife take the floor with the big noise of the evening, and he felt there wasn't anyone in that hall to touch her.

He had insisted on her buying a new gown, and it was a beautiful thing; soft apple-green velvet. It had a full skirt and a low bodice and had looked as plain as a pikestaff before she put it on. But as she had said, it was the cut that made the dress. That might be so, but she was cut out for it. She looked beautiful, and he asked himself now, as George Ferndale had asked of himself a short while before, how on earth had he come to win her? He could see that Ferndale was impressed with her. And it wasn't only Ferndale who had been impressed with her tonight. She'd had requests to dance from three men who weren't of their table, but were apparently known to the company. All horsemen, he surmised. He started slightly, then said, 'What was that you said, Mrs Ferndale?'

'I was saying, Mr Bailey, that some men are too hard on their children. They forget they were young once themselves. And men always want their sons to follow in their footsteps, don't you think?'

'Oh, I don't know so much about that, Mrs Ferndale, because if I'd had a son, my own son, I would have wished him to take up whatever profession he liked, so long as he was going to be happy in it.'

The dance finished, George Ferndale led Fiona back to their table. They were both laughing and when they were seated, George Ferndale leant across to Bill and said, 'Your wife's just been telling me your daughter is a Down's Syndrome child.'

At this Bill cast a quick glance at Fiona and she smiled at him. Then he looked back at George Ferndale, who was now saying, 'My sister has a Down's Syndrome daughter, well, she is my niece. And as your wife said, such a child brings happiness into a home, because you'll never find a happier home than our Lorraine's. Betsy is now fifteen. She is a lovely child. The strange thing about it, Bailey, is that these children have gifts. Do you think along those lines?'

Bill, now full of enthusiasm, said, 'Yes. Yes, I do indeed. Our Angela can sculpt practically any animal she looks at, in plasticine, of course.'

'No!'

'Yes. Yes.'

'Well, Betsy now, she cannot talk as distinctly as one would wish, but she can sing. And when she sings, really it's delightful to listen to her. And dance . . . well, I'll tell you something in confidence—' His voice dropped as if it were meant only for this corner of the table, yet there were other ears cocked in his direction as he said softly, 'Lorraine had lost four babies through miscarriages, and she was on the point of losing her husband. Oh, yes. Yes, she was. Hugh is not a very patient fellow at any time, but you know, from when that child came on the scene, you wouldn't believe it, you would have thought they had just been married and life was a bed of roses. It was, wasn't it, Elsa? Wasn't the house different?'

'As you say, George, as you say, it was different.'

'Yes. Yes, of course, it was different.' His voice was raised now. 'It was a happy home.' He looked at Bill again. 'They take her everywhere with them, and she's always welcome.'

He liked the fellow. Yes, indeed, he liked the fellow. Bill was practically nodding to himself now, and for the rest of the evening he nodded to himself, and all the way home in the car, he nodded to himself. And when he reached the house, the first thing he said was, 'I like that fella Ferndale.'

'So do I.'

'Well, as long as you like him for the same reason.' He leaned forward and kissed her, and she said, 'Shh! You'll wake the house.'

They were making for the stairs when the drawing-room door opened and a sleepy-eyed Mark said, 'You've got back then?'

'Mark! Why on earth have you stayed up? What's the matter? Anything wrong?'

'No. No, of course not. I just wanted to know how it went. Did you enjoy it?'

'It was lovely. Lovely.'

'She made a hit.' Bill pushed Fiona before him into the sitting-room, then closed the door softly behind him. 'You should have seen them, Mark: you would have wanted to punch their noses; they were all after her.'

'Don't talk rot. But' – she looked at Mark – 'it was a nice evening. And I learned a lot, and I met a lot of nice people; some not so nice; but none to compare with my family and friends.'

'Well, your friends, namely Mr and Mrs Bert Ormesby, were up till after twelve o'clock with their wonderful son, 'cos he was howling his head off.'

'He's teething. By the way,' Bill dropped into a chair by the side of the dying fire, asking as he did so, 'd'you know anything about Roland Ferndale?'

'You mean the barrister's son? The one who gave you the invitation?'

'One and the same.'

'Not much, only that the girls make a beeline for

him, and he can pick and choose where he likes, I think. Because well, he's very good-looking. Blond, tanned skin, the lot.'

'He's just your age, isn't he?'

Mark looked at his mother and said, 'Oh, a bit older, I think. Looking back, I recall he couldn't get into R.G.S. nor Dame Allan's. Supposedly he didn't want to be in either, but that's all my eye and Betty Martin, as our dear Nell would say, because he's at a crammer, isn't he? St Augustine's.'

'Yes. Yes, he's there.'

'What about him? What's he done?'

'Nothing. Nothing.' Both Bill and Fiona spoke together. Then Bill, pursing his lips, said, 'Except that I don't think he comes up to his father's expectations. But then, which son ever does, natural or step? You never will. Going to be a bloomin' doctor.'

'Surgeon.'

'Yes. Yes, surgeon. Who wants to be a surgeon? There's no money in that.'

'Oh, yes there is, Dad. There's a lot of money in cutting up, so I'm given to understand.'

'Yes, but what if there's a lot of you aiming to cut up, and there's only one poor bugger lying on the shelf there waiting?'

Fiona almost jumped from the couch. She made a gurgling sound in her throat, then said, 'You two can stay here and discuss bodies on slabs waiting to be cut up until the cows come home, here's somebody going to bed. I'm going to dream of a fairy prince who took me to a ball, and his name certainly wasn't Bill Bailey. You could never have a prince called Bill Bailey, now could you?'

As she marched out of the door Mark grinned at Bill and said, 'Has she had a drink?'

'Just a glass of wine and two small liqueurs. But I'll know what her medicine is in future, a glass of wine and two small liqueurs. Come on, lad, let's get to bed.' He put his arm around Mark's shoulders, and, like father and son, they went from the room.

4

During the following months the house seemed to return to its more normal routine. In the main, things were harmonious. Bill had made a point of taking Fiona out to a good restaurant at least every other week. They had also met up with the Ferndales again, quite by accident, at the very fashionable country hotel on the outskirts of the town. This hotel sported a small orchestra and an equally small space for dancing, and the food was considered first class. For some reason that she couldn't quite fathom, Fiona hadn't enjoyed that evening so much. Yet everything was provided for a most enjoyable night out; even the moon had shone as they sat on the terrace indulging in their coffee and liqueurs.

On one occasion Fiona had refused Bill's suggestion of a dinner and dance, saying, if it was all the same to him, she would prefer to have him at home for a full evening. Like a good old-fashioned couple, she would have described it. Herself at one side of the fire knitting, he at the other, reading.

The children, too, had brought pleasant occasions into the house, such as when Sammy won his brown belt. On that night they had their own private little disco; for this occasion they had cleared the recreation-room and had a buffet meal provided by Nell and Fiona. Katie and Sammy had given a demonstration of their prowess, and Willie had caused hilarious hoots of laughter when he, too, showed what he could do by fencing with a broom, his opponent being Sammy, whom he managed to topple onto his back more times than Katie had done in the karate combat.

There had been a goodly company of them that evening, but more males than females, as Mark had brought two school friends and Sammy had invited Jimmy Redding and two other male karate members of the club. Katie had asked Sue Bellingham and Marion Cuthbert, while Willie's choice had been Daisy Gallagher, of all people. This had caused Katie to go to Sammy and say, 'I'm sorry, Sammy, but somehow she won't fit in, she'll be uncomfortable.' And for once, Sammy had not corrected her on the matter of class distinction; what he had said was, 'He can ask all he likes, but she won't come.' And when Katie had asked, 'What makes you think that?' Sammy had answered enigmatically, 'Oh, I just know. I know Daisy very well; I just know she won't come.'

In turn Katie questioned herself quietly: How much did he know about Daisy? How well did he know her? And how much did he want to know her? And her dissecting told her, that, in a way, Sammy was nearer to Daisy than he was to her. Even with his benefit of education over the past years, there still remained beneath this the solid figure of the young Sammy Love that she had once known and loathed.

When Willie had asked Daisy if she would come to their little do, she had looked him straight in the face and asked, 'At your place?' And he had said, 'Yes, of course, our place.' And to this she had answered flatly, 'Don't be daft.'

'Why am I daft?' he had enquired in no small voice.

'Because you are: your eyes see no further than your nose.'

'Maybe,' he had said, 'but I thought they had learned to see that my heel stuck out as far as my backside.'

The look she gave him, which could have been classed as disdain, was accompanied by, 'Well, you said it.' And she had come back with, 'Like me granny, I say more than me prayers and I whistle them.' And she had flattened him yet again with, 'There's one thing I'll say for you, you're easily amused.'

It was Fiona who had remarked to Katie, 'Isn't Willie asking the girl whom he fences with?' And Katie had said, 'Yes, Mam, he's asked her, but she won't come.'

'Why? Is she uppish?'

At this Katie had let out a loud laugh; and it had been some time before she answered Fiona's question, by saying, 'She's Daisy. She would say, she's her own self. And by, Mam, she is! Well, you've seen some of them in the town, brogues, football stockings, and pink hair, and everything startling in between.'

'Oh, she's one of those? And she fences?'

'Oh yes. Yes. There's a lot like her down there. Well, not up to Daisy's standard of colour; it's part of the vogue now to be outrageous. But there's one thing I've learned about her, that her tongue is much sharper than any foil; it's more like a rapier edge.'

'How do you mean?' Fiona had asked, and Katie had answered, 'I just can't explain. You'd have to meet her, Mam. And I doubt if you ever will, because she's very level-headed and she's quite aware of where she would fit in and where she wouldn't. If anybody knows their place, it's Daisy, and she would put you or anyone else, Mam, in their place if you tried to move her out of it. She's a character, and there's only one person I know who could get through to her, and that's the assistant fencing master. I've told you about him, Jimmy. Well, he'll be here tonight,' she had ended, 'and you'll see him. And Jimmy's got a theory all his own. But I suppose, at bottom, he's quite right when he says, a person can pass himself in any company so long as he remains himself. He's the only one she seems to take any notice of. But, you know something? Dad would understand her. Oh, yes; I think Dad would understand her.'

'Oh, she's a female Sammy then?'

'Oh no, Mam. She could knock Sammy . . . well, the Sammy that was, into a cocked hat.'

'She uses language?' Fiona's face had stretched

somewhat, and Katie said, 'Well, I haven't heard her go in for the four-letter kind with which our Mr Love greeted you, but she can damn, bugger and bloody like the best of them.'

'Katie!'

'Oh, Mam!' Katie had turned her head slightly to the side before she added, 'You live a closeted life. You always have, you know. You've been lucky and' – her voice dropped – 'I've been lucky, too. I said this to Willie the first time we went to the Centre. I said to him, "You know, we've been lucky to be brought up as we have." None of us, Mam, in this house knows how the other half lives. Even dad doesn't now; he's moved so far up the scale. I bet there's not one of his workmen live like some of them do down at Bog's End. I've had my eyes opened during these past months and have been made to think a lot about why people do things and are as they are. You know what I think, Mam. It's the kind of environment we live in that makes us. In the long run it makes us what we are. Take Daisy for instance. If she had been brought up under you, she would now be having university in mind, for she's as bright as a button.'

'Well, why isn't she still at school? Even now they can stay on.'

'Not with a family like hers. I think there's about ten of them. And as far as I can gather the father hasn't been in work for the last five years. And of the five brothers at home, there's only one at work. I would love to meet them, you know. I really would. And the family next door, they are two maiden ladies who enjoy rescuing the family from the father who gets drunk, mortalious, she calls it, and runs around wielding and threatening them with a poker.'

'O . . . Oh!' The syllable expressed shock, and Fiona was shocked at that time to realise that she was finding out another side to this Fickleworth Leisure Centre, or at least to the people who frequented it. And the latent snobbery born of her mother and buried for years raised its head for a moment as she said, 'Aren't there any nice people go to the Centre?'

'They're all nice, Mam. At least the ones I've met, including Daisy. They're all nice.'

'Katie! Do you know you are shouting at me?'

'Oh, Mam, I'm sorry. I'm sorry.'

When, after a moment of quick thinking, Fiona said, 'And so am I, dear, so am I; that sounded like utter snobbery. And when I come to think of it, your dear friend, Sue, would be classed as a nice girl, and yet I've never liked her. She knew too much too young, and she used to pass it on to you, and you used to come home questioning me about certain aspects of a woman's life which you shouldn't have known anything about at that time. And yet, there you are, Sue Bellingham would generally be classed as a very nice girl, and yet I've never thought so and I never shall. And there's talk of her being married, I understand?'

Then had followed a bit of conversation that actually did shock Fiona, for her daughter had said, 'May I ask you something, Mam?' And it was odd that, Fiona recalled, these were the same words that her daughter had said some years ago when she wanted her to explain a conversation that she'd had with her dear friend, Sue.

On this occasion Fiona had said, 'Come and sit down. Is there something worrying you?'

'No. No. Nothing's worrying me, Mam. There's only one thing I'm sure of, and don't tell me I'm too young to say this, because I'm on sixteen, you know. One thing I'm sure of absolutely, I'll never marry. All right, all right, Mam, don't look like that and shake your head. I know it inside myself. I made a fool of myself once, and yet when I look back it was very real. And to think of falling in love again and going through anything like that, it would drive me to suicide. I couldn't bear it. And look what I did, Mam. Just look what I did. I could have killed that girl. I know now, I could. I was obsessed with him, possessed by him. It could never happen again. Oddly enough I'm not affected at all by boys or young men, no matter how good-looking or attractive they are. There's your new friend's son, Roland Ferndale, causing half the girls in our form to have heart attacks. They're always on about him. And from what I hear he can pick and choose, and he does, and drops them like spent matches all over the place.'

'Oh,' Fiona laughed now, 'I wouldn't think he'd have the time. To go by what his mother says, the poor boy has to spend his time cramming.'

'Probably. But she doesn't know what he crams into his time, by all the things I hear. Anyway, that's not the point. The point is, I want to ask you something. Now you won't be shocked?'

'Oh, I likely shall be, dear, but I shan't say anything, I'll try to cover it up.'

They pushed at each other, then Katie said, 'It's something that Sue said to me.'

'Oh, it would be Sue.'

'Yes,' Katie nodded, 'it would be Sue. I get a little sick of her at times, more than a little sick, but anyway she's going to be married, and she got on about . . . well,' – she shrugged her shoulders – 'what happens. She had been talking to her mother about it.' Katie stopped here now and to Fiona's eyes she looked very embarrassed. Then she almost brought Fiona to the edge of the couch when she said, 'When you first went to bed with Bill, I mean after you were married, of course, was it a long time before you started to think . . . well, to think you're in bed with somebody else? Well, just that, a long time to think you're in bed with somebody else?'

'Katie! What are you saying? What are you asking?'

'Just that.'

'Well, I don't know what you mean. Tell me what Sue said. Tell me what you mean. Did she say what she was talking about?'

Katie leant back, closed her eyes, and after a moment, she said, 'Well, Mam, she said that her mother told her that after a short while she would likely get fed up with what was happening . . . in bed . . . especially if it was too often and made you tired.' Again she stopped and wetted her lips before she said, 'Then her mother said, when that happened she had to imagine she was in bed with someone else. She had to pick someone, such as a film star or a . . . well, a coloured man or . . .'

'Wh . . . at!' Fiona was on her feet now and Katie was sitting up straight, saying, 'I knew you'd be shocked. I knew you'd be shocked.'

'I'm not shocked. I'm outraged that that girl . . . I've never liked that girl. She could have been a bad influence on you; but I feel you're sensible enough to know what she's like, really like.'

They stared at each other; then Katie said quietly, 'It isn't true then, is it?'

'No. No, of course not. But . . . but I'm speaking personally, and I say I know nothing about that side of life. If you love someone dearly, he's all you want, that's if he loves you in return. Katie—' Fiona now plumped down on the couch again, and taking hold of Katie's hand, she said, 'Look! Promise me that you'll drop your friendship with that girl. Over the years, all she seems to have talked about, that seemed of any importance to her, was sex. I can remember the things you used to come in and tell me, and I just dismissed them, because sometimes, quite candidly, I didn't believe you. I thought it was just your own curiosity and you were making out that Sue said this, and Sue said that.'

'She's asked me to be her bridesmaid, Mam.'

'And what have you said?'

'I said no, Mam.'

At this Fiona drew in a deep breath, then let it out slowly before she said, 'Well, on that point

I'm glad. But what made you refuse?'

'Well, I suppose, if I was going into it, I would say I had some of the same reaction to her talking as you've just had to me talking.' But at this point Katie thought, if she had told her mother all that Sue had said to her, and in some parts had become giggly eloquent in the telling, her mother mightn't have believed her, even now . . .

That night, in bed, when Fiona had tried to tell Bill of her daughter's enlightenment through Sue, he had taken her into his arms and repeated what Katie had said earlier, 'You know, you have lived a very closeted life.'

When she had gasped, 'You've heard of this before?' Bill quickly said, 'Oh, it isn't unknown. There's lots of things I've heard of, and lots of things I haven't. But one thing I can tell you of which I agree with you, is that I'm glad Katie has ditched that little hot bitch.'

'What d'you mean? How d'you know? You're referring to Sue?'

'Yes, I'm referring to Sue. Of course, she's older than Katie by a year or so, but still too young to give a fella like me, in my calibre, the "come hither".'

'She didn't, Bill?' When she pulled away from him, he pulled her tightly to him and repeated in her tone of voice, 'She did, Fiona. She did, and not so very long ago.'

'You must have been mist—'

'Remember, Mrs B, I was a middle-of-the-road man. I'm never mistaken in that way. How did I come on to your ken? I was escaping from women. And what did I run into? Your mother, who was there, ready, with open arms. There's all kinds of seduction, you know. You don't have to strip off.'

'Oh! Bill!'

'Oh! Fiona!'

They rocked together with laughter. But some time later, when he was asleep, she lay wide-eyed, thinking. As he had said, indeed he had been a middle-of-the-road man: he knew all about women. Yet, now all he wanted was her, and had threatened seriously what he would do if she ever attempted to leave him. This being so, her life should be full to the brim. Yet, there recurred, and more often during the past weeks, that odd feeling of want. But of what? Yes, of what? One thing she knew she didn't want, was to spend what spare time they had dining and dancing, or going to meet people like the Ferndales. And lately more of them seemed to have been popping up on their horizon. So, what did she want? Yes, what did she want? . . .

5

Mamie's behaviour was erratic, as usual. For weeks on end she would behave herself, no tantrums: no, she wanted this and she wasn't going to do that. And when there was an upset with her, it was mostly to do with her friend Nancy Polgar. She would want Nancy to come to tea, not tea up in what was the old schoolroom and now was a play-room, but with the others, with the family in the sitting-room. Or she wanted her to come and stay for the weekend. Should Fiona say it wasn't convenient, sparks would fly: she would threaten to write to her grandfather. She would, she would. The whole family were tired of listening to this threat which was never carried out.

On the occasion when she came home and said Mrs Polgar had invited her for the weekend, Bill thought that Fiona would visit this Mrs Polgar's house. Of course, he had met her once at the parents' meeting and found her, as he had said, all right, a very talkative woman but otherwise all right. But little was known of her except that her husband was a commercial traveller and that she, herself, was an expert at making stuffed toys, animals and such. So Fiona had visited the house and found it very ordinarily furnished; comfortable, what she had seen of it although this was only the sitting-room. She had been given a cup of tea, and Mrs Polgar had talked at great length of the pleasure she felt with regard to the friendship between Mamie and her daughter, because, as she pointed out, her daughter, a year or more older than Mamie, was still very shy.

The visit resulted in Fiona finding no fault about allowing Mamie to stay for the weekend with her friend, even though she herself would not have termed the girl shy. In fact, if she were feeling critical, she would have said, somewhat sly, because the girl's eyes always seemed to find difficulty in looking you straight in the face: she had noticed they were very sharp and had taken everything in, but when the girl was spoken to, they would always be directed downwards.

An incident occurred that caused her to be somewhat suspicious of Mamie, too, so much so that after she found she was in the wrong, she had made herself be very lenient and loving towards the child for some time afterwards. The incident concerned money missing from Willie's bank. Willie had always been a saver and when he wanted something he would not ask for it, but save for it, if possible out of his pocket money; and the box, an antique inlaid Victorian lady's sewing box, given him by Fiona some years previously because he had always admired it, became known as Willie's bank. And when Willie came to her one day and said, 'I'm

. . . I'm worried about something. I thought last week that I had made a mistake in the counting, but when, just now, I put another fiver in, and counted it, I found there was one missing.'

Bill had been informed, as had Katie and Sammy, and Mamie came under suspicion from each of them. That was until Sammy, lifting Angela's plastic box down from the shelf, saw something sticking onto a piece of the clay. It was a five-pence piece, and there at the bottom of the box was some more loose money, ranging from a penny to a fifty-pence piece.

This discovery seemed to speak for itself. Angela was used to trotting in and out of all the rooms; she had likely lifted up the box lid and seen the money and had taken some coins and a piece of paper. They could find out, but nevertheless Sammy's discovery seemed to have solved the matter. But when they searched further they did not find the five-pound note.

It was some months later, on a Saturday afternoon, and Sammy, Willie, Katie and Daisy had, with other members of the club, been in the Centre since ten o'clock that morning, showing off their prowess with a TV unit for a publicity advert that was to promote the Centre still further by the addition of hard tennis courts on a piece of adjacent land. The committee's idea was to interest the public into subscribing towards the cost of the proposed venture. And now, the four of them were standing near the park gates engaged in an argument which had started as a discussion. And Willie was saying, 'Can you give me one good reason why you won't come?'

'Yes,' replied Daisy, 'because I don't want to.'

'You're frightened?'

'What would I be frightened about?'

'You're frightened to leave this ghetto.'

Sammy pushed Willie, none too gently now, saying as he did so, 'Enough of that.' Then it was Katie who spoke: looking fully at Daisy, she said, 'I asked you to come to my birthday party because you're one of the team. All the others have accepted, so there must be a reason for your refusal, and all Willie is saying, is he would like to know what it is. And so would I. But Sammy there, he'll put on his Indian guru's monastery act and say, "You have your reason and your reason is yours alone, and therefore no-one should attempt to . . ."'

'If you don't shut up! I'll attempt to lay you out, Miss Bailey, and in the street.'

Katie laughed at this, as did Sammy, but Willie's face was as straight as Daisy's, and he continued to look at her now, saying, 'You go to discos. You go out with Jimmy. And we don't care how often you dye your hair, or that you wear trainers, or . . .'

'Of all the thick-heads on this planet, Willie, you beat them all.' Sammy appeared angry now. And to this Willie answered, 'Thank you! Thank you very much. And you, I suppose, consider yourself a bloody oracle.'

The result of this exclamation was to make Daisy laugh out loud, and for Katie to join her. And as

Katie looked at the two sheepish faces now, saying, 'Oh, I wish Dad had been here,' Daisy stopped laughing, and turning to Katie, she said, 'Would he have laughed an' all?'

'Oh yes. Yes. Just to hear the way Willie said bloody.'

'Would your mother have laughed?'

'Well, she would have been amused. But she likely would have said, "Willie!" She used to do years ago whenever he would come out with some nicety that the oracle was in the habit of expressing.'

They all turned to Daisy now, as she said, 'Yes, I thought your mother would look at things differently from your dad. And that's one of my reasons for refusing. I know oil doesn't mix with water, except in places like over there.' She thumbed back towards the large building they had just left. 'And even there it can look streaky at times. And if I had accepted your invitation,' she looked at Katie again, 'What would have happened? You would have expected me to invite you back to our place, wouldn't you?'

'No! No!' This came from both Willie and Katie. Then Katie added, 'Not necessarily, although I don't see why you shouldn't invite us to meet your people.'

They were all staring at Daisy again: her head was back and her eyes were cast heavenwards, a pose she maintained for some seconds before, lowering her gaze on to Sammy, she said, 'They don't know what they're talking about, do they?

They're really more foreign than foreigners.'

'Why don't you try them?'

'What!' Daisy stared at Sammy, and he repeated, 'Yes, why don't you try them? It's Saturday afternoon. You said yourself your place is as packed as a football stadium on a Saturday afternoon when there's no money kicking around.'

'D'you know where we live?' Daisy's question was quiet. And Sammy's reply was equally quiet as he said, 'Yes, you live in Forty-five, Brompton Grove West. It's a three-bedroomed house with sitting-room, big kitchen-living-room, scullery and bathroom, and a strip of garden at the back. Me granny used to live in a similar one, not a kick in the backside from Brompton Grove West. I know that part well because I had to stay with her. And I liked living there as much as I liked her, and that wasn't much, I can tell you. When we moved to the High Flats, that wasn't a move upwards, but it seemed like heaven to me because me granny wasn't there.'

He looked towards Katie now, and with a grin on his face, he added, 'I used to say a Hail Mary every night for her and pick some disease she could die of, and it was never a painless one.'

They were all laughing now, and Katie was thinking he sounded just like his father; and it wasn't often he did these days.

When the laughter quietened, Sammy took a handkerchief from his pocket and wiped the tears from the bottom of his nose. Then, still rubbing the handkerchief round his face, he looked at Daisy, saying, 'What about it? Why don't you accept the challenge?'

Daisy sucked so hard on her bottom lip that she left it clean of its red coating. Then she muttered, 'OK, but I'd better warn me mother.'

'Oh, no. No.' Sammy shook his head. 'No warnings. They take us as we are, and vice versa.'

'But what if me da's had a drop?' She was addressing Sammy. 'One thing sure, he won't have had a skinful, because things are tight. But when he goes in for a pint, some of his mates who are still in jobs stand him a round or two. He comes in in his talking mood, and then it can be anything.' She now nodded from Willie to Katie, and exclaimed, 'Anything from blasphemy to black eyes, and of course the Browns next door. And what he says about them at times would make a blue comedian blush. So, there you have it.'

'Well,' – Willie was grinning now – 'let's take it. What d'you say, Katie?'

'I . . . I would like to meet your people very much, Daisy. I mean that. I'll be honest with you, I wouldn't have said that when we first met, but after all this time, I can now.' The two girls stared at each other. Then Daisy, shrugging her now blonde hair back from her shoulders, said, 'What's keeping us? Let's get it over with.' . . .

Forty-five, Brompton Grove West, had a green painted door. It had a letter-box at the bottom and its knocker at the top. There was no bell. If there had been, Daisy wouldn't have used it, or the knocker to give those inside warning of the visitors.

And it seemed, at this moment, as the chorus of raised voices came to them, that some warning was indeed needed. But Daisy, as if she were alone entering her home, pushed open the door, walked straight into the crowded room, turned and held the door open and said, 'Well, come on then!' And so she ushered the three strangers into the family circle. Which of them showed the more surprise was hard to say.

A man in his shirt-sleeves was sitting at the far end of a table, and a smallish woman with a thick mass of auburn hair stood gripping the near end, her body bent towards him, as if she were in the midst of expressing herself with emphasis. At each side of the table sat a young man, the two of them apparently engrossed in a game of cards. That the game was serious was evident to the onlookers, because on the table was a small glass dish holding a number of coins, the largest being a ten-pence piece.

On a long and worn Chesterfield couch set against the far wall and running at right angles to the fireplace, were sprawled two youths who had been reading magazines but were now sitting bolt upright, staring at the visitors.

The door closed with a slam behind Willie, making him jump slightly. Then Daisy pushed past him saying, 'These are my friends from the Centre. They wanted to come and say . . . say, hello.'

'Oh!' The exclamation had come from the man; and he repeated, 'Oh! Well, it would have been nice, Miss Gallagher, if you had given us notice, wouldn't it? And I could have, at least, put on a clean shirt or a jacket. And my offspring there,' – he thumbed down the table – 'could have hidden their gambling. And those two layabouts on the couch could have wiped their snotty noses and got to their feet. As for me wife there,' – he pointed – 'as the song says, if she had known you were coming she'd have baked a cake. Wouldn't you, Annie?'

'Come off it, Da,' said Daisy. 'You've got your dry tongue on the day. Anyway—' She turned now to those she had called her friends and was about to say something when Katie forestalled her. Having taken in the whole situation, and having asked herself what Miss Armitage, the headmistress and lady of ladies would have done in a similar situation, she took a step past Daisy and, looking towards the man still seated in the chair, she said, 'It's unforgivable of us, Mr Gallagher, and I apologise. We should have given Mrs Gallagher,' – she now turned to the round-faced, staring woman – 'we should have given you, at least we should have asked you if it would be convenient for us to visit you. One doesn't think, you know. So, we'll go now.'

'You'll do nothing of the sort. You've just come, so come in and take a seat, if you can find one.' It was as if the little woman had just come to life.

She now turned towards the couch, saying, 'You two, get off your backsides there, and go into the front room and bring out a couple of chairs. And me man, here, is right, for if I had known you were coming I would have baked you a cake. And you would have had it in the front room with the fire on. But it's dead out it is in there, so it'll be warmer here. So, come across here, you two young men, and plant yourselves on the couch. And you, Frank,' – she addressed one of the card players – 'move your ar—, yourself out of the only decent chair in the kitchen and let the young lady sit down.'

The young man rose slowly to his feet, all the while staring at Katie. Then he pushed the chair towards her as if he were saying, take it. And Katie said, 'Thank you. But . . . but there was really no need,' – she looked about her – 'I could have sat on the couch.'

She sat down on the chair and found herself within an arm's length across the table from the master of the house. And she smiled at him and said, 'If we had brought an unexpected avalanche into our house, my dad would have reacted much the same way as you did, Mr. Gallagher.'

'And what is your dad's name, and what is yours?'

'I'm Katie, and my dad is named Bailey.' And she now pointed towards the couch, saying, 'That's my brother, Willie, and that's our friend, Sammy, Sammy Love.'

'Sammy Love? Love? There's not many people called Love. And you don't see much of that these days either. Would you be Davey Love's lad?'

'Yes, Mr Gallagher, one and the same.'

'Well! Well! I knew Davey Love. He would go to

Mass only when he was dragged there, but fight for the Pope up to his last breath, like all the mad Irish.'

'*Len!*'

'Oh, I know, I know.'

'No, you don't know. And when you don't know keep your mouth shut. Don't you remember? His was the big funeral not so long ago when Father Hankin spoke so well of him from the pulpit in the Mass later on on the Sunday.'

'Oh, aye, aye.' He was nodding at his wife now. 'But what I maintain is, death doesn't make saints out of sinners. As far as I can remember, Davey Love was a bruiser.'

Willie's elbow in Sammy's side did not check the retort he was about to make, but Katie's voice did, for she was saying, 'Oh, you couldn't have known our Mr Love, Mr Gallagher. Because he was . . . well, to use a pun, a lovely man. Of course, he could use his fists, and from what I understand, the first time he used them was on the man who ran off with his wife. Now I'm sure, Mr Gallagher, if anyone had attempted to do that to you, oh, I could see you would have stood on your hind legs.'

She was smiling at him, and after a short silence, she went on, 'I know he was given a prison sentence for this, but, as my dad said, it was a miscarriage of justice; he should have had a medal.'

When there was no response to what she had said, she glanced towards the occupants of the couch before, turning back and looking at Mr Gallagher, she added, 'You see, Sammy there was very small when his mother left him, and he missed her. It was after this that he came to visit our family, and his father came too. Oh, yes. Yes.' She nodded now at the face staring at her as if she had been contradicted. 'Right from the beginning Mr Love became a friend of our family. Oh, and I know he hit that workman; but wouldn't you have, Mr Gallagher, if someone had called you a big, loud, Irish galoot, or some such?'

At this there was a stir in the room and smothered laughter from here and there.

'Now, wouldn't you?' Katie pressed the man.

Len, who now seemed bemused, drew in a deep breath, pushed his shoulders back and then replied, 'It remains to be seen. Drunk, yes, I would. Sober, I would have hoped I would have the sense to fight him with me tongue, knowing of me record and that if I used me fists I might be sent along the line again. He might have been a lovely man, in your opinion, but he hadn't much sense.'

'Oh, yes he had, and wisdom.'

Her voice had changed, for she had practically snapped the words at him. And again she had the attention of the room, especially that of Daisy whose mouth was open as she looked at this swanky piece leaning towards her father and saying, 'I'm telling you, Mr Gallagher, he was . . . he was the wisest man I know, or any of our family will ever know. And we all miss him.' Then, suddenly sitting back in her chair she looked about her at the silent group and, closing her eyes, she drooped her head slightly, saying, 'Oh, I'm sorry. Yes, I'm very sorry.'

89

'What you sorry about, girl?'

Her head came up and she again looked at the man opposite her. 'I should say, you've got nothing to be sorry about,' he was saying. 'Meself, I've only met you minutes ago and you've had the bloody nerve to put me in me place, while at the same time praising a fella that I felt was no better than meself, or not as good as. Well, you've spoken your mind and that's something. And you've kept your own opinion of the man, and that's something. Speak as you find. I would say, always speak as you find.' And now looking towards the couch, he said, 'Your escorts haven't much to say for themselves, have they?'

'You haven't given us much chance.' The retort, of course, came from Sammy. And he, taking his lead from Katie and using diplomacy, went on, 'I know something. If me dad had been alive, he wouldn't have had far to go for a mate, in all ways.'

The man at the table said nothing. It was as if he didn't know exactly how to take this. But glancing at the girl opposite him, he remembered that she held big Davey Love in high esteem, and so he met the fella's son halfway by saying, 'Well, as the poor fella's dead, there'll be no proving that. But' – he nodded from one to the other – 'you lot up at that Centre, you don't use your fists, except them in the ring, you use your feet. Topple people over onto their backs. That one there,' he pointed at Daisy, 'I tell her it's indecent, and I mean it, it's indecent, to bring a man or boy low by turning him on to his back. She's had a shot at me, but I'm still a match for her. Oh aye.' He squared his shoulders now. Then glancing around the room at the members of his family before again addressing Katie, he said, 'Today, this lot don't know they're born. With the exception of Harry there, they're all living on the state. And he's starting on Monday, the first time for a year, and two years out of school. My! In my time . . .'

'Oh, in your time.' This had come from the young man with the cards who was still seated at the table, but who did not lift his head, and his father now bawled at him, 'Aye! Mike, in my time they wouldn't have been sitting there playing for ha'pennies on a Saturday afternoon, they would have been outside kicking a football, anybody's football, or on our old bikes scouring the country, not sitting on their arses from Monday morning till Saturday night waiting for work to come.'

'Len!'

He turned on his wife now and shouted, 'Aw! don't Len me in that tone, Annie. I'm solid and sober, and I'll speak me mind. If this young skit across here, who's come into the house uninvited, can have her say, I can have mine.' He was point-ing at Katie. Then, his voice suddenly changing and his manner, too, he said, 'I didn't mean that, miss, young skit. You're no young skit. It's just a habit one gets into, but it makes me wild when I think back. You see,' – he leant towards her – 'the day I was fourteen, I was pushed down the pit. Aye, on me fourteenth birthday I was pushed down the pit; and I was there until I was twenty.

And I said, by God! I don't know how much longer I'm going to live, but I'm going to see the sun set and breathe fresh air all day long, at some job or other. 'Cos I'm not going down that hole any more. And I didn't. I went into the shipyard and from there to the steelworks. Oh, aye.' Again he pushed his shoulders back. 'I was a steel man. For years and years I was a steel man, and proud of it. Look,' – he punched his cheeks with his middle finger, saying 'see the blood veins. You never lose them; that's with the heat. And the blue ones on me brow are from the coal. You never lose those either. But oh, to be a steel man, it was something in those days. Fifteen years I was there; and there's no greater sight than to see steel being born. We had a fella, you know, worked in our shop, and he used to make poetry about it. He said it was conceived like any child. And it was that. And when it was born, there it came out. Beautiful! Beautiful! Aye, it was that. But this fella used to say, it was a treacherous baby. And he was right there because it could take the skin off you. I saw it happen once.'

'Len! No more of that; we've heard it before,' and, straightaway looking at Daisy, Annie said, 'Go and put the kettle on; I'm sure your friends could do with a cup of tea.' . . .

When Daisy brought in the tray holding four cups of tea and placed it on the table, the young man, named Mike, rose quickly and gathered up the cards and coppers from the glass dish, while Annie called to Willie and Sammy, saying, 'Would you two men like it there, or would you like to come to the table?'

'Give it here, Mam.' Daisy quickly picked up two cups and took them to the couch. 'D'you take sugar?' she said.

'Yes, please.' Willie smiled at her; but Sammy said, 'No, thanks, Daisy, no sugar for me.' And at this Daisy leant down close to Willie's ear and in a hoarse whisper said, 'Now don't you say, he's so sweet he doesn't need any, or I'll skelp you.'

At the table Mrs Gallagher handed Katie a cup of tea, and she asked, 'D'you take sugar?' And Katie replied, 'No, thank you.' But she watched the little woman spoon four large spoons full of sugar into the next cup, give it a stir, and hand it across to her husband, who took it without any remark about the tea, but continued as if he hadn't been checked by his wife about describing events in the steelworks. 'I was strong in those days, miss,' he said. He was holding the cup and saucer almost under his chin. The steam from it was wafting over his face, in Katie's eyes covering the red marks and blue blotches on his skin. And through the mist she glimpsed him as he might have been in his youth, a strapping young fellow, proud of his strength. She wondered why he was in this condition now? But only for a moment, for he was now telling her.

'I could lift a bar in those days,' he said, 'that would take two or three of the skinnymalinks these days to even move. And I was well known. Oh, yes, miss, I was well known. I was a steel man.' And then after a longer drink from the cup he enquired of her, 'Does your dad drink?'

'He likes a glass of whisky.' She smiled at him again. 'He comes foaming in at times after a busy day, and if my mother or Nell, she's our friend, asks if he could do with a cup of tea he answers, sometimes very scornfully, "Tea! No, I want something harder than tea." So he has a whisky, sometimes two.'

'Lucky man. Lucky man. One who can take it and know when to stop. But' – he wrinkled his nose – 'luckier still one who has it there when he needs it. Me now, I used to be able to down six whiskys and chasers, that's a pint after, you know, and not turn a hair. But . . . well, since I had me accident things have been different. Your body changes, you know, after an accident.'

When a voice mumbled, 'Yes, he tried to swim,' the man made a movement as if to rise from his chair, and again his wife spoke, not to him this time but to her son, and her voice was harsh as she said, 'That's enough of it, Mike. I'll talk with you later and you'll be able to hear me voice, you will that.' Then looking from Katie to Willie and Sammy, she said in a different tone, 'We know your names but you don't know ours. Well, the one I've just been addressing is me eldest, that is me eldest here. Me real eldest is John, and he's in Australia. And me eldest daughter, Lucy, is away too. And then there's Frank.' She pointed to the other card player. 'As for those two layabouts,' she had swung round now to where the earlier occupants of the couch were sitting on the front room chairs, and she grinned at them as she said, 'these two layabouts are Sep and Harry. And Sep,' she nodded at Katie now, 'is starting work on Monday, and if I'm to believe what I hear through Daisy, your dad is Mr Bailey, the contractor, isn't he?'

'Yes. Yes, he is.' Katie now turned and looked at the young man who was smiling shyly at her, and she said to him, 'Who are you going to be under?'

'I . . . I don't know yet, miss. I just met a Mr Ormesby. He comes into the club, you know, and he says he'll have me set on. I'll have to do odd jobs at first, run around, you know.'

'Tea boy.' This came from Mike.

'Tisn't tea boy, Mike. I won't be a tea boy. Mr Ormesby said I could be apprenticed, either carpentry, or bricklaying, whichever I'm needed on most. You—'

'Now, now, Sep.' His mother waved towards him; then swung round on her elder son, crying, 'I'll slap your mouth in the open for you one of these days, I will that. Why don't you get yourself to hell out of it and look around? But no, you're too big for your boots.'

The young man now turned on his mother, and in a voice as loud as hers, he yelled, 'I was apprenticed, Mam, don't forget. Three years I was apprenticed, and look at me. For two years I've been going the rounds, and the big boots are worn out. Well, I'm going round no more. They can bloody well keep me.'

'I'm sorry. I'm sorry about this.' The little woman was nodding towards Sammy and Willie now. Then turning to Katie, she muttered, 'I am indeed, miss. I'm sorry about this. Family rows should be kept for private times. But . . . but apart from being bone idle, some of my lot are bone ignorant, and it's me that says it.' She now put her forearm under her high breasts and heaved them up, before ending in a softer tone, 'Drink your tea, lass.'

Katie was about to take a drink from the cup when she gulped on it as Daisy's voice, from behind her, said, 'I told you, didn't I? I told you.'

Katie now laid the cup and saucer down on the table in such a way that the tea spilt over from the cup. And turning on Daisy, she said, 'Yes, you told us. Well, I can say the same to you when you come and visit us, because as Sammy's father would have said, "There's often the divil's fagarties," if you know what that means, Miss Gallagher. And it goes on in our house, I know. I've got an adopted sister, much younger but she causes ructions. Willie there . . . well, when he starts, he doesn't know when to stop. As for my dad. Oh!' She turned from glaring at Daisy now and, her gaze and voice softening, she looked at Mr Gallagher again as she said, 'As I said, as for my dad, I bet you couldn't hold a candle to him when he gets going. Bawling Bill Bailey, they call him at the works. And Bawling Bill Bailey he is at home at times. But there's another one of us, and that's my brother who is now in London, studying to be a doctor. And all I can say about Mark is, God help his patients, because he hasn't patience with himself or with anybody else. Willie and he' – she now thumbed over her shoulder – 'used to go at each other's throats. So, you see' – she looked about her now – 'it's nothing new to us, family get-togethers. As for myself, in my time I think I have caused more ructions than all of them put together.' She gave a little laugh. Then, turning to Sep again, she said quietly, 'If Mr Ormesby recommended you, you'll be all right. And you'll get on like a house on fire, if you're willing. All dad's foremen on the different jobs want young lads who will work for them. He's very loyal to those who are loyal to him. Anyway, we would all like to know how you get on.'

'Thank you, miss. Thank you.' The pale-faced boy nodded towards Katie as he asked, 'D'you know Mr Ormesby well, miss?'

'Oh, very well. Yes, very well.'

Sep nodded at her; his eyes were bright. And when his mother said, 'There you are now, there you are. It's good to have friends at court,' Daisy put in, 'Especially in the police station.'

Only Mike did not join in the ensuing ripple of laughter. He was standing near the window staring out into the street. Then the family's attention was on their father again, because he was having a bout of coughing which sounded as if it were tearing his chest. And, as if apologising for the bout, he looked towards Katie as he tapped his chest, saying, 'I hate the bl— winter and dark nights.'

'Oh, now, now.' His wife gave him a sharp tap on the shoulder as she passed him on her way to the fire. 'You're lucky to be alive. Many a less strong man would be in his grave the day.'

The placating tones of his wife seemed to have a soothing effect upon the man, and Katie couldn't imagine her ever throwing a dinner in his face, as Daisy had described.

Len now nodded at Katie again, saying, 'Six hours, I was, in the freezing water of that dock afore they got me out. Almost stiff, I was. Well,' – he tossed his head to one side now and grinned at her – 'I'd had a good night out, you see, miss, I was bottled up to the eyes.' He was saying this now as if it were something to brag about; and she realised he thought it was, as he went on, 'I could carry it in those days. Boy! I could carry it. But it was the wind; it lifted me clear off me feet and over I went into the dock. And I was never any swimmer. In fact, to tell the truth I hated the water. I abhorred people who even put it in their whisky.' The little woman who had now seated herself next to Katie, put in, 'Pneumonia, he had. Bad. Very nearly croaked.' She nodded towards her husband who was sitting with his eyes cast down, his fingers drumming on the table edge as if he were beating out a tune, and she went on, 'A solid year it was, before he was on his feet. So, I say 'tis lucky he's still alive.'

'I don't know so much. I don't know so much.' Len's head was up again and he was nodding. 'It gets me gall up when I think of that bloody steelworks going bust, but more so when I think of those buggers who had only been there not even ten years being given golden handshakes. Set some up for life it did. Others, it turned their heads. But there was me, fifteen years I had worked there, and what did I get? Not a brass farthing.'

'Oh, but' – his wife was looking at him again – 'you know you couldn't have gone back there; of course, you do. And it was three years later when the steelworks went bust. But anyway, I don't envy any one of them that got the money. Although it went to some of their heads, to tell the truth, money, too much of it, can be a curse in some cases. Oh, yes, it can. It can break up a family.'

'Oh, for the curse to drop on us.' It was an intoned voice as if coming from an altar, and on it Mike Gallagher turned from the window and marched out. And no-one spoke until they heard a door bang.

On this, Daisy drew up a chair and sat down next to her father and, nudging him with her elbow, she said, 'Just you wait, Da, till me coupon comes up. We'll show them.'

The look he bestowed on her, Katie could have termed, was one of love; and his voice was soft as he said, 'Aye, that'll be the day, lass. We'll show them. We'll show them.'

'Oh, listen to that! The rips have come back,' Mrs Gallagher suddenly burst out. 'I wonder what they've got this time. They're beachcombers, you know, miss. They're me youngest, they're twins. They'll likely have been picking things up from the shore. They'll likely come in as black as sweeps . . . What did I tell you?'

Two small figures, a boy and a girl, had appeared in the doorway, their hands black and their faces not much cleaner, and their mother cried at them, 'Just look at your coats!' And the little girl cried back at her, 'Aw, Mam, shut up! Just look what we've found.' She held out one of her hands and her brother did the same.

'Put them on the table here. And look, we've got company; say hello.'

The two children stared wide-eyed at those sitting on the couch, then at Katie, and they said together, 'Hello, yous.' And Willie, Sammy and Katie simultaneously replied, 'Hello, you two.'

'This is Jean,' said Mrs Gallagher, pointing to the small girl; and this is Dan, Devil-may-care Dan,' she added as the young lad grinned back at her. Then, looking at Katie, she said, 'Did you ever see two human beings that represented imps, and them all of eleven years old?'

'What have we here?' Len Gallagher was looking at the shell, and the small girl said, 'We washed it in the river, Da. It's pretty, isn't it?'

'Aye, it is that. It looks like mother-of-pearl. Look at that, Annie!' He handed the shell to his wife. And she, after examining it, said, 'It is mother-of-pearl, and it's a bonny piece. But what have you got in the box?'

'We don't know. We found them both together. We couldn't open the box.'

'Oh my! Oh my! Oh my!' Practically all the

family were around the table now.

'Hand me a knife,' said the father, and when a knife was thrust into his hand he tried unsuccessfully to wedge it under the lid.

Presently he said, 'It's locked. Now you don't lock a box, do you, unless you've got something good in it? Well! Well! Well!' He looked at the last great effort of his life and the two children returned his look eagerly, and the little girl said, 'Danny said that, Da, you only lock things up that are good, I mean worth something.'

'You've said it there, my dear, you've said it there. Well, we haven't any spare keys round here small enough to get into this, so what's the general opinion? Shall I force it?'

There was a chorus of, 'Oh, yes. Yes, Da. Go on. Go on, man.'

Len did not immediately carry on with the operation, but he looked at Sammy and Willie who had joined the throng, and said to them, 'What kind of thing would you put in a box and lock away, young men?'

'Money,' said Willie without hesitation. 'I do that when I'm saving up for anything.'

'And you?'

Sammy thought a moment, then said, 'It could be jewellery. Yet, on the other hand, it could be a will or a document of some kind.'

'Yes. Yes.'

It seemed to all of them round the table watching the man handling the box that he was putting off the moment of revelation as if he were savouring it.

Then he said, 'Mind, whatever it is, it's the young-sters who found it. And if it's share and share alike, they get the biggest cut.'

'No, Da, you get the biggest cut.' It was the little girl speaking now. ''Cos you're the biggest, so you should have the biggest cut.'

'Get on with it, Da, for God's sake!' Daisy's voice expressed the impatience of them all; and so the knife was thrust into the box, and there followed the sound of breaking wood. It came like the cry of a small animal. Then the lid was loose and when Len lifted it, they all strained to look down at the contents.

For some seconds there was no sound at all in the kitchen, until Len Gallagher dropped his head onto his hands and let out a deep, choking laugh, which acted as a signal to the rest of the family and the visitors.

'Who would put hairpins in a box like that, and so many of them?'

Mrs Gallagher looked at Daisy, saying, 'At one time, lass, even when I was young, people still wore their hair up. And it took a lot of hairpins to keep a lot of hair up, if you know what I mean.'

'But there must be hundreds there, Ma,' Daisy cried.

'They could be covering something up. There might be something else of value underneath.'

All eyes were on Sammy now, and it was Mr Gallagher who nodded towards him, saying, 'You're right, lad, you're right. We're just sitting here like stooks, thinking the hairpins'll get up and tell us their history.' At this, he took the box and tipped it upside down, spilling the contents onto the table.

But there was nothing in the bottom of the box. He now brought it close to his face, then moved it away again as he said, 'There's a name been burnt in the bottom of it though. Me eyes aren't very good.' He passed the box over to Katie, and she had to look closely at it before she read out, 'This box is the property of Eliza Fair . . . child'. And she repeated the name, 'Eliza Fairchild. Born, 1841'.

'Is that all it says?'

She nodded from one to the other. 'But 1841, that's last century.'

'It doesn't say when she died, miss?'

Katie looked at Sep, and said, 'No, Sep, it doesn't say when she died. But she herself must have burnt that in because if somebody else had done it they would likely have said when she died.'

'It's a very nice box.' Sammy was now holding it. 'I . . . I think it's teak. It's a pity the lock's broken, because, perhaps, it could have been of some value. People collect things like this, you know.'

'Collect boxes?'

Sammy nodded towards the man at the other end of the table now, saying, 'Oh yes, they collect all kinds of things. But because her name's been burnt in, it would make it valuable, I think . . . well, of some interest to somebody.'

'Mr Slater, in the junk shop, you know, Da, he's good at fixing things. He used to be a joiner or something at one time. We could take it down there and see what he says. And he sells all bits of things an' all.'

'Yes, you're right, Frank.' His father was nodding at him. 'We'll do that. But whatever it goes for, little or much, and I should imagine it'll be little, it's the bairns'. You understand?'

'Oh, aye, Da. Oh aye. I'm not out for anything. Aye, it's their's.'

'I think the shell could be worth something.'

The attention was on Willie now. And Daisy, looking at him, said, 'What makes you think that?'

'Because of the mother-of-pearl, I'm sure. Some people collect shells, as others do coins and stamps. What d'you think, Sammy?' He now handed the shell to Sammy, and he said, 'Well, I don't know very much, in fact, I know nothing about mother-of-pearl, only that when you do hear it mentioned, it seems it could be expensive. I wouldn't take it to any junk shop. I would give it another good wash and get somebody . . . well, say you yourself, Mrs Gallagher, to go to a jeweller's and ask its value.'

'You think so, lad? It may be . . .'

'I don't know. But as Willie here said, Mrs B . . .' he smiled now, 'that's what I call his mother, she has a trinket box inlaid with the same stuff. I've seen it. What d'you think, Katie?'

'Yes, Mother has a mother-of-pearl trinket box. But I wouldn't know its value. I've never taken much notice of it. She keeps odds and ends of brooches and ear-rings and things in it.'

'Well, I can tell you from experience,' again Sammy had their attention, and he went on, 'what

I know of Mrs B, she wouldn't have anything cheap on her dressing table. So, I'd have that valued.'

'Oh, well then,' Len Gallagher drew in a long breath. Then, putting his hand out, he patted first his young son and then his daughter, saying, 'Your journey has not been in vain.' Bending down to the two smiling faces he went into a sort of rhyme and song, singing,

'He raced across the open space,
But never reached the end,
For he fell down a cliff
And was found there stiff,
For he forgot to take the bend.'

The two children had joined him in singing the last line; and, again patting their heads, Len turned from them and looked at Katie, who sat staring at him.

'It's like a lot of us, isn't it?' he said. 'We forget to take the bend, and although we're alive, we lie stiff at the bottom of the cliff.' He smiled wryly now and, jerking his head towards where his wife was thrusting the two children into the scullery, he said, 'They like that one. They don't know what it means, but they like the sound of it.' Then, in turn scrutinising her, he said, 'It's been a funny afternoon. Just afore you came I thought to meself, what else is there for me but to go and lie down? But in you three come; hauled in by the wife of the demon barber.' He jerked his chin to where Daisy appeared to be in deep conversation with her brother Sep. 'She's a star, that one, you know. But she's got principles and she sticks to them. She says what she means. I often feel like telling Father Hankin he should come and take lessons from her, for if ever there was a two-faced bugger, he's one. He hunts with the hounds, the moneyed ones, but doesn't even walk with the hare. D'you know him?'

'Not really. He visited our house once,' said Katie; then inclining her head towards Sammy, she said with a smile, 'but Sammy knows him well.'

'Oh, yes,' – Sammy was grinning across the table now – 'in Father Hankin's opinion, he knows where I'm going, but as the song says, "Who's going with me?" It's hell and damnation and I'm to be given the chief guide.'

'He hasn't put the fear of God into you then?'

'No, sir. No. Nor of the devil either.'

'Ah, well,' the man nodded towards him, 'you and our Daisy will make a fine pair. You should get at him together, because she makes his hair stand on end. Oh, my God! There was one day here, not a year gone, when I would have sworn he would have her excommunicated. Not that that would bother her either, would it, you there? If Father Hankin excommunicated you, Daisy – through the Pope, of course – he would have to go there first, wouldn't he? Would it bother you?'

'No, Da.'

Len Gallagher now leant sideways and said quietly to Sammy, 'D'you know what she told him?'

'No. No, Mr Gallagher, I don't.'

'Well, she told him they should alter the second part of the Hail Mary.'

'Why just the second part?'

'Why, begod! Why just the second part? But you know what it says there?'

'Yes, "Holy Mary, Mother of God, pray for—"'

Len Gallagher interrupted him by lifting his hand. 'That's it, the Mother of God bit. You didn't see how that could come about, did you, lass?'

'No, Da; I didn't; and I still don't.'

'Well,' – Len was nodding towards Katie now – 'she told him that she could understand Mary being the Mother of Jesus and that's how it should be said: Holy Mary, Mother of Jesus, and so on, because Mary being a human being, she could have carried Jesus for nine months, but never anybody like God, who we are told is every-where, bigger than this world, in the heavens, on the sea, on the planets, in the stars, everywhere. So how could an ordinary woman carry Him? There was no reason in it, you said to him, didn't you now? You said that was just a prayer made up by old fogies, men in monasteries and dried-up women in convents.' He was nodding round the table again. 'Every word of it is true, what she said to him. And you know something?' He was nodding again. 'He's a ruddy-faced man, you know, fresh complexioned, but he went out of that door as pale as a piece of white lint. Oh,' – he sat back chuckling – 'we have our amusing moments in this house, especially when somebody decides to speak the truth. 'Tisn't often, mind, but, nevertheless, it's something to look forward to when the past lies heavy on your mind. You know,' – he was addressing Willie and Sammy now – 'I was thinking earlier on, if I was a man again and young, I'd make it me business to work at preparing for a bright past, something I could look back on when I was old and enjoy. But you never have the sense of the old when you're young. If God made us, as we're told, he didn't give us the wherewithal, each one of us separately, to cope with the life He threw us into. It's difficult, you know, for many of us to build up a bright past when we're having a hell of a job tackling the present. D'you follow what I mean?'

Both Sammy and Willie inclined their heads, but it was Sammy who spoke, saying, 'I follow you, Mr Gallagher, and I'm with you in all you say. But sometimes from an unknown quarter you do get a helping hand. You won't believe it, Mr Gallagher, but I'm where I am today through using bad language.'

'You don't say?'

'I do, Mr Gallagher, and I'll tell you about it some time. I was very . . . cognisant' – he bowed his head – 'as my schoolmaster would say, with the 'b's, oh, all the 'b's; the 'f's I didn't have much practice at because me lugs were nearly knocked off by me da.'

Now he had Mr Gallagher laughing.

'Me da nearly knocked bloody hell out of me. He belted me and boxed me ears, until sometimes I had to hold me head on with both hands, and all to stop me cussing. And all the while he would use the book on me extending my knowledge, far beyond that for which he was knocking me down. Then one day I went to his house,' he indicated Willie, 'and trampled all the daffodils down in his mother's garden, while I yelled at him as many four-letter words as I knew. But imagine how his lady-mother reacted when she heard her son give me back as much as I sent. That was a day never to be forgotten. Then his dad came on the scene, lifted me by the collar and shook me like a rat, then took me into their house and gave me tea. And that was the beginning. There was a lot after that. Oh, a great deal. If I can come back sometime, Mr Gallagher, I'll tell you all about it. And, Katie, there, she'll tell you of the rows we had. Oh my! She hated my guts. To her I was a common, little, snotty-nosed snipe. I think I still am.' He turned and smiled at Katie, but she didn't smile back at him. Her face was straight but was sending out a warning. And as he pushed his chair back, saying, 'Well, we'd better be making our way.' Len Gallagher bent towards Katie, asking her quietly, 'You all right, lass? You've been quiet of late; you were all mouth when you came in.'

Katie stood up and she gulped in her throat for a moment before she said, 'Yes. Yes, I'm all right, thank you, Mr Gallagher. And . . . and I've enjoyed meeting you and your family. If I may, I . . . I'll come again.'

Glancing at his sister, Willie thought, good gracious! She's not going to, is she? And then he joined Sammy's voice in saying his thanks and goodbyes to Mrs Gallagher, not forgetting to mention the tea she had provided.

Len Gallagher had risen to his feet and Katie saw that she had to look up at him. She hadn't realised he was so tall. But he was gaunt, all of him was gaunt, and his shoulders were stooped. And again she thought, Surely this couldn't be the man who had so often frightened his family to the extent that they had to flee into a neighbour's house. And a further thought struck her, Yes, he was the same man, for only a short time ago he had been for murdering his daughter who had come home pregnant, and for the second time. Nobody had mentioned her. She wondered where she had gone. This knowledge had been imparted by Daisy on their first meeting outside the Centre. The child must have been born by now. But where was it and the girl? There was so much tragedy in this house, what you would call simple everyday tragedy. Of those at home, only Daisy and one of the younger men were in work. She felt she couldn't stand any more, she would have to get out. But she remained looking up at the man, until she held her hand out to him; and he not only shook it, but he covered it with his other big boney palm. Then she was nodding goodbye to the rest of the family. But at the door, where Mrs Gallagher was standing, she muttered, 'It's . . . it's been most kind of you.'

'Not at all, lass, not at all.' Then bending forward, the little woman said, 'Well, it's still amazing to me, it brings a bright spot into me life to know that Daisy has such friends as you and the two . . . young gentlemen. Jimmy had told us about you and your grand place, but I never believed we'd meet you. It's been a pleasure, lass, it's been a pleasure.'

'And for us, Mrs Gallagher.' Katie's voice was very small.

The young man Sep was at the door now, saying, 'Will I come with you, our Daisy?'

'No, Sep; I'm only setting them to the bus. And if I keep well under the lamps nobody will ever pick me up, will they?' At this derisive remark about herself, Willie was for answering, 'I would.' But it wasn't the time for being funny. There was something wrong with their Katie. Nobody had said anything to upset her. He couldn't understand it. She had been full of chatter earlier on; he had never heard her go on as she had.

They had reached the end of the street, and were now about to pass over a piece of open land bordered along one side by a stark brick wall that had yet to be demolished. And when Katie suddenly stopped and turned her face to it, her head crooked in the corner of her arm, Willie exclaimed, 'What is it? What's up with you? What's the matter?'

'Leave her! Leave her!' Sammy pulled Willie to one side as he was about to turn Katie from the wall, and again he said, 'Leave her for a minute.' But he did not check Daisy when she went and stood by Katie who was now sobbing audibly; and she put her arm around her shoulder when she said, 'There! Have it out. Your place will likely have the same effect on me and the people in it an' all when I come to your party.'

Willie now peered helplessly at Sammy through the dim light from the lamp at the end of the wall, and he whispered to Sammy, 'D'you know what's happened? I mean, what's up with her? Everybody was so decent, I mean . . .'

'I know what you mean, Willie. Yes, and everybody was so nice, decent. But she saw something that I know all about and you've never experienced. She saw poverty. And what was more disturbing, she saw a failed human being, a wasted life. That's why Daisy didn't want us to go. She knows it all, she feels it all.'

He stopped muttering when he heard Daisy say, 'Come on. Come on, lass. It's all over now. You know what it's all about and you'll understand in the future. Perhaps you'll understand me a little better. Come on, dry your face. I should think, if you go into your house looking like you do now, your bawling dad will be down here to know who's upset you.' She was talking lightly now, and when Katie muttered, 'I'm sorry, I'm sorry, because I . . . I did enjoy being there, meeting . . . meeting them all. But there was just something.'

'Yes, there was just something,' said Daisy slowly now as she linked her arm in Katie's and drew her over the bare ground, the boys following. 'And Da knew there was something, because he took to you from the beginning. I could see that. He's not the fool people take him for, you know, the drunken, one-time great steelworker, as he still puts himself over to be. And, you know, I bet you wouldn't believe it, he makes up rhymes, sad kind of rhymes, like the one he sang all about failure. Some of them are deep, with double meaning. But there's one thing about it, he's got Ma. He's always had her and he always will. There's that something between them that will keep them together. He's a coarse man, yes, but he's not ignorant. And yet, when I think back, it was his ignorance that stopped John from going to the High School, because even in those days, he could have applied for help, but he wouldn't. But then, perhaps it was the best for John. He went to Australia, you know, and in his going he was supposed to help the family by sending money home. But Ma only had a letter twice with money in it, very small amounts, and that's some years ago now. He picked up with a girl and married her. Me da never mentions him, nor our Lucy. Oh, Lucy could be dead and buried, like the child. This one, too, died, like the other one. Last time we heard anything of her she was down in Brighton. She was working in a convent. They'll have her in afore they finish and she'll be tied to the kitchen for life, like some of the nuns I've seen. But likely that would be the best thing for her. As long,' – she started to giggle now – 'as long as there were no young priests about, because she can't see a pair of trousers but her mouth waters.'

There was a combined giggle from behind, and at this she turned and said, 'You two must have cuddies' lugs!' . . .

At the bus stop they said goodbye to her with, 'We'll see you on Tuesday night,' and one last plea from Katie, 'You'll come next Saturday then?'

'What d'you think?'

Daisy had pushed her up on the step, then stood and watched the bus move away, before turning for home again, thinking, Well, that was a turn up for the books. I never thought I would cotton on to Katie Bailey. But she had got through to me da, hadn't she? It was funny that.

When they reached home, Katie puzzled Fiona with her reticence regarding the uninvited visit they had made to Daisy's house. All she would say was she felt tired and had a bit of a headache, and she would tell her all about it tomorrow.

Although Willie's description was vivid, it still left Fiona, and even Bill, wondering because Willie had said, 'Mam, I've never heard her go on like she did. We were hardly in the house when she began to chatter. Not only did she talk to, but she talked at, Mr Gallagher, if you know what I mean. She contradicted him when he got on about Sammy's father being a bruiser. Sammy was going to get on his high horse, but I stopped him. And she took it up and said that Mr Davey was a lovely man and Mr Gallagher didn't know him. But then she became very tactful, you know, smarmy in fact, saying that he would have liked Mr Davey if he had known him, and that he and you, Dad, would have got on like a house on fire. And so on, and so on.'

To this, Fiona said, 'She said all that?'

'Oh, yes. I've never heard her go on like it. You'd think she had rehearsed something. And it was all so unexpected, I mean the visit. We went because Daisy had said she wasn't coming to the party next week, and gave the reason why, which Katie couldn't see, and so Daisy yanked us all to their house to show us the reason. She said, if she accepted our invitation to come here, then we would expect an invitation from her family. So she was going to show us what kind of a family she had. And boy, she did! But then a number of things happened. Oh, it was a funny afternoon. You wouldn't believe it.' Then he went on to relate about the box of hairpins and the shell, and the attitude of the eldest son. 'It was towards the end, but quite a while before we came out, that she closed up like a clam. She was still sitting at the table opposite Mr Gallagher, and he was talking to her, but she made no come-backs at him. I happened to look at her: she was biting her lip as if she were making an effort to stop herself from crying. And she did cry, but not until we reached a piece of waste land and a wall that hadn't been demolished, where she turned and laid her head against it and practically howled.'

Fiona and Bill had looked at each other as if bemused, and Bill said, 'Nobody had been rude to her then?'

'Oh, no. No. Just the opposite. I've told you, she held the floor. Then she dried up like a clam.'

'Well, somebody must have said something.'

'No, they didn't, Mam. No, they didn't, they

115

were as nice as pie. Well, as nice as pie as they could be. They're a rough lot, especially the old man.' . . .

It was later that night that Bill, taking Sammy apart, asked him, 'What really happened at that visit this afternoon, Sammy? I mean, what happened to upset Katie?'

Sammy had looked at Bill for some seconds before he turned away and went and sat on the couch opposite the fire in the small sitting-room. And still he didn't speak for some time. But Bill, seating himself at the further end of the couch, waited. And then Sammy said, 'It's . . . it's hard to describe feelings, Mr Bill, but the only way I can put it is, for the first time she sensed the feeling that must be in a failure, because Mr Gallagher is of the type. He's bad now with bronchitis, I think. He's had pneumonia and has been a heavy drinker. He was fifteen years in the steelworks. And he gave her all this, how he fell into the dock one night and was nearly frozen to death. He couldn't swim and was off bad for a long time with pneumonia. And from that time I don't think he's worked, which must now be four or five years. So there was a bitterness running through him and a sadness. She . . . she picked this up. And I think she was comparing it with her own life. You know, Mr Bill, Katie thinks a lot. Perhaps too much for her own good at the present time. But there's nothing on the surface with her; she wants to dig deep into everything. I know what that feels like and I understood her crying. But, of course, Willie was somewhat upset, too, because . . . well, Willie's different from her altogether. I can say this to you, Mr Bill, every-thing's black and white with Willie, isn't it?'

'Yes, I suppose so, Sammy. I suppose so. But I don't know where you come in, whether you're black or white.'

'Oh, half in, half out at times.'

Bill now asked, 'Is the girl Daisy coming to the party next Saturday then?'

'Oh, yes. Yes. And you're in for a shock, because, defiantly, she'll come in her best rig-out. Did Willie ever tell you what she said to him on their first meeting, when she was trying to teach him the rudiments of fencing?'

'No. No, he's never mentioned it.'

'Well, apparently, he couldn't get the right posi-tion for his feet, and she asked him whether or not he knew where his heels were, for there were only two protrusions at the back of him and they were his backside and his heels.'

Bill said, 'I'm going to look forward to seeing this piece.'

'Oh, you'll get on with her, Mr Bill, and she'll like you.'

'Now what d'you mean by that? By the sound of it, she's a brash, outrageously dressed little spitfire. And you think we'll get on together?'

'Oh, yes. Yes.' And at this Sammy had risen from the couch, saying, 'Well, here's another one for upstairs. But I'll have to do an hour or two swot-ting before I go to bed.'

'Don't take it too seriously. By all accounts, you're doing fine.'

'Fine isn't enough, Mr Bill, not in exams. Fine are Bs and Cs; I want As.'

Bill sat on for five minutes more, in fact, until the door opened and Fiona came in in her dressing-gown, and, sitting down close to him, she said, 'Bill, I've got to talk to you about Mamie. Something must be done in that quarter. I didn't mention it before because I didn't want the day spoilt. But she cheeked me last night, brazenly. And there's something else: I smelt smoke from her.'

'Smoke?'

'Yes. Yes. I asked if she had been smoking, and she denied it and said, there had been some company at Mrs Polgar's, and they had been smoking.'

'Well, that could be. You know how it is when you sit next to anyone smoking, or even being in the room where there's smoking.'

'I'm not so sure in her case. You know something, Bill, I really think she should go to her grandfather for a time. He's a strict Baptist, and he might be able to do something with her. Oh, and another thing, I don't like this girl, Nancy, that she's seeing so much of. I think she's a bad influence. But how am I going to cut them off?'

'Just write the woman a note and say you don't think the association is suitable, that Nancy is so much older . . . and so on.'

'I can't do that.'

'Well, honey, we'll have to sleep on it, because here's somebody who's dying to go to bed with a woman, and if she refuses to accompany him, then she can just stay put here all night. You have your choice.' He stood and, taking her into his arms, he kissed her, and as they went upstairs, their bodies linked tightly, Fiona asked herself again, What more could she want? But tonight there was no need of an answer.

6

For the past four years, Katie had attended a school which had developed from St Catherine's Academy for Young Ladies, started by a Miss Gregson towards the end of the last century. Today, it was known as St Catherine's, a private school. It was set in deep grounds and looked like an enormous country house, with its own small chapel attached.

A bus heading for Gateshead passed the gates every half-hour, and on this particular Tuesday night, Katie was waiting for it at the indicated bus stop some yards from the main gate. She guessed she would have five minutes to wait, and, as it was bitterly cold, she began to stamp her feet up and down on the frost-rimed path.

Usually, if she were coming straight home, she would be met by either Fiona or Nell. But on this particular Tuesday night, she had arranged to meet Sammy at Mr Fenwick's bookshop, from where they would go on to do extra practice at the Centre.

Willie wasn't to be with them on this particular evening as he had a part in the school play and had stayed back for rehearsals. So, when she saw a car drawing slowly up as it passed the gates, in order obviously to come to a stop near her, although it certainly wasn't her mother's car, she had thought for a moment it would be someone from home.

When the window was pulled down, the blond head was poked out towards her, saying, 'Hello, there. Can I give you a lift?' She took a step back on to the pavement, saying, 'No, thank you.'

'Come on, come on. What's the matter with you?'

'I've told you before, I don't need lifts.'

'I'm not asking you to have lifts, I'm only saying, have this lift. I'll run you to wherever you're going. Are you going home?'

'No, I'm not, and if I were you wouldn't be driving me.'

She realised that the ignition had been switched off and then the car door opened. Then he was standing before her, saying roughly, 'Look! I want to ask you something. Do I smell?'

She could have answered, Yes, you do, to me, but instead she said, 'Look! Remember, I once accepted a lift from you, and what did you do? You stopped the car in a side road behind the station and expected payment.'

'I did nothing of the sort. Expect payment? What d'you mean? I merely put my hand on your arm.'

'Yes, on my arm with the intention of putting it round me. And I told you then, flatly, that I wasn't your sort. But you didn't seem to hear and you continued to be deaf.'

'How d'you know you're not my sort? You've never given me a chance.'

'Look, I wouldn't have thought you needed to make a set for me when it's known you already have a harem.'

He laughed, a self-satisfied laugh, as if he weren't displeased at the description. Then the laughter slid from his face as she said, in no small voice, 'Now look here, Roland Ferndale! Our people might meet at intervals, but that isn't to say that I want to meet you. Now have I made myself plain? And if you don't stop pestering me, I'll take matters into my own hands and then you may get a surprise.'

'Oh yes? Well, we might have to put that to the test, mightn't we?'

'Yes, we very well might. Now once and for all, I don't want any lifts and I don't want any invitations to dances, pictures, or anywhere else. And I'll tell you something else before I'm finished; you're only after me because I must have been the first one to refuse to neck with you. And all I can say for the girlfriends you've had, and dropped, they're a lot of silly bitches to put themselves in that position.'

'Well! Well! So this is the result of being at St Catherine's, is it?' he countered, sneeringly. 'But then you should know all about bitches, because you're the daughter of one. My mother took her measure right away, if you want to know. Upstart, even above her betters. That was her impression.'

She sprang back from him now, her voice rising, 'You do, and I'll have you on your back before you know where you are.' She had taken up a stance with her forearm held straight out in front of her and her leg ready to kick.

'God!' He moved swiftly towards the car door now. Yet before opening it he stood there for a moment and said, 'If you had tried that on, miss, you would have found yourself on your back quicker than your leg could have come up. And you are what you said, a bitch. Why I ever saw anything in you, God only knows: you've got a face on you like nothing on earth. And your figure's yet to be born.'

He managed to get the car started as the bus drove up; but she found she was trembling so much that she could hardly step into it.

Like its owner, Fenwick's was an unusual shop. Stretched above two display windows was a board on which were the letters, in fading scrawl, 'W. Fenwick & Son, Confectioners & Tobacconists', and, hardly discernible, the date '1899'. The rest of the outside woodwork was smartly painted in a mahogany brown. But Mr Fenwick refused to have the original board touched.

Having entered the shop through the double doors, to one's right was a long counter. This was given over entirely to sweets of every kind, and the racks behind the counter showed an assortment of glass jars. At the far end of this counter, facing the door, was the cash desk, alongside which ran the original counter of the shop, put there by Mr Fenwick's grandfather or great-grandfather. It was made of mahogany and slightly curved, and behind it were pigeon-holes in which different types of cigarettes, tobacco and cigars were on display. And on the top shelf, almost touching the ceiling, were five brown jars. On the centre one, there could easily be discerned the word, 'Snuff'.

To the left there was only half of a wall, the rest being an open archway. But covering this half-wall were two stands of paperback books. The original shop had once ended here, but the enterprising and present Mr Fenwick had bought the shop next door which had once been a private lending library, and had turned it into what he called his treasure trove, but what others termed Fenwick's junk room. Two of the walls held the original book-racks, and these were filled with an amazing assortment of hard-back books, in haphazard array. Along the third wall was a counter and, resting on this, was a conglomeration of odd china figures, plates of all sizes and patterns, a large assortment of tins and tin lids, and glass bottles of all shapes, sizes and colours. It was a present-day collector's treasure trove. Then, to the short side that backed on to the array of paperback racks in the main shop were four wash-baskets. And in these, again an assort-ment, but of kitchen utensils. And the last odd thing about this room was the two mirrors set at angles above the steps on the left-hand side of the entrance. One gave a view of those down in the shop, while the other presented a part-view of what was going on in the junk room. Mr Fenwick had had them placed there some years ago, for he might be a man whose heart was set in the past, but he was one whose mind was open to the present.

Although there were nearly always three people in attendance – this being himself, his wife and his daughter, not counting the paper boy – things from both departments disappeared frequently. The junk room was open only from Tuesday to Thursday, because Mr Fenwick's business and work, which was a pleasure, took him to sale rooms, mostly into the basements where the odd bits were to be found. He also dealt with Mr Parker, who was a removal man in a small way. Mr Parker would clear a house for a stated sum, a very profitable sum, and so he could afford to let the bric-a-brac and scores of tattered volumes go to his friend, Mr Fenwick. The rest of his goods would go either into the sale room or for sale at his antique stall in the market . . .

It was here, in Mr Fenwick's shop, that Katie was to meet Sammy. She was well known to Mr Fenwick, although she was anything but a frequent visitor, whereas Sammy had, for years now, even as a lad, visited the junk room, that was when he had any money to spend. In earlier years he would have patronised the tips. Nowadays, he visited the room in order to sort among the books, hoping that here or there he might come across an early edition of one of his favourite authors.

As Katie crossed the shop towards the archway, she turned and smiled in acknowledgement to Mr Fenwick's nodding. He was serving a customer. But she was a little puzzled when he lifted his hand and put his finger up and wagged it towards her.

There were five people in the junk room, but

Sammy wasn't there. Well, she would look around.

As she pulled out what looked like an almost new book from one of the racks, Mr Fenwick appeared and beckoned as he hissed, 'Missie!' And when she approached him, he said, 'You are looking for young Master Love?'

He had given Sammy this title years ago, but it had been a derisive one then, because he was then an urchin, and they have light fingers, urchins. But over the years he had come to know the boy, then the young man, and there was no derision in the title now. 'He . . . he's gone not more than three or four minutes ago. He had found what he wanted. I have it on the counter.' And now he nodded as he said, 'I think it's a find, too. Anyway, it's a ninth edition, which isn't bad. He scooted out quickly as if he had forgotten something and he asked me to say he'd be back in a few minutes. All right?'

'Yes, thank you, Mr Fenwick. Anyway,' – she looked back and around the room – 'I won't get bored.'

'No, indeed, you won't, miss. Indeed, you won't. Not in my shop.'

They parted, laughing, and Katie began her browsing through the books while she waited . . . and waited . . . and waited.

Sammy had come to the shop a good half-hour before he was due to meet Katie. As Willie had been chosen to take part in the Christmas play and had stayed behind for a rehearsal there had been no argument about why he wanted to go to that stinking shop again: Willie wasn't interested in books, even if they were clean. He had enough of them at school to contend with, he said. But he made one exception: if they dealt with cars, then that was different.

Sammy was happy to be on his own, especially in Mr Fenwick's. His love of books had grown over the years. He had a tendency towards ancient history, and also, whisper it even to himself, poetry. And a short while ago on these shelves he had discovered what was left of a book of Donne's poems. It had been scribbled over here and there, and there were pages missing. But someone, at one time, had read the book and likely loved it; for in the margin he had written:

> I too have done a brave thing;
> But a braver thing still I have done,
> I haven't spoken of it.

A new batch of books had been thrown on to the shelves near the archway. They looked a poor lot, and he liked going through poor lots; it was here that you found the treasures. There were regulars who came here, but never spoke to each other: they were out for the same thing, first editions. And yet he had never heard of anyone finding one. But an early edition of any kind was valuable.

There had been children in the house where these particular books came from. They hadn't been scribbled on, but they were well-thumbed, and some pages were torn. He laughed as he read a rhyme in one of the books and at the way it had been set out;

Fix It

He said the clock wanted taking to bits
And when I did it he nearly had fits.
Funny,
People never say what they mean;
Fancy
Making such an enormous scene.

He was still smiling at the scene the little rhyme presented to his mind, when, his hand picking up another book, he almost said aloud, never! But yes, it was. Yes, it was. What edition was it? Oh, the ninth. But, nevertheless, it was a find, and it was volume three, so there must be two other volumes here somewhere. My! My! *Lord Chesterfield's Letters To His Son*. He had read bits and pieces here and there about him whilst reading up about conditions in England leading up to the Napoleonic battles. He rubbed his fingers over a page. It was the original paper all right, beautifully thick and deckle-edged, and which had browned in part with age. Oh! Good! Good! He put the book under his oxter; he wasn't going to put it down: there was a wide boy along there and he was a searcher too. He now thumbed quickly through the rest of the books on the shelf, but to no avail. But there was a higher shelf. There could be some up there. Mr Fenwick might sort out all his utensils but he didn't do anything about the books he gathered. His head went back as his hand went up to the higher shelf. Then his whole body was arrested, for in the mirror set at an angle, seemingly above him from where he stood, he saw a passing face. It was Mamie's. What was she doing here? She was supposed to be doing rehearsals at school. His hand came down from the upper shelf and he moved a step to where he could get a better view of her. He was seeing her back now. She was at the paper counter, but there was no-one serving there: Mr Fenwick seemed to be on his own this evening. Then his mouth dropped into a gape and he moved his head a little to the side. Now he could see all of her. She had picked up a thick magazine and was moving along the counter to where the evening papers were stacked. And that which she did next kept his mouth agape, for with a quick movement she placed a magazine in the middle of the paper, then bent it double. Now she was standing next to a taller girl. He could see her profile: it was her friend Nancy. Then he saw Mamie do something that made him gasp aloud: her right hand hovered close to a standing grid that held Mars bars, Polos and such. Then, before he could blink, he saw her twice slip a handful of packets taken from the grid into the open school bag of the girl standing close to her. And at this, the girl turned and walked slowly down the shop and out of it. But Mamie waited at the counter until Mr Fenwick had returned from serving another customer. Then, as she passed some money to him she also presented the paper lengthwise. He watched Mr

Fenwick nod at her, and then she walked out.

Shoplifting! Dear God! And she was supposed to be at . . . Oh! There was something fishy here. He now dived into the shop to where Mr Fenwick was about to attend to another customer, and pushing his find at him, he said, 'I . . . I found this. I'll be back in a minute. I'm . . . I'm waiting for Ka— Miss Bailey, she's to meet me here.' He gulped.

'Will you tell her I'll be back in a minute? I've just remembered something.'

'Yes. Yes, indeed, Master Love. I will give her your message. Yes. Yes. And you found something? My! My! Let me have a look.'

Sammy did not wait for Mr Fenwick's comment on his find, but hurried out of the shop and was just in time to see the two girls disappearing round the end of the long street to where there was a cross-road. And when he reached it, there they were, going down Pembroke Avenue and acting like silly little kids, pushing at each other.

His first idea was to go and grab them, and from this distance he could do just that. But then, where were they going? And what were they going to do with their spoils? Oh my goodness! Mrs B would go mad when she heard about this. As for Mr Bill, Lord! But that girl had been acting strangely for a long time now: everybody in the house seemed to be fed up with her. But shoplifting! And so expertly done, it was obviously not the first time. No, that was the result of experience and practice. He saw again, in his mind's eye, the taller girl lifting the flap of her school bag to allow Mamie to drop in her spoils. Well, he would get to the bottom of this. And if he didn't wring her neck for her, someone at home would. They were walking up Woodbine Grove now. Well, Woodbine Grove went nowhere. It ended in a narrow piece of wasteland, beyond which was a larger building and, attached to it, another house. A joinery business was carried out here. It was through the gate leading to the house that, in the lessening daylight, he thought the girls had disappeared.

Before crossing the space he paused, and when he reached the gate and gently pushed it open, his hand came in contact with a heavy iron chain with a lock on the end, which suggested that this gate was usually kept closed.

Slowly now, he went up by the side of a blank wall, then into a large yard that was partly illuminated from a window at the far side of a door. Quietly, he passed the door, to stop to the side of the window. There were curtains down each side of it, but they hadn't been closed. Slowly bending forward, he looked into the room and if his mouth had given evidence of his surprise at what he saw through Mr Fenwick's mirror, now it simply gaped open, for he was looking on to a table on which was spread an assortment of chocolate bars, Polo mints, and small cards to which were pinned brooches, ear-rings and such. The woman was moving them around a table as if sorting them out, smiling as she did so and talking. He could hear her voice, but not what she was saying. Then the expression 'Good God!' came from his lips as he saw Mamie, who was standing at the far side of the table, lighting a cigarette and doing it deftly. When he saw her draw on it and puff out the smoke, he could contain himself no longer. It seemed that he sprang from the window, kicked the door open and was into the room in one leap. And he so startled the occupants that they almost fell to the floor. One staggered back against a cupboard, crying, 'What! Oh! What d'you want? Get out! Get out!'

'I'll get out all right, and you'll go with me, missis. You bloody, dirty bitch, you.' Inside himself, he seemed to be back in Bog's End, for now he was spewing out words that he had not used for years. 'By! Mamie, you've got something to answer for, and you will.'

'I won't! I won't! I'm not coming back. She'll go for me; they'll all go for me. I'm going to me grandfather's. I hate you! I hate you all!'

'You'll go to your grandfather's all right.'

He was about to grab her when the woman came at him with fists flying. But turning on her, he brought his arm up swiftly and the next minute she was on her back. Mamie was disappearing through a door at the far end of the room; and when he, too, rushed through it, he was surprised to find himself in a broad stone-paved passage, the other side of which he straightaway surmised as being the end wall of the factory. At the same time a man dropped a box he must have been carrying through the door, in order to grab at Mamie by the neck of her coat and drag her through the doorway.

Without hesitating, Sammy rushed into the

room, to stop dead at the sight of what he was now gazing upon. But it was a momentary flash only before the man, having thrown Mamie to one side, came at him and knocked him sideways with a blow to his shoulder.

What followed was pandemonium. Someone screamed, 'Shut that bloody door!' Then another man came at him, only to find his head knocked backwards from a blow under the chin, and then to double up when a foot came into his groin.

Sammy had learned some time ago that the gentle art could be anything but gentle, when circumstances demanded. And now, indeed, circumstances demanded, for yet another man came at him. He had actually laid him on his back when the bottle hit him on the side of the head. Had the man's aim been true he would have gone down immediately; it knocked him dizzy and he reeled, but it was enough. It was when he hit the floor face downwards and felt his arms wrenched behind him that he came to fully again. And then his legs were bent back from the knees and tied together. When he was kicked onto his side, and his mouth opened in a yell of pain, it was choked by a gag of net cloth.

He was lying against the wall now and looking towards the table over which hung a green shaded light, similar to those he knew were used in newspaper offices. He could see a man gathering up little bags from the table and throwing them into a box, while another carefully picked up glass tubes. He couldn't see where these were put, but recalling his first glimpse of the table, he guessed what had been afoot in this room.

When he heard the door open the woman's voice came to him, saying, 'God Almighty!' And a man's replying, 'Aye, God Almighty! This is you and your bloody sideline, missis.'

'Be careful who you're talking to, Johnny Hatter. My sideline has paid well before and it will again. In the meantime, get yourself into the house and clear the drawers, and not into boxes but into the travelling case. And take them to the Brunch.'

'Oh, no, Mrs Polgar. You know what the boss said before: he's got his name to think about and his business.'

'If he upsets Polgar he knows what'll happen. So, get going. And you, Napier, clean this place up as you've never cleaned a room before, for when that thing down there is missing, they'll even be looking under the flagstones.'

When the door behind Mrs Polgar closed, one of the voices said softly, 'We can't take all this lot to the Brunch.'

'Well, you heard what the lady said, didn't you? God! How I hate women. Anyway, all this must be cleared, as she said, because when the boss comes back, there'll be double hell to pay. And also her bloody market stall. He should have put his foot down about that.'

'It's a good cover-up, but she must have a pile stacked away just from that.'

A voice broke in on the other two, crying angrily, 'This is no bloody time to go on about finance.

What are we going to do with that bugger down there?'

'Well, you heard what she said.'

'Aye, and she's right. He's seen the lot of us.'

'Well, he won't be able to remember much. Get a dose ready; the sooner you give it to him the better. And the other one too.'

'Will we leave him here?' said Breezy.

'Why did they ever give you such a nickname; your bloody brains blew away years ago.'

There was a short silence before a voice said, 'You've got the day's paper there?'

'Aye.'

'See what time high tide is.'

There was another silence. 'One o'clock.'

'Aye, well, that'll just give us time. Is that needle ready?'

When the dark shape bent over Sammy, he wriggled within his bonds. But when he felt the top of his trousers torn down and the needle jammed viciously into his buttocks his groan became audible. A voice above him asked now, 'Was it a stiff 'un?' And the answer was, 'Well, if I'd given it to a horse, he wouldn't be running the morrow.'

There was a swimming in his head; then his body jerked when he imagined he saw his father kneeling by his side. 'Dad! Dad!' he muttered. 'Get me out of this!'

'You walked into it, lad. You walked into it.'

'I didn't, Dad. I didn't. It was Mamie.'

'Yes, it was Mamie. But what you should have done was to go home and tell them first.'

'Oh, Dad. Dad. You wouldn't have done that, would you?'

'No, lad. No, I wouldn't have done it.'

'Dad! Don't go away. Don't go away.'

'Here's my hand. Hang on.'

He felt the hand in his as he said, 'I . . . I can't see you, Dad, I can't see you. Don't go away. I'm . . . I'm sleepy. They've drugged me. This is a drug set-up. Packing it to sell in the streets, Dad. To sell in the streets, Dad. To sell in the streets, Dad.'

'Yes, lad. Yes, lad. Yes, lad.'

His father was going; he was leaving him. He wanted him to go and tell Katie. 'Oh, Katie. Katie.'

Then the apparition had gone and there was nothing. It was as if he had never been born . . .

Breezy looked down on Sammy now, saying, 'He's off! Now what about her?' His head jerked backwards.

'Oh well; just give her a good stiff 'un too; then leave her to the missis. She's her responsibility.'

7

The Gallaghers were pushed for space in all ways, but mostly in their sleeping quarters.

In what was described as the third bedroom, but should have had the title of box room, were two bunk beds, one on top of the other. Mike Gallagher had the lower bunk and young Danny the upper.

Danny liked this room for a number of reasons. First, because he was sharing it with a brother who didn't talk, whereas when he had been in the main bedroom he'd had to take the foot of a bed; and here he could listen to his old CB radio without disturbing Mike. He loved listening to the lorry drivers, but more especially to the police. If he could pick up the right wavelength, he could hear the police chasing the car thieves, and passing messages to one another. It was exciting. Sometimes he fell asleep with the earphones on. He had bought it from a fellow for twenty pence, who had said it was worth thirty pounds. His dad had been angry about it; 'Who but a fool would sell an article worth thirty pounds for twenty pence,' he jeered at him, 'and who but a fool would pay for something that had been thrown away as useless?' Anyway, it went at times, and tonight was one of the times: the police had been chasing a load of fellas in a car. He turned the tuning knob to find a local station.

It must be twelve o'clock now because the late news had just started. He liked listening to the news. It wasn't often they had news on downstairs on the telly, because his da got aggravated about things and would shout about them, so his mother would switch over.

But the news he was listening to now brought him up in his bunk, and he said aloud, 'Eeh!' That lad was here on Saturday. He came with the girl and her brother. His da had got on well with the girl; his ma couldn't get over how his da kept talking about her.

His chin dropped lower and lower, as he listened. The police were taking it very seriously and they had found the girl. Not the one who was here, but the adopted sister. She had been drugged. And the announcer was saying that the police thought the young man was in danger. His eyes widened as he listened. It was about drugs. The police had raided the house and found the girl drugged. She was in hospital now but hadn't come round. They had been searching the river.

He suddenly shut off the man's voice. The river. The river. Yes; he remembered now. Those men they could just make out in the dim light near the jetty, probably dumping something, before hurrying away in a van. He had wanted to go down straightaway to see what they had been up to, but

Jean was frightened and she had said, 'Don't tell me da, but we'll go early in the morning before we go to school and have a look.'

He turned on to his knees, then put his thumb in the end of his mouth and gnawed on it. Their Mike had been snoring for the last hour. But . . . but he wouldn't be able to sleep if he didn't tell somebody, and Mike rarely went for him, like he did for the rest of them.

He dropped down from the bunk and, bending over Mike, shook him gently by the shoulder, saying, 'Mike! Mike!'

Mike grunted, made a spluttering noise in his throat, then said, 'Who? What? What is it? Oh, you! You sick?'

'No. No, Mike. Listen!'

'It's too late and I'm tired. Listen to what?'

'It . . . it could be serious, Mike.'

Mike pulled himself up on his elbows and peered at Danny, and he said, 'What could be serious? What's the matter with you? Had a nightmare?'

'No. No, Mike. But . . . but we came by the shore road tonight when we came back from the pictures, and we're not allowed to come that way. And . . . and . . . well . . .'

By the time Danny finished talking, Mike was sitting on the edge of the bunk, saying, 'You heard this on the police news?'

'No, on the local news.'

It seemed to Danny there was a long silence before he heard Mike say, 'Get into your clothes.'

'Yes, Mike.'

A few minutes later, he said, 'Where are we going?'

'Into Da.'

'Into Da?'

'Aye, of course. We're not going out of the house on what could be either a fool's errand or the real thing. We'll leave it to him.'

They went quietly out on to the landing and gently opened their parents' bedroom door and switched on the light.

It was his mother who woke first, saying, 'In the name of God! Am I seeing right?' She was peering through sleep-rimmed eyes. 'What's the matter with you two?'

Mike was whispering now, 'The young 'un here has heard something on the radio and it's to do with the visitors we had on Saturday.'

'Ah! Ah!' It was a grunt from the bed. Then Annie Gallagher, pushing her husband, said, 'Wake up there, Len, and listen to this.'

Len Gallagher pulled himself slowly up on the pillow and he blinked at the two figures standing to the side of him, and he asked quietly, 'What's wrong with you?'

'I want you to listen to this, Da. He'll tell you what he heard on the news just now. But it's the last bit he's got to come out with. He and Jean have been where they shouldn't have been. But they saw something. Anyway,' – Mike nudged Danny – 'tell Da.'

The boy started where he first heard the announcer. But when he said, 'I know we shouldn't go by the shore road at night,' Len said, 'No, begod! You shouldn't. You haven't, have you?'

There was a pause before Danny admitted softly, 'Aye, Da. After we came out of the early pictures we went that way.' But before Len could come back with any reproach, Mike quickly put in, 'They saw men carrying something under the jetty down to the water-line. And it's high tide tonight, or this morning, and I think we should inform the polis. What d'you think?'

'Yes, we should, and quick, because, you, boy, know more about that jetty than is good for you. But at this moment, perhaps we should be thanking God. Let me get up and get into me things.'

'You're not doing any such thing, Len. You're not going out this night, not in that freezing cold. It would finish you.'

'Ma's right, Da. But look; we've got into our things; I'll take the lad to the station. It might be a wild goose chase and they'll laugh in my face.' Then he muttered, 'But for their own sakes, I hope they don't.'

'Now, now, our Mike. Whatever happens, keep your temper. You know the polis.'

'Oh, yes, Ma, I know the polis.'

'And . . . and you wrap up, both of you.'

Len put in, quietly, 'Take my top coat off the back of the door, it's thicker than yours.'

'I'll do that, Da.'

'And put another scarf around Danny there,' said his mother. 'Anyway, I'll come down and let you out the back door, because you don't want to waken Daisy, for as sure as two pins, she'll be down to the station with you. And don't either of you speak until you're out of the house. If they hear me, they won't get up, any of them, 'cos I'm used to trotting about in the middle of the night looking after your da, aren't I?'

Within a matter of minutes they were in the street, and ten minutes later they were entering Fellburn's main police station.

The night policeman stared at them, and said, 'Yes? What's your trouble?'

And Mike, being Mike, had to retort, 'It isn't our trouble, it's your trouble, and we may be able to help. I don't know, but we thought we'd better take a chance.'

'Well, if you tell me what you want me to decide on, then I might help you, sir.'

That 'sir' got Mike's dander up immediately. God! How he hated these buggers.

'Me brother here, saw something that wasn't for his eyes apparently, when coming along the beach road earlier on the night: men dumping something rather heavy. It could have been rubbish or it could have been a body. He was listening to the midnight news when he should have been asleep, and he hears the announcement about the missing young lad and the girl, and being bright he puts two and two together. How bright he really is remains to be seen, but I thought I should come and tell you. Have you got that?'

The policeman stared at him for a moment and said, in a different tone now, 'Take a seat over there, please. I'll get in touch with the sergeant.'

Five minutes later the sergeant came into the office and, addressing Mike, he said, 'Good evening, sir.'

Dear, dear! What a change of front. Mike made no retort to this and the sergeant went on, 'The officer tells me that your brother might have some lead that will help us in our search for this missing young man?'

'Aye, that's why we're here.'

The sergeant was looking down at Danny and he said, 'Could you take us to the exact place and the particular jetty where it happened?'

'Yes, sir.'

The sergeant now turned from him, said something to the officer, who then picked up a phone, and it would seem that almost instantly the door opened and two policemen entered.

'Take this gentleman and this boy to the car,' the sergeant said. 'I'll be with you in a minute.' He again turned to the night officer and said, 'Get Fuller and Stoddard. Tell them to meet us on the shore road, the jetty end.'

Within fifteen minutes, Danny and Mike were leading the policemen down the bank to the jetty, and Danny was seeing it as he had never seen it before, illuminated by headlights and powerful torches. The tide was within twenty minutes of reaching its height when they climbed through the girders. The sergeant flashed his light from side to side, but saw nothing at first, then concentrated his light along the edge of the rough rising water splashing against the timbers, and almost immediately let out an exclamation: there below him, already half-covered with sea water and moving slackly, was a long black bundle, distinguished only by a lighter patch sticking out at one end. He was up to his calves in the mud and water when he yelled, 'Come on! Get down here!'

It took three pairs of hands to drag the bundle from the hungry incoming tide and over the mud to where Mike and Danny were standing as though rivetted, their mouths open, as they stared down at half of the illuminated, dead-looking face.

8

All the lights were on in the house. Fiona and Nell and Katie were in the drawing room. But the door was open to the hall while they waited for the sound of the car.

Bill, Willie, Mark and Bert Ormesby had been out searching since seven o'clock, when Katie had come home in distress, saying she had waited and waited for Sammy until six o'clock when Mr Fenwick closed the shop. So, something was wrong.

When Bill had come in, he had phoned Mr Fenwick and heard that gentleman relating how young Master Love had hurried out of the shop as if he were running after somebody he had just missed. But the two previous customers to leave the shop had been just young girls.

The lead had started there, because when Fiona got in touch with the school to say that they would be a little late picking up Mamie, she had been informed that Mamie had left school at the usual time. And, no, there had been no rehearsal arranged for that evening. This new piece of information given to the police, who had been informed that the young man and the girl were missing, had led them to Mrs Polgar's house, only to find the house empty, but with signs of a hurried departure showing. It was when they broke into the joinery factory that they found the particular windowless room behind the joinery shop, and the girl, drugged and trussed up.

Bill had phoned to tell them this. Also that he was at the hospital, as were the police, waiting for Mamie to recover. She had been washed out; otherwise she would have surely died.

Fiona was saying to Katie, 'You go to bed, dear; you've got to go to school tomorrow.' And to this, Katie replied quickly, 'I am not going to school tomorrow, Mam. If anything's happened to Sammy, I'll never go to school again. I mean that . . . I mean that.'

Both Fiona and Nell stared up at her. 'He's been my friend,' she was saying vehemently, 'the only real friend I've got, or had. If anything's happened to him, I'll give up, because then there'll be nothing decent or good in the world. His father had to go, but he had experienced life. But Sammy had hardly started on his, and he had so much to give. You don't know, you don't know. We talked.'

'Yes, dear, I know you did.' Fiona had risen to her feet. 'You're going to be in no fit state for anything tomorrow if you don't have some rest. We'll all have to rest.'

When the phone rang, Katie darted from them and into the hall, and there, picking it up, she said, 'Yes? Yes?'

'Katie?'

'Yes, Dad. Yes.'

There was a long pause before Bill said, 'They've found him.'

'Oh, Dad! Oh, Dad! Where? How is he? Is he all right?'

'We don't know yet. He's in hospital. He's been knocked about somewhat, but he's—' There was another long pause before Bill said, 'He's alive. But listen, put your mother on the phone.'

Fiona was already standing at Katie's shoulder and she took the phone, and she said simply, 'Bill.'

'Yes dear; they've got him. Is . . . is she still there?' Fiona turned and looked to where Katie was walking slowly towards the drawing room, her head held in her hands, and she said, 'No, Bill.'

'He's . . . he's in a very bad way, dear. They haven't got much hopes of him. He's been heavily drugged and he was left in the freezing mud waiting for the tide to take him out.'

'Is he in the hospital?'

'Not in Fellburn; we're here in Newcastle, the General, and there's a lot of fuss going on. It'll be in the morning's paper. You won't believe it. There's reporters already kicking around. They must never sleep, these fellas. I'm tired of trying to be civil to them. Listen, dear, Bert and Mark are coming home. I wanted Willie to go with them, but he won't.' He did not add, 'I'm staying, too,' because she would know that went without saying.

'Can . . . can you get some rest?'

'Oh, don't worry about that, woman. They've

put nice big leather reclining chairs into the waiting room for us. They've been very good. But anyway, I . . . I want to be here when he comes round. I'm sorry that I have to put it like this to you, Fiona . . . if he comes round. God!' – she heard the break in his voice – 'How that lad got under my skin right from the beginning. I'm going to say this to you, Fiona. We have a daughter, you and I, and you have sons and a daughter, but . . . but I feel and always have done from the day I first met up with him that he could be mine, my son.'

There was silence on the line, and then she said quietly, 'Oh, I've always known that. Yes, I've always known that . . . When he comes round, or if there's any change, will you phone me?'

'Of course, of course. Good night, love.'

'Good night, Bill.'

The tears were running down her face as she turned to Nell, and Nell said, 'He's safe?'

Fiona swallowed deeply before she glanced towards the drawing room and then she said softly, 'Just. By the sound of it, it's touch and go.'

9

The morning headlines gave a sketchy account of the incidents:

> Eleven-year-old twin leads police to drugged and battered body of a student, Samuel Love. Mr William Bailey's adopted daughter, Mamie, was found earlier. She was also drugged but otherwise, unharmed. Police are sitting by her bedside in Fellburn hospital, hoping that when she can talk, she will throw some light on the matter of who her assailants were. Samuel Love was taken to the General Hospital in Newcastle where he is still in a very critical state.

Another paper waxed more lyrical:

> The terrible twins, Danny and Jean Gallagher, were where they shouldn't have been and where they

saw something they shouldn't have seen. And it's lucky for young Samuel Love that these eleven-year-olds disobeyed their father's orders never to go near the old jetties, especially the derelict one on the southern side of the shore. But they did, not once but a number of times, and they had a find last Saturday. It was a box of hairpins. However, this time, and in the dark, they made out something happening, but kept quiet about it in fear of their father's wrath. Then what should happen but Master Danny is listening to the twelve o'clock news, his head under the bedclothes, when he hears that they are searching for Master Sammy Love. And he knows Master Sammy Love because that young man had visited their house on Saturday. So, the terrible twin braves his brother's wrath by waking him up. And they both brave their father's wrath by waking him up. They enter the police station at twenty past twelve and Mr Michael Gallagher explains to the officer the reason for their errand, with the following result: the great black bundle the twins saw men thrusting through the wood supports of the old jetty turned out to be the drugged and battered Samuel Love. And, by accounts now coming out of the hospital, he was found only just in time.

The local radio gave out the story in a plainer fashion. But the following day the story was head-lined on one or other of the pages of the national dailies, not so much concerning the twins' escapade, but that the Fellburn police had discov-ered what they had been looking for, for a long time, the storehouse for the street-trading in drugs in the town and city. And they hoped that when Samuel Love was fully recovered, he would give them enough information to lead them to the ring-leaders.

It was when Mr Gallagher read the newspaper that he said, 'You talk about silly buggers. The ring-leaders of such a business as they had won't be bloody fools and sit waiting to be picked up, they'll be scattered country-wide now.' And to this, his taciturn son Mike said, 'No, Da, they're not bloody fools, they won't sit waiting to be picked up; they are mere tools, the ones who make and bag and push the stuff. I'd like to bet their bosses are living somewhere on Brampton Hill here in Fellburn, or Jesmond in Newcastle, respected citizens, doing good work here and there. Remember the case last year of that insurance agent who did so much for the Boys' Club, and he's doing a stretch now. No-one could believe that such a nice man was in the drug trade on the side. Never touched it himself, of course. And they had some job in convicting him. You know me, how I love our dear constabulary, but I was with them over him.'

Len Gallagher looked at his son and laughed now, saying, 'Oh, but you've changed your opinion about the polis, haven't you, lad? You could have called those two that were in here this morning brothers.'

'I was merely being civil, or trying to be.'

Len laughed again as he said, 'You'll have your picture in the paper the morrow. See if you don't. Flanked by the terrible twins. 'Tis a pity though, there's no money as a reward.'

'I don't want any bloody money,' growled Mike. 'I wouldn't take it if it was offered, not from them lot. But anyway, I was only the spokesman. If there is anything to come out of this, it should go to Danny. But I don't see from what quarter there'll be any reward.'

'You never know, lad, you never know. You never know where a blister might light,' his mother said.

'Oh, Ma.'

'Never mind the Ma. Anyway, I don't know about money coming in, but money is going out. There's our Daisy, she's lost a day's pay: she's been hovering round that hospital all day. And if he's not round the morrow, she'll likely lose another day's pay.'

'Oh, but Ma, why are you worrying about her losing a day or two's pay?' There was a sarcastic note in Mike's voice now as he went on, 'For where is she at this minute, but up in the Bailey mansion? And who got her up there? Well, no other than their stinking, snobbish daughter that she couldn't stand. Oh, things are changing on the Gallagher horizon. We're going up in the world. Oh, yes. Yes.'

'Many a true word spoken in joke.'

'Oh! Annie.' This came from her husband, and she turned on him and said, 'When you're at the bottom, there's no way out but up; and even skimmed milk has got a skin on it.'

When laughter came from the scullery from Frank and Sep, their mother yelled back, 'I'll knock the sniggers off both your faces, if I come in there to you.'

There was a short silence in the kitchen until Mike, speaking as if to himself, said, 'Sep can afford to snigger.' His mother's voice, equally soft, said, 'Ah, Mike, lad; give over, give over. Things can't remain as they are for ever. Believe me, lad, believe me.'

When Bill entered the waiting-room and saw Daisy sitting there, he said, 'I thought you had gone home for a bite with Katie.'

'Yes, I did, Mr Bailey. But Katie was all in and

her mother said she must go to bed for an hour or so.' And Daisy smiled as she added, 'Mrs Bailey wanted me to lie down an' all; but I said once I put my head down I'd lie there till the morrow. Anyway I must look in at home; they'll be thinking I've left for good, but I couldn't go without calling in to see if there was any change.' She paused, then added, 'Is there?'

'No, lass. But now you get yourself off home and to bed. I'm staying for an hour or two; then Mrs Bailey will relieve me. And don't worry; if there's any great change I'll get word to you right away. Willie's with him now; but he's another one who must get his head down for an hour or so, else he'll be finished. Go on now, lass; get yourself away, and keep hoping for the best.'

After she had gone, he stood thinking: that lass had been on her feet for more than twenty-four hours. He had first met her yesterday morning and within a short time had learned much about her and her family. What surprised him more was that she seemed to have an influence on Katie, who had simply gone to pieces; she would not stop talking about Sammy. Neither Fiona nor he could do anything with her, but this Daisy lass had talked back at her, about her own family and what had happened to them over the years, more than she had heard last Saturday. She had told Katie she knew how much she thought about Sammy, but that she wasn't the only one who cared for him; in their own ways they all loved him.

One thing was certain in his mind: whether Sammy lived or died, he felt duty bound to do something for that family.

He wasn't a praying man, but he had the wish now to slip into the hospital chapel, not to pray in the ordinary way but to ask a power higher than that any of the doctors possessed to bring the lad round.

When he remarked to the sister that Sammy seemed to be sweating all the time, she had said, yes, that wasn't very good; and that he may be heading for pneumonia, but let them tackle one thing at a time. And, apparently, the thing they were tackling now was the effects of the drug that had been washed out of him. Of course, lying in that ice-cold water for hours would lead to pneumonia, and in his present state, pneumonia would be dangerous . . .

In the chapel, Bill found himself alone and ill at ease. He did not kneel but sat in a pew, and stared at the gleaming brass cross standing on the little white altar.

It was odd, but he could not think of one thing he had intended to ask.

He later recalled he did not know how long he had continued to sit before he seemed to come to himself by emitting a deep sigh. Then, as if he were talking to someone in that altar, he heard himself think, you know what I'm after, but I can't put it into words; so I suppose it's as good as said.

He remained seated, feeling a strange sort of

peace on him now, something he had never experienced before. Then he rose slowly and walked out, and stranger still, there came to him the thought that there could be something in this God business after all.

10

It was the following day when Daisy burst into the kitchen and to the surprise of the whole family, who were seated round the table finishing their evening meal, gasped at them, 'I'm . . . I'm going up to their house for a meal, Ma.'

'What!' Annie Gallagher got to her feet.

In a much lowered voice, Daisy said, 'He's . . . he's outside in the car. He asked me to go up and keep Katie company. Somehow I think it was just an excuse. But anyway, I'm going.' She now nodded down at the menfolk, who were staring up at her as if they had said something to which she must give a reply.

It was Sep who rose from his chair and in an awe-filled voice said, 'You mean Mr Bailey, the boss? He's outside in the car?'

'Aye, he is.'

A smothered bark from his mother halted Sep: 'Come away from that window, else I'll swipe the lugs off you.'

Daisy was looking at her father now; he hadn't spoken and she said, 'They're kind, Da, they mean well. Not patronising or anything. And the way he talks at times he's as rough as you.' She grinned at him, and for answer, he said, 'How's the lad?'

Her face went into its usual stiff pattern and she bowed her head as she said, 'Pretty rotten.'

'He hasn't come round yet, then?'

'No, Da. But . . . but if it's all right with you, I'd . . . I'd like to go back with them.'

'It's all right with me, lass.'

Daisy now bobbed her head from one to the other of the family and, her face becoming bright for a moment, she said, 'I'll give you all the news of the palace the morrow.'

'Aye, do that. Do that, Daisy.' This was from Frank. 'See if they want a butler. I wouldn't even mind being a footman, I'm sick of navvying.'

She smiled at her brother now as, making for the door again, she said, 'I'll keep me eyes open and drop a word.'

'Do that, Daisy. Do that.' Frank laughed back at her . . .

When she took her seat in the back of the car, Bill leant his head back as he drove off, saying, 'Everything OK then?'

'Aye. Yes. Thanks.' Then she couldn't resist being herself for a moment for she added, 'They were a bit peeved because they weren't all invited. But, as me da said, he couldn't have come anyway, his dinner jacket was at the cleaners.'

'Now, now! Daisy. Let me put you in the picture. You're going to a big house standing in its own grounds, but it's a home you're going to an' all, and it's full of very ordinary people. By God! Yes, very ordinary people, fighting, squabbling, worrying, ordinary people. The only difference between our house and yours is a bit of money, and money isn't everything . . .'

My God! What was he saying? Money isn't everything? Money *was* everything in these days.

Look at this area he was driving through now in this big, posh car; it was as it was through the lack of money; not that there wasn't money about and being wasted by many people, and in this district too, for booze and betting would often be found top of the list. Oh, aye, they must have their booze. Yet most people found at the bottom of the list would be there because there was no work. What would happen when this scheme of his closed and he had to lay off two hundred or more, he did not know. Oh, what the hell was he thinking about! The scheme would last for almost three years. And he was working on getting other plots, even though they'd be far afield. The old trouble would then start, a lot of them didn't like to travel . . . What in the name of God was he on about? He was going home to have a bath; he was worried to death about the lad; and also, don't let him forget, about that damn little monkey. If only they could get her to speak the truth: she would keep saying she knew nothing, even insisting that she had been to school and to the concert practice. Oh, he was going to get in touch with her grandfather and he would have to take her on; Fiona was fed-up to the teeth trying to do anything with her . . .

When Daisy entered the house, she tried to stop herself from gazing about the hall; she tried to stop herself from gazing about the drawing-room; she tried to stop herself from gaping at the dining-room, especially the way the table was set out.

After saying, 'Hello,' to a very surprised Willie and a slightly gaping Mark who, for a moment, forgot his manners, the only one she seemed to relax with and who saw nothing strange in her was Angela, for the child made straight for her, held up her arms and put them around her neck, and was hugged in return. When the child kissed the face under the blonde hair, Daisy felt a lump in her throat.

Looking on at this greeting was Nell who thought, they're two of a pair, loving oddities in their own way. She could understand how Willie was smitten by this girl. His pleasure at seeing her when she entered the house had been evidence of this. And if Sammy had been all right, she would have said that this, in a way, was a good thing, no matter how it turned out, for then Sammy's spare time would become more his own.

Willie was saying now, 'Dad, why don't you have a few hours sleep and I'll go down and sit with Mam until twelve, then you and Mark could come in.'

'And where do I come in?' Katie looked from one to the other, and it was Bill who answered her, saying, 'Katie, dear, if you're wise, you'll stay here, go to bed and be fresh for tomorrow morning when you can take over all day. None of us can go on without sleep and . . . and when Sammy does recover, we won't be able to crowd in on him at all hours. They're letting only one at a time sit there now so he'll be able to see someone he knows when he comes round, and perhaps speak to them, tell them what happened. He's more likely to tell us than the policemen, at least at first. But I bet your bottom dollar, whatever he's got to tell us will be about that little cat who is still lying.'

The result of this discussion was Willie got his way. And it was Bert who drove him and Daisy back to the hospital, where Daisy stayed long enough to ascertain if there was any change in Sammy. She had realised that if she stayed longer it would be in the waiting room and she would be alone with . . . the woman, Willie's mother, at least until she replaced her son at Sammy's bedside. And she knew she wouldn't have to be long with her, for they both found out they weren't bouncing their balls against the same wall, that they were two people who couldn't play together: as in the wall game she had played as a child, your partner had to be one of your own lot, not someone from another street. And being no fool, she knew that Mrs Bailey, of all of them, was certainly from another street. So, she asked Mr Bert Ormesby if he would drop her at her house, and she, too, would have a sleep and then return early in the morning before she went to work.

'And you think the cutlery was silver?'
    'Well, I don't know, Ma, but it was heavy.'

'What was the dinner like?'

She turned to her father now, saying, 'Well, I suppose you would call it ordinary, but it was very tasty. Their friend, Nell they call her – she's Mr Ormesby's wife, you know, the man who does part-time at the Boys' Club, and got Sep set on – she seems to be like one of the family. And she's got a baby an' all – she did the cooking. There was soup first, then a sort of shepherd's pie. It was different from yours, Ma.'

'It would be,' – her mother nodded at her – 'fresh beef likely.'

'There were three other vegetables. They were in dishes and they were passed round from one to another; you helped yourself.'

'My! My! No grabs?'

She smiled at her father now and said, 'No grabs there, Da. No grabs there.'

'Have they got any servants?'

'There weren't any kicking about, but apparently there's a Mrs Green comes in from Fellburn every morning. When the woman, Nell, went for Willie – yes, she did, she went for him about leaving his room like paddy's market – she said Mrs Green had only just cleaned it, and so he had to go and tidy it up himself.'

'And . . . and young Willie took it?'

'Oh, yes, Da. Mrs Ormesby, or Nell, is a power there, I think. Always has been, as far as I can gather. But somehow, I wasn't listening to them; there was so much to see, you wouldn't believe. Oh, Ma, you know me, I don't care for things, at least so I've said up till now. But the hall, it's a beautiful hall. It was tiled-like, I suppose what you would call mosaic-like. But the drawing-room was carpeted wall to wall, as was the dining-room, in a lovely deep pink with a pattern on it. In the drawing-room, you'll never believe it, the colour that matched the carpet, the upholstery and the curtains was a sort of golden-yellow; brocade stuff. It was like something you would see on telly.'

'Did they take you all over the house?'

'No; well, not all over it, Da; Willie took me to the recreation-room. He knew I'd be interested in that. They've got everything in it. As Willie said, they only need horizontal bars and a trampoline.'

'You said there was a swimming pool?'

Daisy looked at her mother for a moment now without speaking, then she said, 'Yes. Aye, Ma, there is. But I couldn't stay there looking at it. I couldn't bear it, 'cos I was imagining what it would be like to get up and swim in there every day. My! I got a bit bitter at times, thinking, this lot don't know they're born. But then Katie took me upstairs and her bedroom wasn't as posh as I expected. In fact, it was a bit old-fashioned. To me, the bed-room suite was outsize. She said quite openly that it had come with the house, but it was of such beautiful wood the mother wouldn't part with it. And the bathroom was a bit old-fashioned, an' all. It had a standing iron bath, Da, you know, with little legs on, curved legs. I bet you it was six-foot-six, if it was an inch. But it was just one of the bath-rooms. I think there were three up there. And the main bedroom had what you would call a dressing-room going off.'

'She took you in there?'

'No, Ma, not really. She didn't purposely take me in, but she had to go in to pick up a warmer coat to take to her mother. And we went through the bedroom and into this other room that used to be the dressing-room but is now all wardrobes. The bedroom too had old-fashioned furniture in it. Nothing what you would call smart. Well,' – she tossed her head – 'it's a matter of taste, isn't it? But you would have liked it, Ma, and you an' all, Da. Aye, you an' all. But there was none of the beds canopied, or any of them in modern brass, they were all just wooden or padded backs . . . but oh, downstairs it was lovely! I have to admit, Ma, it was lovely. And you would have gone crackers over the kitchen. Thirty feet! Oh aye, thirty feet if an inch.'

'The kitchen was thirty feet long?' Len poked his head out towards her.

'Yes, Da. It was as long as this room and the front room put together.'

'Never!'

'It is.'

'But the main thing,' put in her mother, 'is, how did you find them? As a whole, how are you finding them?'

Daisy looked down at her hands and she drummed her fingers on the table for a moment before she said quietly, 'If I'm being honest, I would say they're a decent lot. You know how the swanks get up my nose; and when I first met Katie I thought she was one of them, but she's not. As for Willie. Oh, no; he's no high-hat. I think perhaps his older brother, Mark, might be a bit. But he was nice enough to me, although quiet and stared a lot.'

'Could you blame him, lass,' her father said, 'could you blame him. That hair! When are you going to stop messing your hair up? Come on, now; it's gone out of fashion, you know. I might not get out very much, but I read the papers, and the woman's page,' – he laughed at her – 'and it's gone out of fashion, as have your football socks.'

'Well, I don't go with the fashions, Da; never did. And I'm me, and it you don't like me, you know what you can do.'

'Aye, madam; and if you raise that tone to me again, you'll know what I'll do.'

'Now, now, both of you!'

'Well, Ma,' – Daisy tossed her head – 'you know for a fact you've got to make yourself stand out else nobody takes any notice of you. You're just one of a crowd to be humped together, to be treated like scum or made pregnant and live in one room, or land up in the police court, or . . .'

'Enough! Enough, lass! Enough.'

'Well, Da, you started it. Just leave me and me hair alone. Anyway, none of them passed out when they saw me. Although the woman . . . Nell grinned at me, and she called me lass. We seemed to be on common ground then. And Mr Bailey . . . well, I've told you. He can be as rough as a sheet of emery paper one minute and then be speaking Mr Fowler's English the next.'

'Who's Mr Fowler?'

Daisy tilted her chin and laughed, saying, 'Oh, Ma! Ma! He's nobody I know; he's just a man who wrote a book, and our English teacher at school, you know the barmy nun, Sister Felicia . . . Well, we all said she used to go to bed with Mr Fowler 'cos he spoke correct English. Oh, what a lot of time she wasted on us.' She now turned her laughing face towards her father. He didn't return her laughter but said, 'And what a lot of time you wasted, lass, in not listening to her.'

'I can speak as good as the next, Da.'

'You can speak in a certain way as good as the next, but not as good as the next.'

Daisy got to her feet abruptly, saying, 'You always hit me on the wrong spot, Da. Anyway, I'm off to bed now, 'cos I'm getting up early in the morning and going to the hospital.'

'Aren't you going to work the morrow, lass?'

'Yes . . . Ma . . . Yes, I'm going to work the morrow, don't worry. And they won't sack me 'cos I'm the best they've got in our department. There's some lazy buggers in there. If I was in charge I'd give them the sack.'

'Mr Fowler's English! Mr Fowler's English!'

'And the same to you, Da, and the same to you!'

As she went out of the room and they heard her going up the stairs, Len said quietly, 'As I see it, Annie, she's got a chance in a lifetime, getting to know that family. But . . . but being her, she'll bungle it, and not so much through her get-up, but through her tongue. I've never known her be concerned about anybody so much as she is for this lad and the condition he's in, 'cos she couldn't have known him all that well.'

Danny's voice came from the end of the table, where he had been quietly playing tiddlywinks with Jean during the whole of the conversation, and he was saying, 'Our Sep says, it's 'cos she's gone sweet on him, and that she was just trying to get her picture into the paper along of me, just to show off her hair.'

His mother now turned on him, saying, 'Then all I can say is, you're a silly little idiot to think she wants to get her picture in the paper. But your brother Sep is a bigger idiot saying what he did.' She turned now and went towards the fire, and as she poked it vigorously Len said, 'I don't know so much about Sep's idea being that of an idiot. The particular lad in question is no relation whatever to the Baileys. He's still the son of Davey Love. And, as I've openly said before, and maintain, that Davey Love, at best, was a rough customer. But by what the lass said when she was here on Saturday, the Bailey family, from top to bottom, seem to love him. And I give it to you, that everybody has another side. I've seen Davey Love in action and he knew every letter of the 'no holds barred' term. So I cannot see any difference between the lad in question and our Daisy. Except that she will dress outrageously, I admit that. But put her in some decent clothes and put her where she can talk and she'd be as good as the next, at least on that young man's level. Although again I admit that he's having an education well above her own. But to my mind, that's her fault; she could have stayed on. Now I've said that, haven't I, Annie? She could have stayed on.'

Annie said nothing. Len was right about many things. He was also right that if their Daisy would change her rig-out she could pass herself in some company. But, by her description of the Baileys and the house they lived in, she could never really mix with that lot. Not in a way so as to become close to them, as Sep had suggested, because the young lad now lying near death's door mightn't be a Bailey, but he wasn't a kick in the backside off it, class-wise, because he had been with them for years. And the way he spoke was practically in the same tongue as that of the young fella Willie. So if their Daisy was wise, she would stick to her own class. But who was to tell her that? Oh, yes, there was the point, who would have the nerve to tell her that?

II

Katie was feeling very tired. This was the fourth day Sammy had been in a coma.

At the other side of his bed sat a policeman. He, too, looked weary.

A nurse came into the room, and Katie moved aside for her to take Sammy's temperature and blood pressure. It was as she recorded these on a chart that there came from the bed a sound that brought the policeman from his seat and caused Katie to exclaim loudly, 'He spoke! He spoke!'

'Hush!' said the nurse as she stared down on Sammy.

When the sound came again she said quickly, 'Don't fuss him, I must get Sister.'

Once the door closed on the nurse, Katie could not restrain herself from putting her fingers on Sammy's cheek and saying, 'Sammy! Sammy! It's Katie. Do you hear me? Come on, Sammy! Wake up! Come on! Look!'

The policeman's head was close to hers, and he said, 'Quiet a minute, miss; he's trying to speak . . . What did you say? What is it you said?'

They both watched Sammy's lips move: it was as if he was saying, 'Mama.'

When Sister came hurrying into the room, hissing, 'Leave him alone! Get out of the way!' and went to push the policeman aside, he checked her, saying, 'He's trying to say something Sister, and if you don't mind I would like to hear what it is.'

For reply, he was greeted with a further hiss, 'And if you don't mind, constable, you will move to the side until I attend the patient.'

The policeman stepped aside and looked across the bed at Katie, who had also been pushed aside.

'Come along, Mr Love! Come along,' sister was saying. 'You're all right. Everything's all right. Open your eyes. Now, come along, Mr Love.'

Had she omitted the 'Mr', Katie thought, she would have sounded affectionate, whereas, she made the 'Mr' sound like a command. Then she did exclaim when Sammy's eyelids fluttered; and she actually did speak aloud when he half-opened his eyes, 'Oh, Sammy! It's me . . . Katie,' and when sister remonstrated, saying, 'Miss!', she in no way put Katie in her place, for she replied, 'He's more likely to respond to me than to a uniformed—' she almost said, 'individual', but managed to bring out, 'nurse'.

The sister straightened up and, looking across the bed at Katie, she said in a voice just above a whisper, 'He will respond to no-one for some time. He must not be disturbed or agitated any further at the moment,' and she turned to confront the policeman and added, 'Do you hear that, officer?'

His reply was as soft, but as vehement, when he said, 'Yes, Sister, I hear it. But I'm on duty here, and this patient holds valuable information, which' – his voice dropping still lower, he added – 'might be the means of helping a great many people, or destroying a great many. It's how you look at it.'

Sister's neck seemed to stretch from the collar of her blue uniform; then, looking across the bed, she addressed her subordinate, saying, 'Remain on duty in this room for the time being, nurse.'

She might as well have said, 'See that these two do as I've told them.'

After the door closed on her the policeman muttered softly, 'She's like one of the old tartars. I thought they were all retired.'

The nurse grinned at him before saying softly, 'Like you, she knows her job.' Then turning to Katie, she pushed a chair towards her, adding, 'Don't expect any change yet a while. But it'll come.'

In this case, however, both the nurse and the sister were mistaken, for it was less than half an hour later when Sammy again opened his eyes. He blinked and his eyes moved from side to side while his head remained still. This time the name was distinct, 'Mamie!'

'She's . . . she's all right, Sammy. This is me, Katie. You're going to be all right.'

'Mamie!'

The policeman was hanging over him now, saying, 'Yes, sir, Mamie is all right. Can you remember anything?'

Katie put out her hand and pushed at the policeman's shoulder as she hissed, 'Give him a chance. It'll come.'

'He could go off into a coma again . . . Can you remember any names, sir?' the policeman persisted.

'If you don't leave him alone,' the nurse said, 'I'll call Sister back right now.'

The policeman straightened up, and he said stiffly, 'Every word he says will mean something and could be a lead.'

Before the nurse could respond, Sammy spoke again, 'Ka . . . tie,' he murmured.

'Yes, dear?'

'Mr . . . B.'

The policeman was all ears now, saying nothing, but listening intently until Sammy said, 'Ma . . . mie . . . Bunch . . . powder.'

When Sammy closed his eyes, the nurse said, with some agitation, 'Leave him alone, please! Let him rest.'

They both straightened up and the policeman, after rapidly making some notes, said, 'Well, that's a start,' to which Katie stressed, 'Mr. B is referring to my father.'

Slightly disappointed, the policeman said, 'Well what about Bunch? Did you recognise that?'

'No,' said Katie.

'Sit down!' said the nurse to both of them, 'and be quiet, please.'

By eight o'clock that night, Bill had taken Katie's place and there was a different policeman sitting there. When Bill had entered the room, the policeman introduced himself, saying, 'Police Constable West, sir.' Bill had nodded to him before turning to Katie and saying, 'Your mother's waiting for you,' and she whispered, 'Dad, he spoke. He said Mamie and another name that sounded like Bunch.'

'Oh, yes? Yes?' He nodded at her, but pressed her towards the door.

In the corridor he said quietly, 'He likely wanted to say something about that little bitch. I've got it in my mind that she's been the instigator of all this. She still won't speak except to say she wants to go to her grandfather. I can tell you, she can't get there quick enough for me. Anyway, don't let your mother come out again; Willie's coming to take over later on.'

As Bill sat down by the side of Sammy's bed, the policeman said, 'He's been knocked about . . . the young fella, hasn't he?'

'Yes. Yes, he has,' Bill said; but when the policeman said, 'You can't believe the things that happen these days,' and went on to relate them, he wished to hell the man would shut up.

He sat back in his chair, and closed his eyes, only to jerk forward again at the sound of Sammy's voice, saying, 'Mr Bill . . . Mr Bill.'

'Yes, Sammy, I'm here. Take it easy now.'

'B . . . Bill.'

'Yes? Yes, lad, this is Bill.'

'Shop . . . lift . . .'

Both Bill and the policeman exchanged glances.

And the policeman said, 'What did you say, sir?'

They had both heard what he had said, and when it came again, 'Shop . . . lift,' and then after a gasping breath, 'Mamie lifting,' the policeman repeated, 'He said, shoplifting.'

Bill had heard the words but was actually shocked by Mamie's name being associated with them.

Sammy had moved his head slightly on the pillow and now he looked at the face above him and said again, 'Br . . . Br . . . Brunch.'

'What did you say, sir? Brunch?'

Sammy's eyelids drooped, but as they did, he repeated, 'Brunch.'

At that moment the door opened and the nurse came in, and as she made for the bed Bill said, 'He's spoken, nurse.'

'Good.' Her voice was noncommittal. 'But he mustn't be pressed. He wants sleep now, ordinary sleep, and then tomorrow he will likely be quite lucid.' She now went through the procedure of taking Sammy's pulse, blood pressure and temperature; then said 'I'll be back in a minute or so.' Then, turning to Bill and her voice softening, she said, 'Unless you'd like to stay in the waiting room as before.'

'Yes; if you don't mind, Nurse, I'll do that.'

'He won't do any talking until tomorrow, as I said.'

But Sammy did. The door had hardly closed on her when the policeman, bending close to Sammy, said, 'Is it the name of a man, sir, Branch?'

'Bru . . . Bru . . . Brunch.'

'It sounds like Brunch, not Branch,' said Bill quietly.

Then his head moving slightly again, Sammy looked at Bill and said, 'Garage, Bill.'

'Garage, Sammy?'

'Johnny . . . Johnny Hatter.'

Bill straightened up for a moment. 'Garage? Johnny Hatter?' The name recalled a young fella whose name was Hatter, to whom Rupert had given the push some weeks ago. It wasn't concerning his work, but that he took too many days off. He was always sick or there was somebody in the house sick, if he remembered. Yes, that was the name.

'Drug . . . drug.'

'Yes, sir, that's what we want to know about, the drugs.'

Sammy pulled in a long breath. Then as his head seemed to sink back into the pillow, he breathed the name again, slowly, 'Bru . . . nch.'

It was at this moment sister came bustling into the room and, looking from one to the other, she said, 'Would you kindly wait outside?'

'It's my . . .'

Sister now stared at the officer, saying, 'I know what you're going to say, constable; it's your duty. Well, he's not a prisoner, but he's a very sick young man and' – her voice dropping – 'for your information, he's going to sleep. And hopefully, he'll be much better tomorrow . . . hopefully, I say. But if you choose to sit here all night, that's your business.' She turned and looked at Bill, her glance saying, the same applies to you.

When the two men were in the corridor, the officer said, 'She is a bossy boots, that one, isn't she?'

'Yes. But I suppose she's right.'

'What d'you make of the word Branch, sir?'

'I don't think it was Branch, but Brunch.'

'Brunch?'

'Yes. Brunch. There's a little restaurant in town, called The Brunch. Do you know it? A board outside says, "Come and have a brunch for your lunch." I think it's Americans who use the word brunch for lunch.'

'The Brunch?' The policeman's face had stretched now. 'Yes; yes, you're right, sir. And he said drugs, didn't he?'

'Yes.' Bill nodded thoughtfully. 'Yes, he did.' And then he added to himself, he also said shop-lifting. My God! Fiona will go round the bend if that's true. As for myself I'll want to take the skin off her if she's been the means of causing this business. And I'll likely not be able to stop myself if anything happens to him . . . 'What did you say?'

'I said Johnny Hatter. He mentioned that name.'

The policeman now took out his radio and spoke into it, saying, 'Is the inspector there?' There was a pause, then he said, 'Well go and get him, and put him on.'

Presently, he spoke again, 'Is that you, sir? The young fellow has spoken. It seems that the name Brunch or Branch is connected with a restaurant in

Fellburn. He also spoke the name of a man he must have recognised, Johnny Hatter. Apparently some weeks ago this man was dismissed from Mr Bailey's garage. He also associated the girl Mamie with shoplifting.'

There was a further pause before the policeman said, 'Yes, sir. Thank you, sir,' before returning the radio to his pocket and saying to Bill, 'That's given them a lead, anyway.'

12

The next morning Sammy had come around somewhat, although he still imagined his father was with
him and holding his hand. 'Da, I'm paining.'

'Well, you would be, lad, wouldn't you?'

'But why?'

And his Dad had said, 'You'll know soon
enough, lad. Just rest easy.'

'Da, are they going to kill me?'

'Well, they had a good try, lad. You'll hear all
about it later.'

When Davey's hand went to leave his, Sammy
grabbed it, saying, 'Don't go, Da. Don't go. I'm . . .
I'm frightened, Da.'

The hand left his; but another hand took its place
and a voice said, 'You awake, Sammy lad?' He
opened his eyes and looked up into Bill's and on a
whimper, he said, 'Oh, Mr Bill.'

'Oh, lad, it's good to see you back.' There was a
break in Bill's voice.

'I'm aching, Mr Bill; I can't move.'

'You're bound to ache, lad, but you'll soon be
better.'

'Me da's been with me, Mr Bill.'

'Well, you couldn't have a better man by your side, lad. Do you think you could talk to the policeman and tell him what you remember?'

'Policemen . . . policemen?' muttered Sammy. 'They didn't come.'

'No, but they're here now, lad, and you can help them.'

Following Bill's pointing finger, Sammy's eyes slewed to the side to the face peering at him, and Bill said, 'This is Inspector Mason. Can you tell him what you remember?'

Sammy sighed, as if trying to recollect what had happened. Then he muttered, 'Kitchen . . . Thieves' kitchen. Table lit . . . littered.'

As Sammy gasped for breath, Bill said, 'Take it easy, boy,' and he stroked the wet hair back from Sammy's brow, the while raising his hand, indicating to the inspector to go slowly.

However, the inspector said, 'His every word, sir, could give us a lead. The Brunch information certainly gave us a start. There won't be any more brunches there for a time. If you could have seen that cellar and the camouflage, you would have been amazed. He's part Greek, the owner; but his subordinates are certainly not foreigners: lads from your own doorstep. We've got one, but there must be others. And if he can only remember names . . .'

Again Bill held up his hand for Sammy's eyes were open again and he was looking at the inspector. 'Polgar,' he said.

'Yes, sir,' the inspector acknowledged. 'She had been in the house, Gertie Polgar; at least, that's the name she is going under now. She's got a record, that one, and she's as slippery as an eel, but we'll find her, because she's trailing her daughter with her this time. She's another one, that young lass.'

He looked across at Bill, but at this stage he was tactful enough not to make mention of the daughter's companion.

'Hatter and, I think . . .' Sammy paused and drew in a deep, long shuddering breath before he said, 'Breeze . . .'

'Breeze? You mean wind?'

Sammy closed his eyes. He wished he could remember clearly. If only his da hadn't gone. Then he saw a man's face and another man going for him, and on a quick note he said, 'Breezy. M-M-Morley. Yes, Morley.'

The inspector now said eagerly, 'Breezy? Oh, we know a Breezy. He's in and out like popcorn.'

Sammy closed his eyes again: he wanted to go to sleep, for his da had come back, but he had hold of his hand and was saying to him, 'Remember Pembroke Place? D'you remember that, lad; Pembroke Place and Mr Campbell? Mr Campbell?'

He opened his eyes slowly and muttered now, 'A man, Mr Campbell; they were going there, or wanted to go there, Breezy said.'

'Go where? Go where, sir?' The inspector's voice was urgent.

'Pembroke Place, I think.' Sammy closed his eyes. 'Is that it, Da? Then he said, 'Pembroke Place.'

'I . . . I think he's had enough.' Bill again looked

across at the inspector, and he, straightening up, said, 'He's done splendidly to remember those names, because he's still rather concussed, I would think. By! He's had a narrow escape.'

Turning now to the sergeant who had been taking down notes, he said, 'Let's get on with the business. Campbell will take over,' and turning to Bill, he added, 'You never know what else he may remember.'

When the nurse came in she looked from Bill to the new policeman and, smiling, she said, 'Those two look pleased with themselves.' Then addressing Bill, she said, 'Your wife has come. She's in the waiting-room with the young girl.' She did not say 'that weirdy', because she was puzzled that such people could be associated with someone like her. Perhaps she was a friend of this young man. Yes, it was more than likely, because it was said that he had once lived in Bog's End in Fellburn, and she understood you couldn't get much lower than Bog's End.

In the waiting-room he greeted Daisy, 'Hello, lass,' he said.

She stood up, saying, 'How is he?'

'Quite a bit better, lass. I'd go along now; there's nobody there except for the polis, as usual.'

Daisy turned now and, looking at Fiona, she said, 'Be seeing you,' and Fiona answered in the same vein. 'Yes, Daisy; be seeing you.'

As Bill sat down next to Fiona and saw her hands gripping the top of her handbag, he said, 'What is it, dear? What's the matter?'

She looked up at him. 'It's . . . it's her, Bill, Mamie. I . . . I can't have her back in the house; I wouldn't know a minute's peace. I went to see her this morning and she still lied barefacedly: she had never stolen anything in her life, and that when her grandfather heard of it, what he would do to us. And she wouldn't shut up; she went on and on, gabbling. Yes, she admitted she had been to Mrs Polgar's, but she still maintained it was only after she had been to the practice. Her story is that some men had burst in and they had tied her up and stuck a needle in her, and they had taken Mrs Polgar and Nancy away with them. As for shoplifting, oh, that brought her to tears. I was so mad, Bill, I shook her by the shoulders. We were in the side room by ourselves, but a nurse came in and upbraided me. You . . . you'll have to do something. I don't know what. But I'm not having her back.'

'Don't worry, dear. I'll do something, and I'll take a policeman along with me. I'll put the fear of God into her. She'll come clean or else. In any case she has only two choices, that of going back to her grandfather, or into a home for wayward girls. Anyway, it's out of our hands now. However, I'll get on to her grandfather and get him here quick. He's made no move since he was told.' He bent down and kissed her, saying, 'Come on, honey, don't waste your tears on her. You've wasted years trying to make something of her. It's all my fault, playing the big-hearted Bill, taking on somebody else's kid.' He now drew her to her feet, saying, 'Come on now. I'll take you along and pick up Daisy and drop her at the factory.'

On opening the door of Sammy's room, he nodded towards Daisy, saying softly, 'Come on, Minnehaha; I'll drop you off at your factory.'

They had walked some way in silence along the corridor when she startled him, by saying abruptly, 'You're lucky, you know.'

'Oh? And how d'you make that out?'

'Well, you've got her. She's uppish, but she's the right sort.'

'Oh, she'll be pleased to know that.'

'Well, you should tell her, and often. Men are fools; most of them, anyway.' She glanced sideways at him as they divided to let the food trolley through, and when they were walking together again, he said, 'And from where, miss, have you learned your deep wisdom about men?'

'From our kitchen.'

'Oh! Oh!' He nodded his head, then said, 'Could be. Yes, could be. Any particular member? Or just the bunch of the males?'

'One, really; me da.'

'Oh, you don't say. And he knows how to treat women?'

'Well, one at least, they fight like hell at times, but it's not so bad now as it used to be. When he was in work you could look for a bust-up with your dinner in those days.'

'And that's the man, you think, who knows how to treat a woman?'

They were crossing the forecourt of the hospital now to where the cars were parked, and she didn't speak for some time; but then, thoughtfully, she said, 'Well, for his type of woman and her type of man.'

He glanced at her. She looked a pickle: she was still wearing the short coat that came above her knees and was pulled in tightly round her waist with a belt. Then there was the face above it: eyes made up with mascara, dead white cheeks, which he thought might be natural, but set off by scarlet lips; then the hair, partly covered now with a thin gauzy scarf; and her legs, not with football stockings on today, but definitely bright ones. And she wasn't wearing trainers. Strangely, her footwear looked like an ordinary pair of black shoes. Yet, there she was, spouting theories, theories riven from experience, but which wouldn't have come amiss if spoken by some modern sage, such as a psychiatrist was supposed to be, with his knowledge of life garnered only from books. Otherwise how could he know anything about real living, the way in which the majority of mankind existed? Oh dear, dear! He would soon have to bracket Mark, Willie, and Katie with that lot. Yet Katie was already wise in a way. Aye, well, perhaps after all women had more up top than they were given credit for. And, as this one had suggested, there were women wise enough to keep quiet about it . . .

'Get yourself in.'

'Back or front?'

'Well, madam, if I were chauffeuring you, you would get in the back; but as you seem to have become a member of my family, you'll have to ride with me. Any objections?'

She grinned at him, saying, 'I could think up some.'

'Get yourself in!'

It was indeed as if she had become one of the family, and he hadn't set eyes on her until five days ago. But he had heard quite a bit about her, and from Willie. Oh, he could see how Willie was attracted to her, because, in a way, she was another Sammy. Well, as Sammy used to be, and still was underneath. But what really was Willie's interest in her? Oh, dear me! Dear me! Well, that was in the future. Yet, put her in a different rig-out and she could pass. But was she the type to go into a different rig-out? He cast a sidelong glance at her. She was looking out of the windscreen and she said quietly, ''Tis a lovely car. The lads would go mad about it. But I can tell you this,' – she turned towards him and, almost as if she were ready to do battle, she stated – 'not one of our lot has been a car thief. No, not one. We had a car . . . I mean, our Frank had. It was an old jalopy, but he had to give it up. It was the insurance, and it was always going wrong in a way he couldn't put right. And they've never gone for joyrides either, not one of them. They wouldn't dare; me da would murder them. With his last breath, he would murder them. But around our way they do it all the time. I think our Sep, at times, used to wish he could join such a gang, but now he's set up in a job. Oh, aye, it's at your place.'

'My place?'

'Yes. Mr Ormesby set him on.'

'Oh, well, if Mr Ormesby set him on, he must be all right.'

'Well, yes, he is all right, our Sep. And he's got it up top an' all, but there's no place to use it. He left school when he was sixteen and got into a decent job in Bryants, in the storeroom. He was going to work up to be a clerk. Then they went bust. So he hasn't done anything for nearly two years. He was getting desperate and he just might, oh, aye, yes, he just might have joined one of the gangs and gone car-lifting, because there's money in it. Pinch enough cassettes and radios in a day and you've got a week's wages.'

He pulled up sharply, then exclaimed, 'Why don't they look where they're going?'

'And they saunter over as if tomorrow would do.'

'What did you say?'

'Nothing.'

'You said something, and it wasn't complimentary to me or the car.'

'I just said, what's the hurry, they're not in a posh car.'

She's a tantalising piece this one.

They passed through Gateshead and Low Fell without exchanging further words. Then, when they entered Fellburn, she said, 'D'you know where the factory is?'

'Yes, miss, I know where the factory is.'

There were a number of women passing through

the gates when he drew up the car alongside the kerb; and they stopped and gaped as the passenger stepped out of the car. They watched her bend into it, but they didn't hear her say to the driver, 'Thank you, mister. But don't you call me Minnehaha again, else I'll have Big Chief Running Water after you. He's my minder and they call him Jimmy. And he puts people in their place.'

'Get out!' He stretched his face so he wouldn't burst out laughing. Then, as she closed the door, but not properly, he bent sideways, pushed it open, then banged it; and for a moment he paused there, and returned the wide stare of the women standing on the pavement.

Well, she'd get some fun out of that: there'd be some hot cross-talk in her section today, if he wasn't mistaken.

Throughout the drive back home he found himself chuckling. He had much the same feeling as he used to have when leaving Davey Love's company; there was that quality about her. Sammy had it, too, although Sammy didn't let himself go as he once did, because education was building up a façade about him. And in a way, that was a good thing.

However, once he was in the house his mood changed: he was going straight into battle with the old grandfather of that brazen piece.

Bill got through to him straightaway.

'Yes?' the querulous voice greeted him.

'This is Bill Bailey here.'

'Oh! Oh! Haven't heard from you for some time. How's the child?'

'The child, as you call her, is a girl not yet thirteen, and she is in dire trouble.'

'What!'

'You heard what I said; she is in dire trouble. She has almost caused the death of a young man; in fact, it's touch and go yet whether he'll live. And, into the bargain, it turns out she is a shoplifter.'

'Well! Well!' The words came as a bawl. 'You've trained her all right.'

'Shut your mouth about training; we've done everything possible. She was sent to a good school, private. But she's a polished liar. And I ask you where she got that from, because she didn't get it from her mother and father; they were a decent couple. That's why I gave her a home when she was three and you refused to look after her, but you hung on to her money. Well now, I wash my hands of her. You get yourself over here, and make the choice: either you take her back with you, or she goes into a home for wayward girls and her money will go with her. I've done my utmost for her and so has my wife. She must have bad blood in her.'

The voice came over the phone now, yelling, 'If I was at that end, I'd make you eat those words. Bad blood, indeed! You, who've never put your foot inside a chapel in your life.'

'Shut up about you and your chapel and get yourself over here! If not, I'm leaving her in the hands of the police. When I took her, you made it definite that you were her legal guardian. You thought of the money, didn't you? in case I might claim it and use it on her upbringing. And let me tell you something: if you're not here by this time tomorrow, I shall get the police here to contact your local office. Finally, I'll leave you with the further knowledge that there are drugs in this case, and she's implicated.' He banged down the phone.

He stood for a moment, his hands covering his eyes; he didn't know just where he stood: was he or the old man her adoptive parent? He, himself, had never had control of her money. Then, angrily, he marched away and along to his study, saying to himself, 'Don't be such a bloody fool. You adopted her; you're responsible for her. Both of you took on the role of parents.'

In the office, he sat down at his desk, put his elbows on the table and lowered his head into his hands. There's one thing certain: Fiona wouldn't have her back. And the very thought of her being in this house again was nauseating to him. Well, this being so, he'd have to come into the open. There'd be a court case anyway, because the doctor had found a trace of drugs in her blood. 'Minute compared,' he had said, 'but nevertheless, there.'

Compared with what? The drug addict which she would soon turn into? Oh, yes; once she had started on that, and at her age.

He sat back in his chair and breathed heavily. There was only one spot of light on the horizon; she didn't want to come back here. She had told him openly she wouldn't come back here; she would go and live with her grandfather. Well, then, let her confront the old man with that. And if he would have none of it, then he would see that some arrangements were made for her to be sent to a strict school. There must be such places. And that's if she wasn't recommended by the court to be put in a place for unruly girls like herself; somewhere dealing with drugs and stealing.

He couldn't believe the thieving part. She had everything she wanted, within reason that is, except for gold charm bracelets and spangles! Lately, she had been sending letters to the old man, and had received answers from him, likely with postal orders in, for he would have been unwise to refuse her money. If he remembered rightly there was a clause written into the trust fund that she would not have the sole use of her money until she was sixteen. She could draw upon it for special items. Well, if she had to go into that school or wherever, he would see that she drew upon it, because he wouldn't pay another penny towards her keep.

He got up quickly from the desk and, nodding to himself, said, 'That's that! as far as it goes.' He had work to do.

13

He left his office on the site at half-past four, and made straight for the hospital in Fellburn. And now he was sitting by Mamie's bed. Her head was lowered and she seemed intent on cleaning one fingernail with another.

He had been talking to her for at least five minutes, and she had taken no heed of him. 'Well, now, I'll put it plain to you,' he went on. 'My wife,' he did not give Fiona the usual name of Mrs B that the girl used, but repeated, 'my wife won't have you back in our home. Nor do I want you back. That part being clear, it might be news to you that your grandfather and his cousin don't want you in their house either.' He did not know why he said this, only he knew, in his mind, it was true. But this statement brought her nail cleaning to a stop and she said, 'He will! He will want me . . . he does!'

'Well, he'll likely tell you out of his own mouth tomorrow when you meet him. But let me emphasise to you that it will all depend upon the police; Sammy has come around and given them further information, apart from your shoplifting . . .'

'I didn't! I didn't!'

'You are a liar, and you know it. And when Sammy comes fully around, he'll prove it, and in court. D'you hear? And in a police court, because he has already named some of the men concerned with drugs and whom you know. It is already known to the doctors that you have taken drugs.'

'I haven't! I haven't!'

His voice was a growl now, 'Don't be stupid, girl! The nurses found two punctures on the top of one arm and some in your hip.'

'They're scratches! I haven't!'

'Well, you tell that to the magistrate when you come up before him.'

With some satisfaction, he now watched the scarlet flush cover her face.

'I'm going to my grandfather's; he does want me; nobody can stop me.'

'Well then, you tell him that when he comes.' With this, he got up and walked out.

The following afternoon found two men sitting opposite Bill in his study. They had both been made almost speechless by the size of the grounds and the house, and more so after they had entered it.

As blunt as ever, Bill said, 'You're surprised, aren't you, that this is where she's been brought up?'

The older man, his lips now moving one over the other, muttered, 'Houses don't make characters.'

'You're right there. You're right there. As I said to you on the phone, what's in her has come out from way back. But again I'll say, not from her mother or father, for neither of them would have bred the lying little thief she's turned out to be, and all underhand. Oh, yes, for the first we heard of it was when she went missing. And when my lad went after her, having seen her shoplifting with her pal, what happened to him? He was led into what is now known to be a den of drug-pushers, and afterwards was almost murdered. Thankfully, he's lucid enough today to give the police the whole picture.'

'Well, all I can say now,' said the elderly man, bristling, 'is that somebody in this house was very amiss not to notice the condition she was in.'

'She was a girl of almost thirteen; and she was cute enough to know that my wife might have noticed something if she had gone into the pool. But she hasn't used that for some weeks now, saying it would give her a cold. Always some excuse. But none of us twigged.'

It was the younger man who was bristling when he said, 'Well, now, when she's in this dreadful condition, what do you expect us to do?'

'I expect you to do nothing, sir, but I expect her grandfather to act as a grandfather. And, let me tell you, she wants to go back to him.' He was nodding towards the older man now. 'Yes, she wants to go back to you. She says she will never come back here. Nor would we have her. Anyway, you are her legal guardian; and you saw to it when you took charge of her money.'

'Well,' the younger man was putting in now, 'why should my uncle be expected to—?'

'Will you please keep out of this? You didn't

want anything to do with her ten years ago, did you? Oh no. So, I am dealing with your uncle.'

'He's an old man.'

Bill looked at the older man and said, 'Old? But not too old to carry on business, are you, sir? I don't see you as old. But still, if you think you are too old to take her, the magistrates will decide where she is to go, and her money with her.'

When he saw them both moving in their seats, and the younger man glance quickly at the old man, Bill said, 'Anyway, the money was put into trust, and that can be gone into and easily dealt with. As yet, her money should hardly have been touched. And then there is the accrued interest.'

'There have been expenses,' the old man said.

'What expenses?'

'Well, she's had sums from time to time, and there has been correspondence . . .'

'Sums? There's been five pounds, ten pounds, and not very often. I go through the post before anybody gets letters in this house. And last year I should say she had a letter from you twice. As for expenses; what d'you mean, expenses? There's no expenses in running a trust like this unless you . . . Did you have a secretary, such as your nephew here? Whom I thought, when I last met you, was your cousin or your son-in-law, or some such.'

'There had to be things signed at the bank, and correspondence and—'

'Shut up! Don't you try to cover up to me. D'you know who you're talking to? I'm a businessman: I have secretaries, I have accountants; I know how things are run; I am now working on a contract from a trust left by Sir Charles Kingdom. I am also on a committee that deals with a trust for cancer relief.'

'Those . . . those are different trusts.'

'They all come under the same laws; and we'll look into the laws, won't we? And that's one of the first things I'm going to do when she's sent into a home.'

'I don't want to see her going into one of those places.'

'You don't?' Bill poked his head towards the old man. 'Then what is the alternative, if you're not going to take her?'

'I haven't said I'm not going to take her. Well, what I mean is, you haven't given us a chance to speak.'

'Uncle, what about room?'

The old man almost barked at his companion now, saying, 'Will you leave this to me, Owen. Please!'

Again Bill was looking from one to the other, and now he repeated, 'Room? What d'you mean, room?'

To this the old man said, 'Don't worry. If we have to make room, we'll make room.'

'All right, you'll make room. But what is all this about? You had, I understand, a very nice house. What are you talking about,' he had turned to the young man, 'not having enough room? Is that what you're saying?'

The old man drew in a long breath, and said, 'My

. . . Owen and his wife are living with us temporarily.'

The younger man, who was glaring down towards the end of the desk, now had all Bill's attention. 'But you and your wife were going up in the world, weren't you?' Bill said. 'You were moving from some village in Wales to The Hill, or the equivalent, into a fine house; and you had made up your mind you didn't want any children. Apparently it was children or the house, and the house won. You were in big business of some sort, weren't you?'

The man still kept his gaze on the end of the desk as the older man attempted to explain, 'It's . . . it's only temporary. There was a bit of a slump and . . .'

'Oh! Oh! He's gone bankrupt, has he?'

The younger man's head came up quickly and he snapped, 'It's a temporary thing, just temporary. It'll be all over in no time.'

'Not bankruptcy, lad, not bankruptcy. I don't know how long ago it is, but you know it's three years before you can start up again. And then it's difficult. Well! Well!' His tone now changing, he went on, 'Well! Well! You wouldn't have him down as the secretary to Mamie's trust, would you?' A flush crept over the boney face, and the old man spat out, 'You . . . you should be careful what you're saying, what you're suggesting.'

'Oh, I am careful. I'm very careful.' He said no more until, after a silence, he asked the old man quietly, 'You are going to take her, then?'

The old man's head came up, but he kept his eyes

lowered as he replied, 'Yes. Yes, I suppose you could say we are going to take her.' Then he added sharply, 'At least for a time. At least for a time.'

'Well, I don't know how long you mean by a time, but she comes into her money when she's sixteen. And if there's nothing accounted for before, it will be then. And she's very money-conscious, you know. She's a spender.'

'She . . . she will have to conform if she's under my care. And this I will see to. Oh yes.' His head was bobbing now. 'Yes, I will definitely see to it.'

He rose now, and the younger man with him; and when he said, 'We will go back to the hospital and get her.' Bill held up his hand and said, 'Oh, no. It can't be done as quickly as that. We'll have to see the police, because there's bound to be a case later on. They've got two of the scoundrels already. They're looking for the woman and Mamie's friend, Nancy.'

It seemed that the two men were unable to speak a word, and so Bill said, 'You could go to the hospital and see her, and you'd better take some of her things with you, I'll have the rest sent on.'

As he passed them to go out of the room, it seemed for a moment that they weren't going to follow him. Then they were in the hall and he was calling, 'Nell!'

When she appeared from the drawing-room, he said, 'Will you please take these gentlemen upstairs to Mamie's room, and pack a couple of cases with her dresses, or what clothes she'll need. Then would you mind driving them to the hospital?'

Nell, falling in with Bill's tone, said, 'Yes, Mr Bailey,' then led the men upstairs.

Fifteen minutes later, when the three of them came downstairs again, the younger man was carrying one small case, and on Bill's look of enquiry, Nell said, 'The gentlemen didn't think her clothes are suitable for her. I have packed some of her . . . plainer underwear, and a dress and coat, also some stockings and walking shoes.' She was looking straight into Bill's face, but he said nothing to her. To the old man, he said, 'She won't like that; I mean, not having her own clothes.'

For the first time the old man spoke to Bill through the Bible, saying, 'Vanity is the breeder of sin; and in this way alone you may have a lot to answer for.' And on this he marched out, to Nell's voice saying, 'Hang on a minute. If I'm to take you in I must get my coat,' and, on the run, she called to Bill, 'Tell Fiona, will you? She's up in the nursery.'

Bill stood at the top of the steps and watched the two men standing on the gravel drive, their backs towards him. They didn't move until Nell approached them, when they turned and followed her towards the garage. Bill then closed the door and went back to his study. And once again he put his elbows on the desk and held his face in his hands. 'Vanity is the breeder of sin. And in this way alone you may have a lot to answer for.' Does any good deed one ever does turn out right? He had taken Mamie as a child of three and it had taken only ten years of soft living to turn her into what she was today. He had taken Sammy, not only into his house, but into his heart, and although there was nothing legal about it, he knew he had adopted him as a son, and look what had happened to him and what the doctor had said this morning. Even when he got back on to his feet, it would take him a long time to get back to what he had been, for through the kicking he had received, there might be some damage to his kidneys. His ribs were broken, but they would heal in time.

Time. Time. Oh, he was tired. They were all tired. But this business was only really starting. Wait until the papers got their teeth into it.

As Bill slowly mounted the stairs, he repeated to himself, vanity is the breeder of sin . . . you do a good turn, and this is the outcome of it, drugs, shoplifting, and sin.

14

Expectancy is more trying than the event itself.

Who said that? Somebody had; he had heard it somewhere. And it was right, because the headlines hadn't come down on him regarding the girl in the way he had expected; in fact, in a way, some of them had been kind. And after praising Sammy, the schoolboy, as some of them called him, who had tried to get the young girl in question away from the house of Mrs Polgar, at least that was the name the known drug runner had been living under for some two years in a respectable quarter of the town, what had happened to him in trying to get the girl away? He had come across a drug set-up and immediately recognised one of the men as having worked in a garage. Being a member of a karate club, the young fellow had used all his expertise, only to be felled by a blow on the back of the head, then pounced on. He had then been tied up and put in a plastic bag and left under a jetty to the mercy of the tide.

The whole report had ended by saying that the young girl was now in the care of her grand-father . . .

There was no upbraiding of either him or Fiona. Only one paper mentioned that the girl had been before a magistrate and was told that she had the choice of going into a rehabilitation home, or being placed in the care of her grandfather, for apparently she had stressed she didn't want to go back home and live with her adoptive parents. Although she had been brought up almost in the lap of luxury for the past ten years, the girl herself wasn't without means: when she was sixteen she would come into a large sum of money which was held in trust by her grandfather.

So they had got over that. The next headlines, he supposed, would be dealing with the further charges of drug running. But there were still the Polgars to be traced.

But tomorrow was Christmas Eve, and it was hoped they would have Sammy home. He had been in hospital for almost three weeks, and although he had been on his feet for the past week, he had found difficulty in walking. But he had been assured that this was simply because he had been, and was still, badly bruised all down the left side. And no matter what he thought, he must, for the time being, make use of a wheelchair.

He had said to Bill, 'Wheelchair! I'd rather go on my hands and knees.'

And to this Bill had retorted, 'You'll do as you're told; you'll use a wheelchair. We've got one at home all ready for you.'

'Well, you'll not get me into it, Bill.'

'D'you know something, Sammy Love?'

'What?'

'You're not treating me with respect.'

'Oh, I know what you're going to say . . . I've forgotten the Mr.'

'Yes, you forgot my title.'

'D'you mind that much?'

'No lad,' – he punched Sammy on the shoulder – 'of course I don't; I like it. There's another title I'd like better. But you only had one da and I wouldn't want to replace him. What am I saying? Who but an idiot would want you for a son anyway? If you had been bred of me, you certainly wouldn't have walked into a den of thieves and drug addicts, pushers, murderers, the lot; no, you would have had more sense. Anyway,' – he had stood up, embarrassed now – 'I'm going to see the doctor now about getting you home tomorrow.'

'I *am* coming home tomorrow; I'm sick to death of this hole. And the nurses, they're as brazen as brass: the things they say would make your hair stand up on end.' He grinned as he added, 'One's proposed to me, and I'm thinking about accepting her. She's classy an' all. She's not from these parts, she's from Somerset, and she talks well off. I'm definitely thinking about it. I mean, if you can get a car when you're seventeen, you can get married when you're seventeen, can't you?'

By now, Bill was at the door and he turned about and, trying to suppress a wide grin, he said, 'I've only got to tell two females about that, their names being Minnehaha and Katie Bailey, and your Somerset lady would find herself scalped.'

'Who's Minnehaha?'

'Well, I ask you, who of your acquaintance would look like a Minnehaha?'

'Daisy?'

'Yes, Daisy.'

'Oh, my Lord! You're barking up a wrong tree. I'd better not step in that direction; I don't want another bout with Willie.'

Bill had pushed open the door a little when he stopped again, saying, 'Willie and Daisy?'

'Who else?'

'Don't be daft!' And he closed the door, if not with a bang, then none too quietly.

As he walked out of the hospital, he said to himself, there it was again, Willie sweet on Daisy. Dear! Dear! But wait a minute. He almost stopped in his stride. She had never been away from the hospital. She had been here some part of every day since Sammy had been brought in. Was he thick-headed? Didn't he know he was in the running? And who was this Jimmy fella that Daisy had said was her minder? Oh, what a tangle. Well, he supposed, it would sort itself out. It would have to. Before going back to the site he would have to phone Fiona . . .

'That you, love?'

'Well, who else do you expect, Mr Bailey?'

'It could be my mistress . . . Nell.'

'Shut up! And tell me what you want; I'm very busy. We're up to the eyes here.'

'Have you got everything arranged for the Gallaghers?'

'Yes, dear, right to the last member, from Mr Len and Mrs Annie, down to Jeannie with the light-brown hair.'

'Funny! Funny! But, lass, I would like to be there tonight when all that stuff arrives.'

'So would I, dear.' Fiona's voice was soft. 'And, you know, I may as well tell you, I got great pleasure out of seeing that hamper packed. And Mr Graves promised that the other parcels would be dressed up to the eyes. I told him it was your idea, and . . . now hold your head in case it swells . . . he said he had heard you were a good fellow. Ah, but wait! For he added, "at bottom"; he wasn't saying what was on top.'

'Careful, Mrs Bailey, careful.'

'No; seriously, dear, he thought it was a wonderful gesture, and he could understand why you wanted to make it. And I told him about one or two other things you intended to do, and he was so interested.'

'You should mind your own business about that, Mrs Bailey.'

'I'll try, Mr Bailey, I'll try. What time will you be home?'

'Well, as we're closing down tonight, I want to stay on to see what type of guards they're sending this time.'

'You have to be there, and the managers?'

'Yes, I know they'll be there, dear. But you know me; and this is a new firm we've taken on, don't forget: I'd like to tell them myself what will happen to them if they kip down on the job.'

'You're an awful man, but canny in your way.'

He laughed now as he said, 'You're canny yourself, Mrs Bailey. Be seein' you, lass.'

When Fiona put the phone down she looked towards her mother who was entwining holly in the wrought-iron balustrade of the broad stairway, and she said, 'Bill's saying he wishes he could be at the Gallaghers tonight when the hamper and parcels arrive.'

Mrs Vidler paused in her work and, sitting down on one of the stairs, she said, 'And you know, Fiona, so would I. Yes, so would I, if it was only to see that girl again. She intrigues me; I've seen nothing like her. I was thinking about her the other night and I thought she must be absolutely fearless to walk about dressed up as she is. And that hair, you know, has all gone out of fashion.'

'Not quite, Mother. I understand that when they go jiving or whatever, a lot of them go round like that.'

'And, you say she fences and does ju-jitsu?'

'Yes, and very well, from what I've been told.'

'My! My! As they say, you shouldn't judge people by their dress.'

Fiona gave no answer to this, but she went to the large open fireplace at the end of the room and placed another log in the iron basket, thinking my, my! for her mother to say, never judge people by their clothes! At one time, that's all she went by except, of course, their accents. If there had been a change in anyone in this world, it had taken place within her mother.

Her mother's voice came to her now, saying, 'I'm so looking forward to Sammy coming home tomorrow. And you know, Fiona, I've been thinking a lot about his father recently. Whether you believe it or not, I had a great affection for him. I had.'

'Yes, I know you had, Mother, and he appreciated it.' Even as she said this she conjured up Davey Love, Sammy's father, a man so opposite to her mother it was impossible to imagine. Her mother so prim and correct before her unfortunate, or perhaps, fortunate experience in America that brought her back to England a chastened woman. And then there was Davey, half her age, who could hardly say three words without two of them being curses, even if they were laughable ones. And he, poor Davey, scared out of his wits by her mother's attention, so much so that he had come and appealed to them for help. It had been laughable in those days. She stood looking down into the blazing logs, thinking, they had laughed a lot, they had all laughed a lot when Davey was alive, because he had played the part of God's idiot. That's what he had called himself, 'God's idiot'. He had been such a wise man underneath it all. But during this last year they hadn't seemed to laugh very much. There had been little merriment in the house, family merriment, and it was all due to that girl. And she had tried. Oh, how she had tried, and all the time it had been useless, for there she was, shoplifting and taking drugs. Dear, dear God! She closed her eyes tightly for a moment as she thought, well, things would be different from now on: she was with her grandfather and likely to stay there, because he would hang on to her, if for nothing else for the money that was coming to her. But knowing what she did about Mamie, once that girl got her hands on her own money, she doubted if even her grandfather would see much of it. Anyway, Sammy was alive, and he was coming home tomorrow. Like his father, but not so much, because he didn't now decorate his language with colourful adjectives . . . and nouns. Nevertheless, he created laughter, did Sammy. And pray God, from now on laughter would once more return to the house.

She was diverted from her musing by the voice of her small daughter, who was now coming down the stairs, saying, 'I help, Grin? I help, Grin?'

'No, darling, you'll get prickles in you from the holly.'

'Pickles?' The childish laughter rang out. And as Fiona looked up the stairs, there she saw someone who, in her own way, created laughter; and not only laughter but love, binding love, a love that threaded the family together. Yet even this had been tested during the past year through that girl. Oh! why couldn't she . . . ?

She swung round and made for the kitchen, saying almost aloud, why couldn't she forget about that girl? She was gone from their lives never to return. Never! Never! Never!

15

'D'you want your suet puddin' with your stew, or are you goin' to save it for afters, our Sep?'

'For afters, Ma.'

'Me an' all,' put in Danny, 'with sugar, Ma.'

'We'll see about the sugar when the time comes.'

'Well, if I don't have sugar, I'll have butter and jam on it.'

'This is what comes from gettin' your name in the papers.' Frank was nodding down the table at his small brother. 'If I had my way with you, I'd scud your ear every time you opened your mouth.'

'When I'm big enough, Frank, I'll remember what you said, and you'll be too doddery then to stand up to me. And I'll remember you're always shutting me up because of me lip. So, don't forget.'

With the exception of Daisy and her mother, who were serving the meal from a side table, the rest of the family joined in the chuckles and laughter.

After placing the last soup plate of mutton stew in front of her mother at the bottom of the table, Daisy took her own place, yet no-one started to eat until Annie said, 'Well, let's go.'

They had been eating in silence for a while, when there was the sound of choking and spluttering from a different quarter of the table and Annie's voice came, admonishing her youngest daughter, 'Stop playing about with your dinner, girl! Put that spoon down. You'd be glad of that if you were hungry. You're getting too finicky by half. You only get it once a week now.'

'But it's always fatty, Ma.'

There was another splutter. Then, from the far end of the table, Frank said, 'You tell her, girl! You tell her, and ask her why she can't give us sirloin once in a while, and a rump steak. I like rump steak and chips meself.' And to add to this, Harry put in, 'Me an' all, Frank. There's nothing can beat a rump steak and chips and plenty of tomato sauce on it.' Then lowering his voice and his head going forward in order to look at his brother, he added, 'She's stingy with the tomato sauce, isn't she?'

Again there was a splutter. But Annie said nothing; she just continued to take her spoon around the side of the plate. And when Sep, in a quiet, almost refined tone, said, 'Roast lamb is very appetising, served with green peas and new potatoes. I remember once in the far, far past, having partaken of such and . . .'

His voice was cut off by the scraping of a chair, and in amazement now they watched their mother hurry across the kitchen and push open the door into the front room. It was at this point Mike got to his feet and, looking down the table, he said,

'You're an unthinking lot of buggers. That's what you are.'

'Sit down. Sit down, Mike.' Len patted his son's arm. 'Another time she would have taken it, but with Christmas coming . . . well, she's a bit touchy. Sit down, sit down.' He now tugged Mike back into his seat.

But as Mike sat down, Daisy rose from her seat, saying roughly, 'If you want fancy meals, then you should tip up fancy money,' and with this she, too, went into the front room.

Frank now turned to his father, saying, 'I tip up a decent share, Da. Always have done.'

'I know, lad, I know.'

'Mine isn't all that big to tip up.' Sep's voice was again quiet, but expressing a note of regret.

It was a good ten minutes later when their mother returned to the kitchen. And there, Frank going up to her, said, 'Sorry, Ma. It was all in fun.'

'I know, lad. I'm just gettin' thin-skinned in me old age. I should have more sense. D'you know something?' She looked about her. 'I hate Christmas. I really do, I hate Christmas. Oh,' – she went over to the side table now, saying on a lighter note – 'you would like your suet puddin' with sugar, Master Danny, wouldn't you?'

'It doesn't matter, Ma,' the small voice answered her now. 'I'll have it plain.'

'You'll have it with sugar, and like it.'

'I would like hot syrup on mine, if you don't mind, Mrs Gallagher.' Len now winked at those of his family who were looking at him in some surprise, as it wasn't often their da took up a joke. And there was a pause before their mother answered him. 'You know what I'd like to do at this minute if I had any syrup in the house, don't you, Mr Gallagher?' And when their father answered, 'Yes, I've got a good idea, Mrs Gallagher,' there was laughter in the kitchen again, but slightly subdued now . . .

It was a good half-hour later when, the table had been cleared and Daisy, helped by Jean, had washed up the dishes, Frank came into the room again dressed for going out.

Speaking to Mike who was sitting to one side of the fireplace reading the paper, he said, 'Come on down to the club with us; I can afford to stand you a pint the night, it being pay day.'

'No, thanks.' Mike hadn't even looked up from the paper, until Frank's voice came at him, barking, 'Don't be so bloody miserable! It'll get you nowhere. You're not the only one who's having to sit on his arse.'

Mike sprang up from his chair and, flinging the paper to the floor, he cried back at his brother, 'I don't sit on me arse. I walk the streets, the roads, every bloody day.'

When Annie pushed in between them, one hand on each of them pressing them apart, she said, 'For God's sake! Give over, both of you.' Then nodding towards them, she tossed her head backwards and indicated where Len was going quickly out of the room, and she hissed at them both, 'How d'you think he feels? He's sitting there because he can't do anything else . . .'

The knock on the front door drew them apart. It wasn't just a knuckle knock but more like a bang, which caused Annie to march to the door and give the visitor, whom she imagined would be a Christmas collector, a mouthful.

March to the door she did, but she didn't speak. Two men confronted her, and on the pavement between them was a very large hamper. And beyond the pavement she could see a van.

'Mrs Gallagher?'

'Yes.'

'Well, we had better bring this in.'

'Wait a minute! Wait a minute!' She stopped the men from lifting the hamper. 'I think you've got the wrong house. *I'm* not expecting any hampers.' She recalled the adverts sent through the post advertising hampers, and she had been more than vexed just by the sight of them.

'This is Forty-five, Brompton Road West?'

'Aye, it is.'

'And the name's Gallagher, Mrs Gallagher?'

'Yes, you're right again.'

'Well, this hamper is for you.'

Slowly, she moved back, pulling the door with her, and the men had to edge the hamper in sideways. And after placing it on the floor near the table, they looked around at the staring faces, which caused one of the men to smile and address Mike, saying, 'I think we'll need a hand to lift it on to the table.'

Mike hesitated for some seconds before he

moved forward as if in a daze. Then, when the hamper was on the table the men, looking from one to the other, said, 'This isn't all, there's more odds and ends to come.'

Only the door opening and Sep coming back into the kitchen broke the silence, for it was as if the other occupants had been struck dumb.

When the men returned they placed a large square cardboard box on the table, together with four parcels in Christmas wrapping.

Both men, nodding to the occupants, exclaimed awkwardly, 'Happy Christmas! then. Happy Christmas!' They were smiling widely, but it seemed they weren't going to be answered until there was a joint chorus, some voices high and some low, saying, 'Same to you! Same to you!' and from Annie, 'Many thanks. Many thanks.'

She saw them to the door. Then, when they were on the pavement and making for the van, and pulling the door after her, she went quickly towards them and in a whisper she enquired, 'Who . . . who sent this lot?'

'Mr and Mrs Bailey.'

She nodded now silently, but didn't repeat the name. And when the men got into the van, they both leaned forward and looked at her again and one of them said, 'That lot should help you over the holidays, missis.'

All she could do was nod her head. Then the van drove off and she was left standing in the street, to hear a voice from the door calling, 'Come in out of that, Ma; you'll be frozen.'

Slowly she walked back to where Daisy was holding the door open, and she said, 'Mr and Mrs Bailey.'

At this Daisy just shook her head. Then they both joined the mêlée round the table.

'God in heaven!' It was Frank who, seemingly having recovered his good humour, made the statement, 'I've never seen a hamper that size in me life. Who's it from?'

'Mr and Mrs Bailey.'

All eyes now were turned from the hamper on to Master Danny who, his head wagging, was saying, 'Likely it's because Mike and me saved that fella.'

'You big-headed, cheeky little brat.' His father's hand came out and cuffed his ear.

'Well, open it, Ma, the hamper; open it.' Harry pushed his mother towards the table. 'Me mouth's watering already.'

'Hold your hand a bit, lad,' Annie said; then turning, she looked at Len and said, 'Your da will do the opening. Anyway,' she added on a slight laugh, 'it'll take him to undo that leather strap. See to it, Len.' And Len came forward as if he were one of her children answering her bidding.

After undoing the leather strap and lifting up the lid, he stood for a moment gazing down on a galaxy of bottles and jars surrounding a wrapped article in the middle of the basket. Quietly now, he said, 'There's a lot of jars here; I'd better take them out one at a time.' He looked at his wife. Then he handed her a jar, and Annie handed it to Daisy, and

Daisy handed it to Sep, and together, they said, 'Pickles.'

But Frank, looking more closely at the jar, said, 'Walnuts! Pickled walnuts! Eeh gods! Pickled walnuts.'

One jar followed another: honey, two jars; strawberry jam, two jars; then two tins of apricot preserve; two tins of half-peaches; two jars of brandy mince. As the articles mounted on the table the whole kitchen began to buzz with voices, all exclaiming at and repeating what their father was handing to their mother, who in turn was passing them into the various hands reaching out.

Now came a large tin of tongue and two tins of salmon, and when Len paused in the magical process, Harry said quietly, 'You could lift that middle part out now, Da.'

When Len lifted it up, a space on the table had to be made for it. It was unwrapped to reveal a turkey; and what a turkey!

'I can't believe it's happening to us,' Annie said.

'No; and neither can I,' said Daisy. 'It's like something you read about and scoff at because you know it could never happen to you. Is there anything else, Da?'

'Yes, there's plenty more I can see.' Len's voice was thick. And from each corner of the hamper he lifted up a bottle: the first was sherry, the second was whisky, the third white wine and the fourth red wine.

No jokes were made about the bottles as they were placed on the table; to every member of the family it was now seeming too fantastic to take in. Then with an effort, Len lifted a box from the hamper, and more space still had to be made on the table to accommodate it. When its contents were revealed the word that resounded round the room was, 'A ham,' but echoed like 'Amen!'

It was Mike, speaking now for the first time, who said, 'There're more packages in the corner, Da.'

'I thought it was just straw, son.'

Again Len was reaching into the basket and among the straw. He brought out several packages which, on inspection, turned out to be cheeses.

When the hamper was lifted down from the table and put to one side, Little Jean said, 'And there's all those packages, Ma.'

Annie answered her quietly, 'Yes, hinny. Bring them here to where the hamper's been.'

There were four wrapped parcels, varying in size. And as they all stood round expectantly waiting for their mother to unwrap them, Annie surprised them by saying, 'Give me that chair.' And at this Daisy pulled a chair quickly from the side of the fireplace and placed it for her mother. And when Annie sat down, she drew in a long slow breath before, looking at her husband, she said quietly, 'It's odd, you know. I thought it was only bad news that knocked the stuffing out of you.'

'Aye,' he nodded at her, 'I know what you mean, lass. Aye, I know what you mean. But . . . but what about lettin' the youngsters open the parcels?'

At this Annie said, 'Aye. One at a time though! Let Jean have first pick.'

Jean had first pick. It was the longest parcel, and when she opened it, to reveal twelve beautifully decorated Christmas crackers, Len muttered, 'It appears they haven't forgotten anything.'

Danny was the next to open one. This proved to be a large flat box holding an assortment of chocolates by a very good maker.

It was his father who said to Mike, 'Come on, lad, you have a turn. But for you, nothing like this would have happened.' The box contained a display of glazed fruits.

There was now one parcel left. They all turned and looked towards Daisy, and her mother said, 'Last, but not least, lass.'

Quietly and without any fuss, Daisy undid the parcel, picked up the box and held it in her hand for a moment. Then lifting up the lid, she stared at the contents.

There were obviously nine plain envelopes, not those usually holding Christmas cards.

When she lifted them out she flicked through them before turning swiftly about. Then, to her mother, she said, 'They're named, all nine of them.'

'Good Lord!' Frank made a sound like a giggle as he asked, 'Is my name on one?'

'Yes,' and Daisy handed him the envelope. He did not open it immediately; he looked around at the others saying, 'I'll leave it until we all have one.'

'Well, well! Who's going to open theirs first?' Len said.

'I will,' cried Danny, 'because it's what I did that's brought all . . .'

Before he could get any further Daisy dropped her envelope on to the corner of the table and sprang forward, to grip her brother by the shoulders and shake him, the while yelling, 'I'm sick of listening to you blowing your own trumpet! Well, let me tell you, nothing would have come of your find if it hadn't been for our Mike being quick enough to get up and go to Da, and then run to the polis. If he hadn't done so, in another half hour there would have been nothing to find of Sammy.'

'Daisy! Daisy! Give over,' her mother cried, only to be interrupted by her husband, saying, 'She's right, Annie. I'm sick to death meself listening to his twaddle of what he's done.' But then turning to his youngest son, he said, 'But go on. Let him open his envelope.'

Danny, quiet now, and not only having been literally shaken but mentally so, too, by the fact that his favourite sister could rough him up, opened his letter and drew out a piece of paper and a small card. Holding the piece of paper before his face, he seemed fascinated by the sight of the twenty-pound note. It was his father's voice, saying, 'Who's it from?' that made him move his eyes to the card and slowly to read out, 'I owe you more than this, Danny, but I'll never be able to repay you . . . Sammy Love.'

He looked up at his mother who was now staring at the twenty-pound note. And being the little boy he still was, he said, 'Can I spend some of it, Ma?'

'You can, indeed, son. You can, indeed. But let's

see what Sammy Love says to Mike?'

All eyes were now turned on Mike and he, as if obeying an order from his mother, opened his envelope. In his case it was to extract a fifty-pound note, and, like his younger brother, he just stared at it. And his colour rose until it reached his black hair, but still he didn't speak.

It was Frank who said, 'Fifty quid! God! Fifty quid, and me offering to stand you drinks. Well, turn and turn about.'

'What's in the letter, lad?'

Mike did not answer his father, for he was reading the letter. Then, it seemed as if he was about to crush it in his hand; instead, he handed it to his father. And Len, taking it, said, 'D'you want me to read it . . . read it aloud?'

When Mike still made no reply, Len began, '"Like Sammy, I owe you and your brother a debt that can never be repaid. He, to me, is like a son and his loss would have been as grievous. I understand you are out of work. I don't know what your particular line is, but there are many trades at work on my development, and if you would look in at my office on the third of January, around 10.00 o'clock, we can have a talk and perhaps I will be able to fix you up with something. Ever gratefully, Yours, William Bailey."'

They were all looking at Mike now where he was standing with his head down, still holding the fifty-pound note. But when, quite abruptly, he turned about and, pushing Sep and Harry aside, made for the stairs, his mother thrust out towards Frank a warning finger, which said plainly, shut it!

It was Sep who broke the silence, saying, 'I'm glad. I'm glad for him. They are a decent lot there. I've been pushed around from one unit to another, but they're all all right.' He nodded towards his father and Len said, 'I'll have to sit down. It's all too much for me.' And he smiled wanly around the rest of his family. Then, looking towards the bottles on the table, he said, 'It's at this minute I could do with a reviver. But it's no use asking for it, Mrs Gallagher, is it?'

And Annie answered him with a smile, 'Not a bit of use, Mr Gallagher, not a bit of use. Christmas Day you'll have your share, the lion's share. But not until Christmas Day.'

'Well, I think I'll open my packet and see what luck has dropped into my lap.'

'No! No!' His wife was again wagging her finger at him. 'Yours and mine, leave till the last. Let the others have a go. You, Harry.'

Quickly Harry opened the envelope, and he, too, drew out a twenty-pound note and a card. And his face bright, he said, 'It just says, "Happy Christmas, Harry, from Willie Bailey".'

'From Willie?' Daisy had their attention again, and she looked at her mother, saying, 'He's the one who was here that Saturday, you know.'

'Eeh! That is kind, isn't it?'

'Now you, Sep. Come on, let's see what you've got.'

Sep, too, drew out a twenty-pound note and a

small card, and reading it aloud, he said, 'A very happy Christmas, Sep.' Then, his eyes coming from the card and a wide smile spreading over his face, he said, 'It's signed, "Katie Bailey". Coo! What d'you think of that, Ma, eh? The sharp-tongued one that was here that Saturday. D'you think I could cock me hat for her?'

There was laughter all round now. Then his father said, 'Well, come on, Frank, open up.' But before Frank slit the envelope, he looked back at his father and said, 'I'm in work. It'll be "A Happy Christmas", and that'll be all.'

'Well,' Sep put in now, 'so am I at work, and . . . and he's paying me, her da . . . father.'

Frank drew out the similar twenty-pound note, then read slowly from the card, '"A Happy Christmas, Frank, from Mark Bailey",' and he looked hard at his mother before he said quietly, 'They've gone to some trouble, haven't they, Ma? I've never known anything like it. I mean, well, sending me twenty pounds. I had nothing to do with it, and as I said, I'm in work. It looks as if they've all got their heads together, or him or his missis drew them all together. But whatever, I'll say this for them, it's bloody . . . well, I will say it, it's bloody kind of them.' Now he turned to the girls, saying, 'Your fingers are burning both of you. Come on, Jean, open up.'

From her envelope she extracted a ten-pound note, the card saying, 'Happy Xmas, from Angela'.

Jean looked at her mother, and her lips were

trembling when she said, 'Isn't that nice, Ma?' And Annie answered, with a break in her voice, 'Yes, it is, me bairn.'

Slowly from her envelope Daisy also drew out a note; then for a moment she held it at arm's length towards her father. After reading the accompanying card she closed her eyes for a moment, before saying, 'No, no! Well, Ma, look at that!'

Annie looked at the card. It was a Marks and Spencer voucher for fifty pounds.

Lastly Daisy drew out a smaller card, and when she read the simple words, ' "To our friend, with our warmest regards, Katie and Fiona Bailey",' she almost rammed the three pieces of paper back into the envelope and, swallowing deeply, she addressed her father, saying aggressively, 'It's too much, Da! You can get too much of a good thing. Makes you feel . . .'

'Now, listen to me, lass! You listen to me!' Len's voice was as harsh as her own now. 'Don't you start bringing out any of your modern arguments this night. And about this gesture. That's more than a gesture, let me tell you: I'm looking upon it as a miracle, and I haven't opened this envelope yet, and neither has your ma. Every one who has written a note in these letters has taken some pleasure in doing so. And, by God, everybody in this house has felt pleasure at what they have received! Now don't you start, I'm telling you, with your high-falutin arguments. I'm not the priest, or any of that crazy crowd you get in with: independence and modern thinking, and so on, I've heard it all. Now, you be grateful.'

'Open your letter, Len.' Annie's voice was quiet. 'I've opened mine and I feel like going down on me knees at this moment. Just look at that.' She was holding out a note for fifty pounds, saying on a small chuckle, 'And what d'you think it's signed? Just "A Happy Christmas. Bill Bailey". Can you believe it? I would sing that to him meself if he was here at this minute, "Won't you come home, Bill Bailey." Well, he's brought some pleasure into this home this night. And you, Len, what's yours?'

Len looked at her and said quietly, 'The same, lass, just the same. But how is anybody going to thank them for this lot?' He spread his arm out wide, taking in the laden tables. 'Little notes or a letter don't seem right to me; somebody should go.' He turned and looked at Annie, and she said quickly, 'Well, you know I can't, now can I?' Then there was a pause as they both looked at Daisy, and it was her father who said, 'What about it, lass? Will you go up the morrow and tell them . . . well, what we feel?'

'It's Christmas Eve tomorrow. They'll be up to the eyes; they have quite a do up there at Christmas, so I understand.'

'Well, what about slippin' along the night, lass?'

'Oh, Da, d'you know how often the buses run out there?'

'Buses, be damned! We've all got enough money to afford a taxi.'

'I'll come along with you, Daisy.' Frank was grinning at her now. 'I'd like to see that set-up.'

'You'll do nothing of the sort.' His father had

turned on him. 'If anybody is to go with her, it should be Mike.'

'Oho!' said Frank. 'You can see Mike going with her, can't you?'

'There's more in Mike than his stubborn temper, I can tell you.'

'Well, I wish I could see it, Da, I do. I wish I could see it at times.'

When Jean's voice piped in, 'You know something, Ma, what's missing?' She had all their attention and her mother said, 'No, miss. What d'you mean, something that's missing?'

'There's no cake, no Christmas cake.'

'Well, well.' Harry punched her gently on the head, saying 'She's right, you know, she's right. Better phone them and tell them.'

Daisy had been making for the stairs, and she turned and looked towards her mother, saying, 'I . . . I told Mrs Bailey about the Misses Browns always bringing in a Christmas cake on Christmas Eve. She did not go on to explain that she had made Fiona laugh by telling her that the Browns had been a bolt-hole for them for years whenever her da had been on the rampage, and that the last time had been when her eldest sister had come home, once again saying she was pregnant. She knew that she had told her all this, and in the process had elaborated in parts, because, like herself, the woman was very upset about Sammy.

She now went upstairs and knocked on the box-room door, saying quietly, 'May I have a word with you, Mike?'

When the door opened he was standing there in his shirtsleeves. 'They're wantin' me to go up and thank them,' she said, 'to take a taxi. But I don't want to go by meself. Our Frank has offered to come with me, but me da thinks it should be you. Will you come?'

'Up to their house?'

'Aye. Yes.'

'Oh, Daisy, no. I don't know anybody there.'

'I didn't know anybody there either. But they're . . . well, I can't say they're ordinary, but there's no style. And him, the boss, I tell you he's as rough as a bit of sandpaper. And I give him as much as he sends.'

'You give him as much . . . ?'

'Yes.' She nodded at him, smiling now. 'He calls me Minnehaha, so, I "ha-ha" him a bit.'

He turned back into the small room and she followed him. Then, looking at her, he said, 'It's impossible to take in there are people like that. That lot of stuff down there the night . . .'

'Well, Mike, it's their way of saying thank you. Let's face it,' she said, 'without you there'd be no Sammy Love the night, and they know it. You know something? I walked down there the other day and looked down the mud slope on which they threw him. And it's true, in another half-hour the tide would have rolled over him, then gently taken him back down!'

'You went there?' His voice was soft. 'So did I. On the quiet, like.'

They shook their heads at each other; then she

said, 'Come on, Mike, Time's getting on.'

'Oh, Daisy! My clothes aren't decent.'

'They won't look at your clothes. Anyway, I was thinking you're in need of a rig-out and have been for some time. Well, I'll tell you what: the Oxfam have opened a shop near Brampton Hill, and they get a lot of stuff from there, mostly men's. One of the storemen from the factory goes there. You should see the lovely overcoat and things he wears. I told our Frank about it, but he's too big-headed to go. I want a few things an' all. So, what about popping in the morrow, that's if it's open, eh?'

'I'll do that, Daisy. Yes, because I know what I mean to do with this money and that's to get meself a decent rig-out.'

'Well, roll on the morrow. But come on now, get your coat. Put a scarf on, because it'll cut you in two out there.'

He laughed now, quite a merry laugh, as he said, 'Look who's talking about being cut in two, you with your backside bare. How on earth are you not frozen, lass, in that get-up?'

'Me tights keep me warm.'

'They can't. Anyway, between you and me, you've grown out of that kind of rig-out, haven't you?'

'Mind your own business.' And she laughed as she added, 'Funny! If I came in the morrow with a frock on and me hair brown, it would shake them, wouldn't it?'

'It would that. Yes, it would that. But don't do

it all at once. It's like trying to give up smoking; you'd only be back the next day in your shorts.'

'Oh, you don't know, you don't know. Come on. Come on.' . . .

In the kitchen, her mother made no remark on her son appearing with Daisy. 'Well, you're off,' she said. 'Now listen, both of you. Just tell them,' – she nodded now – 'in your own words, just tell them that it's been the greatest night of our lives.'

'I'll tell them, Ma.'

'Wrap up, lass.'

Daisy looked at her father and, her voice cocky again, she said, 'I *am* wrapped up, Da, or I'm going to wrap up.'

When the door closed on them, Len said to Annie, 'D'you know something, lass? They must be a very unusual family to take her as she is, at least outwardly.'

'Yes, Len; but perhaps, like you, they can see beneath her surface.'

There were lights streaming from all the windows at the front of the house as they walked up the path to the front door. Her hand on the bell, Daisy whispered, 'Don't look like that, Mike. It'll be all right.'

There was the sound of voices and laughter from the other side of the door, and when the ringing of the bell caused one voice to rise above the rest, saying, 'Well, you're nearest; see to it,' they glanced at each other again; and then the door was pulled open and Willie gasped, 'Daisy!' Before yelling over his shoulder, 'It's Daisy! Mam . . .' Then putting out his hand towards Daisy, he pulled her over the step. And when the man with her followed, he looked at him. 'Mike?' he said. 'It is Mike, isn't it?'

'Yes, I'm Mike.'

Mike had taken off his cap and was trying to take in the effect of the surroundings. The hall was beautifully lit. There was a roaring fire at one end of it and holly was draped round the top of the pictures.

A man was coming towards them, saying, 'I'm Bert Ormesby.' Then a girl was shaking his hand saying, 'I'm Katie. Remember? Throw your cap down there,' and she pointed to a chair; and turning to Daisy she said, 'Take your coat off, Daisy. You'll feel the benefit of it when you go out.'

'We're not staying,' Daisy said, 'we just came . . .'

'You've just come, girl. Mam!' Katie was yelling up the stairs now.

'What's all the fuss?' added a big booming voice from the drawing-room; and Willie called back, 'It's Daisy and her brother, Dad!'

'Oh, well, I'm not getting off these steps again until I get this damn thing fixed.' Bill was perched half-way up some standing steps. And then at the top of his voice, he yelled, 'Fiona!'

But Fiona, followed by Nell, was already hurrying down the stairs, and on seeing Daisy, she called 'Why, hello there! This is a nice surprise.' And it certainly was when, as Daisy said, 'This is my brother, Mike,' he said, 'How d'you do, ma'am.'

'Very well, Mike. It's nice to meet you.'

Daisy was smiling from one to the other now: she

was proud of Mike. He hadn't said, 'Pleased to meet yer,' but, 'How d'you do, ma'am.' That was nice.

When they entered the drawing-room Bill was stepping on to the floor, and he looked down the room and cried, 'Oh, hello there, Minnehaha!' And she, moving towards him and her face bright now, retorted, 'Hello, Big Loud Buffalo Horn!' The whole room became alive with laughter, and Bill stood with head lowered and bobbing as if talking to himself, while at the same time drawing tightly on his lower lip to suppress his own laughter.

When he cried at her, 'What d'you want here at this time of night?' She answered, 'I'm after a loan,' which caused more laughter.

Bill now turned to Mike, who was standing with a look of amazement on his face. He was seeing his sister in a different guise and he couldn't believe it, not her coming back at this man. Bill was now confronting him, saying, 'And which one of the tribe are you?'

'I'm Mike, sir; and we've only dropped in to . . . well, to try to express our thanks, my mam and dad's, for all your kindness.' He cast his glance towards Fiona. 'You don't know . . . well . . .' As he swallowed deeply, Bill said harshly, 'Look, as I said, that debt can never be paid. That was nothing.' Then he was surprised to hear this young fella come back at him, saying, 'It might be to you, sir, but to our family it was indeed a gift from the gods, as also' – again he swallowed – 'was my letter.'

'Oh! Oh, that. Well, we'll talk about that on the

third of January. That's another thing.' He now nodded around his family; then his eyes coming to rest on Bert Ormesby, he said, 'It's a bloody scandal . . .'

'Bill!'

'All right, woman, all right. Anyway, I repeat to you, Ormesby, it is a scandal: weather dry as a bone; they could have been working this week. No, they have to have a holiday . . . to the third, mind. No good expecting your lot back on Boxing Day, is it? Or even the day after? But, let me tell you, if they're not there on the third . . . well, they'll know what to expect.'

'Bill, this is Christmas. Will you forget about work! Look . . . sit down. Please, sit down.' Fiona pointed to the couch.

Daisy's voice was different now as she addressed Fiona, saying, 'We just dropped in, Mrs Bailey, just to convey my mam and dad's thanks. He would have come himself, me dad, but he's not well.'

'And . . . and we've got a taxi waiting.'

'Oh, begod! You've got a taxi waiting. Well . . .' Bill now pointed to Willie, saying, 'Get outside and tell them . . . have you paid him?' He was now looking at Daisy who answered, 'No, but I'm going to when we get back.'

'You're not going back yet, miss. Look, get outside, Willie, and see to it.'

'Please!' Mike's voice was low but firm. 'I'll . . . I'll see to him. I happen to know him.'

'Well, go on then, do it!' Bill jerked his head, and Mike went out.

Then, looking at Katie, Bill said, 'Is Nell still in the kitchen?'

It was Fiona who answered, 'No, she's up in the nursery arranging a cot for Andrew.'

At this Bill turned a steely gaze on Bert, saying, 'Why don't you two and your offspring move in altogether? Your own house must be going mouldy.'

'Yes. Yes, Bill, it is. Now you've said it, exactly what I said to Nell: our house is going mouldy because we're at the beck and call of that fella and his needs. Oh, for the day when I come back from work and find my wife in her rightful place.'

'What's that?' Nell was coming into the drawing-room now and she put in, 'I'm always there when you come back from work. What are you talking about? What I do with my mornings and evenings is my affair; but I'm always there.'

When Mike came back it was into a babble of voices exchanging what appeared to be insults. Slowly he made his way to where Daisy was sitting on the couch and sat down beside her; and almost instantly Katie, too, flopped down by him, exclaiming, 'It's no use me apologising. The only word for this family is not bad mannered, but uncouth. That's the word, uncouth. Anyway, it's very nice of you to come.' But Mike didn't answer her; he just stared at her. Then Fiona, who was sitting in a chair to the side of the fireplace looked at them, saying, 'We'll have Sammy home tomorrow; at least, I hope so. He hates the idea of a wheelchair, but as I said, better a wheelchair here than a wheelchair there, to which his retort was, that was the place for wheelchairs, not here.' Then she added, 'Would you like a drink? Sherry?' She looked at Daisy, then turned her gaze on Mike and suggested, 'Something stiffer? Or a coffee or tea?'

'Oh, for the Lord's sake don't bring in coffee or tea again,' Bill said. 'I want something to drink. Look, let the females have what they want.' He was now bending down towards Mike, saying, 'What's your poison? Mine's whisky.'

'Suits me fine, sir, whisky. Yes.'

'Well, that's settled. Your weak-kneed sister here will likely want tea.'

'His weak-kneed sister would like a gin.'

'No!' Mike's voice had become loud and he looked around apologetically. Then, nodding up at Bill, he said, 'She's only trying to be clever.'

'I'm not, our Mike. I've had a gin, haven't I, Willie?' She looked across at Willie who was smiling widely at her. And he nodded and said, 'Yes.'

Looking at her son, Fiona asked in a stiff tone, 'When did you have gin?'

'We all had a gin one night. Well, Jimmy, that's one of the instructors, and Sammy, and Katie, and . . . well, Daisy and me; after the practice we all went into Jimmy's club and had gins.'

'Well! Well!'

They looked at Bill, and Willie nodded at him and said, 'Yes, gin and lime.'

'So, what are you going to do about it, our Mike?' Daisy asked. 'Going to tell me da?'

Mike did not answer his sister but looked across at Fiona and said, 'Our . . . dad can drink like a whale. Yet he can't bear to see me mam having a drink. A glass of beer, yes, but never spirits. Our elder sister was banned from the house because she took to it . . .'

'Oh! It wasn't through that, our Mike,' Daisy cut in. Then she looked across at Fiona and explained, 'It was because she was fool enough to come back the second time in a certain condition.'

At this Katie, turning to Daisy, almost spluttered, 'And it wasn't St Michael The Archangel this time, was it?' At which Daisy pushed her as she said on a high laugh, 'No, it wasn't. You remember that . . . from our first meeting? I was in a hell of a . . .' Quickly she closed her eyes, gulped again, then cast a glance around the company. And her gaze coming to rest on Bill, she said, 'Well, I was, I was in a devil of a stew that night. There had been divil's fagarties in the house.'

The room seemed to rock with laughter, and Bill, wiping his cheeks quickly with his hand, said, 'I want that drink. We all want a drink,' before muttering again, 'Divil's fagarties! It's years since I heard that one, divil's fargarties.'

The laughter subsided; Mike looked at Fiona and said, 'There's always one in the family that lets you down. You know what I mean, Mrs Bailey?'

The laughter still rumbling in her throat, Fiona didn't answer him for a moment, then she said, 'Well, it all depends, Mike, on what you mean by letting down.'

Daisy did not take this up directly but, looking at Nell, she said, 'There's so many hypocrites kicking about, don't you think?'

Nell, rather surprised by the question being directed to her, answered, 'Yes. Yes, you're right. Hypocrites, yes.'

'Well, no-one could take you for one, could they, Daisy?' said Willie, and she came back at him quickly, saying, 'You're getting at my gear again, aren't you?'

'No. No.'

Daisy turned to Fiona and said, 'He's half ashamed to be seen with me in the street. It's all right when the others are there.'

His face straight now, Willie said sharply, 'Don't talk nonsense! I'm not! I'm not!' and Mike added, 'It wouldn't be surprising if he was ashamed to be seen with you. Who could blame him? And you know what Da's threatened to do with your gear?' His gaze was soft on her as he added, 'And he will one of these days, mind.' He now turned to Fiona, saying, 'He's threatened to burn the lot.'

'Yes' – Daisy was nodding back at him – 'and you know what I told him I'd do. And I would. I'd walk out starkers, or wearing anything he had left me.'

They were all roaring as Bill entered the room, carrying a large tray of drinks. 'What's that about starkers?' he bawled.

Bubbling, Katie answered him, 'Daisy and I are going to run starkers across the cricket field one of these days, just to give the old fogies a treat.'

'Oh, that will be nice. Let me know when you're prepared to do it, and I'll join them.'

Endeavouring to change the subject, Fiona asked of Mike, 'You keep Christmas Day just for the family?'

'Yes,' said Mike; 'but this one will be different. Oh, so different.' He moved his head from side to side, and they all knew he was again expressing his thanks.

As Bill handed Daisy her glass, he asked her, 'How old are you?' And she, repeating his question, 'How old am I?' said, 'Well, Mr Bailey, in twenty years' time I shall be thirty-seven. That answer would be called facetious, wouldn't it, Katie?' And Katie, her eyes wet with laughter, answered, 'Yes. Yes, I suppose, Daisy, you could say that. But it was right on the spot.'

Making an uneasy movement on the couch and, drawing himself to the edge, Mike drank the last of the whisky from his glass before addressing Bill, and saying, 'We'd better be on our way, sir; we're holding things up. You were all very busy. Come on, up with you!' And he put a hand out to Daisy. 'You've done enough back-chatting.'

Daisy drew herself to her feet, and looking towards Fiona, she said, 'I always do what I'm told.'

When Fiona smiled and Willie laughed outright, Bill said, 'Why didn't you bring your minder with you?'

'Minder?' Willie was no longer laughing. 'What d'you mean, her minder?'

'Well, she told me she had a minder, like that Cockney bloke on the television.'

Mike was looking at Daisy now and he gave a short laugh as he said, 'Minder? Who is your minder?'

'Jimmy.'

'Jimmy Redding?'

Before Daisy could speak again, Willie put in, 'He . . . he's an instructor. Well, part of the time he's an instructor; he's also a friend.'

'He's my guru.' Daisy's face had lost its smile now and she glanced round the company, but she looked at Willie again as she added, 'He took me in hand when I was twelve, and since then, what he says goes.' They were all staring at her now. 'Well, I mean, up to a point.'

This caused Mike to shake his head and say, 'It's the first I've heard of it.' Then he added, 'The point, I suppose, is stopped at your rig-out.'

A short silence ensued, until Willie broke it, saying, 'Jimmy's a pal to everybody. He helps in the boys' club; he's likely minder to all of them.'

Daisy now nodded towards him, saying, 'I shouldn't be surprised. He's like that.'

A further embarrassing silence was prevented when Bert said, 'Well, it's my turn for washing up, I'm told by Mrs Ormesby; so, if you don't object, I'll have your glasses.'

Looking at Fiona, Nell said, 'He does go on, doesn't he? But I'd better go and do my own clearing up if I want it done properly.' Then, turning to where Mike and Daisy were now standing, she said,

'I'll say good night. You see how things are; you've got to work for your grub in this house, let me tell you. Anyway, we'll be seeing you.' She smiled from the one to the other. And Bert, stepping towards them, said quietly, 'Never get married if you can help it. Jimmy'll make a good minder, Daisy, nobody better. He has a family of his own to see to, and he does a good job there.' He held out his hand to Mike, saying, 'Be seeing you. Oh, by the way, d'you have any spare time?'

'I've had a great deal of it up till now.'

'Well, if you've ever got any you don't want, I'd be glad of it.'

'Get yourself into the kitchen, you!' It was a bawl now from Bill. 'He's starting work after the holidays.'

A few minutes later they were all in the hall and Bill, pulling on an overcoat, said, 'I won't be a minute; I'll get the car out.'

He had just left the hall when the attention of the others was drawn to the stairs and to Mark slowly descending them.

When he paused on the second step Fiona called to him, 'Finished, dear?'

'Yes, Mam, for the present.' He stepped down into the hall and looked towards Mike and Daisy, and Fiona, taking him by the arm, led him towards them. 'You have met Daisy,' she said, 'but this is her brother Mike.'

Mike held out his hand and it seemed that Mark hesitated for a second before taking it and saying, 'How d'you do?' And this time Mike responded with, 'Pleased to meet you.'

'Dad's just gone to get the car,' Fiona explained.

'You swotting?' Daisy asked.

There was another pause before Mark answered her, 'Yes. Yes, you could say that; swotting.'

'I used to swot when I was working for my GCSEs, didn't I, Mike?'

'Well, you went through a great many books, as I remember, and your temper was worse than usual.'

'Yes, it was,' she acknowledged, and straightaway nodded towards Fiona and said, 'Goodbye, Mrs Bailey, and a happy Christmas. And thank you once again for . . . for everything you have done for the family.'

'Yes. Yes, I second that, and I speak for everybody in our house,' added Mike.

'Oh, say no more about it,' said Fiona. 'It made us happy to do it. As my husband said, we'll always be in your debt, and Sammy, too. Oh, yes, Sammy, too.'

'Could I come across next week and see him?'

'Of course! Of course! Any time.'

Immediately Katie commented, 'If you didn't he'd be sending for you . . . and you, too.' She nodded at Mike.

The loud blast from the car made Fiona bustle them all to the door, saying, 'Oh, whatever you do, don't keep him waiting,' and Daisy and Mike went out on a chorus of good nights and Happy Christmases all round . . .

'She's a character, isn't she?' Nell was walking

by Fiona's side now. And when Fiona said, 'I'll say. I've never met anyone like her,' it was Mark who took it.

'I shouldn't imagine you would, Mam,' he said.

'What d'you mean by that?' Willie turned on his brother as he was entering the drawing-room, and Mark answered, 'Just what I said. Shockers like her are ten a penny . . . Who you pushing? What's the matter with you?'

'Nothing's the matter with me, big fella, but something's the matter with you. You can't see further than your nose. And let me tell you that some of the shockers, as you call them, could beat you for brains any day. If they'd had half the chances you had they wouldn't have fluffed like you did last year.'

'I didn't fluff last year.'

'Willie! Mark! Stop it! Stop it this minute.'

It seemed that neither of them heard their mother, for they took no notice and stood just within the door, facing each other. And Willie, his voice now loud, cried, 'If Daisy had been in your place, she blooming well would have got more than Cs. As she said, you're swotting, yes, and you have to keep at it if you're ever to be fit to join your uppish friend in the London hospital. You're an upstart stinker, that's what you are . . .' Nell had gripped Willie by the shoulder and was pulling him back into the hall, saying now, 'Give over! Else I'll swipe you one meself.'

And as Fiona banged the drawing-room door closed, saying 'What's come over Willie?' Katie put in, 'It isn't what's come over Willie, Mam, it's what's come over him.' She thumbed towards Mark, and he rounded on her, saying, 'Now you start and I'll soon put you in your place.'

'Mark! Stop it, this very minute!'

'Oh, leave him alone, Mam. Leave him alone. As for putting me in my place, he would need some spunk, and that's what you're lacking, isn't it, Master Mark? And I'll say as Willie said and add a bit more, if you'd had half the brains of that shocker, as you called her, you would have come through on top.'

'Katie! Now you stop it! Please! You stop it! It's Christmas. Oh, my goodness!' She put her hand to her head, and at this Katie said quietly, 'It might be Christmas, Mam, but this has been blowing up for a long time because he's been absolutely insufferable. And you've made excuses for him all along. That's nothing new though; you have done that over the years.'

'Nonsense, Katie! Nonsense! What's come over you?'

'Well,' put in Mark quickly now, 'one thing Mam can say about me is, I haven't caused her any heartache, as Willie did years ago with his choice of friends. And you did with your love affair.'

Katie's response was to go and sit down on the couch, from where she glared at him, while he, bending towards her, said, 'How would you like the shocker for a sister-in-law?'

Katie neither moved nor answered, but Fiona

shouted, as if in alarm, 'What? What d'you mean? What are you talking about?'

'I'm just talking about my younger brother and that specimen, because that's what she is, a specimen, she who has just left the house. Haven't you listened to him over the past weeks, going on about her? But that's nothing to what I've been given: he's collecting all the one-liners she comes out with. He's absolutely besotted with her. Why d'you think he's unglued himself from Sammy?'

As Fiona stared at her son, Katie got up from the couch, saying, 'Don't worry, Mam, it may never happen. Anyway, put her in some ordinary clothes and she'd pass muster anywhere. There's more to be seen in her than her thighs.'

When the door closed on Katie, Mark said, 'She wants slapping down, if anyone does.'

'Mark! You're talking about your sister. Now, listen to me.' Her hand was on his shoulder and pulling him round to face her. 'I'm saying this to you – not to her or to anyone else – you have been rather a trial over the past months. You used to be so understanding. Another time you would have understood and been helpful with Mamie, because you know the trouble I've had with her over the years. But you've been so absorbed in your own affairs.'

'Mam!' His voice showed he was deeply hurt. 'I've been swotting. Yes, that's the word she used, but I've been swotting for months past.'

'Only since you got the results in the summer

term, Mark. Before that you were your usual thoughtful self.'

He swung away from her now, saying, 'Yes, too thoughtful for the others; I didn't pay enough attention to what I really wanted, and that was to work.'

'Don't be silly, Mark; nobody stopped you from working. You spent too much time playing tennis and squash and such with Roland Featherstone.'

'Well, he spent the same time on sport and he got through and he's no better than me.'

She just stopped herself from saying sharply, oh, yes, he is: learning comes easy to him, and he's got a retentive memory. Moreover, you couldn't bear the thought of him getting into the London hospital before you.

Fiona walked away from her son and sat down in a deeply upholstered chair to the side of the fire. She was tired. She was always tired these days; not so much physically but mentally. Yet at times her mind seemed empty and groping for something, that elusive something. She had thought that when she got over the business of Mamie, they would all return to being a laughing, happy family. But it hadn't come about. Sparks had always flown between the two brothers. They were such opposites. One could say that Willie was all heart, and Mark was all head. Yet, Willie had got nine O levels last year, whereas all the trouble was because Mark had only three Cs at A level, and he needed at least three Bs to gain a place at the London Hospital Medical School.

She could never understand him wanting to be a doctor; but then, he didn't just want to be a doctor, he wanted to be a surgeon. And Bill had said that there was a coolness in Mark that would fit him for the surgeon's role, whereas he could never see him as a general practitioner adopting a bedside manner.

But careers apart, all she wanted for her family was for them to be happy. Yet not one of them was happy. But was ever a teenager happy, going through this period of mixed emotions? And these erupting unexpectedly, some with terrifying force. She could recall her own youth and the sick fear that swept over her on realising that she hated her mother. And thinking of her mother she thought, if ever a miracle was wrought on anyone, it had been on her; and she could honestly say now she loved her. Nothing would have pleased her more if she had settled in the annexe. But no, she had her bungalow. Yet, as Bill said, it was a waste of a house, because she spent most of her time here looking after Angela.

Oh, she hoped they would have a happy Christmas, if only for Bill's sake. He worked so hard, he never seemed to let up. But now there was a full week ahead. How could it be a happy time, though, with the two boys at each other's throats? She put out her hand towards Mark, where he was standing looking down into the fire, one hand resting on the mantelpiece. He looked a man, although he was not yet nineteen. 'Mark, dear. Go and make it up with Willie.'

'What?' He seemed to spring round towards her. 'Make it up? I didn't start this, and you heard what he said to me. Oh, no! Mam. Don't ask me to belittle myself by saying I'm sorry, when I'm not. I'm only sorry that instead of a shocker I didn't call her a freak. Because that's what she looked like, with her face plastered in make-up.'

Fiona rose from the chair and her voice held a cold note as she said, 'Well, apart from what you think, Mark, and what you have said to Willie, I wouldn't repeat your opinion to Sammy, if I were you, because Sammy is very fond of her.'

'Well, that's understandable, Mam, isn't it? He was from the same quarter as her once, wasn't he?'

Fiona stared at her son. In her wildest imaginings she would never have thought that the day would come when she would look at him, the son who had taken a man's place in her life when she was made a widow, and not like what she saw. And she was also made to wonder just how he looked on Bill now, the man who had been such a wonderful father to him, and still was; paying out thousands of pounds for his school expenses, and would have to continue keeping him for the five years he would likely spend in London in his training, that's if it were not to be longer. Bill put on no airs, he was always himself, and he had been brought up in circumstances similar to both Sammy's and Daisy's. And such was the state of her mind at this moment that she said to Mark, 'Do you class your dad in the same category as Daisy and Sammy?'

He blinked rapidly, then wetted his lips and

said, 'Dad's different. He . . . he's a man.'

Her voice was cool as she went on, 'He's a man who never forgets his upbringing. That's why he understands Sammy and Daisy; he was one of them. Think about that. At the same time, think of what you owe him, and will go on owing him. Also, what he has done with his life, and without the education you've had the benefit of so far. Just think of that, Mark.'

'Mam.'

'Good night, Mark. I'm going to bed.'

She hurried from the room and was making for the stairs when, glancing down the broad corridor, she saw Nell, Bert, Willie and Katie standing together. And she paused a moment before walking towards them and saying, 'What's the matter?'

'Nothing. Nothing.' Nell shook her head; then Bert said, 'Willie's going to apologise. It's Christmas and . . .'

'No!' The word was sharp, and now Fiona, looking at her Willie, said, 'No, Willie; there's no need for you to apologise.'

'But . . . but, Mam, I . . . I know I went off the handle.'

'Yes, and there was more than one handle. Now I'm saying to you, forget about it, ignore it. As everybody is saying, it's Christmas, the time for good cheer and jollity.'

In surprise they watched her toss her head back. And when she turned from them and made for the stairs, Nell said softly, 'They're both fast asleep.'

'And that's where I hope to be very soon,' Fiona

said, 'I'm going to bed. When Bill returns will you tell him I'm upstairs?'

Bert and Nell exchanged a quick glance. Then Nell hurried along the passage to join Fiona on the stairs and, putting her arm about her shoulders, she said, 'Well, if you're going to bed you'll have to be undressed, won't you?'

There was no laughing rejoinder to this. And below, Willie, Katie and Bert stood looking at each other in silence until Bert muttered, 'Dear, dear. Something drastic must have happened in there. I've never known her take an attitude against Mark; Mark above all of you.'

'Yes.' Katie nodded at him, 'Yes, Mark above all of us. Well, perhaps she's seeing him as he really is for the first time, or as he has become, because that's what Dad will label him; an upstart. But I've noticed he's careful what he comes out with in front of Dad; his opinions and that. But Dad would have known what his opinions were had he been aware that he didn't want to put his name to one of the Gallagher parcels.'

As they looked at each other in silence, the sound of the car passing over the drive came to them. And at this, Willie, looking towards the hall, said with a note of apprehension in his voice, 'Oh, I hope she doesn't tell Dad; he'll wipe the floor with him, because it's really all my fault—' He tossed his head now, then said hurriedly, 'I'll . . . I'll go up and ask her not to.'

Both Katie and Bert stood listening to the soft thumping of Willie's footsteps across the landing.

With a small smile on her face, Katie looked at Bert and said, 'He's soft, you know . . . Willie. Remember, we used to fight like cat and dog when we were younger. And I used to be all for Mark. Funny how you change, isn't it, Bert?' Then she asked him a question that bore no relation to what she had just said, 'Does Jimmy . . . you know, Jimmy Redding, does he consider Daisy his girl? I mean, his real girlfriend? You suggested in there' – she thumbed towards the drawing-room – 'that he was married.'

Bert's reply was mumbled, 'Oh, well, Katie, I couldn't really answer that, not truthfully. I only know he looks after a young woman and three children; in fact, he lives in their house. As for his association with Daisy, I know he took her in hand when she first came to the club. She was about fourteen then, and in with a lot of tearaways.'

'Well, she calls him her minder. And it's funny, but he's about the only one she takes any notice of. I mean, she'll go her own way in all things and say what she likes, until he stops her.' She laughed gently now as she added, 'You should hear her at times. If she'd had an education, she would have gone in for politics in a big way. She's very hot on class.'

'Yes, I've heard her. But why do you ask about Jimmy?'

'Well, simply because Willie's gone head over heels in that direction.'

'No!'

'Yes.'

'Oh, my goodness!'

When Bill went into the bedroom, Fiona was lying on her side, her face away from him. Putting his hands on her shoulder, he gently pulled her on to her back, saying 'What is it? What's happened? You've been crying.'

I felt tired. I had a headache.'

'Oh, don't come the "headache" one, Mrs B, not after the jolly night we've had. Anyway, I have a headache an' all. So, we'll call a truce, shall we, on that point? At least for tonight.'

'Oh, Bill!' She pulled herself up on to the pillows, and he, sitting on the side of the bed, said softly, 'What is it, love? Something happened? Well, nothing could have happened since I've been away; it's been hardly half an hour.'

'Mark and Willie went at it.'

'What about?'

She turned her gaze away from him as she said, 'Minnie . . . Daisy.'

'Oh, Willie thinks she's the cat's pyjamas, and Mark thinks she's less than cat's spit. That's it, isn't it?'

'Well, putting it that way, I suppose, yes.'

'And Master Mark expressed his high-class opinion of her, and Willie went for him. Is that it?'

'That's it!'

'Well, good for Willie. But . . . but that shouldn't have made you howl. They're always going for each other, those two. If it's not one thing it's another.' He had hold of her hands now and he pulled them towards his chest as he asked, 'What happened?'

She shook her head and her lips moved as if she were trying to form words; then she said, 'Mark's changed.'

The retort came back quickly, saying, 'Oh, no, he hasn't: Mark is Mark. It's only coming out more now because he's feeling his feet. I think you've got to face it, love; and I've wanted to say this to you for some time now, because I've seen the road Mark has set himself to follow. And it's all on the upgrade. Mark is ninety per cent his father, whereas Willie and Katie are nearly all you. Was his father a snob?'

Again she found it difficult to answer. Then, she said, 'Yes. Yes, I suppose so, mostly about his work and literature.'

'And he wasn't very much good at that, from what I gather. But his son thought he was. Oh, it's some years ago since . . . well, since we came into this house. He was showing somebody the pool, and voices echo from there, you know, and I was in the dressing-room. He was saying, "Oh, he's my step-father. My real father was an author. He wrote travel books and novels. He was well known."'

'He said that?'

'Oh, yes. But he never wrote a book, did he?'

'He wrote articles on travel . . . He wrote articles on all kinds of things. He would read up something and expand on it. We once had very hot words,

249

because I suggested it was a form of cheating; he called it a result of his research.'

'I suppose Mark called Minnehaha common?'

'Yes, and more. It was the terms he used that maddened Willie. And you know what he's like when he gets going. They almost came to blows.'

'I suppose he still thinks of Sammy as common. But Sammy has acquired a façade; thin in places, but it's still there. However, he manages it better than I do, because common I was and common I remain.'

'Oh, Bill. Bill, don't say that; there's not a common streak in your body. You're,' – she now put her hand out and touched his cheek – 'you're brash, loud and dominating, but there's nothing common about you, my dear.'

His voice was soft as he said, 'You really think that, Mrs B?'

'Yes. Yes, Mr B, I really think that. And . . . and it's no exaggeration to say that there's not a day goes by that I don't love you a bit more. Especially on days when you come up with ideas like you did about the Gallaghers' Christmas.'

'Oh, that! Well, that was poor return for Sammy . . . Oh, it was funny when I stopped the car outside the door. I wondered if she would ask me in, and if she had I would have gone. But what she said, in her inimitable way, was, "D'you want me to ask you in?" And at this, her brother put in sharply, "Daisy!" And she turned on him and said, "Look! I know what I'm doing, and he understands." And what I answered her was, "No, I don't want to be asked in. When I want to visit your people I'll make a point of going when you're not there, because then we might be able to talk without you butting in, Miss Clever-Clouts."'

'You didn't say that to her!' She was smiling now.

'Yes, I did, word for word.'

He got up from the bed now, bent over and kissed her hard on the lips, then said, 'I'm going down now to make some hot milk, and I'm going to cool it down with a good dose of brandy, and you're going to drink that, Mrs B; then off to sleep.'

'But . . . but what are you going to do? Aren't you coming to bed?'

'No, not yet. I've got a lot of things to do, such as minding my own business. And look—' He bent over again and now kissed the tip of her nose, as he said, 'It's Christmas, so forget about the irritations of your offspring. Anyway, Sammy'll be home tomorrow, and the atmosphere will be lifted sky-high. He's a chip off his old block, that boy.'

When the door closed on him, she stared towards it: Sammy. His feelings for that boy outdid any he had for her own tribe. Measure for measure, it could be the same as he felt for his daughter. Well, she liked Sammy, too; she even loved him. And yes, the atmosphere would change once he entered the house . . . She was glad she had opened up to Bill about Mark. It had made her feel better. But then, he always made her feel better. And it was true, she did seem to love him more and more as time went on. Yet, what about that lonely spot in her? Was that still there? Yes, strangely, it was still there. It was like an anxiety, one she couldn't explain, and she recalled how she had been aware of it during the time she had gone for Mark. It had appeared then as if she were experiencing a great loss. And she supposed she was, in a way, because never would she look upon her son in the same way again. He had revealed his true character and she didn't like it. She admitted to herself now that he was, as Bill had suggested, a replica of his father. Of a sudden, she sat bolt upright in the bed, asking herself a question: could it be that she wasn't using her mind? Secretly, she had always wanted to do something, something different. But what had she done with her life? Struggled alone to bring up three children; then married Bill and acquired Mamie, and later Sammy. Then, the great event of her life; she had given Bill a child of his own. But what a child. A Down's syndrome child, whom she had hated for a time, but then began to love, even passionately, for she could not return such a love as emanated from the child. But it was only during this last year or so that she'd had this gnawing emptiness inside her. It wasn't that she knew she was going to lose them all, but a want of some kind. But for what? *What?*

16

When the bell rang, Katie, who was passing through the hall, opened the door, then stood almost gaping at the figure on the step. It was, yet it wasn't, the Daisy Gallagher she once knew.

'It's going to snow.'

'Yes, Daisy. Yes, get in.' She almost pulled the girl across the step. Then she stood looking at her, an amazed smile slowly spreading across her face.

'Go on, laugh. Laugh,' Daisy said.

'No. No, Daisy, I'm not laughing. You look . . . well, marvellous!'

'Marvellous, me granny's aunt! I don't know how I got down the street; nobody knew me.'

'Give me your coat here.'

'No; no. I want Sammy to see me like this.'

'Oh, yes. Well, come on then. We've got him fixed up in the little sitting-room until he can make the stairs.'

'Is all the family in?'

'No; there's only Grandma and Angela; they're upstairs. Mother has gone to see Nell; she isn't very well. And Dad and Willie are down in the wood with the gardener, clearing some of the branches that came down yesterday in that wind. Mark is spending a couple of days with his friend, Roland Featherstone.'

At the end of the broad corridor, Katie tapped on the door. Then, opening it just a little way and putting her head round, she said, 'Guess who's here?'

'Male or female?'

'Female.'

'Oh, then it must be Princess Fandango. Show her in, serf.'

When Katie thrust the door wide open and Daisy followed her into the room, the sight of her brought Sammy up straight from the depths of the large, upholstered wing-chair, and exclaiming much the same as Katie had done earlier, 'Daisy!'

'Well, go on, ask what's got into me.'

'I'm not going to; I'll wait until you tell me. But by! you look . . .'

'Well, how do I look? Like everybody else you see in the street; Dizzy-Lizzies all look alike.'

As Sammy swayed on his feet Katie put her hand out towards him, saying sharply, 'Now, you sit down before you fall down.'

'Well! Come here, you!' – he beckoned to Daisy – 'Come here, and let me have a good look at you.'

When she stood by his chair, he looked at her from top to toe; then, again his face smiling, he said, 'Oh, Daisy, you look smashing. How did this come about?'

'It's a long story.'

'Here, sit down,' – Katie pushed a chair towards

her – 'I'll go and make a cup of tea. And take your coat off, and your hat or you'll freeze when you go out.'

'No,' – Daisy shook her head – 'I won't take me coat off.'

'Why not? Still got the old rig-out underneath?'

'No, I haven't. All right then, I'll show you.' She stood up again and began to unbutton the green velour coat with a deep fur collar, and it's length, reaching below her knees, left only a three-inch gap to the top of her long dark brown suede boots.

Her coat she hung over the back of the chair. Then, after pulling the felt hat from her head, she struck a self-conscious pose. And such was the impression she made that neither Katie nor Sammy spoke for a moment. Then it was Katie who said, 'My! My! That's lovely.' And she put out her hand and felt the long sleeve of the pale-mauve woollen dress that was doing even more than the coat to transform the girl they had come to recognise as an individual, one on her own, belonging to no set type. But, here she was . . . really what was the word? She could only think of smashing, upper-grade smashing, too.

'It's lovely. Where did you get it?'

'Oh, as I said, it's a long story. When I've had that cup of tea, I'll tell you.' She now nodded towards Sammy, saying, 'It's beginning to snow and so blooming cold, I don't think I could have worn me bum-freezer the day.'

This was the Daisy they knew, and Katie went out laughing.

Seated once again by the chair, Daisy looked at Sammy and said one word, 'Well?' Sammy shook his head, then after a moment he muttered, 'Remarkable! You look bonny, Daisy, really bonny . . . even beautiful.'

'Come off it!'

She rubbed a finger over her lips, which were no longer scarlet, but a pale pink. And when her eyelids blinked, he could see most of her natural lashes.

'Your hair . . . you've had it tinted?'

'Yes. Yes, I did it meself. So, it's a bit patchy at the back.' She turned her head. And he said, 'No, it's all right. It isn't patchy, just a little darker. But it looks better. Oh!' He shook his head, then said softly, 'Don't go back to the rig, Daisy, 'cos you look lovely. I've known you for a long time and this is the first time I've really seen you. You've been covering yourself up. Why did you go in for that rig?'

'Oh, well, I wanted to be different. My teacher was for me staying on. Well, you know the set-up. Me da was off, and bad; in fact, nobody was in work, and they were offering girls good money at the factory, so there you have it. It's the old ego, you know. I wanted to be recognised as somebody different. And I was different, wasn't I?'

'I'll say. I'll say, Daisy, you were. But you'll always be Daisy, no matter what you wear. Oh,' – he leant back – 'you do look bonny. I can't get over it. I'm so proud of you, Daisy. Wait till the others see you.'

'Don't make me blush. I don't look bonny. The only thing is, I've washed me face. I haven't washed me face for God knows how long. I just grease it, you know. It stops the wrinkles, they say. Anyway, how are you feeling?'

He didn't answer her for a moment, then said simply, 'Different.'

'Different?'

'Yes. I don't feel I'll ever be meself again.'

'Don't talk daft. Of course, you will.'

'I'm not talking daft, Daisy. Between you and me, I feel I've got no spunk left. I can't see me ever doing a back-throw again on anybody.'

'That'll come. You've had a knocking about. It's a wonder you're still alive, d'you know that?'

'Yes. Yes, I know that. And I wouldn't have been if it hadn't been for your little Danny.'

'Well, everybody gives little Danny the benefit, but it was really our Mike. 'Cos if he had told Danny to get back to bed, that's where he would have gone. It was Mike who set things going.'

'I'll have to see him.'

'Oh, you'll see him some time. Anyway, he's going to start work, you know, for the big boss, the big chief Bang-Bang!' She smiled now and hunched her shoulders as she said, 'I give him as much as he sends.' Then, the smile slipping from her face, she said, 'It's funny, you know, Sammy, I always felt at one with you, because originally we were from the same groove, brought up in the toughening school. And then, you know, when he first spoke to me I had the same feeling because I could back-chat him. And now I know why, because he came up much the same way. Our Frank said he was a brickie in Liverpool first, and when he came this end he started with three men. So, that's why, I suppose, I feel kind of at home with him. Although I know how far I can go, and I wouldn't want to go any further, 'cos I admire him. Oh, aye, I do. He's full of push and that's how I used to feel at one time.'

'Oh, Daisy,' – Sammy laughed now – 'you're talking as if you were an old woman.'

'Well, I am in some way, inside, 'cos I've passed through a number of grades. Oh aye, most of them better left buried now. But . . . but you see what I mean about you, me and Mr Bailey? The others are different. Nice, oh aye, nice and kind, but different; even Katie.'

'Katie's not different.'

'Oh, aye, she is, Sammy. She's on the other side of the line, no matter how nice she is. And there's her big brother. Well, I haven't seen much of him, but I class him as a bit of a nowt. A proper snob, that one, I think.'

'Well, that only leaves Willie.'

'Oh, Willie . . . he breaks his neck to come down to my level. But he's still Willie. And . . . and look about you and this place, where he's been brought up by his mother. Now she's the nicest woman I've met, but nevertheless, she's classy. And what d'you think would happen' – she leant forward now and there was an impish grin on her face as she said – 'if he were to go to his dear mama and say he had cottoned on to Daisy Gallagher? Oh my, Sammy!' She pulled a face at him. 'I doubt if Big Chief would stand for that.'

Sammy did not laugh and his voice held a serious note when he said, 'Willie thinks a lot of you, Daisy. Seriously, he does.'

'Well, well! That's his hair shirt; I can't help it; I've given him no encouragement. In fact, I can tell you one thing for nothing; I've gone overboard in me gear just to put him off. Some part of his head must be soft, because it's only made him grin. But I'm serious too now, Sammy, when I say, no, I'm not for Willie and Willie isn't for me, and the quicker he gets to know that the better. I've,' – she stared at him – 'I've got different ideas: I know what I want and who I want.'

'Is it Jimmy?'

Her chin jerked up as she asked almost in a demand, 'What makes you name him?'

'Well, you're always calling him your minder, and . . . and it's evident that he's very fond of you, that he looks after you.'

'He doesn't look after me.'

'Well, what I mean to say is that he advises you, let's put it that way, what to do and what not to do. Oh yes, he does, Daisy, so don't deny it.'

'I'm not denying it, but let me tell you I know more about Jimmy than you do. He sees himself as a universal fatherly figure, because he's got a woman who has three bairns and they're not his. The husband scooted.'

Sammy's eyes had widened. 'Really?' he said,

'How long have you known this?'

'Oh, don't ask me; I can't remember.'

Sammy turned his head towards the door, saying, 'Oh, here's the woodman coming in.'

She, too, looked towards the door as the commotion came from the corridor and Bill's voice could be heard saying, 'Oh, a cup of tea. That's what I want, next to putting my backside on the fire. D'you know it's snowing.'

'We've got company.'

And when Bill appeared, he stared for a moment at the girl in the very smart woollen dress. It was some seconds before he exclaimed on a high note, 'Daisy!'

'At your service, sir.'

She had risen to her feet, and now she was standing not an arm's length from him. And he, looking her up and down, said, 'Well, I'll be damned! I never thought to witness it. You're human!'

'Just as far as me neck, 'cos me mind's still in me rig-out.'

Again he looked her up and down, then said, 'Well I'll say this and in all seriousness, I never thought that that get-up covered such a bonnie lass.'

She took up a pussy-cat pose, flapping a hand at him as if it were a paw as she said, 'Go on with you, Mister; me ma says no.'

'What?'

In her ordinary tone, she repeated, 'Me ma says no. And I'll have to explain that to you later.'

'You've no need, you brazen hussy, you!'

'*Daisy!*'

They all turned to look at Willie, who was standing in the doorway, for his 'Daisy!' had sounded like a choirboy's high C.

Slowly now he advanced towards her, saying, 'You've . . . you've changed your gear.'

'Oh, is it so noticeable?'

Willie glanced towards Bill and said, 'I can't believe it.'

'You've seen nothing yet, sir. But in the meantime, if we're going to drink tea, go and get two more cups, and bring the plate of cakes from the kitchen table.'

Willie shook his head, then hurried from the room; and straightaway his voice could be heard crying, 'I'll have to bring three; here's mam.'

When Fiona stepped into the room she looked first towards Sammy, then to the strange girl sitting by him, and her mouth fell into a slight gape before she muttered, 'Daisy?'

'Yes, Mrs Bailey, me in the flesh.' Daisy had risen to her feet.

'Oh, my dear!' Fiona moved slowly towards her. 'You look . . . well, you look lovely, dear.' She held out a hand to take Daisy's as she said, 'I'm not going to ask the reason, but I'm going to ask why you have hidden your real self for so long?'

'I haven't been hiding meself, Mrs Bailey; these are just clothes. I'm still the same up here,' she patted her head.

'That's enough, that's enough,' put in Bill

quietly. 'Her head's too big for the hat already. Let's have that tea.'

'A cup of tea, Mam? Willie's gone for another cup.'

'No, thanks, dear. I had two just before I left Nell's.' Fiona now went to where Bill was standing near the two-seater couch, and as she sat down, he said, 'How did you find her?'

'Oh, heaps better. But she's had a real flu cold . . . Do you know it's snowing?'

'Yes, of course I know it's snowing; I've been sawing wood in it.'

'You couldn't have; it's just started.'

He now turned to Daisy and said, 'How d'you find our invalid?'

'I think he's looking fine; much better than I expected. But being him, he'll take advantage and hang it out.'

'I'll hang you out,' said Sammy. 'Stand up and put your coat on and show Mrs B your bargains. At least, I imagine they're bargains.'

Daisy, doing as she was bidden, stood up, got into her coat, turned the fur collar well up over the back of her head, then posed again. And both Bill and Fiona stared at her for almost a minute before Bill said, 'Well! where did you come across this rig-out?'

'It's from a second-hand shop. I heard of it being exclusive like, being situated near Brampton Hill. And they weren't likely to get the riff-raff from our way, because it was kind of pricey. I'm afraid them round our way think hand-outs are dear; they won't buy anything unless they're badly pushed. Anyway, I heard about this fella getting a lovely overcoat there, and I told our Mike about it. He was determined to spend some of the money that you gave him' – she nodded towards Bill – 'on having a decent rig-out and an overcoat, and I must confess he was badly in need of the lot. Anyway, I promised I would go with him to this shop; that's if it was open during the holidays. We had a job to find it; it was right at the other end of town and up a side street. We got there about a quarter to ten and it had just opened. Eeh! My!' She smiled from one to the other. 'What an experience! There were two women serving . . . no, they weren't just women, they were ladies of a certain age.' She bounced her head with each word as she repeated, 'Yes, definitely of a certain age. One was called Gwenda. She saw to the first floor and the men's department. I don't know what mine was called, but she was canny. She had been sorting things out of a great big hamper.' She nodded towards Bill, adding, 'It was the same size as the whopper you sent us.' And at this he jerked his chin at her, and she went on, 'She took out this coat and as she held it up she said to herself, "That's nice; but a fur collar. They don't usually have fur collars, not this make." And this was to herself, mind. When she laid the coat across the counter, I looked at it, and I don't know what made me say, "May I try it on?" But that's what I said.' She was nodding from one to the other now. 'And when she saw me in it, she looked solemnly at me and agreed, "Yes, my dear.

Now that's better. That's much better, and it's such a beautiful coat." It's Asquash something.'

'Aquascutum?'

She nodded towards Fiona, saying, 'That's it. I can never get me tongue round it. Aqua . . . scutum. Then I heard meself asking, "How much is it?" And she said, "Oh, it hasn't been priced yet, dear; I'm just sorting. But wait a minute! Give it me here." I took it off and handed it to her, and she went out and along a passage, and I heard her call, "Gwenda!" Then after some prattle she comes back and says, "It's such a good coat and it's hardly been worn, you know. But Gwenda says, and she knows about furs, and she thinks the collar is Russian mink, but that it's been tacked on. You see? At the back.' She began to show me. Then she said, "But I'm afraid it will be six pounds. Because you wouldn't get anything like that under sixty now." And when I said straightaway, "I'll take it," she said, "Oh, that's nice, dear . . . And look at this!" And what did she do but bring this out?' Daisy now took off her coat, then plucking at the front of her dress, she said, ' "This would suit you," she said, "and this too hasn't been worn much either. They go under the arms, dear, you know; it's the perspiration. But this shows no sign of wear."' When Daisy lifted up her arm, they all started to laugh, and she said, 'She was right. No sweat marks. Then out she brings a two-piece. It was brown and a lovely thick material. And it had something in its favour for me. Anyway, the skirt didn't reach me knees.'

'How much did you pay for that?'

'Three-fifty, and I could see then why only a certain type came to this shop: for that three-fifty, in the Oxfam shop in Broad Street, you could buy a complete outfit.'

'Did she bring your boots, too, out of the basket?' It was Willie, and he was grinning at her. And she said, 'Oh, me boots? No. Now they were a bargain. And she told me the history of them. Umpteen people must have tried them on, and she said she always told them not to pull the zip of the right hand one well up, because it stuck; once they got it up, they couldn't get it down. And she said, "You know, it's true, because there was one day if took half an hour to release the customer. And so, since then, when I warn people they must be careful of the zip and not to take it right up, it seems to put them off. So they have lain there this past year, and they're a beautiful pair of boots." She asked my size, and when I said five, she said "How wonderful! Would you like to try them?" Well, I tried them. And look!' She turned her right leg to the side to show them the zip stopped two inches from the top.

'Why don't you try closing it?' said Bill, on a laugh. 'I'll open it for you.'

'Not on your life! I'd have to go to bed in them. But' – nodding towards Fiona now – she said, 'they are lovely inside. Sheepskin.'

'How much did she sting you for those?' asked Sammy. 'Just a pound,' she said, 'I think she was glad to get rid of them.'

Fiona said in amazement, 'A pound! D'you know, Daisy, that quality and that size would cost anything from eighty to a hundred today.'

'That a fact?'

'That's a fact. I paid sixty-five pounds for Katie's ankle boots, and they're nothing compared with those.'

Straightaway putting out her hand, Daisy pushed Katie in the shoulder, saying, 'Well, I've got one up on you at last.'

Before Katie could retaliate Sammy asked, 'What did Mike get?'

'Oh, well, you wouldn't believe it.' Daisy shook her head. 'You should have seen how he came down those stairs; and I've never seen him look so . . . well, the only word I can say is, happy. As you know, Sammy, Mike's always got a perpetual scowl against life; but he looked handsome. He did. Well, he was never bad-looking.'

'I thought he was very good-looking,' put in Katie.

'Oh, you did?' Daisy had turned quickly towards Katie. 'I'll tell him, then.'

'Yes, do. Quite macho.'

'Oh-ho!' Daisy laughed now. 'That'll tickle him.'

'Anyway,' Sammy said, 'tell us, woman, what did he get?'

'Well, he got two pairs of smashing trousers, lovely stuff, and a tweed jacket, the like he has never had. But the main thing was the overcoat, and he kept telling me it was a Crombie, made in Scotland. I've never seen him go over the top about clothes before; but then he's never had anything like that.'

'Well, if it's a Crombie, it's the tops.'

She looked at Bill and said, 'Well, it looks it. It's a fawnish colour, almost a light brown, and you would swear he'd had it made to measure. I tell you, I've never seen our Mike look so happy. He also got two shirts and a pair of boots. Oh yes, and a pair of shoes. And Miss Gwenda must have fallen for him, because she put all his odds and ends in a plain bag. And when me da saw the stuff he was absolutely miffed; and me ma's going there to get him some odds and ends.'

'How much did he spend altogether?' Willie asked.

'Eighteen pounds. And' – again she was nodding at Bill – 'he could only do that because of you. And if over these holidays you've made anybody happier than the rest, I think it's him. I'll never forget his face when he came down those stairs into the lower shop in that coat.'

'And what did all yours cost you?' Katie was asking.

'Fourteen pounds-fifty. But mind, I could have had four of me usual rig-outs for that, and a hair-do.'

'Well, thank God, we've been saved any more shocks.'

'Oh you!' She jerked her head towards Bill, and in answer, he said, 'You, an' all.' And they smiled at each other. Then turning to Fiona, Daisy said, 'You know something? I can't get over the old girl in that shop. She must have been . . . well, kicking seventy herself; the veins on the back of her hands were standing out like pikestaffs.'

'Is that how you tell age?'

She turned to Willie now, saying, 'Yes, it is, in a way. But . . . but there she was, at a holiday time, sorting out all that stuff, and likely would keep open all day. And it's voluntary, you know. Oh, yes, she looked a voluntary type, and I bet she wasn't in need of a penny either. Well, when you wear Chanel, you must have a bit put by.'

'Chanel scent, you mean?'

'Yes, Chanel scent, that's what I mean.'

She jerked her head towards Bill now, and when he said, 'How d'you know about Chanel?' she almost snapped back 'That's my business! Anyway, I bet I know more about it than you do.'

'I bet you don't. I've paid thirty pounds for a bottle of it for her mother. And that monkey there,' he stabbed his finger towards Katie, 'she poured the lot over herself. But' – he smiled now – 'it saved you from being murdered, didn't it?'

'How's that?'

'Oh, it's another long story. But how did you recognise the smell of Chanel?'

'It's a private matter.'

'Well, that's not going to stop you from telling us, is it?'

She looked at Fiona, saying, 'He's nosey, isn't he?'

'Yes. Yes, he is nosey, Daisy. But I, too, would like to hear.'

'Well, all right then. But let it be a warning to you.' She turned back to Bill, making a deep obeisance with her head. 'Well, it's like this. There were three bosses at our place. One we called Highchurch. He was the fellow who built the concern, and he would pop in every now and again. Lowchapel, as we used to call the second, was a stiff-neck. The third one we'll call Mr X. He was very popular. Not that I saw anything of him, for the offices were right over at the other side of the yard, and being down in the basement . . . By the way, did I tell you, I've been promoted? I'm head of the packing section now. Eight under me.'

'Oh, that's good!' This came from all quarters. And as they looked at her, they registered her pleasure, for her face looked bright, her round dark eyes twinkling. Then she said, 'To get on. The Chanel business started, oh, long before that. I've only been in my elevated position for the last five weeks, and it's got one drawback; I can't make any more excuses about going sick, or me ma being in bed, or some other futile excuse, because I was never believed. Anyway, the manageress upstairs has been known to say, "If they are a trouble"' – she now mimicked the voice of the manageress – ' "give them a little power, and it works wonders." So that's what they did with me.'

When the laughter died down she went on, 'I'd never seen this bloke . . . this third boss, more than twice and then from a distance. Until one night I was crossing the yard with the lasses and he was going the other way to get into his car, one of those

BMWs, you know, a smasher, and he smiled at us. The others went all goofy and giggly, but not me. Mind, he was a good-looking bloke and even my mates used to ooh and ah about him. Well, I've never oohed and ahed about anybody and I wasn't going to start about him.' She now pulled a face, 'And anyway, I wasn't like the rest, was I? And he must have noticed.'

'I bet he did.'

Again she was nodding towards Bill, saying, 'Being of the male tribe, you would.' Then turning quickly and almost apologetically, she said to Fiona, 'I can't help it, Mrs Bailey; he asks for it.'

'Well, if he asks for it,' said Fiona, 'you give him back as much as he sends. You have my free permission.'

'Well, that's good enough for me. Anyway, where was I? Oh aye. The night that I was a little late in coming out; it was the Friday and the parcels all had to go out, and I was by meself when I went out of the gates and making for the bus stop, and he comes along right up to the kerb, stops the car and says, "Can I give you a lift?" Well, well!' She drew in a long breath here. 'What did I say to that? Well, I poked me head in the window and said, me ma says, no!'

There was a gurgle from around the room and Bill said, 'What did you say?'

'You heard. I said, me ma says, no!'

'Well was that any kind of answer to give him?'

'Yes, it was. Oh, yes, it was, 'cos I guessed what he was after.'

Fiona leant against the tall back of the couch and her body was shaking and, as Daisy listened to her laughter, she said, 'That's what he did, too, Mrs Bailey. That's what he did. He suddenly threw his head back and he laughed. You could have heard him in Bog's End. And when I was half-way along the road to the bus I could still hear him, and the car hadn't moved. Anyway, I thought that was that. Then, about a week later, there he was again. It was as if he had been waiting for me coming out by meself, because he had stopped in the same place. But he didn't ask me in this time, he put his hand out and pushed a little parcel at me, and said, "A nice smell for a good girl." Then before I could say anything, he had started up the car and was off. Anyway, I didn't open it until I got home, and as soon as I did and me ma saw what it was, and had been told how it had come about, she said to me, "*And your ma says, no!*" And I said to her, "I've already told him that, ma." You see, it was a saying between us, because when I was little, I would say, "I want this," and "I want that," and "I want to go here and I want to go there." And one day me ma shook me by the shoulders and said, "Your ma says, no!" Well, after that it became a sort of slogan with me. Anyway, about the Chanel: we both had a good laugh, and she said, "You keep it and don't you dare open it. You keep it with you and throw it back into the car the next time he stops." Well, I kept that damn package in me pocket all the following week, but no car stopped by the kerb. And then the rumours started. Well, they must have been rife upstairs, but we were the last to get them, down in the packing room. It appears there had been a stinking row upstairs in the head office, and Mr X had been sent off, so one rumour said, to the German end of the business. Another said that one day he just got up and walked out, and there wasn't any row. There must have been because orders came from the boss to clear Mr X's office. But nobody really got to the bottom of it for a month. Some said he had just gone on a holiday and would be back. And it was because of that rumour that I hung on to the bottle. Then it all came out; one of the typists was going to have a bairn, and then we heard his wife was asking for a divorce, because the typist wasn't the first one to rock his cradle. Eeh!' She stopped now and looked from one to the other as she said solemnly, 'Just think what I escaped, just because me ma said no! When I told me ma what had happened we laughed fit to kill ourselves, because, she said, "If you hadn't said the famous words, you would likely have been one of the many." She also said that if I'd had a bairn, she was sure it would have been born fully rigged-out, with a bum-freezer, because that's what must have caught his fancy.'

Fiona leant against Bill; Katie turned her face into Daisy's shoulder; Willie leant over the top of Sammy's high chair; and Sammy, himself, made groaning sounds, saying, 'Oh, dear me!' and put his hand tightly against his side.

It was some time before calm was restored; then Fiona said, 'So, you enjoyed the scent after all?'

'No, it wasn't the real scent, Mrs Bailey; it was Chanel all right, but it was toilet water. It had the scent but it didn't last; you know, not like the proper stuff. It was supposed to be used after washing your hands. Well, I didn't just use it for me hands, I dabbed it all over. But I recognised it on the old dear in that shop, because it sort of clings to you, doesn't it? Not strong, just nice.'

It was Fiona now who asked, while drying her eyes, 'Did you have a nice time at Christmas?'

'Oh, Mrs Bailey, you wouldn't believe it; it was a one-off Christmas Day, all right. And you know, we've got neighbours, the Misses Browns. I think I've told you about them. Well, they came in. Eeh! My! You never know what's under people's skins, do you? The tales they told. You talk about laugh. And you know something? They both liked a drop of the hard, they said. So they had a good measure of your whisky. But that didn't please me da: he didn't mind them having the dinner wine, oh no, but, as he said after, it was a waste giving them whisky. You know, we've always thought they were two dried-up sticks of old maids. Very nice, you know. Oh, always been good to us, but still old maids. But from the tales they told about one another, they vied with each other to see who could tell the worst one. I think they had been two sparks in their early life. I don't think I've ever laughed so much. But some of their tales were far-fetched; you couldn't believe they were ever so innocent. One had a proposition put to her by the head of a school, and she thought it was to be a kind of pupil–teacher. But it turned out he wanted her to be his mistress. It was the way they both came out with the tales, so innocent-like. Oh, yes' – she nodded her head now – 'it was the most wonderful Christmas. And you know something?' She now bit on her lip, then looked around her and said, 'I don't know why I'm telling you lot this. I just don't. I mean, personal things. There should be a law against people dragging personal things out of you.' Again she was biting, almost dragging her lower lip in between her teeth. Then, her voice soft, in fact, her whole expression soft, she said, 'Me da kissed me.'

Nobody spoke. They didn't even move. They just stared at her, all of them stared at her, as she now added quietly, 'He had never kissed me in his life. I'd . . . I'd never seen him kiss anybody, not even little Jean, and she's only nine. Never me ma. But . . . but he kissed me. Mind' – her manner reverted to its old style and her voice became louder as she added – 'it was just a splosher, and on the cheek. And of course, he'd knocked back two double whiskys. But' – her voice sank again and her eyes lowered to where her hands were joined on her lap, the fingers interplaying with each other nervously, as she ended – 'it was nice. It put the finishing touch to a wonderful Christmas.' Her head now coming up, she looked towards Fiona and Bill, and it was as Bill said, 'You're a very kissable lass, Daisy,' there came a groan from Katie. And now it was she who had the attention of them all, for her head was turned away and she was wiping her face hastily with her handkerchief. And when Daisy put her hand on her shoulder and tried to pull her round, as she said, 'Oh, my! What's got into you? Leave off. Good Lord! I shouldn't have . . .' Katie turned on her and said, 'People like you, you know, Daisy Gallagher, should be put down at birth.'

After a moment, Daisy said, 'Oh, I know that. Yes, I know that.'

'You're a stirrer-up, that's what you are. You never keep to one theme.'

'Don't I?'

'No, you don't. One minute you're a clown and the next you're a . . . Oh!' – she tossed her head – 'I'm going to make some more tea.'

No-one spoke as she clattered the cups onto the tray and went out. Then Daisy said quietly, 'I'll have to be going. The bus leaves just after three.'

'Well, let it go just after three.' Bill got to his feet. 'Stay and have a bite. It'll be odds and ends as usual. That's all we've lived on since Christmas Day.'

'It isn't odds and ends; there's a leg of pork in the oven.'

'Oh, pork! Oh, that's all right then. I hope you've done the crackling so it'll crackle. Nell's the only one who can do that.'

'Oh really!' Fiona pulled away from him; then looking at Daisy, she said, 'Do stay, Daisy, that's if you've no other arrangements made.'

'No, I haven't any arrangements made, Mrs Bailey. And, aye, I'd like to stay, if it's not putting you out.'

'Oh, that old line, if it's not putting you out. Of course you're putting us out, that's why we asked you.'

'All right, Big Chief. Last word on the subject.'

'You know something?' Bill poked his face towards her, 'I don't put up with cheek like that from my own, in this house.'

'Well, sir,' – she now poked her face towards his – 'I always give people what they ask for, except when . . . me ma says, no!'

When Bill's hand came playfully across the side of her head she fell for a moment against Willie, and Willie put his arm around her shoulder, saying, 'He struck you, didn't he? He struck you.'

Making to leave the room, Fiona said, 'Come on, Daisy, you can give Katie a hand setting the table. And you, Mr Bailey, can see to the hall and drawing-room fires. So, let's all get moving.'

When Daisy followed Fiona, Bill did not immediately leave the room, but bent towards the two boys and said, 'That's a miracle, if ever I've seen one. She could be a smasher, couldn't she? Well, she is already. And to think she's plastered her face and rigged herself out in that dreadful get-up, when all the time—' He now straightened up and shook his head as he said, 'Women are the weaker sex, you know; they don't reason. She doesn't know she's an attractive piece even without that tongue of hers. But that's definitely good measure.'

It was Sammy, smiling now, who said to him, 'But Mr X didn't seem to mind the bum-freezer.'

Bill now went out laughing, but at the door, he said over his shoulder, 'Come on, you, Willie, and finish your job; we want some dry logs from the shed; that wet stuff'll spit all over the place.'

Willie did not immediately follow this command, but, looking at Sammy, he said, 'I've known all along.'

'What d'you mean, you've known all along?'

'Well, about her being a spanker.'

'Well, not the kind of spanker she looks now; nobody could have guessed.'

'I did.' The tone was arrogant.

'Oh, second sight.'

'No, first sight. I went for her first sight, the gear and everything.'

'Look Willie,' Sammy pulled himself somewhat painfully to the edge of the chair, and his voice was quiet as he said, 'I think you want to get things straight in that quarter. She's got Jimmy, you know.'

'She hasn't got Jimmy. Jimmy's got her, but only like a brother would act towards her; he's sort of looked after her.'

'Well, why d'you think he's looking after her? Not all out of charity. If you say you fell for her straightaway and could see below her plastered surface, then he could have felt the same.'

'He's older than her.'

'Oh, don't be daft, man. Older . . . four, five, six years, what does it matter? Younger or older, when it hits you it doesn't ask the age.'

'What would you know about it, anyway?' For the moment, Willie had forgotten that he was dealing with his friend who was far from well; and he went on, 'You turn your nose up at girls. I think you're frightened of them.'

'Yes, perhaps I am. I'm afraid of them trying to hook me.'

'Is that why you stick to our Katie?'

The voice that answered this issued from no invalid, saying, 'If I was meself, Willie Bailey, I'd knock you flat for that. I don't stick to Katie; I like her company. It's a relief from you and your tactless mouth.' Of a sudden he lay back against the chair and gasped as if exhausted, and Willie, all contrite now, said, 'Oh, man, I'm sorry. I'm sorry. It is me mouth; I should keep it shut. I am sorry, I am. And I know you just took up with her because she was having a hard time after the Rupert "do", when me da stopped speaking to her . . .'

'I didn't just "take up" with her for that.' Sammy's words came slow now, but heavy. 'I like Katie. You could say, we're on the same wavelength.'

'You mean . . . you like her?'

'Yes, I mean . . . I like her.'

'Oh, I didn't think of it that way. Well, what I mean is . . .'

'Well, whatever you mean, get it right in your mind: we are good friends.'

'Oh, well, good friends.'

'Yes! Good friends.'

Again Willie said, 'Oh!' as if that had cleared something else from his mind. And it had, because a girlfriend and a good friend meant two different things. He wanted Daisy for a girlfriend, but apparently Sammy just wanted Katie for a . . . well, friend.

'May I ask you something?'

'You'll ask me whether I want to listen or not.'

'Well, it's just this. D'you think I stand a chance with Daisy?'

'Well, you want it straight, so I'm going to give it to you straight. You stand as much chance as I do. In fact, I stand more chance than you because she and I understand each other. We speak the same language, being out of the same boat, if you take our environment into account. And I'll tell you something else. You'll never change Daisy, not inside. A new rig-out won't touch her real self. She'll always remain amusing, funny ha-ha, to make people laugh, while at the same time being as deep as a drawn well. It'll take someone more clever than you or me to get to the bottom of the real Daisy, because she's got a thinking mind, which she tries to hide.'

'Well, she's all the better for that, as I see it.'

Sammy sighed now as if he were tired, and his voice was slow as he said, 'Willie, you'll see her as you want to see her. You'll see her the same way as you saw me, and you'll aim to keep pressing on and pressing on until you think you've got her as seeing her through your eyes. With me, it worked. Circumstances made it work. Unearthing your dad in the muck heap put the final touches on it. They felt they owed me something and that has worked in with what you wanted. So, let's face it, I'm here at this minute being nursed and pampered because of you. If you work it back you'll see that. And, in a way . . . oh, I'm not going to just say, in a way, I'm going to say simply, and I'm lucky.' And now he laughed quietly as he said, 'I've never said this to you before, but I owe you for the way of life I have now; for my home, because I do look upon this as my home; my education; and all because of you who wanted to cuss and swear like me.' He smiled now up at Willie, but Willie's face was straight. And what he said next proved that he hadn't really been listening to the latter part of the conversation, for his mind was still brooding on the answer Sammy had given him with regard to his chances with Daisy, for he said, 'I'm just going to keep on. And I know one thing; Mam will accept her now. She looks different. It'll work.' He nodded twice towards Sammy, then turned and walked quickly from the room. And Sammy, looking towards the door, repeated, 'Mam will accept her now. She looks different.' And it was as if a voice from the side of him said, Like hell she will! It was his father's voice. And strangely, he heard himself reply to it,

You don't think she will? And the answer he got was, Mrs Bailey is not Mr Bailey, and there's no-one to fight Daisy's case like Mr Bill fought yours. Anyway, Daisy will decide.

Yes, Daisy would decide.

PART TWO

I

Mark had finished his exams in June, but he wasn't to know the results until the middle of August. What he did know was that if he got three Bs, he would be able to take up the place offered him in the London Hospital Medical School, where Roland Featherstone would be about to start on his second year. And Fiona had not known how, in the meantime, she was going to put up with this new-found son of hers.

But time had passed, and tomorrow he'd be gone to start his new life in London. He had been fortunate enough to find a room in the same house as Roland Featherstone, and for the first time in what seemed years Fiona was seeing her son again.

They were all at dinner, the last dinner before the family was to break up and, as Nell had just put it, the first fledgeling was to fly the nest. This had brought no retort from Mark but Willie once again put his foot in it by commenting, 'To start his first year chopping up rats.'

Fiona watched the look that she had hated, and which she could only describe as disdain, appear again on her son's face, as he snapped back at his brother. 'Don't be so stupid, showing your ignorance.'

And Willie, about to retort again in his usual way, picked up a warning look from Nell who was sitting opposite him. And after a moment, he said, 'Well, that's what I understand. Ralph Conway's brother is in his second year, and Ralph says he will stop dissecting rats now and go on to something bigger, such as . . .'

'Enough, you!' put in Bill, harshly. 'I'm eating, or trying to anyway.' And he picked up his wine glass and said, 'Let's drink to the future surgeon.' And when he got to his feet, the others followed, with the exception of Mark, who remained seated looking down towards his plate. '*To the future surgeon.*'

When they were again all seated and there followed a moment of silence, Mark broke it by looking towards Bill and saying quietly, 'Thanks, Dad, for all you've done for me, and are going to do. I do appreciate it.' Then, before Bill could answer, Mark turned to his mother and said, 'I've . . . I've been a bit of a pain in the neck, haven't I, lately?' And immediately two laughing voices, almost simultaneously, shouted out, 'You've said it, boy! You've said it!' Katie and Willie pushed at each other and a ripple of laughter went round the table, which brought from Mark a forced smile as he said, 'Oh, I know you two will be glad to see the back of me. I only hope I'm given the chance to operate on you one of these days.' There was loud laughter, and the tension at the table was broken.

'Right!' Bill's voice was a bellow now. 'Let's away into the drawing-room, Katie has raked out some old ragtime piano pieces and Willie's going to perform on his whistle "Won't you come home, Bill Bailey?" Remember that, Mrs B, when a certain lady got on the phone and sang that to me? The best thing you ever did in your life.'

Fiona put her hands to her head. 'Oh, that man's ego! For goodness sake get yourself into the drawing-room and let us clear up.'

'You're not doing any clearing up tonight,' her mother put in. 'I'll help Nell.'

'No, you won't! We'll all clear it,' called Bill. 'Come on! Pick up your dishes and take them into the kitchen, all of you.' And at this he picked up his pudding plate and a wine glass and marched out from the room, singing, 'Won't you come home, Bill Bailey?'

Katie and Willie and, almost immediately, Mark joined him.

When later, they all stood round the piano singing one old tune after another, with Mark's clear tenor voice now rising above the rest, Fiona gazed at him, thinking how she now wished he wasn't going away, until her common sense told her he had fallen back to his former self only for the simple reason that he was going away.

During the days that followed, the house fell back into what Fiona thought of as its usual pattern before she had experienced Mamie's tantrums,

Sammy's near tragedy, and Mark's insufferable manner.

At least once a week, sometimes twice, Katie, Willie and Sammy went to the Centre and continued with the fencing, karate and ju-jitsu, but, in the main, their evenings were taken up with study. Katie was in her A level year. She had got ten O levels, which hadn't pleased Willie, who, later, had managed only nine. And even Sammy, who had missed quite a bit of schooling, had got nine. Still, he had taken it very well. He was quieter these days, was Willie, and she felt she knew why. It had something to do with Daisy. Daisy had turned out to be a very attractive girl and she often turned up in a new rig-out from what she termed 'her private source'. But according to something Katie had let drop, it seemed that she did not return Willie's ardour. In fact, she had even refused to go to the cinema with him, telling him bluntly she wasn't starting 'anything like that'. And for this attitude, Fiona was doubly thankful.

She liked Daisy, found her very refreshing, very amusing, but as a prospective wife for Willie? Oh, dear! Even she could see what Willie was blind to: it wasn't just that Daisy was strong-willed, had a mind of her own, and, whatever happened, would go her own way, but that she knew her second son and she was able to realise that he would not be able to keep up with her, mentally that is. And then there were her people; and if there was ever an advocate for a family, Daisy was an advocate for hers. There would be no hiding behind a façade for

Daisy. And as much as Fiona liked them, and yes, she did – they were all good people in their own way, and she secretly admitted they and their ways would be acceptable to Bill and to Sammy, and even to Katie – she, too, was herself, and whereas she had accepted Sammy and even loved him, she could not see herself loving Daisy as a daughter-in-law. Still, as Daisy was showing no designs this way, she needn't worry. And Willie would get over her; he was young yet. Young? In another few months he would be seventeen.

It happened to be a Tuesday night and Willie was sitting before the drawing-room fire, nursing a cold. He hadn't been to school for the past two days, and Sammy had come straight home from school to keep him company and, at the same time, to get a bit of work in. He would really have liked to be with Katie at the Centre, where they were practising turning the routine into an exhibition piece for the pantomime that they were putting on for Christmas. As it was, he was to take the six-fifteen bus into the town and meet Katie at Laburnum Walk. From there they would both go to Bill's club, where he was at a meeting which should be over by seven o'clock, and he would pick them up from there.

For the past few weeks, if Katie had been going to practice alone, she had always asked Sammy to come and meet her. He hadn't asked the reason why, of a sudden, she wanted to be met, but he put it down to her not liking to come along Laburnum Walk. Although there was a lamppost at each end, the middle section tended to be dark.

The name Laburnum Walk had been given to the short cut flanked on both sides by high garden walls overhung by the branches of laburnum trees.

Katie wasn't afraid of walking through Laburnum Walk; she had never been afraid of the dark; but she admitted to herself she was becoming afraid of being waylaid by Roland Ferndale, who had taken to pestering her when she was by herself. It had first happened at a charity disco. Sammy, Willie and Daisy were all there and she herself had been dancing with one of the members of the ju-jitsu class. He was only about fifteen, but when he was shouldered roughly aside by a tall fellow, Katie, for a moment, had thought he would react by throwing the big fellow on his back. And likely he would have done, had she not shaken her head at him. Then she was staring at the swaying figure in front of her, but only for a minute, for when he lifted his hand with the intention of taking her arm, she knocked it aside and, turning her back on him, walked from the floor.

For the remainder of the evening, whenever she passed him, he would scowl at her as he had done that night when she had refused a lift from him in no uncertain manner. And twice she had noticed him sitting in a stationary car when she came out of school. However he had not made any move to contact her. The last time she had encountered him was by the park gates, but, that night, she was with Daisy and the boys. Nevertheless, although it was getting dark, she knew he was staring at her. She had heard a rumour he had been engaged but had broken it off, or rather she had, whoever she was.

Tonight, she had come out of the Centre with Daisy. Daisy would be making for home so they parted at the park, and she made for Laburnum Walk and Sammy.

When she turned into the cut she was aware of footsteps hurrying ahead of her as if somebody were anxious to get to the other end, and so when the sound stopped, she took no further heed.

'Well, hello!' When the arm was thrust out and blocked her way, she gave an audible gasp. She had no need to ask whose voice it was, so she cried, 'You let me past, Roland Ferndale, else you'll get the worst of it in the end, I'm telling you.'

'Big talk from a little girl.' The tone was derisive. Then it changed. 'What is it about you that gets me, for you're nothing special, you know, are you? And your people neither. What is your father after all? He's known as a loud-mouthed git.'

The push she gave him actually knocked him against the wall, which seemed to enrage him, for he gripped her shoulder and pulled her round, but in the swinging she jerked herself free. And now, jumping back with the practised step of the fencer, she brought her thick-soled lamb's-wool boot up, aiming at his groin. As he fell sideways, his flailing arm caught her shoulder again, and she in her turn, was knocked sideways against the wall. Now he was tearing at her coat, in spite of the nails clawing at his face and hair, and he continued to rip at her clothes.

The buttons flew from her coat and the top of her blouse; but when his hands grabbed at her breast, she really went berserk, and the same white hot fury was in her again as when she had seen the two naked figures on the bed and had thrown the heavy wooden bowl at them. Automatically, her knee came up again and her hands clawed at his throat. She was unaware that she was screaming.

Before his body crumpled her foot had caught him in the stomach. Then again she heard running footsteps. Now she was leaning against the opposite wall, gasping. She knew that there was blood running into her eyes and that her blouse was wet.

'My God! My God!' It was Sammy holding her up.

Taking a small torch from his pocket, Sammy flashed it down at the prone figure, and again he said, 'My God!' And when he heard running steps and voices, he pulled Katie from the wall, saying, 'Go on! Go on! Get out of this! Quick!'

For a moment he watched her stumbling away into the darkness before he bent down and, gripping the man's collar, brought him into a sitting position. In doing so, he felt the blood running over his hands. His face was in a mess. My God! What had she done to knock him out? Was . . .was he dead?

'What's this? What's this? What have you done?'

He turned and peered at the dim faces of two men and a woman.

'I . . . I found him like this. He's been in a fight,' he muttered.

'Been in a fight? My God! Look at his face. You mean, you've been in a fight too. Look at you! What have you done to him?'

Roland Ferndale's hand came up and gripped Sammy's wrist, and he muttered something.

'What did he say?' the woman said.

'It sounded like, you, you!' said one of the men. While the other, peering at Sammy, said, 'You say you found him here?'

'Yes. Just . . . just a minute ago.'

'Well, how is it that you're covered in blood too?'

'Oh.' Sammy looked down at his hands. They were wet: he couldn't make out whether it was blood or not; but, of course, it was blood.

'Something fishy here,' pronounced the woman.

'I think it's a police job,' added one of the men, 'and an ambulance too, for that poor fellow won't be able to stand. Run back home, Carrie, and phone for an ambulance. We'll keep this one here.'

Sammy now got to his feet, protesting, 'You send for the ambulance, missis, and the polis, but I tell you, I just found him here and straightened him up.'

The man who now spoke to him was a burly type, well into six-feet and a good head above Sammy, and his voice was threatening as he said, 'If you're going to make off, young man, you've got another think coming.'

For a moment Sammy wondered if he could throw the man. But no; he'd better wait until the polis came; they would understand. But when Ferndale comes round he'll find some excuse.

What would he tell them? That a young lass had done this to him when he tried to rape her. There was a point here; yes, what would he say?

A voice came to them now, calling, 'There's a police car in the district, and they're sending an ambulance.'

It was hardly a minute later the big man said, 'There they are now.' Then, turning to Sammy, he said, 'Well, young fella, now we'll find out what's what, won't we?'

'Yes,' snapped Sammy, 'we'll all find out what's what. And it'll likely teach you not to jump to conclusions. As I've told you, I didn't do this.'

Before the policemen reached them the woman called, 'We've come upon a nasty business, officer, a nasty business.'

Neither of the officers spoke until a light was shone on the figure slumped against the wall, when one of them said, 'Well, what's happened here?' And he turned to Sammy, and, taking in his blood-stained light-grey overcoat and also his hands, he asked quietly, 'Had a row?'

'No, sir, I haven't had a row. I came along here and I saw him in this condition. He was bent forward leaning over towards the ground, and I straightened him up to get him to his feet. And then these,' – he made a motion with his hand – 'these people came along; and because they saw the blood on my hands, they jumped to the wrong conclusion.'

Without commenting, the policeman bent over Roland Ferndale and said, 'Do you think you can stand up, sir?'

'My . . . my head . . . it's aching.'

'Yes. Yes, I should imagine it is, sir. Come on, see if you can get to your feet.'

One on each side of him now, the policemen hoisted him and he was propped against the wall; and slowly he put his hand in his pocket and drew out a handkerchief and wiped the blood from his eyes. Then he blinked in the strong light from the policeman's lamp. The light now was showing up two men, the woman and Sammy, and it was on Sammy that Roland Ferndale fixed his blinking gaze. And as he did so, he put his hand to his groin and his upper body came forward from the wall and he groaned.

The policeman was now asking him, 'Have you any recollection of who attacked you, sir?'

Still with his body bent forward and one hand pressed against his groin, Roland Ferndale lifted the other hand in a shaky movement and pointed towards Sammy.

Almost instantly Sammy's shout echoed down the Walk, as he cried, 'No, I didn't! You're a bloody liar, Roland Ferndale. You know I didn't.'

'That's enough. That's enough.' One of the policemen had pushed Sammy against the far wall, saying, 'You know him then?'

'Yes. Yes, I know him, and he's a liar. I told you I came upon him.'

'Oh, you came on him all right.' It was the woman's voice piping in again. 'We saw what was happening when we came up. You were trying to loosen his grip on you.'

Sammy was now yelling at her, 'He was gripping my wrist to support himself. I was trying to get him upright.'

The second policeman now put his hand out and gripped Sammy's shoulder, saying, 'That's enough of that. Stop your bawling.'

'Take your hands off me!'

The policeman did not move his hand, but he said, 'I will when I'm ready. Come along.'

The other policeman, in an undertone to his partner, the while nodding towards Ferndale, said, 'His flies are open.' And, in a conciliatory tone, he said to Sammy, 'Did he accost you, lad?'

'Accost me? No, he didn't! But I don't know about anybody else. And will you please now let go of me.' He had turned to the other policeman, only to receive the reply, 'As I said, I will when I'm ready, and after you've answered a few more questions at the station.'

At the man's tone Sammy experienced what was not an unfamiliar feeling, that his father was again standing by his side, urging him now to put the man on his back, and so when he was pulled roughly from the wall, he turned on the policeman, 'Take your bloody hands off me, or I'll have you on your back.'

'Enough of that, sir. D'you know whom you're talking to?'

'Yes. Two stupid buggers who cannot see any further than their noses. Would I be standing straight and without a mark on my face if I had been fighting him? And he almost twice my size. Use your nap—' He didn't get "napper" out before he was being pulled from the wall.

'Big fella, aren't you?'

'Yes, and if I had you one at a time, I would have you on the floor.'

'Oh! Oh! Ju-jitsu-like?'

'Yes. Ju-jitsu-like.'

The first policeman said to the other one, 'Get through to the office and tell them to direct Ben this way. We've got one for the station and one for hospital.'

'No. No,' Ferndale was gasping. 'Home, not . . . not hospital.'

'All right, sir, all right. We'll get you home.' The officer turned to the two men and the woman, saying, 'Will you give my partner your names and addresses please? Thank you for your help.' Then turning back to Sammy, he said, 'It's no use struggling, youngster; you're not going to throw anyone tonight, so you might as well relax.'

It was strange, but Sammy did relax, because of a sudden feeling of fear . . . he was going to the station . . . station meant prison. His da had been there twice, and really feared it. And he was fearing it now.

*   *   *

When Katie had stumbled to the end of the Walk, she leant against the wall and bent over almost double to stop herself from passing out. She was aware of the commotion going on further down the Walk; vaguely, she thought, someone's helping Sammy with him. Then she was talking to herself: Don't let me pass out. Oh Lord, don't let me pass out! Take deep breaths. Take deep breaths.

When she straightened up, she suddenly exclaimed, 'I'm going to be sick.' Then 'Oh, I mustn't be sick here. I must get to Dad. I must get to Dad.'

Again she was aware of the voices, and she muttered, 'Oh, come on, Sammy! Come on! Leave him! Come on!'

When she heard the distant sound of a police car, she muttered, 'They'll likely take him to hospital. It'll be in all the papers. Oh, Mam! Oh, Dad!' Then, her hand going inside her coat, she winced, and again she was speaking aloud, saying, 'Oh, my breast, Oh, my breast. He would have raped me. He would! He would! He's mad. Oh dear Lord! And I was too. Oh, that terrifying feeling. Oh, Lord! Oh, Mam!'

At this she turned quickly and vomited against the wall. Three times she retched. It was as she staggered on to the path and towards the lamppost that a couple, passing with a dog, paused for a moment as if they were going to commiserate with her. Then the woman said, 'She's drunk. Dear! dear! Tut-tut! She's been sick. Come away from that, Cherry.' There was a tug on the dog's lead now, and as they moved away, the man's voice could be heard, declaring loudly, 'A young lass! Likely drink and drugs. What's the world coming to?'

She actually put her arms around the lamppost and leant her brow against it and said, 'He meant it. He meant it. He meant it. His flies . . . I saw his flies open. Why me! He's had all the girls. Why me? I . . . I must go back to Sammy.'

She now looked down at herself. Her coat was open and her school blouse was ripped down one side, and she muttered, 'Oh, my breast.' She cupped her breast with her hand, then winced. 'Dirty swine! Dirty swine!' The tears now were running down her face. She pulled her coat tightly about her, then again she stumbled into the Laburnum Walk, only to peer down it and realise she could see the lamp at the far end, and more than one light. There was a revolving light, indicating a police car.

Now she was running and when she reached the end of the Walk it was to see what would have been the second of the police cars disappearing into the distance.

Two men and a woman, who had been standing a little way further along the pavement, now walked towards her, talking to each other. And as they went into the Walk, she heard one of them say, 'I'm having different ideas about it now. Perhaps he had attempted something on the young lad and he retaliated. That's why he blamed him.'

She turned and watched the three backs disappearing into the dimness and muttered to herself.

'He must have blamed Sammy.' Of course, he'd have to blame somebody; and he would never say it was her. Oh, no, not the big macho fellow he was. Oh! Oh! The exclamation was loud. And now she turned, and in a stumbling run made her way to her dad's club.

Bristol's Club was the most exclusive in the town and it sported a doorman. But it wasn't until she stood in the small car-park to the side of the building and saw Bill's car there that she asked herself what she was going to say to him. It would happen that Mr Ferndale was one of the men he was meeting tonight. What would happen if she said to him, 'That man's son has tried to rape me?' He was a member of the trust and the trust controlled the development that had made her dad what he was today. But her dad would have to go to the police station and clear Sammy, and Sammy would tell him. As she stood wondering what she was going to do, the door opened and Bill came out, accompanied by another man. She heard them parting and Bill saying, 'Good night, Ralph.' Then he was coming towards her.

'Dad!'

'Oh, you're on your own. Where's—? Good God! What's the matter with you, girl?' He looked at her hugging the coat tightly about her waist, then at her tousled hair and the part of the head scarf hanging over her shoulder.

She whimpered at him, 'Dad! Dad!' He said, 'You've been attacked? Where's . . . where's Sammy?'

'Dad, let me sit in the car for a minute, please!'

After he had helped her gently into the passenger's seat, she said, 'Yes . . . yes, I was attacked, and Sammy . . . came to my aid . . . and he pushed me away. He told me to go because . . . well, Dad, I went mad, and I've hurt somebody again.'

He made no comment, but his grip tightened on her hand as he said, 'Who was it? D'you know?'

'Yes. Yes . . . but, I'm not going to say just yet.'

'Why? In God's name, girl!'

'Don't shout, Dad. Please, don't shout. Sammy pushed me away . . . well, he didn't want me mixed up with this. I know . . . I know what he meant. But now he's having to . . . well, stand the racket. The police took him away.'

'When was this?'

'Just . . . just now, about half an hour ago. Will you go to the station and . . . and get him out, if you can? But . . . but if you can talk to him on the quiet, would you do something for me?'

'You know very well I will girl; just tell me.'

'Will . . . will you say to him that I don't want him mentioned . . . I mean, the one who attacked me. Not yet anyway. We must . . . must talk about it.'

'Good God! Mystery . . . mystery. Well, look; let me get you home.'

'No, Dad. Put me in a taxi and then go straight to the police station.'

'If he's in the police station, he won't rot before I get there. Dear God! Davey's son now. Did he batter him? Because he's got a lot of his father in him.'

'No, Dad. No, he didn't. It was me. It was me. Well, what happened, Dad, was, I went mad. I did, like I did before. But he . . . he was going to rape me.'

'You went mad, girl? When I get him, whoever he is, I'll kill him.'

'Dad! Please do as I ask, please! I beg of you. Say to Sammy, straightaway, she won't tell me who it is and she asks you not to. Will you do that? Don't ask who it is?'

'Well, the police'll know.'

'No, they don't know. They think it was a fight between him and Sammy.'

When Bill started up the car, Katie begged again, 'Dad! Put me in a taxi.'

Bill had never driven so fast through the town. And after he got out of it he must have exceeded the speed limit. Then, he was helping her out of the car and straight into the house because the door was open. And there was Fiona, Willie and Nell awaiting them.

'What . . . what has happened?' Fiona gaped at her daughter, whose coat was open, her blouse in ribbons, and she said, 'Oh, my dear! You've been attacked! You've been attacked!'

When Katie fell into her arms, sobbing, Fiona looked at Bill and said, 'Sammy's in the police station; he wants you to go as soon as possible. What's all this about? How's it happened?'

'She'll likely tell you more than she's told me. There's a mystery here I'd like to get to the bottom of and I will before the night's out. See to her; I'm going back for Sammy.'

'Dad! Dad!' Katie swung round from Fiona. 'Do what I ask. Please! There's a reason. Please!'

He stared at her for a moment, shook his head, then went out.

At the police station there were only two officers present. One looked up and said, 'Good evening, sir.'

Bill did not respond to the greeting, but said, 'I understand you have my boy here.' He had not said son.

'Mr Bailey?'

'Yes. I'm Mr Bailey.'

'We are holding a youth named Samuel Love.'

'Yes, you are holding a youth called Sammy Love, and he's my boy. And I would like to speak to him, please.'

'Yes. Yes, of course, sir . . . you know what he may be charged with?'

'No, I don't know what he might be charged with.'

'Well, sir, he apparently attacked another young man and left him in a pretty sorry plight. This could be described as "assault and battery"; but, more so, he has used language to the police and resisted arrest.'

'Is that all?'

The policeman's face altered, as did his tone, and he said, 'I think it will prove to be enough, sir.' Then he turned and nodded to his associate, who stood up and, looking at Bill, said, 'Will you come this way, please?'

The sight of Sammy sitting in the bare cell on a wooden plank bed, his elbows on his knees, caused Bill to groan inside. It was as if he were looking at Davey again, for the expression on Sammy's face was exactly that of his father's after he had come up against the law.

When the policeman hesitated to leave, Bill said, 'He has not been officially charged yet with any offence?'

'Not exactly, sir. But the victim,' he paused, 'pointed him out. And as you heard, he has resisted arrest, and so on.'

'But has he been officially charged?'

'No, sir, not yet, as I understand.' The reply was snappy and Bill's was equally so as he said, 'Well, then, I would like to speak to him in private.'

When the door closed, Bill pulled up the single chair to the side of the bunk. Sammy was still sitting as if unable to move. But what he said straightaway was, 'I didn't do anything, Mr B. I didn't.'

'I know you didn't, lad.' He put his hand on his shoulder. 'And before you go any further, Katie has tried to extract a promise from me to say to you that you are not to name the culprit who went for her. Now why, I ask you, should she want to keep that a secret? D'you know who went for her?'

Sammy stared up into Bill's face, and it was some seconds before he said, 'Yes. Yes, I know who went for her. And Katie said that?'

'Yes. At least she wants to talk about it first. Can you explain why?'

Again Sammy stared at Bill, and again it was

some seconds before he nodded and said, 'Aye. Yes, in a way, I can. But it'll all come out later; it's bound to.'

'You don't know why she wants it kept dark now?'

'No. No, I don't.'

Bill hitched his chair forward to get closer to Sammy. And what he said quietly now was, 'Did she really beat him up that much?'

'Yes, she did, and some. She must have gone berserk for a time, because he's a biggish fella.'

'But why did she leave you there? Why did she not stay and sort it out with the police herself?'

'I . . . I made her go. It would have made big headlines. And we both knew . . . well, I mean, the consequences. We didn't want that. At least, I didn't think that at the time; it came to me afterwards. But I can tell you this much about him without telling you his name; he's a dirty swine. He pointed me out as his assailant; he couldn't bear the thought that he had been roughed up by a girl.' Then, his voice dropping, he said, 'Can you get me out of here the night, Mr B?'

At this, Bill shook his head slowly, saying, 'I . . . I doubt it, Sammy. Perhaps I could if you told me the fella's name. If you know him and she knows him, then why not? Was it somebody at that Centre?'

'No. No.'

'Anyway, you know you shouldn't have got back at the officers. That wasn't a sensible thing to do, was it?'

'You don't know how they treated me. They just took his word. And, oh,' – Sammy shook his head – 'it's funny. No, it isn't funny, it's odd and it's frightening. But, you know, since Mamie's business, and when I thought I was done for on that floor and me dad came and spoke to me, as I told you, well, he's been back several times, and I'm getting worried. For there he was again, and it was as if it was he shouting at them when I bloodied and buggered.'

'Oh! You bloodied and buggered, did you? Anything worse?'

'No. No. Except that I threatened to put one on his back.'

'Oh, my God, boy! Threatening to toss a policeman. Well, apart from anything else, I think that'll keep you in the night. But I'll be round first thing in the morning. You'll likely have to go before a magistrate, then be bailed out. But, like your da, you'll have to plead guilty.'

'If I plead not guilty, I don't get out?'

'That's about it. Oh, my God!' Bill tossed his head. 'I'm back with your dad, explaining these very same things to him.'

'But I'm not guilty. All right, about the police, yes, but about the other thing, no! And that's the main thing, and I'm not going to say I am.'

'Are you going to say who is, then?'

'No, of course not.' It was a growl now from Sammy. 'What d'you think I am? But . . . but he'll have to say mistaken identity or some such to get me off this hook.'

'Don't worry, lad. You'll be off the hook. In any case, you'll be home tomorrow; I'll see to that.'

As Bill rose, Sammy also got to his feet and, looking at him, he said softly, 'D'you know something, Dad? I'm more afraid now than when I was lying on that floor trussed up and the needle was working on me. I suppose, like me da, I'm terrified of bars and locked doors.'

Bill's arm went about him and he pressed him tightly to him, saying thickly, 'The night'll soon pass. I'll be here first thing in the morning.' Then, pressing Sammy back on to the bunk, he said, 'I'll have a word with the officers. We'll soon have you home.' His own voice was near breaking now; he couldn't stand any more, and, turning swiftly, he went out of the cell, but stood in the corridor for a moment the while the officer locked the cell door.

Following the officer back to the enquiry room, he endeavoured to regain his composure, and to the officer in charge at the desk, he said, 'There's something here I can't get to the bottom of. But I'm sure it'll be cleared up tomorrow. Until then,' he paused and looked straight into the man's face as he added, 'I hope you will deal with him fairly.'

'We always try to, sir.'

Then on a lighter note, and with a slight smile, the officer said, 'I understand, sir, that he's a karate expert?'

'Yes, he is.' Bill nodded at him. 'A brown belt and ready for his next step in that direction.' And now the man, leaning further towards Bill, said in a low and amused tone, 'I understand he offered to throw one of my associates!'

Bill was forced to answer with a smile, saying, 'What a pity the man refused.'

'Yes. Yes, it is in some ways, sir. Yes, it is. Good night, sir.'

'Good night, officer.'

There were decent ones among them. Oh, yes, there were decent ones among them . . .

Back in the house, Fiona met him in the hall, saying, 'You haven't brought him back?'

'No, woman, I haven't brought him back. He'll be in the cells the night, because he's standing the racket for what Katie did to the fella, and rightly so. Oh, yes, and rightly so. But more so than that, he's not only used some of his father's language on the police, but offered them ju-jitsu on his own terms. Now that last bit'll take some getting over.'

'Oh, my goodness! My goodness me!'

'Is she asleep?'

'No. No; she's in her dressing-gown. She won't let me have her clothes. I mean, the ones that are ripped, and they're all bloody. And she says she knows who attacked her, but she won't say the name. Why?'

'Don't ask me why, woman.' He pushed past her and into the drawing-room. 'I've just left one who's given me the same answers. At least, that was after I passed on the message she wanted me to give to him. It'll all be clear tomorrow, she said . . . The things that happen in this house. I wonder what next. Get me a drink, Willie, will you? Oh, I forgot, stay where you are with that cold; I'll get it meself.'

'You won't get it yourself. Sit down.'

Fiona almost pushed him on to the couch, then, as she went from the room, Bill's voice followed her, saying, 'As you say, missis, things that happen in this house. We never seem to be out of police clutches these days. Sammy, Mamie, and now Katie and, of course . . .'

'And, of course, Sammy again.'

Bill now turned to Willie, saying, 'I've never seen him look so lost, Willie. It nearly broke me up. There was his father all over again.'

Willie said quietly, 'Sammy isn't fit yet to tackle anyone with karate, or judo, or anything else. He still has pains in his side, you know, from that do.'

'Yes, I know.'

'Katie must have gone berserk. She says herself that she did. And I'm glad she did else God knows what would have happened to her.'

'Was there anybody after her at the Centre?'

'No, not that I know of. She was well liked. But she never encouraged any of the blokes in either classes and none of them have made a pass at her, I'm sure. They're a decent lot, you know, Dad. Most of them are from Bog's End, but they're better than some of the others; at least, towards girls. Some of those fellas think they're God's gifts, you know.' Then he shook his head, saying, 'No, there's nobody I could think of who would attempt that on her. But it's somebody that she knows and Sammy knows. And why she's keeping quiet beats me.'

'And me. Yes, and me.'

Bill took the glass of whisky from Fiona's hand,

saying, 'Thanks, dear.' Then, 'Has she cried a lot?'

'No. No, not after the first bout. And she says she doesn't want to talk about it. She's had a bath, and I saw—' When she stopped, Bill said, 'You saw what?'

'Oh, it doesn't matter.'

'Mam,' – Willie's voice was quiet – 'I'm not a kid. I was brought up with Katie, you know.'

'He's right,' said Bill. 'What did you see?'

Fiona drew in a deep breath, then said, 'Her breast is all marked, almost black and blue in one part where he gripped her. And his nails have torn the skin, and it must have bled. She has two deep scratches down her chest where her blouse was ripped. Moreover, there's a dark bruise on one shoulder.'

There was a moment's pause before Bill said, 'My God! I wish I could get me hands on him.' And to this, Fiona put in immediately, 'That's what she's afraid of, I think.'

'So I know him?'

'Well, you must in a way. I've racked my brains and I can't think who we know would do such a thing, attempt such a thing.'

'Where is she now?'

'She's in the little sitting-room.'

When he made as if to rise, she said, 'Leave her, Bill. If you go in there you'll only bring it all up. And she doesn't want to talk about it, not tonight, anyway. When I went to sit with her, she asked me to leave her. Yes, she did. She said, "I'll be all right, Mam. Just leave me alone. I want to think." '

'What does she want to think about?'

'Bill! Bill!' She closed her eyes and turned her head away. 'I don't really know. She's got something on her mind . . . There's the phone ringing.' She got up and went out of the room. But within a moment she was back, saying, 'It's . . . it's George, George Ferndale.'

'George? What does he want? I only left him an hour or so ago at the club.'

He marched into the hall, picked up the phone and said, 'Hello, there. Anything amiss?'

There was a short silence before the words came, 'Need you ask?'

'Aye. Yes, I need ask, George, because I don't know.'

'Well, I thought you would know by now. You've been to the police station, haven't you?'

'Yes. Yes.'

'To see that young Irish skit? I can say this because he's none of your flesh or blood. But he's definitely his father's son.'

'Yes, he's his father's son. And his father was one of the best men I've known. All right, he was ready with his fists—'

'Well,' the voice broke in now, 'the son, let me tell you, is not only ready with his fists, but with his feet too. You should see my son's groin.'

'Your son's groin?'

'Yes, that's what I said. It's black and blue. As for his face, I doubt if he'll ever get rid of the marks, nail deep.'

Bill brought his head back from the mouthpiece.

He couldn't believe it. Young Roland Ferndale . . . he had tried it on her, and Katie had beaten him up.

The voice came to him now, saying, 'I feel no compunction in pressing the charge. You'll likely find some excuse and wish to contest it. Well, I'll be in my chambers at half-past ten tomorrow morning.'

Bill was about to bawl into the phone when the line went dead. He'd be in his chambers at half-past ten tomorrow morning. Well, by God, he'd beat him to it! By that time, he'd be at the police station, and not alone. No. He swung about, went to the drawing-room where the door was open and called, 'Come along! You'll hear something.'

Both Fiona and Willie hurried down the room and followed him into the little sitting-room where Katie was curled up in the corner of a big chair. And when Bill greeted her with, 'What d'you mean, you silly little bitch, by keeping this to yourself?' He now swung round to Fiona, saying, 'Roland Ferndale!'

'*What!* You mean? Oh, no.'

'Oh, yes! Yes! What d'you think George Ferndale wanted me on the phone for? It was to tell me what he was going to do with Sammy for knocking his son about. He said that if Sammy had been my own flesh and blood, he might have thought twice, or words to that effect. But being the son of Davey Love, whom he had helped to send along the line, he's going to go the whole hog now and charge him.' Turning now to Katie he said, 'Why, girl, did you keep your mouth shut?'

Katie unwound herself from the chair and, drawing herself to its edge, she looked up at him and said, 'I had my reasons. I knew if I told you who it was, you, in your tactful fashion, would go and raise hell. And he's the big noise on the trust, isn't he? And—'

'Blast the trust!'

'Yes, that's what you would have said, blast the trust! And blasted your future plans with it. I wanted time to think of a way out, and I have thought of something.'

'Well, would you mind enlightening me, miss?'

'No, I wouldn't. You're the last person I would enlighten.'

Bill drooped his head deep on to his chest. And now Fiona said, 'Sit down. Don't you realise that what she's done, she's done for—?'

'Yes; yes, woman, I realise that. Of course, I do. But I'm not depending on George Ferndale; there's other men on the trust. Oh, yes. Yes, he's a big noise and knows the law, and by the sound of it, he means to do something with it tomorrow. He's bidden me to be at his office by half-past ten, and I'll be there. Oh yes, I'll be there. And you,' he now took hold of Katie's hand, 'you will be with me. Tomorrow morning you put on your school rig again. I'll take you to the station and have you examined by a policewoman.'

'You'll do nothing of the sort, Dad.'

'Oh, we'll see who's going to be boss tomorrow morning. Oh, yes, we'll see. In any case, there'll still be two charges of a sort for that stupid young bugger to face,' – he turned to Fiona now – 'for using bad language and aiming to tackle a policeman. Can you believe it?'

'He didn't, did he?'

Bill had turned to Katie again, and his voice was calmer as he said, 'Yes, lass, he did. And by what I can gather from himself, he acted pretty much as his father would have done. In fact' – he now nodded from Fiona to Willie – 'he told me he thought his dad was there with him, as he had been on the night they trussed him up. My idea is, he was suffering from concussion then and the effects of it have remained with him, and he's a bit nervous about it.'

'Poor Sammy.'

Bill looked at Willie now and repeated, 'You can say that again, lad; poor Sammy.' Then turning to Katie, he added, 'I'm sorry, lass, I went for you, but it was out of concern. Believe me, it was out of concern, because I can see now why you were doing it. I would, yes, I would have gone down there and finished off the job that you started on that fella. By God, I would! And if ever I get my hands on him we'll arrange for some reparation. Oh, yes! The dirty pig. But why you? By what I've gleaned from his mother, he's a great favourite with the girls, so why has he picked on you for this?'

Katie drooped her head as she said, 'Because I wouldn't have anything to do with him. He pestered me at one time and I went for him then. But he's a big-head and can't bear to think there's somebody not falling over themselves for him.'

After staring at her for a moment, he patted her hand, then turned to Fiona, saying, 'Get her to bed. It's going to be a busy day the morrow. By, it is!' Then, bending forward, he kissed Katie on the cheek.

When Bill was left alone with Willie, he said to him, 'This town will ring with some news the morrow, boy. Just you wait and see.'

'Dad?'

'Yes? What is it?' He turned back to Willie, but Willie didn't speak for some seconds, then he said, 'Somehow, that's what she doesn't want. That's what she's been trying to avoid.'

'Oh, I know, because she thinks it'll do me harm in the business. But damn the business!'

'Yes, that may be the main point, but there's another, Dad. I don't think she wants it known that she's capable of knocking someone out, a man especially, because that's what he is; he's nearly nineteen and he's big with it. Well, she doesn't want it tacked on to her that she roughed him up in a way that even a man mightn't have been capable of. You see, she possesses all the tricks in the judo and karate games now. And she's hoping that her A levels will get her into university next year, and people being what they are, she could be shunned. I don't think she thought all that out really, but Sammy must have when he made her go away and leave the rest to him. Remember what she did to Rupert's girl, and Rupert himself: she went into a fury that day, and it must have been the same tonight, or even worse, because it would have been a hand-to-hand battle with him.'

Bill looked at Willie in silence. Here was one of the family whose tongue ran away with him at times, yet he had clearly dissected his sister's feelings in this matter, and very likely he was right. Oh, yes, more than very likely. But still he was sorry that, in this case, he couldn't see it her way. To all intents and purposes he was her father, and a father who would put up with his daughter being raped to save his business wasn't worth a spit. No, he was taking her, not to the chambers, but to the police station, tomorrow morning. He continued to look at Willie as his thoughts ran on. Willie was a nice lad, that was the word for him, nice, and strangely, like himself, he had no feeling for class, hence his persistence in trailing Daisy. Funny, he thought, but he could be my own son, because where class is concerned we're both on the same wavelength. And like Willie, he too opened his mouth often and put his foot in it. And there was a third thing; deep down he cared for people. Aye, he did.

He put his hand on Willie's shoulder now, saying, 'We all need an early night; get yourself upstairs. I'll lock up. Good night, Willie.'

'Good night, Dad.'

Two hours later Willie was woken from sleep, and he blinked into the light of the torch as he muttered, 'What is it? Who is it?'

'Shh! It's me, Katie.'

'What's the matter? What time is it?'

'It's a quarter to twelve.'

'Some . . . somebody bad?'

'No. Listen. Do something for me, will you?'

Willie pulled himself up in the bed, ran his hands through his thick hair, then said, 'Well, if I can. What is it?'

'Tomorrow morning I want you to tell Dad not to kick up a fuss or phone anybody, because I'll have gone on an errand. But tell him to be at the police station between half-past nine and ten. He was going to be there in any case. But when he finds me gone, you know him, he'll kick up a dust.'

'You going out now?' Willie pulled himself further up in the bed, and she hissed back at him, 'No! No, I'm not. But I'll be leaving the house about seven. I'll tell you this much, I'll be catching the workmen's bus.'

'What for?'

'You'll know later, Willie. I . . . I know how to straighten this thing out without it affecting Dad. Because, you know, once he gets going, he'll say things he's sorry for. And it's all right in the house, but he's got a business to carry on.'

'He doesn't care a damn about the business. Well, what I mean is, that comes second to you.'

'I know that. But there'll be no need if you'll only do what I tell you.'

'Where are you going in the morning?'

'I'll tell you later. You'll know all about it then. Just leave it to me. And do this for me, will you? On no account let him go to the station before that time. Anyway, I'll likely be waiting for him outside, if not inside.'

'What're you up to, Katie?'

'I'm up to nothing. But I can straighten this thing out in my own way if I'm left alone. Will you do that?'

'Yes. Yes, of course, I'll do that. But I can tell you, it'll be like keeping a tiger in a rabbit hutch.'

She put out her hand now, saying on a small laugh, 'A good description.'

He caught at her hand as he whispered, 'Well, whatever you do, I'm with you. You know that, Katie. And I'm glad you laid him out.'

'Good night, Willie.'

'Good night, Katie, and don't worry, I'll do as you say and hang on to him.'

The seven o'clock bus was the first bus of the morning, and it was full of workmen who all seemed to know each other, and, without exception, eyed the young lass in the long mackintosh and woollen hat.

She had to go to the back of the bus where sat three men, and they moved along the seat to make room for her.

'A sharp morning, miss,' said one of them.

'Yes. Yes, it is very cold.'

'Get fed up with dark mornings,' said another. 'Can't see your way to work.'

'A good excuse for being late,' put in a laughing voice. 'But you wouldn't need that, would you, Dickie?'

She sat listening to the back-chat, mostly put on for her benefit. And when the bus reached the market place she was the only one who rose to get off.

The three men on the back seat all said, 'Goodbye, miss.' And one added, 'As the Americans say, have a nice day.'

She turned and smiled at him, and what she said, was, 'I intend to.' Which left them not a little puzzled.

She knew that the Ferndales' house was called Willow House and that it was situated in Lime Avenue. This had come to her knowledge some time ago. It was when her Dad had been remarking on the number of law people that lived in this district and that the police inspector's sumptuous house was only four large gardens away from George Ferndale's. And this, she was thinking as she covered the ten minutes walk from the town centre to the avenue, couldn't be better for her purpose.

She had entered the gate and was halfway up the drive and in sight of the front of the house when it was suddenly illuminated by strong beams of light, and she knew she must have passed a trigger point. This kind of protection was being taken up by a lot of people in the town, so it didn't deter her. But it showed her up in the bright light when the door was opened to her knock and a maid peered at her, saying, 'Yes? What is it? What d'you want?'

'I wish to see Mr Ferndale.'

'Eeh! Who are you? He doesn't have visitors at this time in the morning. Are you selling something?'

Katie's voice soon disabused her of the idea that she was the kind of person who would be selling something when she said, 'No, I am not selling something. And will you kindly tell your master that Miss Bailey is downstairs and wishes to see him?' Then she put her hand out, saying, 'Don't close the door on me.' And, stepping into the hall, she said, 'I'll wait here.'

The maid, who was dressed in a blue-print dress to which was attached a working apron, now stooped and picked up a dustpan and brush from the floor, all the while keeping her eyes on Katie. Then she muttered, 'He won't like it. He's just finished his shower. He's . . . You had better wait until he comes down.'

'I'm not waiting till he comes down. If you don't go up now and tell him, I will present myself in his bedroom. How does that appear to you?'

The girl, who was in her late teens, stared open-mouthed at the visitor; then turning, she hurried towards the stairs, but remembering what she was carrying, she again laid down the dustpan and brush. And it was only a minute later when she heard a man's voice saying, 'What?'

Then a woman's voice saying, 'What is it? What is it?'

'The Bailey girl is downstairs.'

The man's words came clearly to her and she nodded to herself, saying, yes, the Bailey girl is downstairs.

When George Ferndale reached the bottom stair, he stood peering at her; but there was no need to peer because the hall was brilliantly lit by a chandelier. Then stepping down, he took three paces towards her before he stopped and said, 'May I ask the reason for this early visit, Miss Bailey?'

'Yes, you may, Mr. Ferndale. I've come with a proposition.'

'Of what?' His head moved to the side and his eyes narrowed.

'I'll repeat the word: proposition. First of all, I must tell you that your son is not only a liar, but he is a coward and a dirty swine.'

She watched the man's face stretch and his jaw come out, and as he was about to speak she unloosened the belt of Fiona's raincoat, and so exposed her partly naked top: her school blouse was hanging as it had done last night; her brassière strap had been torn from the material and one cup of it was hanging loose over her left breast. Then letting the raincoat drop to the floor, she pulled the sleeve of her bloodstained coat to the side to expose her shoulder. And lastly, she pulled the middle of the brassière down and pointed to the two red weals marking her breast. And now she said, 'Look at me! This is how your son left me last night when he tried to rape me. But he didn't expect what he got. And let me tell you, sir, it's a wonder I didn't throttle him, and I could have done.'

'What on earth are you talking about, girl?' The voice thundered almost as loudly as Bill's would have done, and she said, 'Do I have to explain? Your cowardly son tried to rape me. He waited in Laburnum Walk for me, right in the dark part at the middle, and snatched me. And I soon realised his flies were already open.'

'Oh, my God! Oh, my God!' The man now turned and looked at his wife who, by now, was standing two steps up from the hall and supporting herself against the balustrade.

'Yes, you can say that, Mrs Ferndale: Oh my God! Oh, my God! That's what I yelled out. And my friend, Sammy Love, whom I was to meet at the end of the Walk, heard me, and it was he who tore me off your son, and saved him from being throttled. Then he pushed me away and I was on the verge of collapse. And, quite candidly, I didn't know where I was until I reached the end of the Walk, and there I vomited. If you want proof of that, you'll likely find it there this morning!'

'She's . . . she's mad! It's lies! She's mad! She's mad!'

'I'm not mad now, Mrs Ferndale, but I was last night. Your son has trailed me for weeks. Oh, longer than that. I repulsed him last year with one of my ju-jitsu tricks, and he has been on the look out for me since. But last night I used every trick I knew, and if he's alive it's Mr Sammy Love you've got to thank for it. But your cowardly son couldn't bear to let anybody think that he had been done over by a girl not half his size, so he pins it on Sammy.'

'I don't believe it! I can't believe it!'

'Shut up, woman! And you, get yourself away!' he yelled at the staring maid. Then, drawing in a long deep breath, he said, 'Come in here a minute, miss. And you, too!' He turned on his wife.

'No! No! I must go—'

'You must damn well not go to him. I'll be the one who'll go to him. Come down and into the drawing-room this minute.'

Katie watched the tall, thin woman step down into the hall and follow her husband, very like an automaton would have done, for each movement was stiff, as if she had to force her feet forward.

'Sit down.'

'No, thank you. I've more to say, and I'll say it standing. I'll begin by telling you that I kept your son's name from my father last night, because I was afraid of what he would do; more than likely he would have finished what I began. But it was you, yourself, who came on the phone and gave him the name that I had withheld. It then took my mother all her time to stop him from coming over here.' This wasn't quite true but it added to the effect. Then she went on, 'But what he intends to do is to have me at the police station between half-past nine and ten this morning, an hour before your demand that he should meet you in your chambers, by which time he would have laid a charge of rape against your son. With this evidence.' She flapped her hand against her chest, and, as she did so, she was aware that the woman's face turned away as if in disgust. Then she went on, 'I've no need to apologise for my father's manner. But I'll leave you to guess what will happen in that police station; and as there's always a reporter kicking around a police station, so this town would be ablaze before the day's over. And my father would leave out no detail, from my torn clothes to my bleeding breast, and his flies, as I said, already open.'

'Girl! Girl! You're indecent!'

The woman had been seated, but now she was on her feet, and her husband, turning on her, yelled 'Of course she's indecent. She's been made so by your son . . . our son. God forgive me that I've got to say he is mine. And I've warned you for years, haven't I? Oh! Go on up, now, and bring him down.'

'I can't! I can't!' Her voice now was firm and cold. 'He's not well. You've seen how he is.'

'All right: he won't come down, then we'll go up. Come on, girl.'

'You can't! I forbid it.'

Katie watched the husband and wife facing each other, and for a moment she felt sad as she saw the actual hate that emanated from each of them.

'Come on.' He beckoned Katie towards him, and she hesitated for a moment before following him.

When she reached the galleried landing, her whole body began to tremble. She felt like putting her hand out to the man in front and saying, 'No. No, I don't want to see him. I can't.' But then the bedroom door was thrust open, and she could see the man propped up in bed. He'd had a cup in his hand, but he now thrust it on to the bedside table, and pulled himself up straight, then stared wide-eyed at his father. And when the man yelled, 'Come in,' she was unable to move until the father took her arm and pulled her into the room.

She looked at the figure in the bed. There were red weals down both sides of his cheeks. One eye was slightly discoloured and his lower lip was swollen. But the expression she saw on his face was indescribable, going beyond fear into terror. The skin had turned so pale that the scratches and bruises stood out as if they had been painted there. He now fell back against the bedhead, and was drawing in his breath as if he were gasping, and what he muttered was, 'I . . . I didn't. I didn't. I mean, well . . .'

'What do you mean?' His father was standing by the head of the bed now. 'Look at her breast. The nipple's the size of a walnut. And you drew blood there, didn't you?'

'Mother! Mother!'

'Oh, don't pass out. She got you out of playing rugby, but she won't get you out of this. A jug of water will soon revive you.'

'She's . . . she's mad.'

'Well, who made her mad?'

'I . . . I only tried to . . . to k . . . kiss her.'

'With your flies open?'

'They . . . they weren't!'

'You're a liar.' The words were forced from Katie. She now moved a step towards the bed and added, 'And you're a dirty coward. You couldn't bear to be beaten up by a girl, could you? It would take some living down; and if my father has any-thing to do with it you never will.'

George Ferndale turned now and, taking her arm, he said quietly, 'Come along. Come along. As you say, it will take some living down.'

Downstairs once more, he said, 'I'll put things right.'

'Oh, yes. Yes, I know you will. But there's something more.'

'More?' His voice had risen again. 'What more?'

'Sammy Love will not only be accused of assault and battery, or whatever terms they use, but, because he was so enraged when they wouldn't believe that he had just come across your son and was helping him to get to his feet, he swore at the police. More than swore at them, I understand. But what is even worse in their eyes, he threatened to throw one and, I think, actually attempted to.'

She watched the man before her close his eyes, then say, 'Dear, dear! Well . . . well, that's another case, isn't it?'

'No. No, it isn't. It's all the same case.'

'What do you mean?'

'I just mean this. I must get Sammy out of that place before my father reaches it this morning, and I've made arrangements with my brother to keep him at home until half-past nine, to beg him to stay there until then; and only to come to the police station when I expect Sammy will be free, and through your intervention.'

'I cannot go against the police.'

'No, but the chief inspector can, and he's a friend of yours and lives four doors away.'

George Ferndale's eyebrows seemed to strain towards his hair as his nose tended to move downwards, while his mouth opened, then closed. He did not speak, but just seemed to be waiting for her next words. But when she uttered them, saying, 'You could slip along and ask him as a favour to inform the men of the Dene Street station, that last night never happened, or whatever way he likes to put it. But if Sammy isn't freed from that charge too, and is not at liberty by half-past nine, then I promise you my father will be there and I will do what he is dead set on me doing, name your son as my assailant and attempted rapist.' She watched the big head move slowly from side to side, and then he uttered one word, 'Now?'

'Well, the time's going on. It's getting on for half-past eight, and I'm not leaving until I get what I came for, and that is, to use a word with which you are familiar, justice, for someone who has been wrongly imprisoned.'

'He hasn't been imprisoned yet.' There was a terseness in the tone.

'He's spent a night in jail. If that isn't imprisonment I don't know what you would call it. Anyway, there it is.' She turned now and picked up her mackintosh from the chair, and, putting it on, she tightened the belt while he stood staring at her quite speechless. Then, as he made for the stairs, he paused and turned to her again, saying, 'What guarantee have I that if you get all your demands your father won't still go to the station?'

'I can assure you he won't if Sammy is outside by the time he arrives. And to be on the safe side, that should be half-past nine. From then on, some time will be taken up by him going for me; then the rest is up to you.'

'The rest?' It was an enquiry, and she answered it swiftly, 'Yes, the rest.' She added, 'You ordered my father to be at your chambers at half-past ten, likely to give him a dressing down for championing his adopted son. But now the boot's on the other foot: he will tell you where you stand.'

When, in a sarcastic tone, he said, 'Will you grant me time to dress?' she did not answer, but as she watched him going quickly up the stairs, she put her hand out and groped towards the wooden hall chair, and sat down.

In less than five minutes he reappeared, dressed in a dark blue suit with a grey-striped tie, then went to a hall wardrobe and took out a dark overcoat. He did not look towards Katie – it seemed to be agreed that she should sit there and await his return – but he had just reached the front door when his wife appeared from a further door across the hall, and she called to him, 'Where are you going? Your breakfast is ready.'

'I don't want any breakfast.'

She came hurrying towards him. 'Where are you going?'

'To Arthur's.'

'To Arthur's!' The exclamation came in a high voice, and she repeated, 'Arthur's? Why?'

'Because I want his help. Without it, I'm informed' – he now nodded slowly to where Katie was sitting – 'we'll be headlined in the papers by this evening. Would you like that, madam?'

The woman now turned and looked at Katie, and she actually cried, 'She wouldn't dare.'

'Oh, yes, she would, my dear. That young lady is an unusual individual. So, I am going to Arthur, and Jean can come in and console you later.'

With that he stepped past her, pulled open the door and went out, while she, turning, walked slowly towards Katie, and when she stopped, she was wringing her hands.

She spoke as if the words were being forced through her teeth. 'You are a wicked girl,' she said. 'Wicked! He would have never attempted any such thing if you hadn't encouraged him. He could get any girl he wanted, so why should he want to take you?'

'That's what I've asked him, Mrs Ferndale. The only reason he wanted to take me was because he couldn't get me. I wasn't easy bait. And he couldn't bear the thought of any girl turning her nose up at him. Oh, no! And I've always turned my nose up at him, because I've known from the first that he was no good. To put it in common parlance, your son is an empty nowt.'

The woman's teeth were actually clenched now, and she swallowed twice before she muttered, 'And you, girl, are like your father, as common as dirt, and as pretentious as your mother with her act of false refinement.'

'Well, if that's how you see them, that's your opinion. But I wouldn't want to hurt you any more than you have been this morning by telling you their opinion of you. But I'll say this: it's mainly to do with your lack of intelligence.'

She thought the woman was about to drop at her feet, because she swayed now and gasped a number of times before turning away.

If Katie could have been amused at anything while she sat waiting, it would have been the sight of the young maid making frequent visits across the hall, and always her look directed towards herself, as if she were a creature from another planet.

She was shivering again. Her insides seemed loose within their casing. She knew she had been very rude to the woman. What she had said would have been applauded by Bill, but not by her mother. She asked herself now what the next move would be if the chief inspector found it impossible to help his friend and stop that particular section of the force from making charges? Yet, she was aware there were wheels within wheels: she had only to listen to her dad talking to her mother about the workings of the trust, and the hand-outs here and there so that things should run smoothly. Bill had a saying, 'You can't have too many friends at court.' But one of those friends, Mr George Ferndale, barrister, would definitely be one no more; nor would the inspector of police, who had been, if not a friend at court, on the list of court acquaintances, being a member of the same club.

She glanced at her wrist-watch. It showed twenty minutes to nine.

When the hands had moved to ten to, she got to her feet, and as she did so the front door opened and George Ferndale entered. After he had closed the door he leant against it for a moment before straightening up and saying, 'Well, you'll be pleased to know your plan has worked. And, in a strange way, I suppose I've got to thank you for going to all this trouble. But I quite understand it wasn't to save my face, and certainly not that of my son, but in the main I see it as your attempt to quell the reactions of your impetuous stepfather and the consequences of his outburst which might have affected his business. Am I right?'

'Yes,' she nodded at him, 'you're right. I wouldn't have wished to see him lose all he has worked for over the years. Not that the trust could have taken the contract away from him, but they could have squashed his further plans, which you will undoubtedly have already heard of, concerning the ten acres of building land on Bishop's Farm.'

'You're very well informed.'

'We are a close-knit family.'

'Yes. Yes, you are that.' He nodded at her slowly. And, as she looked at him, again she felt sorry that she'd had to take this stand, because he looked and sounded weary. Then he said, 'By the time you reach the station, your friend will have been released.'

'Thank you.' She was now making for the door when he said, 'Have you got your career mapped out?'

'Not really. I'm sitting for my A levels in June.'

'How old are you?'

'Eighteen next birthday.'

'Why don't you try the law? You've got all the makings of an advocate. There are lots of women barristers these days.'

She did not know whether or not he was laughing at her, so she answered pertly, 'Yes, I could give it a try. I'm not likely to make more of a hash of it than the rest.'

He actually smiled at her now, then quietly he voiced his real thoughts by saying, 'Whatever you do, it must be something where you can use your voice and your rational reasoning.'

They stared at each other. Then she answered him quietly, saying, 'Thank you, and . . . and I'm sorry that I have had to act as I have done.'

She had to blink quickly to stop the tears spilling from her eyes. And now he put his hand out and lightly touched her arm as he said, 'Don't worry, my dear. I too am sorry that you have had to act as you have done, particularly so that you have had to suffer under my son's hands. Believe me, particularly so about that.'

She drooped her head. Then he opened the door and she went out.

She did not hurry towards the police station because she was endeavouring to calm herself. All she wanted to do now was to cry, to lie down and cry. She felt utterly tired, sapped. She only hoped her dad wouldn't make a scene when he arrived, because that would finish her. She couldn't cope with much more.

When she entered Dene Street it was to see Sammy in the distance. He was standing on the kerb, and on the sight of her he hurried towards her, his hands outstretched. And she just stopped herself from falling against him.

'They've . . . they've just let me out. They said I . . . I had to wait for you.'

'That's all they said?'

'Oh, something about pending, case pending. Oh, Katie! Oh, Katie! am I glad to see you. I know what me da went through in there. Oh, I'll never do a wrong thing in my life; it puts the fear of God into you. Where's . . . where's Mr B?'

'He should be here at any minute.'

'It's a long story. I . . . I can't talk now. Oh, there's the car. Oh, thank God!'

He looked at her, then took her arm. And when the car drew up against the kerb, she put her head in the window and said, 'Dad, don't get out. Please, don't get out! Mam, let . . . let Sammy sit there, and you come in the back with me, please. Please!'

'Look here! I want . . .'

It was almost a scream she let out as she stuck her head through the window now and cried, 'Shut up! For God's sake! Dad, shut up and let me get home! You can do all the shouting you like then. Just drive me home.'

When Fiona left her seat, she opened the back door of the car and pressed Katie in. Then, when she herself sat down, she said quietly to Bill, 'Get us home.'

He said nothing, but started the car with a jerk, and almost at the same time Katie turned and buried her face in her mother's shoulder and began to sob uncontrollably.

Katie's crying did not stop when they arrived home. It did not stop until the doctor, two hours later, gave her a sedative, declaring she was suffering from delayed shock. And it was more than twenty-four hours later when, once again seated downstairs, she related all that had transpired. And when she was held in Bill's arms, he, too, brokenly related what had transpired since she had been asleep. It was to do with a meeting with George Ferndale, and the punishment the man intended to mete out to his son.

2

Vague rumours were fleeting through the town. One concerned the big contractor's daughter: that she had been raped and had turned up at a barrister's house early one morning.

What was known for certain was that the barrister's son was to start work in the court offices, in a position no better than a tea boy's. It had been assumed he would have been off to university, but the fellow had not had enough guts to refuse.

Yes, there must be something in the rumour. Somebody's palm must have been well oiled to keep quiet about it. That's how things were worked these days, in all ways. You could get away with murder, if you had enough cash.

Funny, too, it should be that man Bailey's family again. Not so long ago there had been that drug business, in which one of the family had also been concerned . . .

Oh, what did it matter after all? The trains were still running, there was water in the mains, and nobody yet had thought of cutting off the town's electricity. Although, when one of the bright lads found out a way to shin up the pole to those wires without being electrocuted, undoubtedly they would have a shot at it. And you only owed four hundred and sixty-five pounds in back rent. So, why worry? All they could do was put you out, then find you another place where you could start all over again.

So was Daisy's opinion of rumour and the condition of the country. And when her father shoved her so hard that she fell against the chest of drawers, she cried at him, 'Don't you start knocking me about, Len Gallagher. I'm not your wife, I'm only the result of a skinful of beer.'

'Our Daisy!'

'Yes, our Ma. Well, you said so yourself, and I remember the time you said it an' all. You were laying on to me bare backside and you said that I showed fear for neither God nor man. And it was all because of him,' she thumbed towards her father, 'because he came in roaring that night, full up to the gunnels. And you always said he had fear of neither God nor man when he was in drink. Well, he's passed it on.'

She cast a laughing glance at Len now and he shook his head slowly at her, saying, 'By God! I did an' all; and we've all had to pay for it since.'

'What's brought you home at dinner-time, lass?' Annie now pushed a mug of tea towards Daisy, where she was sitting at the corner of the table close to her father's chair. 'Well, it's about the only time I guessed that the house would be empty except for you two,' Daisy replied. She looked down into the mug of tea before she explained quietly, 'I want to ask you something, both of you, and it's serious.'

She had their attention now; they were both staring at her. And when she didn't go on, Annie pulled a chair from under the table and sat down; and she said, 'What is it, lass? Something worrying you?'

'Yes, you could say that, Ma.' Daisy nodded towards her mother. 'Yet, it's all cut and dried in my mind; it was just that I wanted to know what you think about it?'

'You're not thinking of leaving home, are you?' It was almost a growl from Len, and Daisy, looking at him, said, 'Not for a while, anyway, Da, and not in the way you mean. No.'

'Then, what is it?'

She now looked from one to the other, then said, 'If you fell for somebody, you know what I mean, and . . . and you knew he didn't want you, never would in that way 'cos he had somebody else in his eye, would you think it a good thing to take second best?'

She watched her parents exchange glances. It was her father who answered, 'That, in a way, is a tough question to answer, lass, but as it happens, I can answer it from personal experience.' Now he had turned his gaze fully on his wife as he said, 'Isn't that so, Annie?'

Annie did not answer, but she lifted up her mug and took a long drink of tea. Then, looking at Len again, she said, 'Well, go on with your tale.'

He turned back to Daisy, saying, 'I was knocked for six when I was let down by someone I thought I couldn't live without. I was a young fella, and the day she married another bloke I got drunk. I'd hardly touched it afore; it didn't appeal to me. All I could think of in those days was saving money to make a home fit for a bride. Huh! Well, I went on the razzle. Then I met' – he now jerked his head sideways – 'her. She was a shoulder to cry on. I liked her, but I didn't love her.' He now turned and his look was soft on the bowed head. 'But I wasn't married to her long before I knew her value. I also knew if I had got the other one, I couldn't have put up with her five minutes. By that time, she was already leading the other fella a life of it. He was working time and a half to keep her in clothes. And they parted within two years. I was working in the yard then. When I went into the actual foundry the thirst, at times, got the better of me. And so I'd get a skinful and I'd raise hell. Yet, in between times, in my sober senses I knew that the second best, as you would call it, was the best thing that had happened to me.' He now put his hand out and took one of the hands that were clinging to the mug and, laying it on the table, he patted it as he said, 'I've never been any use with words, except swear ones, but she knows what I mean.' He was nodding at Daisy the while, and he finished, 'Life works things out for you if you let it. So, have you got your answer?'

'Aye, Da, in a way, that is.'

Her mother was looking at her now, saying, 'Who's let you down, lass?'

'Oh, nobody, Ma. Nobody's let me down. I've let meself down. He's never been other than pally, and I saw the red light ages ago, but wouldn't take any notice. But, in his own way, he swung the lantern in me face, if you know what I mean.'

'Who's he, lass?'

She lowered her lids before she said, 'Sammy.'

'Sammy Love?'

'Yes, Da, Sammy Love. I only know one Sammy.'

'Well, all I can say, lass, is, he's a blasted fool. He must be swinging the red light before his own eyes.'

'No, Da. No.'

'Has he got somebody else?'

She looked at her mother. 'Yes, and always has had, I think.'

'Well, I've got no need to ask who your second choice is.'

'Haven't you, Da?'

'No, it's that Willie, isn't it?'

Daisy gave a short laugh as she said, 'No, it isn't that Willie, Da, although he would like it to be. And sometimes, in a way, I wish it was, 'cos he's got spunk. Well, I mean, he was never afraid to be seen with me in me rig, and he's a nice lad. But I'm not daft or blind, and if I did like him that way, I know there would be opposition. Not from the big fella, or Katie, or Sammy, but as nice as his lady ma is, I don't think she can see me as a daughter-in-law. And then there's his big brother, the one that's in London learning to be a doctor. Oh, he was snuff up your nose, if anyone was. He used to look at me as if I was a cabbage snail and should be trodden on.'

'The bugger; he did?'

'Yes, Da, the bugger; he did. And many a time I wanted to give him a mouthful. I don't know who he takes after in that family. Of course' – she laughed now – 'Big Chief Running Buffalo isn't his da, else I think he'd have had the upstart knocked out of him afore now. But stepfathers have to watch their step; at least that's what I think.'

'Who's your second choice, lass?'

The question was quiet and she looked at her mother and answered as quietly, 'Jimmy.'

When they both said together, 'Jimmy?' she nodded from one to the other, saying, 'Yes, Da, that's what I said, Jimmy.'

'Is that why you brought him here this last twice or so?'

'Aye, in a way, Ma, so you could pass an opinion. It would just be a surface one because you don't know him, only what I've told you about him. But he was the one that pulled me up and stopped me being daft that long while ago.'

'Does he feel for you?'

'I don't really know, Da. Well, yes, he does in a way, because he's always seemed to look after me in the club and that. And I've laughingly called him my minder.'

'How d'you really feel about him?'

'Oh, I like him. I've always liked him, and if there

was any second best, well, he could be it.'

'Why must there be a second best, lass? Why can't you wait?' Annie was shaking her head slowly at her daughter, and at this Daisy said, 'There's a reason, Ma, and you would say I wasn't doing things for the right reason. But, if Sammy waved a red lamp at me, I feel this is the only way I can wave a red lamp at Willie, else there'll be a showdown shortly and it won't be pleasant. It might mean that I'll have to break, well, sort of cut off from the family, and I like them. But if I could show him I was really going with somebody else, well, it might dampen him down.'

'Oh, lass! Oh, lass!' Len's head was bowed now and he was shaking it slowly. 'I thought you'd have more sense than to play that game. And,' he now wagged a finger at her, 'I'm telling you this. From what little I've seen of this Jimmy, and how he talked when he was here, he was trying to put it over that he had kept an eye on you for years and would still continue to do so. And to my mind, if he had any feelings for you other than that of, as you call it, a minder, you would have known about it before now, because . . . how old is he? Twenty-one?'

'Twenty-three,' Annie put in.

'He's not, Ma, he's not twenty-three.'

'He is, lass.' Annie let out a long drawn sigh before she added, 'And up to a few months ago, he was living with a woman in Pilot Road.'

Daisy's chair almost toppled backwards on to

the floor as she sprang up, crying, 'He wasn't! He's never lived with any woman. Who told you that?'

'Mrs Anderson, from two doors down. I know she's a gossip, but there she was in the supermarket and she said, "I see that Daisy's taken up with Jimmy Redding. He's a nice lad. I knew his people when they lived in Dene Street. They were a bit cut up when he went to live with that piece in Pilot Road. But now he's back at home again, I see." You like him that much, lass?'

'No. No. But the fact that he's been living with a woman and I didn't know.'

'What you talking about?' It was her mother speaking now and harshly. 'Why should you have known? Except that he was lodging there. And he's a young man. It's his life, and everybody's living with somebody else now, and they don't wait until they're twenty-three. By that I don't mean . . . or that kind of man is for you. No, I don't! You're young and clean and . . . Oh!' She tossed her head now and walked towards the sink, and as she clashed the crockery into it, Daisy said, 'I'm . . . I'm not gone on him in that way, but I never thought he was that sort.'

'Look here, girl!' Len's finger was wagging at her again. 'You were going to make him a second best choice, and you made no bones about it. Now I'll tell you something. What impression he has given you and others at the Centre, to me is much more underhand than him going to live with a woman, because it's calculated. In our case' – he pointed to Annie – 'there was nowt calculated; it just happened. But you're working things out aforehand, going to have them your way, and the man has to fit in. Oh, lass, I'm surprised at you, I really am. Well, you came home to ask our advice and mine is; don't go in for your second choice, 'cos if he's had one affair like that, he could have another. And it's his life, so who's to blame him? And as far as I can see he's done nothing wrong to you, only looked after you and stopped you being a young tearaway years ago. 'Cos that's what you were.'

'Thank you very much, Da. Thank you very much.' She now went and grabbed up her coat from the settee. It wasn't the Aquascutum with the fur collar, but it was a warm-looking coat of reasonable length, one which had come from her private source. Then, she rammed her woollen hat on her head before making for the door. But there, her mother stood blocking her way, and quietly she entreated, 'Don't be mad, lass. Your da's right, and' – she now put out her hand and pushed an errant piece of hair under the woollen hat – 'you're much too bonny to throw yourself away on second best. Wait a while; think it over in that cute mind of yours, and it will straighten things out for you.' Then, looking into the brown eyes that were expressing deep hurt, and as if applying a salve to the hurt, she said, 'I'm making a big pot-pie for dinner the night and a spotted dick for afters, and' – she now added more salve – 'if you wouldn't mind taking me with you to your shop the morrow, 'cos I'm almost threadbare in lots of ways, I'd be grateful.'

'Oh, Ma!'

The two words spoke volumes, untranslatable to anyone other than their two selves and the man who stood watching them. Then Daisy went out.

PART THREE

I

'I'm lonely, Bill, and I'm going to be more so. Katie's ensconced in Durham, has been this past year, and whereas Sammy could have chosen Newcastle University, he plumps for Durham, too. So, by October, who will I have left? I'll have Willie for another year, then he'll be off.'

'You've still got a daughter.' Bill's voice was cold.

'Yes, I still have a daughter. But am I now to tell my mother I don't need her to come here every day to see to Angela? You don't understand, Bill, how much she has come to mean to mother. The child has given her an aim in life, a meaning, and the love she showers on her is reciprocated. I . . . I feel jealous at times. Yet, in a way, I am glad for them both, because, as you know, Angela needs company all the time. She must be with someone. Nell used to take a turn with her, but now her time is taken up with her own son. It's understandable she can't keep running backwards and forwards here every day.'

'And you're too busy yourself to see to her?'

'Don't speak to me like that, Bill. You're inferring what you're afraid to say. I love the child, Bill; I love her dearly. You come in at five, six, or seven at night and make straight for her and give her half an hour. Then you have a bath and your meal, and five nights out of six you settle in the study with your papers. Oh, yes, you want me to be with you and sit there. And what will I do? Knit, crochet or wait for you to throw me a word or two, and ask me how my day has gone.'

'Ah, now, hold your hand a minute. Hold your hand a minute, woman.'

'And please don't call me, woman. You know I don't like it.'

'All right, lady. Well, take your mind back. It's only a few days ago that I asked if you'd like to go out to dinner, and what did you say?'

'I said, no, because you asked me while sitting in that chair there' – she pointed to a deep armchair to the side of the couch on which he was sitting – 'And you were stretched out and yawning. And when I said, no, I didn't want to go, you got yourself a drink, settled down again and dozed off.'

'Oh, I'm terribly sorry, really I am; I shouldn't be tired, the easy life I've got.'

'Sarcasm doesn't suit you, Bill.'

A pained silence fell on the room. Then in a low voice she said, 'It's now more than a year since I dared to mention that I would like to take up a career. And I was informed, in no small voice, that you were my career. Well, I've worked at it, but I am still left with a gaping loneliness in me. I love you. I couldn't stop loving you if I tried, but what do I see of you? You're out of the house every morning before nine; you don't come home to lunch; you sometimes phone me, not so often as of yore, but sometimes. And then there's your routine of the evening. Except for the weekend, and even then, I've known you to spend the whole of Saturday morning in the office. As for Sunday, you keep out of the way mostly, as one or other have their friends here. The only time, I may say, when you willingly show your face is when Daisy comes, because you like to banter with her. But up till now I fill my time with the family, seeing to food, seeing to their clothes, and, when Mrs Watson has been off, doing the chores. But now, since my family is going to be greatly depleted come the end of September, I can see myself passing the time answering phone calls, preparing our meal in the evening and, for a break, taking a run over to see how Nell's faring. Well, all that won't fill the gap, Bill. So, whether it vexes you or pleases you, I have made a decision.'

His head jerked towards her, the look in his eyes hard, his mouth a tight line, and he waited. And she, looking him straight in the face, said, 'I'm going to take a course at the Open University. I'm going to try for a degree.' She watched the pink flush on his face deepen. She watched his Adam's apple jerk up and down in his throat. Then, she watched his mouth open twice before he said through gritted teeth, 'You wouldn't like to go to college with the others, would you?'

And when she dared to answer him fearlessly, saying, 'Yes. Yes, I would love to do that, Bill. It was a chance I missed in my youth and I would simply love it, and people of my age are doing it every day. But I have a home to see to, and a *daughter*.' She stressed the word. 'Moreover, I would like to be here when different members of my family might need me, if ever they do.'

She could feel the force of the anger rising in him. It was like a heat emanating from him – but she urged herself to go on, so she said, 'We've been married eleven years, Bill, and I have never crossed you in any way. And this desire of mine appears to me such a simple matter; however, simple or otherwise, I have made up my mind to carry it through, and so much so that I have already applied.'

As she watched his doubled hand tapping against the side of his thigh, she was fully aware that if he had been dealing with a woman of his own type, that hand would have come across her face. Bill Bailey was Bill Bailey. Slowly she turned from him and walked out of the room.

The sun was shining and dappling the ground where the trees thinned out towards the edge of the wood. When a light breeze brought down a small shower of leaves, Katie looked upwards, saying, 'Who was it said,

> I cry with each leaf that falls,
> Although I love the drying of the year

350

And dance round the burning pyre
That was summer's glorious array.'

'I wouldn't know . . . Well, who wrote it?' asked Sammy.

'I don't know either. I just remember reading it somewhere, and it was brought back to mind when I saw those leaves falling.'

They reached the end of the wood, then stood looking across the low fence towards the open farm land. Then turning to Sammy, Katie said, 'How do you feel about this being your last day; I mean, starting a new life? Because that's what you'll be doing tomorrow.'

And to this, Sammy answered, 'I can't explain it, except that I'm sad, and glad. I seem to have lived in this place all my life, been with the family all my life. That is the sad part, because after tomorrow, nothing will ever be the same again. Didn't you feel like this when you went up last year?'

'I suppose so; well, I was homesick for a time, and everyone seemed far away. And yet it was only twelve miles. But it will be different this time for you, because you will have' – and she did not say, me near you, but – 'one of the family already there.'

When she felt her hand caught and held, and saw the look on his face, she knew the moment had come for which she had been waiting . . . oh, yes, waiting. Even so, she put out her other hand and gently laid it on his lips, saying, 'Let me say something first, something that's been singing in my mind for a long time. I love you, Sammy, so very, very much.'

She watched him close his eyes tightly and bring his teeth down on to his lower lip and, for a horrifying moment, she thought, No, no! Have I imagined it? No. Oh no.

Then she was startled as his arm shot out and pulled her to him. Pressing her close, he muttered, 'Oh! Katie. Katie. To hear you say that. I . . . I had hoped; and yet had thought because we were such pals that was as far as it would ever go. But I meant to tell you what is in my heart and I meant to do it today.'

Her eyes were moist as she gazed into his face so close to her own. The well-known face that was neither handsome nor plain, but was different. Her dad had once said that he had the ascetic look of a budding priest. Sammy had thrown a cushion at him, and had then put up his fists in a sparring attitude. But his face was different from any other boy's or man's she had seen. Likely it was because of her feeling for him. He had a longish face and the skin had a tinge of tan. His eyes were round, his eyebrows, like his hair, brown and thick. His nose was slightly wide at the nostrils, and his mouth, although not full-lipped, had shape to it, and would go very much out of line when he was annoyed. And the top lip seemed to aim to press the lower one down towards his straining chin. He always looked funny then, nicely funny, and he used to get mad at her when she laughed at him at such times. But it was a long time since he had been mad at her.

His voice was soft as he said, 'At school, you were known as my girlfriend. We all had girl-friends, and, as you know, a lot of snogging went on. But I used to think, here we were, real pals over the last four years, and we had never . . . we had never kissed.'

When their lips came together it was a tentative gesture until their arms tightened about each other. Then, such was the force of their embrace, they both fell against the tree that was to the side of them. Their lips parting, they lay against the support of the comforting oak and rested there, gazing at each other, until the breeze again brought another shower of leaves down on to the path. And as she watched them she laughed gently as she said, 'I've never thought to feel like this in my life. Never. After that stupid and terrifying business with Rupert, followed by that year when Dad sent me to Coventry and never spoke to me unless he was obliged to, that was terrible. And I was so sure then that nothing nice or decent would ever happen to me. Then, the night your father was buried, you came and told me he had suggested you to talk to me because I was lonely. Oh, that broke me up. For a long time after I used to cry every time I thought about it. But I think I started to love you on that day. And you will remember you took my hand, and we were going downstairs holding hands when we suddenly realised that if we went into the drawing-room like that, all eyebrows would be raised in large question marks.'

Sammy laughed and said, 'Oh, yes, I remember

that. To me it was a red-letter day, that I could hold your hand while going downstairs. I think I began to hope then. Before that, I had given up hoping.'

'What d'you mean, given up hoping?'

'Well, you see, my first memory of you was sitting in your kitchen and experiencing a very odd sensation. It was a mixture of anger, a desire for retaliation, and something else which I couldn't understand, because, you know, you were looking at me as if I was something the cat had brought in. In fact, your cat would have had more sense. That was your opinion, wasn't it?'

Her shoulders shook with laughing now, as she said, 'Oh, yes, it was. Yes. I couldn't stand you. Mam was dead nuts on breaking up the association between you and Willie. And she had a good lieutenant in me. Every time I looked at you, or saw you coming, I said the two words to myself and with disdain, "Bog's End". Oh, I was a little bitch.'

'Yes. Yes, you were. You know something? It's amazing, but you've . . . you've lost all class-consciousness. You're just like Willie in that way, and your dad. Not your mother. Oh, no, she'll always be class-conscious. Yet I love her because she took the place of the mother I hardly knew, but missed all the time. But after that good turn I did for Mr B, she couldn't do enough for me, could she? I wonder what she'll say about us? D'you think they twig anything?'

'No. No, I'm sure they don't; we're just pals. Well, that's all we have been to all appearances, anyway. But they'll welcome it. I know they will.

Dad will . . . and Mam, too, because, you know, you are no longer "Bog's End", but someone she is very proud of. I heard her talking about you to Mrs Watson. It was when her son was sitting the exam for the Royal Grammar School. She was saying how wonderful it would be if her son got in there because Mr Willie and Mr Sammy were both brilliant. And Mam was kind enough . . . surprisingly kind, I considered at the time, to say that, well, they weren't both alike: Mr Willie was what you would call a plodder, he would get there but he would have to work hard, whereas Mr Sammy was what was termed a flier.'

'Flier?' And Sammy laughed. 'I had the real jitters in the last exam.'

'Well, you didn't show it; you never do. And you have never shown what you feel for me; you have never, Sammy Love, used your surname to put into words your feelings for me.'

'Oh, Katie.' Again she was tightly pressed close to him. 'Do I have to? To say "I love you" wouldn't suit my bill. The words are too prosaic. And yet when you said them they were so beautiful, so wondrous, so . . .'

'Oh, Sammy, shut up! Just say, I love you, Katie. Go on, just say, I love you, Katie Bailey.'

His face straight now and his tone flat, he repeated, 'I . . . I love you, Katie Bailey. I adore you, Katie Bailey. You are the most wonderful girl in the world to me, Katie Bailey. But I can explain my feelings better through the Bard.'

'Damn the Bard. I'd much rather hear the fella

from Bog's End now and again. Not always, mind,' – she shook her head – 'but now and again. And over the last year he has fast disappeared; I've not heard you curse for months.'

'Well, I've been practising self-control. You don't want me to go up there, do you, and speak perfect Bog's English. Mind, it isn't that I wouldn't like to, and who knows, if I get worked up I likely will sometime. But in the meantime—' he stopped and, cupping her face in his hands, he said very, very softly, 'How long d'you think it'll be before we can be married?'

'Oh, Sammy, Sammy. I hate to think of it, but there's another two years up there for me before I get my degree, and then another year in the teacher's training department. And you, there's a full three years for you. And you say you don't want to go in for teaching, but into the commercial world. That means, in both cases, it's three years at least before we can do anything.' She drew her head back from him now and looked down the avenue between the trees. She kept her gaze directed on it as she said, 'Unless we decide on anything else.'

She waited for an answer or a comment, and when none came she turned and looked at him again. What he said was, and slowly, 'Yes, we could do that. We could set up somewhere; that is if both of us had money, which we haven't; and what is more important still, we could do it tomorrow. But two of the best people we'll ever know in our lives would be shocked. Your mother might accept it as being commonplace today, but not Mr Bill. Funny that, isn't it? But I know deep down in me that this is true. He would see me as the leader in this business and despise me ever more for bringing, what he would call, disgrace on his daughter. He wouldn't consider that half the population, at least those over sixteen, are shacking up today; no he would be blind to all that, and you know it, don't you?'

Again Katie looked along the path and her voice was low and slightly weary as she said, 'Yes. Yes, I know it. But I'll say this in our defence, in defence of all those whom we've mentioned, we've only got one life. It's a very commonplace saying, but the youth of today know it to be true; so many things have happened to point it out to them. Anyway, half the parents don't deserve consideration. But, like ours, when they do, you'd like to say to them, "But you've done what you wanted to do. You've gone your way and you're happy together. You're enjoying your lives. But anything could happen to us tomorrow, never mind in three years' time," although we wouldn't say that, would we?'

He kicked the trunk of the tree with his heel and let out a slow breath before he said, 'No, we wouldn't say that. But to pick up what you said just a minute ago; that they're happy. They always have been, but lately I've thought that your mam might be worrying about something. She's been very quiet. I thought it was, perhaps because of Nell having another. But she's got used to that.'

She was looking at him again as she said, 'You . . . you think there's something wrong? I've noticed too that she's quiet at times. But then she always has been like that. Her broody periods, she used to call them. Some time ago when I asked her if there was anything wrong, if she had a pain, she said she was just going through one of her broody periods. Like the hens, they stop cackling and she stops talking for a time.'

He smiled widely now, saying, 'It would be nice if all women had broody periods.'

'Oh, are you telling me I must adopt broody periods?'

'Yes, just that, woman.'

She had her arms around his neck now and her body pressed back from him, and she was laughing as she said, 'I like that; to be called woman. I'll be twenty next year, then you can say I'm a woman, I suppose. Funny, I'm more than a year older than you, but I've always thought that you were, oh, years older than me.'

'I am. Oh, yes, I am in all ways: in worldly affairs, work capability and, of course, women.'

Now she was shaking him . . .

They remained locked together against the trees for some minutes more. It was then that she said, 'D'you think we should go and tell them?'

'Yes. Yes, I suppose so.'

They walked between the trees with their arms around each other, and it was when they were clear of the wood and were entering the cultivated garden, she stopped and said, 'You saying about Mam being quiet. Now that I come to think about it, last weekend, just after Willie and Daisy left, I heard them; I mean, Mam and Dad in the drawing-room. I thought they were going at it in some way, so I didn't go in. But I wondered if it was over Daisy, because, you know, although she's decently dressed now, she's still Daisy. Of course, Dad thinks the world of her, he really does, but not so Mam. Oh, she likes her, but I'm sure she can't see her as a daughter-in-law. The fact is, I would like her as a sister-in-law; she's real good fun, with no pretence about her. She wouldn't know how. And I won't ask your opinion of her. D'you know something? At one time she was sweet on you.'

'No!'

'Yes, she was.'

'Oh, I wish I had known, I'd have done some-thing about it. She would have been a comfort.'

'Look out where you're pushing me; I've stood on that azalea. My, my! Arthur will have my guts for garters if he finds out. Funny about gardeners. As Dad says, they always imagine they own the gardens they work in.'

Within sight of the house they glanced at each other, joined hands, then began to run. In the hall, they stopped and leant against each other for a moment before crossing the hall and thrusting open the drawing-room door. Then just within the room they halted, and Sammy, raising his hand and pulling up Katie's with it, exclaimed loudly, 'Hail! Behold! We are the bearers of news.'

Bill had been leaning back in the corner of the couch, a newspaper across his knee. It was evident he had been dozing. But Fiona was at a side table pouring out tea into a second cup. And she turned, the teapot in her hand, and gazed at them. Then, after putting it down with somewhat of a clatter, she looked towards Bill. He had now pulled himself to the edge of the couch, and he blinked and peered towards them as he said, 'Aye, aye. What's this?'

'I think you'd better have a cup of tea, both of you.' Katie now tugged her hand from Sammy's and went towards Fiona, saying, 'Here, go and sit down, I'll bring it to you.'

Fiona did not speak, but just stared at the pair of them, before going to the couch to sit down, but not close beside Bill, as was her wont. And when Katie, following her, handed her a cup of tea, then one to Bill, he pointed to a little table and said, 'Put it down there.' Then he added, 'What's all this in aid of? Practising for something?'

'You could say that, Mr B. Yes, you could say that.' Sammy was looking straight at Bill now. 'I'll put it this way.' He now turned to Fiona and in a softer voice, he added, 'We hope it's the first step towards getting married.'

'Good God!' the exclamation spoke of Bill's astonishment. And now he added, 'Well, you two? I thought you were pals, just pals.'

'Not on my part, Mr B, not for a long, long time.'

And now Katie, taking a step closer to Sammy, said, 'Nor mine, Dad. It would appear we've both been holding back from each other while all the time knowing how we felt.' Then, looking at Fiona, she said, 'Well, say something, Mam.'

'I . . . I just don't know what to say. Once or twice

I've wondered a little . . . well, about you, Sammy, and your feelings. But I suppose my mind has mostly been concerned with . . . well, I must admit, Willie's affections. Willie's the kind of person who must always glue himself on to someone. It was you for years, and now it's Daisy.'

'And you don't like that, do you?' Bill did not look at Fiona as he said this, but he turned and picked up the cup of tea from the table and drank half of it, before replacing the cup. And now he did look at her and say, 'You didn't, did you? And you don't.'

'What I feel about it is entirely my business, just as what you feel about it is yours.'

Both Katie and Sammy experienced the chill that was between these two lovely people, as they both thought of them. But whatever it was that had caused it, it was lessening any surprise at their news and, apparently, any opposition to the word marriage.

Sammy now said to Fiona, 'She's a good girl, Mrs B. She only needs a little polish.'

'She needs nothing of the sort,' Bill's voice had a snapping edge to it. 'She's all right as she is, and if she suits Willie she has no-one else to suit. But about you two. Well, all I can say is, it's a surprise, but a glad one. Yet, at the same time, if you want to do the thing properly, it's going to be a while before you can really talk of getting married. Have you thought of that?'

'Yes. Yes.' They both nodded at him, but Katie added, 'We've been into that.' Then on a laugh she added, 'But, of course, Dad, if Mam and you are agreeable, we could, well, we could shack up.'

'Shut up! I don't want to hear any such talk. You'll shack up, as you call it, when you have a proper house to go to and a wage coming in to support it.'

Sammy's voice now was almost as rough as Bill's as he said, 'You've got no need to press that point, sir. We've been into it and into the pros and cons. And we're not asking anyone for anything or looking for hand-outs. What we're going to do, we'll do it off our own bats. But let me put it this way; if we did feel like shacking up, nobody could stop us now, could they?'

'Sammy.' There was a plea in Fiona's voice, and he turned his head towards her but bowed it, muttering, 'Don't worry. I'm sorry.'

'You've got no need to be sorry. No need whatever.'

Fiona did not glance towards Bill, but her further words spoke for her as she said to Sammy quietly, 'Go and fill the teapot up again for us, and bring in a couple of cups.'

Before Sammy did what was asked of him, a request made in order, he knew, to get rid of him, he stared enquiringly at Katie, and she, trying to smile said, 'Do as you're told. For once, do as you're told.'

With the room to themselves now, Katie, looking at her father, said, 'We could an' all, you know, just do exactly what he said. And what could you do about it? Just stop our allowance. Well, we'd find some way out. Half of them in the colleges have to take a job at night and nowadays there's always the banks.'

'Katie!' Fiona was on her feet. 'Stop it now! Stop it! Please!' She glanced at Bill, who was staring wide-eyed at the tall, indignant young creature before him. And now, pushing Katie down into the corner of the couch, she said, 'That's no way to act. That's no way to talk. We are . . . are just surprised, that's all . . . but pleased. Oh, yes, my dear, I'm so pleased.'

'Well, that's something to hear, Mam,' Katie said quietly.

When Fiona took her place on the couch again she had to sit close to Bill, but he gave no sign that he noticed her presence, nor did one of them speak until Sammy entered the room again carrying a tray. As he put it down on the table, he turned towards them with a smile and said, 'You should go into the hall. There's a singing contest going on: Grandma and Angela are in the conservatory, one singing *Hickory, Dickory, Dock*, and the other *Three Blind Mice*, but they are both harmonising.'

Fiona smiled, saying, 'That often happens. And as you say, they do harmonise.'

Sammy now asked Bill, 'May I fill your cup up?'

'What? No, no, thanks.'

'What about you, Mrs B?'

'No more for me, dear.'

Sammy poured out two cups of tea and took one to Katie; and again there fell a silence among them until Fiona asked, 'What time are you leaving tomorrow?'

'Oh, about ten,' said Sammy. 'I'll have to present myself to my landlady and get my things arranged. It's all right for some people,' – he nodded towards Katie – 'privileged, living in hall.'

'It has its drawbacks,' put in Katie.

'I'm going to miss you both,' said Fiona.

'Yes, I know. We were talking about that last night,' Katie said, nodding towards Sammy.

'It would happen that Nell's time is taken up more than usual, and Grandma seems a permanent fixture up in the nursery.'

'There'll only really be Willie and Dad to see to, so you'll be lonely for a time.'

'Oh, no, not really. No, we've . . . we've got a new arrangement.'

'Yes?' Both Sammy and Katie looked at her, and she nodded her head at Katie, saying, 'Your father's idea.'

There was an uneasy movement to her right. But Fiona didn't turn towards Bill, she continued to look at Katie as she went on, 'He knew I'd be at a loose end with all the family gone, Mark included; then next year Willie will be joining you, unless he goes to Newcastle, so he thought it would be a good idea if I took a course at the Open University. It would give me something to do. Perhaps I, too, could contemplate a de—' Before she could finish the word she felt Bill about to spring from the couch, and her arm went out swiftly. Her hand gripping his leg, she said, 'Don't say it, Bill. Please, don't say it!' She had turned towards him and was smiling, and his face, which had almost depicted rage, was now covered with a red hue. And when his head drooped slightly, Katie, straightening up, said, 'I think that's wonderful. It's the best news. It's made my day. And I know it has Sammy's too, because for some time now we've been talking on and off about how the house would be depleted with one and another of us going. Oh Dad, that was good of you!'

Bill now pressed her gently aside; then getting on to his feet, he looked down on Fiona, and she, looking up at him, said, 'Thanks again.'

When Bill gave her no answer whatever, especially such a one as they would have expected, but just left the room without a word, they both looked at Fiona.

Her chin was pressing into her chest now and she was biting on her lip. And Katie, putting her arms around her shoulders, said, 'What is it, Mam? What is it?' Fiona answered, 'I shouldn't have done that.'

'What? What d'you mean?'

'Say that it was his idea about the Open University.'

'Well . . . well, wasn't it?' Sammy had asked the question.

And now Fiona swallowed deeply, as she said, 'No. No, it wasn't. He's . . . he's dead-set against it. I wanted to do this nearly two years ago, because I do get lonely, you know.'

'Oh, Mam! Mam! Yes, of course. We've all been

very unthinking, really, up till lately; but Sammy and I have talked about you being left alone. And Dad was against it?'

'Oh, yes. Yes, it's impossible for him to share.'

'What would he be sharing?' There was a puzzled note in the question from Sammy; and Fiona looked at him and said, simply, 'Me.'

'Oh, no! That isn't him.'

Fiona didn't say, 'Yes, that is him.' But Katie said, 'Yes. Yes, I can see. He would think that . . . well, he would be losing you in some way. He . . . he's always known you were superior.'

'No. No, Katie.' Fiona turned quickly on her. 'No, I am not superior.'

'In his eyes, and in everybody else's, you are superior, Mam. You were brought up differently. Sammy knows what I mean, don't you, Sammy?'

'Oh, yes. Yes, I do. And I see his side of it. Oh, yes. If I was the Sammy Love I once was, I would feel the same about Katie. But with his and your help, I've been given a façade and I've been able to realise I've got a mind. This wouldn't have happened if I'd still been in Bog's End.'

'But Bill is a very clever man, Sammy.'

'Yes. Yes, he is, he is a brilliant man when it comes to his kind of work. But he also knows, for instance, that he couldn't sit and discuss the arts with anybody. Not as you could. If I spoke of John Donne to you, you would know that I was referring to the great writer and poet. Likely, if I spoke to Bill, he would ask me who he was. Was he local, or something like that? And if one dared to laugh, my God, he would level them! He's a man who can hold his own with any other man in his own line, but he's conscious of his drawbacks, not compared with anyone else, but with you. Yet, as I said before, he's the best man I know or will ever get to know. And to me, he is worth all the learned professors that are likely to come my way during the next few years. And I can say this; had he been given the chance when he was young, the same as I was given by him and you, he, too, could have been a flier. As for you, Mrs B, you couldn't even stand the smell of me, could you?'

When Katie and he laughed, Fiona said with a deep sadness in her voice, 'No, I couldn't, Sammy, and that proves a great lack in my make-up. And I'm as much aware of that side of me as he is of himself, because I lack his humanity.'

'Oh, no, you don't, Mam. Oh, no, you don't.' Katie's protest was loud and Fiona, tapping her daughter's flapping hand, said, 'All right, all right, I don't.'

'But you're not going to let him put you off, are you, Mam?'

'No; strangely, no. I'm standing up to him about this, and I find it very, very difficult, because I love him dearly. I loved him when I married him. I knew what kind of man he was then, because he told me quite seriously if I looked at anyone else, he would shoot us both.'

'Oh, Mam!'

'Oh, yes. It wasn't in fun. I knew that. The only man I've really ever spoken to as an equal is Rupert, you know.' She nodded at Katie now. 'And Bill was so jealous of him, he insulted him and practically told him to get out. And it was at the time I was carrying Angela. I was an awful-looking sight and very unattractive. I think that he would have thrown Rupert out of the house bodily if it hadn't been that he was connected with Sir Charles Kingdom. And you know something? Since then I have never had an interesting conversation with anyone outside the family; I have to watch my ps and qs when we eat out.'

'I . . . I can't believe it,' Katie said.

'Oh, shut up, you!' said Sammy. 'You can't believe it. Well, I, in my own way, will prove it to you some day if I catch you in deep conversation with some polished individual.' This caused Fiona to smile at him now and to put her hand out to him and say, 'Sammy, he's likely in the garden. Go on out and have a natter with him in your own way. I think you understand him better than any of us.'

'Yes, I think I do. I suppose it's because we are both from the same nest. But I must have developed a double shell. And you must realise that that's why he is for Daisy, too, because we are a trio. Mr Bill will always remain himself; but I have hopes for Daisy.'

'Oh, Sammy,' Fiona pushed him, 'I now know what your career will be; it will be in the diplomatic service. You'll be up in London before we know where we are.'

'Of course, of course.' He nodded his head at her. 'That's my intention, to have a house in Belgrave

Square. Oh, yes.' Then assuming a strutting pose, he went from the room.

He did not find Bill in the garden, nor in the wood, but when he re-entered the hall and heard high squeals of delight coming from upstairs, he took the stairs two at a time and made for the nursery, where he found Bill sitting in the old basket rocking-chair, with his arms about his child and hers tightly about his neck.

Mrs Vidler turned to him, saying, 'Hello, there, Sammy. These two will be on the floor in a minute.'

'Well, it looks as if it will serve them both right.'

Going close to her, Sammy whispered in her ear, 'Mrs B's got some news for you.'

'Fiona? News for me?'

'Well, it's news about me and another person.'

'Really?' Her head to one side and a slow smile spreading over her face, she said, 'Now, I wonder what that could be? Yes, I do, I do. May I have a guess?'

'No: I wouldn't try. But there's some tea going downstairs.'

'Oh, then I can't wait.'

She turned from him and went towards the door, then came back, and, in her turn, whispered in his ear, 'Some people are blind. But I've always had good eyesight. Congratulations.'

He pushed her gently on the shoulder. He liked the old girl. He hadn't at one time, oh no, but she grew on you.

The rocking had stopped. Angela had climbed down from her father's knee, and now she rushed towards Sammy, saying, 'Sam. . . my. Sammy. Sammy.'

'Yes, milady? What is it?'

When she held out her arms, he lifted her up, saying, 'Oh my! You get heavier every day. You'll soon need a crane to lift you.'

She laughed into his face, her round eyes gleaming with happiness and love. She was a child who oozed loving emotion, but even more so did she pour it out on Bill. Her voice had a lisp to it, but her words were strung together coherently, as now when struggling down from Sammy's hold she said, 'Look! Imadecat.' She ran towards a table on which was an array of plasticine animals, some quite recognisable, a box of coloured crayons, and some wooden tools.

Angela was pointing to a longish roll of plasticine, on one end of which was stuck a ball, and on the other a long tail, and, looking up at Sammy, she said, 'Pawsanwhiskers.'

'Yes. Yes.' He smiled down at her, and she said, 'What?'

Bill said softly, 'She's asking you what you think it is.' And Sammy's voice was terse as he replied, 'I know, I know.' And he did know because he had played longer with the child than Bill had, in spite of his open adoration for her. And now he scratched his head as he looked down into her bright face, then said, 'Kanga . . . roo?' And now he put both feet together, formed his arms into two legs and began to hop, while she squealed with delight, crying, 'No! No!

Notkanga . . . silly!' Now he was galloping.

Still laughing, Angela turned to Bill, saying, 'Dada tell Sam, tell Sam.' And Bill, coming out of his bitter reverie for a moment, said, 'It's a pussy cat, you dumb-head.' And she repeated, 'Pussycat, dumb head.'

'Oh! Oh, yes, of course. Well, go on and finish it, then I'll know what it is.'

Immediately now she sat down on a low chair and began to roll up bits of plasticine into narrow strips.

They both watched her for a moment; then Bill walked slowly back to the rocking-chair. And when Sammy went and stood by his side, they exchanged glances, but neither of them spoke. And it was evident to Sammy that Bill's mood was black, perhaps the blackest he had ever seen in him, and so his voice was low and quiet as he said, 'I have a number of things to say to you, but I'll ask you a question first and it is this, how d'you feel about me having Katie?'

Bill's eyes were narrow as he looked up at the tall, smart young fellow this 'Bog's End' lad had grown into, and his answer was noncommittal: 'What would you like me to say?'

'Oh, Bill.' No mister now. 'Oh, Bill, that tells me nothing, not one way or another, and . . . and it is important to me how you feel about us; because you are important to me, always have been. Although verbally you have been Mr Bill, inside, like the others, I, too, thought of you as Dad. And tomorrow I'll be leaving your protection and the security you and this house have given me, even before my dad died. It will never be in my power to repay you for what you have done for me. And now when, apparently, I've given you a bit of a surprise, if not a shock, by declaring that some day the girl you look upon as your own daughter has promised to marry me, it might seem to you that I'm repaying you badly for all you have done for me. But I hope it isn't like that with you. I want to hear you say you're glad and that, through Katie, I'm to remain in your family.'

'Oh, well, that remains to be seen.' Bill sat back in the chair. 'Yes, by gum, it remains to be seen, for if you did decide to shack up together before marriage, there'd be no welcome in this family for you.'

Sammy stared at this man, this man whom he considered big in all ways, generous to a fault, and, because of his dealings with men, he had imagined he'd be broad in his outlook too. Yet, within the last hour he had shown, to his surprise, two flaws in his make-up. First, he was so dominant and possessive that he wouldn't allow his wife a career. Secondly, were he and Katie to break the moral code, he would be banned from this house.

Part of him was so incensed that he dared to say, 'What if it should happen that we both can't hold out and should come together without shacking up, as you call it? You wouldn't know a damn thing about it unless she became pregnant. And that can be easily dealt with. They're selling preventatives in schools today because the kids are at it. Yet, here are we, two young people, being told what will happen to us if we do what is as common today as chewing gum.'

When Bill sprang up from the chair, he almost knocked Sammy to one side, and stalking to the fireplace, he gripped the top of the high fire-guard and actually shook it before turning about and growling, 'My God! I've listened to everything now. To think that you, of all people, could stand there and talk like this to me. And you know something?' He stabbed his finger towards Sammy. 'I've put you before the others, except her.' He nodded to where the child was still working at the table. 'Yes, above the others. They are my stepchildren.'

'Yes. Yes, I know you did.' Sammy's voice was as rough as Bill's now. 'And I thought of you as a father, so I thought I could speak plainly, not as someone who owes you a great debt, and who, as I said, can never repay it but as someone, like a son, who would be free to speak his mind.'

'Free to speak your mind!' It was as if Bill had spat out the words. Then he added, 'Every bloody one in the house is after speaking their mind. Apparently nobody needs me now; everybody's going their own way, my wife included.'

'All because she wants to take a course at the Open University.'

'So she put you wise?'

'No, not at first, not until you did, the way you took her suggestion and stalked out.'

'Well, let me tell you, young man, what is between my wife and me remains between my wife and me, and I am not going to discuss it. And it's none of your damn business or anybody else's.'

They stared at each other in hostility across the room. Jerking his head up out of his collar, Sammy marched towards the door. As he opened it, he turned and said, 'It was in the papers the other day about a man finding a diamond. It was a huge one. It was intimated it would be worth millions, that is, until they found a flaw in it.'

Bill's hand went out to the wash-hand stand and grabbed a jug standing in a basin that was used for the child washing her hands, and the sound of the china splintering into myriad pieces against the closing door was almost matched by the child's screams.

As Sammy reached the top of the stairs, it was to see Katie and Fiona about to rush up them. He stayed them with a lift of his hand, and Katie cried, 'What was that noise?' Fiona appealed, 'What's the matter? What's the matter?'

'Oh, that noise that you heard was likely meant for my head. We had some plain speaking.'

'Oh, Sammy! You and Bill? Oh, no!'

'Yes, Mrs B, me and Bill. Impossible, isn't it, when you think of it? Anyway, it's a good job I had closed the door. But I asked for it.'

'What did you say to him to make him do that?'

'Oh, I just quoted a bit that I'd seen in the paper the other day.'

He didn't go on. And when Katie said, 'What was it? Go on, tell me, what was it?' He said, 'Oh, I finished my say by telling him about the diamond that was supposed to be worth millions, but then they found it had a flaw.'

Fiona's mouth opened wide. When she did speak her voice was a whisper, 'You didn't liken him to that?'

'I'm sorry, Mrs B, but I did. Well, it all led up to that, Mrs B. You see, Katie and I were threatened with excommunication from the house should we come together before marriage, whether shacking up or not.'

'Oh, Sammy!' Fiona was now standing with her hand across her brow, then looking at them both, she said, 'Go on, both of you, get yourselves out. Go and tell Nell and Bert the glad news. Because it *is* glad news.' She put her hands out to both of them, and as she did so, Katie said, 'No, we won't go to Nell's, not straightaway. We'll go and join Willie at Daisy's, because I want to laugh; if I don't I'll sit and howl.'

'Well, get away.' She pushed them now, then held on to Sammy's arm for a moment, saying, 'Oh, Sammy. When you come back, make it up with him, will you, please? Because he's had enough through me.'

'I'll do that. Yes, I'll do that.'

As they went out, Mrs Vidler came from the open kitchen door, and she and Fiona stood looking at each other for a moment before Mrs Vidler said, 'I'm sorry, my dear, but I heard it all. Imagine me being sorry for Bill; but I am, you know, especially over him rowing with Sammy, because he's been his blue-eyed boy, hasn't he, all these years?'

'Yes, Mother, and he's done so much for him. Oh, dear me!'

'Don't worry, dear. Like everything else, it'll pass. But I must go up now and clear the debris, whatever it is. And that'll give him a chance to come down and take it out on someone, because he won't take it out on me. He's so polite and kind to me, it's unbelievable. And I . . . I know I don't deserve it, but I'm grateful. Anyway, here goes.'

Fiona watched her mother go up the stairs, before she herself returned to the drawing-room, there to await the avalanche that was now certain to come.

The house had an unearthly feeling, with no movement or sound in it at all. She longed for the telephone to ring. Before returning to London, four days ago, following the long vacation, Mark had promised to ring her when he got there. But he hadn't. Mark, she had found, only rang her when he wanted something. She wouldn't admit to herself that her once beloved Mark was a disappointment to her; indeed over the past holiday his attitude towards the family had irritated her. From Willie to Katie he had scorned their activities. And she could count on one hand the times he had joined in an evening meal. He had seemed to live at the Featherstones and had accompanied them on holiday to France and Italy.

Katie had a word to describe her brother but her mind rejected it. It was 'insufferable'. Bill, she knew, would have another word for him and that would be 'upstart'. But she hadn't heard him voice it yet.

Fiona had a desire to cry, but were she to indulge herself in this relief and Bill should happen to come in, he would call it female blackmail.

She would wait no longer. She would go and prepare the evening meal.

She was crossing the hall, when she glanced towards one of the long windows, and through the twilight she saw Bill crossing the drive in the direction of the woodland. He was walking slowly, his head down. She stood and watched him for a moment. He must have gone out the back way.

She set the meal for two on the corner of the dining table. She laid out the cold meat from yesterday's roast, put it on the middle of a large serving dish and surrounded it with salad. After putting this in the fridge, she mixed up a treacle sponge pudding and put it on the stove to boil. He always liked a boiled pudding after a cold meal, and he was particularly fond of treacle. Not that she hoped its sweetness would do anything to soften his temper tonight . . .

By now, it was quite dark and she had switched on all the necessary lights in the house and had gone into the little sitting-room. And there, after banking up the fire with logs, she sat in one of the two armchairs that flanked the fireplace. She chose the one where she would have her back to the door because she didn't want to be met by his expression as he entered the room, calculating that by the time he was seated, and this would be after him taking a pipe from the rack to the side of the fireplace, filling it with shag and lighting it from the fire with a spill, she would be ready for whatever he had to throw at her.

She picked up her magazine from the fender stool and began perusing it lightly. And after fifteen minutes she brought herself forward in the chair and almost exclaimed aloud, 'Oh, he's not going to keep this up, is he? He's waiting for me to go and apologise and say, "All right. I'll not do it. I'll sit in this great empty house, for it *will* be empty, and wait for you coming in, tired and ready only for a meal, a bath, an hour's work or so in your study, and bed. And in bed, you will likely know I am there." ' But no. She reared up. She would do nothing of the kind. She would stand out for something she thought was just, as any reasonable man would consider just . . . But then, Bill wasn't a reasonable man where she was concerned. She lay back in the chair and at that moment the door opened and she closed her eyes. She was aware he didn't go to the pipe rack, but had immediately sat down opposite her and was looking directly at her.

She opened her eyes now and met his gaze. He looked tired, worn. For the first time, she realised that he looked his age, a man in his fifties, not one who could be taken to be in his middle forties.

'Well?'

She didn't answer the syllable.

And now he asked outright, 'Pleased with the day?'

She forced herself to say, 'Part of it. I was pleased to hear Katie's and Sammy's news.'

'Oh, you were? Well, that was another surprise to me. A "Bog's End" product and your daughter. Oh, we all know he's got a veneer, but he's still Sammy Love under the skin.'

'I don't consider that a bad thing, remembering his father.'

'"Bog's End" coming into its own at last. You'll be telling me shortly that you are all for Willie's association with Minnehaha. Although that one has started to dress differently, she won't create a façade. Oh, no. So, what you going to do about her?'

'I'm not concerned about her at the moment.'

'Oh, you're not? Well, doubtless you'll get back to being concerned about her after you stop being concerned about us. By which time, you will have expected me to have given you my blessing to your education stunt.'

'I never expected any blessing from you in that direction. But I did expect you to be fair and to see my side of it: the life I will lead in this house from tomorrow onwards.'

'Many a woman would be damned glad to be in your place, and leading the life you talk about living in this house in the future, let me tell you.'

'Well, let me tell you something, Mr Bailey. I am not any woman, I am myself, and I'm not damned glad to be mistress of this house at the present moment. And for that matter I will add something else: nor am I glad to be Mrs Bailey at this moment, at least not the Mrs Bailey I have come to know lately.'

She saw the colour drain from his face. She saw his hands gripping each side of the armchair. She knew he was making a great effort at this moment to control his temper. And when he didn't bawl, or even shout at her with his next words, she knew how far she had hurt him. And what he said was, 'You knew the type of man you were marrying. As you are yourself, so am I. And now when we're facing facts and the truth is out, I will tell you this much: you've always made me feel bloody inferior, and no man should feel inferior to a woman, especially his wife. I, as a man, feel inferior to no other man, no matter of what station, nor to any other woman but you, right from the word go. Not, mind, that I think you have brains above the average. Oh, no, that didn't come into it. It was just something about you, that middle-class aura that clings to you and your tribe. It's a false thing, and it isn't worthy of notice, because it doesn't come through lineage or breeding, and definitely not brains, but it's there, created by money and superiority. Your mother's got it, too. But funny, I don't have the same feeling with her. The only emotion she once created in me was hate. But now we're all pals together, and, oddly, I like her and I know she likes me. And it is not with the intention of putting any lightness on this matter when I say that I could have married her and you would have been my stepdaughter. What about that? But at the present moment I can't see the funny side of anything. I only know that you're going to step away from me in a different direction.'

He leant back in the chair now, and she was so shocked by his outburst and what had been in his mind all these years that she could find nothing to say. Then he began talking again, quietly now. 'I've taken extra pride,' he said, 'in being known as "Bailey, the big fella", builder and contractor, who swiped the biggest deals that this town has known in years, and who is a name to be reckoned with in the business world. Bill Bailey, who has men toadying to him for sub-contracts. Bill Bailey, who had been invited on to the council, but was big enough to refuse. Yes, he's got a nice wife. She was a widow with three children when he took her. Then he adopted another, one of his men's bairns. Then, you could say, he fostered a young fella from "Bog's End", a rough piece, and look at this young fella now, going to university the morrow. Oh, he's done well, not only for himself, but for everybody connected with him, has "Big Bill Bailey". And what do they know about "Big Bill Bailey"? Bugger-all. They don't know that he has an inferiority complex, as the degrading condition is so-called. And now his wife is determined to overwhelm him by it, and what he'll hear in the future is, "Oh, his wife's a different kettle of fish from him. Dragged by his shoelaces, he's been, but she's got degrees."'

He stopped speaking. And now she saw his eyes were tightly closed and his teeth were grinding one against the other, when he said, 'Why have you made me appear so small, even to myself, that I have to talk like this to you? It proves I have reached bottom in self-estimation. And what you felt like, listening to me, I don't know. But listening to myself has made me feel sick.'

She could not suppress the groan; it was riven from the depths of her. And when the words, 'Oh, I'm sorry, Bill. I'm sorry. I didn't know,' spiralled from her throat and as she attempted to rise she was almost knocked back by the force of his body against hers. And there he was, kneeling at her side, his head on her lap and his arms about her. And she bent over him and held his head that lay against her . . .

How long they remained in this emotional embrace, neither was aware. But, after some time, when she said, brokenly, 'It's all right, dear. It's over. I . . . I won't do it,' this brought his head up, and the fact that his face was wet caused an agonising pain that seemed about to put her heart into a cramp. And when he said, 'Oh, no, you don't. You don't give it up. No! You're going on with it.'

'Bill, it's all right. I . . .'

'It isn't all right.' Now he moved his body until his elbows were resting each side of her on the arms of the chair, and he gripped her hands as he said, 'Don't make me feel any worse than I am at this moment. You're going to go through with it, even if I have to apply for it for you. Sammy threw something at me before I levelled the jug at him. It was about a man discovering a big diamond, only to find there was a flaw in it. And it would seem that everyone in this house, with the exception of Willie, has discovered a flaw in me today. But your mother's been the kindest of them all, for all she said to me was, "Bill, that was such a nice jug. But then, what's a jug?" Even the child became afraid of me and she took some pacifying. I think that was the last straw.'

When he drooped his head, she shook the hands within hers, saying, 'Bill, look at me. Look at me! All you have said isn't news to me. I've always known how you have felt. Yet, at the same time, I wondered how such a big creature as you are, and in my mind you're away above any man I know, or will ever know, could really hold such an idea in his head. And I'm hurt to the very soul of me by the fact that you would, even for a moment, think yourself in any way . . . in any way at all, inferior to me. And the reason I wanted to take up this course wasn't only because I would have a lot of time on my hands in the future, it was because I know so little. My view of the world and everyone in it is so narrow, and I can never widen it by travel, because I don't like travelling. So I could only turn to books. But I know so little about literature, so I felt I needed a guide in that way. I wanted to have an interest as you have in your work, designing, planning, arranging, always having something to look ahead to. In that world you are looked up to, adhered to, and it brings you satisfaction, I know it does. But I had nothing like that to look forward to, except my children coming back from university and, in the main, talking over my head. So, you see, dear,' – she smiled wanly at him – 'we all have our inferiority complexes. But, oh, my darling,' she now cupped his face with her hands, 'the relief, the wonderful relief that it's over, this awful feeling between us. I could never have believed that it could happen. Yet, in a way, I know now we'll understand each other better.'

He did not reply as she leant forward and pressed his lips gently to hers. And when she said, softly, 'Let's go upstairs and see Angela,' he nodded at her. Then, getting to his feet, he said, 'You go along, I'll follow you. I'm—' Then, half-shamefully, he added, 'I must sluice my face.' At this he took a handkerchief from his pocket and rubbed his eyes as he muttered, 'There's a first time for everything, and I've proved it today. Yes. Yes, I've proved it today.'

2

'Mam. What would you think if I asked Sep to dinner on Sunday; tea would be too late, because Sammy and Katie will have to get back early in the evening and there would be no time to have a game or . . .'

Fiona was busy at the kitchen table, preparing a fruit salad, and she stopped the process of peeling an orange and, looking across to where Willie was sitting, she said, 'If you would like to explain who Sep is, and why you want him to dinner, and what game you want to play, then we can discuss it.'

'Oh, Mam. It's Sep Gallagher, Daisy's brother. The one, you know, who works for Dad.'

'Oh, Sep. And you want to ask Sep Gallagher to dinner?'

'Well, yes. You see, we never have tea before about six o'clock . . .'

'You've said all that. But you've never before expressed a wish to invite any of the Gallaghers to a meal, except Daisy.'

'Oh! Well, I thought I might have mentioned it to you some time about Sep being an expert table-tennis player. We have a table, you know, Mam,'

– he thumbed over his shoulder – 'in the recreation-room.'

'Now, now, Willie Bailey . . .'

'Well, Mam, it should happen that Sep has won the competition at the club. It's been quite a big thing. He's a wizard at it. He started at the club when he was a lad and then he dropped it when he was out of work. But since he's had the job at Dad's place, he's picked it up again. And, as he said, just out of the blue he went in for the contest, and the champions from different clubs were also competing, and one after another were eliminated, leaving only him and the American still unbeaten. And I'd better explain who the American is. He is the son of an American who apparently came over during the last war. Well, he talks like a Yank; at least, I suppose, as some Yanks talk. Anyway, he was a crack player and Sep beat him and won the trophy. But, as Daisy said, the others in the house just made a joke of it, even his dad, although he was laughing as he said, "What's the good of a silver cup if you only hold it for a year? Together with a free ticket to an international match of your choice, but not a penny to get you there." So, I thought, Mam, it would be nice and it would make him feel that it was an honour – well, it really was, of a kind; and of course, it would please him and Daisy, if he could have a game with Sammy, because Sammy is hot stuff at it, you know.'

Fiona looked down into her son's face. He was a nice boy, was Willie. Thoughtful and kindly.

Impetuous, oh yes: spoke without thinking at times. But when he did think it was nearly always about other people. And here he was, suggesting inviting another of the Gallaghers to a meal, just to make him feel good. So opposite to Mark; he was more like Sammy; they could have been brothers, those two.

Thinking of Sammy for a moment she was so glad he was going to remain in the family, because he and Katie would always remain close to her and Bill. Oh, yes, and Bill. As yet, however, she couldn't come to terms with accepting Daisy. But then, with regard to Daisy, Willie was tenacious. And it was odd, but during this last year, so Katie said, Daisy wasn't pushing him off as she had done previously. It was as if she had changed her mind about him. But what she herself did know was that if she refused to accept Daisy, she would lose Willie.

Still, Daisy was hard to accept, because in spite of all the change in her dress, she remained herself. In fact, she seemed determined to remain herself, and she would go out of her way to impress this attitude when she was in her company.

'All right, Mam, if you'd rather not.' Willie got up from the chair and was about to walk away when she said, 'Wait a minute! Wait a minute! I . . . I wasn't thinking about him, but about something else that's on my mind. Yes. Yes, of course, invite him to dinner. But it'll be the ordinary Sunday do, mind. And Nell and Bert will likely be here, and the children; then there'll be Gran and Angela.'

'Oh, he certainly won't mind that. He's used to

a crush. They can hardly get round their table; they're packed like sardines.'

'Well, if he comes, that'll be a round dozen here.'

'Thanks, Mam.'

Suddenly he went round the table and, putting his arms about her, he kissed her. Then, holding her at arm's length, he said, 'You know something? You've looked happier these last weeks than I've seen you for a long time. And you know something else? I've felt happier, too. There was a period when the house turned gloomy, didn't it? But now we seem to be back like we were when Dad first came on the scene. Remember? Won't you come home, Bill Bailey? Bill Bailey, won't you please come home?' he sang to her. 'I look back, you know, on those days, as simply marvellous. There was Mr Bill always creating excitement, and Sammy, whom you couldn't stand because he swore like a trooper; but you always gave us grand teas. And exciting things used to happen, didn't they? Like Katie being kidnapped and Dad being nearly murdered; and Sammy's father going to jail and Dad getting him out. Then Angela coming, and how she made us all love each other for a time. She did, an' all, didn't she?' He nodded at her. 'Then things got serious. Katie trying to brain Rupert and the girl, and Mr Davey dying. Life changed from his going. I suppose we were all growing up. But it isn't life that changes, Mam, is it? It's people. Mark, Katie and I, we've changed. Even Sammy has. But he's like Daisy, in a way; he'll always be himself underneath. People brought up as he and Daisy were are tough in some ways. Don't you think so, Mam? They're stronger somehow. And yet that isn't the word.'

'I think it is, dear. They're made strong by their environment. Refinements of any kind in some odd way appear to dilute the personality.' And she smiled now as she added, 'Take me for instance. I'm an example.'

'Oh, Mam, I could take you in any form, personality or not.' Again he was hugging her; and when he went to dance her round the kitchen, she laughed and said, 'Give over, you fat-head. If you want to be helpful, you'll take those dishes out of the sink and put them in the dishwasher. I'm beginning to think that your father's right about dishwashers. You've got to practically wash the stuff before you put it in. Mrs Watson won't go near the thing since it knocked the handles off those two cups.'

'She's daft. I believe in using everything. I used to loathe it when it was my turn for the washing-up. When I marry I'll have the whole house electrified. Everything, right down to my pyjamas. I'll have them made like an electric blanket.'

As Fiona laughed, she thought, when he gets married. My, my! It must be on his mind. And he's going to have everything electrified. Well, that should complete the picture, because he'll certainly be marrying a live wire if he takes Daisy. Dear, dear! She grabbed up a pear, put the knife in the top in order to peel it, but brought it down too sharply and cut her finger.

Dinner turned out to be a very jolly meal. It seemed that Sep competed with his sister to make the whole company laugh.

Fiona had been surprised by Mr Sep Gallagher, not only by his appearance, but by his voice. He used the idiom of the Northerner, but it wasn't thick and stressed as it was generally spoken, and his inflection, too, was somewhat modulated. You could say he had a very pleasing voice and a manner to go with it. Moreover, he had finely cut features and must be close on six feet tall. And she understood he wasn't yet twenty. He had been set to work with the plasterers. When he was told to go to the main office and ask for a chit for two buckets of lime for the plaster, at that moment he knew no better than to obey them. In fact, he had not hesitated in doing so because he knew that lime was an ingredient for plaster and they were using a lot of it. His precise orders were to go to the main office and ask for the chit, then take the buckets to the store and have them filled up.

The main office was a set of huts with a large caravan just beyond them. He had sense enough not to go into the caravan, but he didn't know which of the huts would be the office. So he stopped two men and said, 'I'm new here. I have a chit for some lime.' He nodded down to the buckets and the men dug each other and one had said, 'Oh, a chit for some lime. Which house are you doing?'

'It's number seven on what they call, I'm told, a new patch.'

'Oh, aye,' said one of the men, 'number seven on the new patch. Well, laddie, you see the big caravan there, well that's the boss's office. Now don't go there, but to the hut nearest it; they'll fix you up with what you want.'

He pushed open the door of the office, only to be slightly abashed by the sight of two typists sitting at desks. At the end of the room, by a long table, stood three men. One he recognised immediately; Mr Ormesby. The second one he knew nothing about, but of the third he knew quite a bit. The three were staring at him, as were the two typists, and he looked from them down to his muddy feet, wondering how he dare step on to the hessian-matted floor. He was nearest to one of the typists, and it was to her he stammered, in a voice almost little above a whisper, 'I've c . . . come for a chit for . . . lime.'

What he noticed next was the three men at the table turned their backs on him; and the typists, after gaping at him, put their hands over their mouths and bowed their heads. Then the bark that hit him made him almost jump back; and there was the boss in the middle of the room, an arm outstretched, yelling, 'I'll lime you if you don't get out of here and get back to your squad, and tell them to be at this office at five o'clock tonight for their cards. All of them, d'you hear? All of them, and you an' all! And that's the payment for wasting time. Now you go back and tell them that . . . this instant.'

Sep had imitated Bill's voice except for the bawl.

And when the laughter subsided a little, he ended, 'I never knew how I left that hut. I came to myself standing outside in the middle of a muddy patch, and the two men who sent me in there leaning helplessly against each other. Well, I went for them first. "Silly" – he paused and looked to where the two children were perched – "Bs, the pair of you, and not you alone," I said. And you know something?' He looked round the company, then back to Bill seated at the head of the table, 'You know, sir, you couldn't have beaten my bawl when I got back on the job. I was really sick, because I had just started, and there I was for me cards. It was Mr Ormesby, there,' he nodded towards Bert now, 'who said it would be all right, but to keep me wits about me in future, for the men in that gang were known to be practical jokers.'

Looking down the table towards Bert, Bill said, 'Those two on the road would be Partridge and Kennedy, I suppose?'

'Yes. Yes. But I'll tell you one thing that you mightn't know, neither that gang nor those two ever waste a minute. They work like machines. No rushing or hurrying, just steadily. And it's amazing what they get through in that way. Also, they are the kind who don't grab their coats when the whistle goes. And if anybody's wasted time through them, like Sep did that day,' he nodded across the table to Sep, 'they stay behind and help clear up.'

Daisy looked up the table towards her brother, sitting to the left of Fiona, and she felt a wave of pride pass over her. Their Sep was passing himself. She had always known he was different, but not that he could tell the tale as he had done. He had made them all laugh over something quite simple. If it had been Mike, he would have sat mute most of the time. And Frank . . . oh Frank would have butted in, either causing an argument or saying something stupid. As for Harry, well, he too would have been mute, but in a different way from Mike. Unless the conversation touched on sport, you didn't get much out of Harry. But there was Sep holding this table as she herself could do at times. They were alike, she and Sep; yet not alike, because they should each have possessed the other's nature: there was no roughness in Sep, and he was kind; whereas, she was afraid of softness. Yet deep inside she wanted the comfort of it. And she, too, was kind, but she didn't want people to know she was kind. There was only one person who seemed to know her inside, and that was her da. But wait, there was him across there who was smiling at her now, as if, in a strange way, he was proud of her. He knew all about her, because she had opened her mind to him. She had intended it to put him off, but it had only made him cling closer to her; and now the sensible part of her was beginning to appreciate it. Oh, not just now, but for some time past she had been grateful that he should think of her as he did.

That time she had asked her mam and dad about choosing second best, she now knew to have been stupid, because here was Willie, and he was the third one, and he wanted her. Sammy, the first one, didn't want her. Jimmy. Oh, Jimmy. She felt wild with herself that she had ever thought of Jimmy, considered Jimmy as second best. But Willie now, she could have Willie. Oh, yes, she knew she could have Willie. But there was an obstacle, two obstacles. One was his mother, and the second one . . . well, that was another thing . . .

'Well, if we're going to see this contest, let's make a move,' said Bill. 'Everybody up with their utensils and into the kitchen. Mrs Watson wants to get home some time today, it being Sunday. Yet, you wouldn't think she had a home to go to, the way she sticks around here so much. She must get double pay. D'you give her double pay?' He looked at Fiona.

'No, I don't,' she said. 'When she comes on a Saturday or a Sunday, I deduct it from her wages, because she tells me she likes to come. And everybody must pay for their pleasures, mustn't they?'

There were giggles as they gathered up the dishes and marched into the kitchen, and Nell cried after them, 'I'll be with you in a minute. Mrs Vidler will see to these two, but I must just go up and see if the other one's still asleep,' only immediately to be brought to a stop with her foot on the second stair when the front doorbell rang. The others too, had stopped and looked expectantly towards the door. And when it was opened, there, over their heads, she saw a man and a woman and a young girl.

It was the sight of the young girl that made her gasp. But no! Mamie? No! It couldn't be. Yet, it was and it wasn't.

She saw Bill move towards the door and she knew he was not only staring, but gaping at the visitors, and particularly at the girl.

'You Mr Bailey?' It was the woman speaking. And when he did not answer, she went on, 'I . . . I had to bring her. It was only common charity, but I had to bring her.'

Bill pushed the door wide, and his voice sounded like a croak as he said, 'Come in.'

The woman pressed Mamie over the step, and when she came close to Bill, she looked up into his face and said, 'Oh, Uncle Bill.' The voice sounded small like that of a child, the words spaced.

Bill now looked at the others in a helpless fashion before, seeming to come to himself, he called to Willie, 'Go and bring your mother.' Then turning back to the man and woman, he said, 'Come this way, will you?'

As they passed Mamie, the woman took her arm and said, 'Come on, dear. It's going to be all right. Come on.'

Bill ushered them into the drawing-room; but with his hand on the door, he stopped and looked back at Nell, saying, 'See to things, Nell, will you?' Then he closed the door.

The man and woman were standing in the middle of the room gazing about them, but Mamie was looking at Bill, and when he approached her, she said, again in the same nulled tone of voice, 'Oh, Uncle Bill.'

He was telling the man and woman to be seated when the door opened hurriedly and Fiona came in, but she didn't move up the room but stood with her back to the door and, after glancing at the man and woman who were now seated stiffly in chairs, her gaze came to rest on this girl who had caused her so much trouble, caused them all so much trouble and unhappiness. But she wasn't looking at the same girl. This girl was much taller and terribly thin, and there was a strange expression on her face. There was no colour in her cheeks, and all she could say about her clothes was that they looked very drab, from the flat felt hat on her head to the dark-grey coat that reached her calves.

She had to force herself to walk up the room. And when she came within an arm's length of the girl and heard her say, 'Oh, Auntie Fi,' her face actually screwed up in perplexity. There was such a depth of pain in the voice; yet, it sounded like that of a weary elder.

'I'll be good, Auntie Fi, I will. I promise. I promise. And I won't go out. Never! Never! I won't go out.'

Seeing that Fiona was beyond words, Bill put his hand on Mamie's shoulder, meaning to direct her to the sofa; but when she jerked her body from him, he gaped at her, saying, 'It's all right. It's all right.'

'I'm . . . I'm sorry, Uncle Bill.'

The woman put in, 'She's got like that. She can't . . . well, she can't stand men . . . I mean, touching her.'

'My God!' Bill looked at the girl who had now seated herself in the corner of the couch, and it could be said that the same thought was passing through both his and Fiona's mind, and it was laden with guilt. What had they sent her away to? Something had happened to her.

The woman was saying, 'You'd have to know about it. You see, we lived two doors down and we are of the chapel as well, but as me mam says, there's moderation in all things. And Harry . . . my husband here' – she thumbed towards him now – 'he said from the beginning that something should be done. But you don't like to interfere, do you? It isn't your business. But when she first arrived' – she nodded towards the wide-eyed, staring girl – 'she was spritely. Oh, too spritely. But she soon had it knocked out of her. It was chapel twice a day on a Sunday, like with all of us, but one or other of them would take her to the Bible reading on a Sunday afternoon. But she was never taken to the choir practice. They all used to come at one time, but one or other was detailed to stay back to see to her. Then it got round the village that they were out to reform her from her bad ways. What her bad ways were nobody got to the bottom of. Then there was school. There were only three teachers there. Well, there's only thirty-five children, you know. Two of the teachers were chapel, the third wasn't. Our ones were told to keep a strict eye on her. The third began to open her mouth about what was happening to the girl. Nothing very serious at first, only that if she was defiant she was locked up in the attic, and her meals were cut down to one a day. This seemed to happen more during the holidays. But the third teacher . . . well' – there was a little toss of the head here – 'her name was Blackett, and she said the girl had to pray before she was allowed to take a swallow of water. Of a sudden she stopped going to school, and they had to get the doctor, because the authorities began to make enquiries. It was then stated that she had a rash all over her and it was a bit catching. It wasn't the doctor that said that, was it?' This was a question applied to her husband, and he shook his head and said, 'No, well, not about it being catching, because Mrs Edwards took her Glenda to him because she had been sitting next to Mamie. Well, not exactly next to her, because they had her stuck at the back of the class by herself, except when she was in Miss Blackett's class. She was tolerant, was Miss Blackett.' His wife's expression changed as she looked at him, saying, 'She was nosey, known to be nosey.'

'Yes. Yes, perhaps it was just as well in this case. Well, it was from about this time that my mam noticed . . . You see, we weren't living there then, not with me mam. We were married three years ago, and we had shifted to Cardiff. But when we visited me mam, she would give us details of what had been going on. And when she told us for the first time that she had heard screams coming from two doors down, we didn't take much notice, because she tells a good story, does me mam, and we thought she might have been imagining it. It was no good going to Mrs Wilkins who lived right next door to them, because she was as deaf as a stone. And as the Pearsons' house was the last in the block and there was nothing on the other side, except the playing fields; well then, there was nobody else to bear out the fact that they heard screaming. And we visited Mam at least four times following that before she said again that she had heard screaming. Another thing that me mam noticed during this time was that the old man's nephew, Owen, and his wife were spending money like water, with new rig-outs, and of all things they had got a car. It wasn't much of a car; it was second-hand. But the bus had been good enough for them up till then, because there's a good service from the village, very good. And it was passed round the chapel that no matter what they did, they couldn't get rid of her rash. Then, she must have really taken bad, and it was the night before, me mam swears, that she heard the lass screaming again. Anyway, there was the doctor and he was there every day for four days running. And on the Sunday they had prayers said for her at the chapel, because the old fella . . .' She turned to her husband now, saying, 'I could never stand him, could I?' And he said, 'No, dear, not many could, not many people could.' She now sighed deeply and looked from Bill to Fiona, and said, 'Could I have a glass of water, please?'

'Oh. Oh.' It was as if Fiona were coming out of a trance. 'You . . . you must have some tea,' she said. 'I'm . . . I'm very sorry. Just a moment. Just a moment.'

She ran to the door and into the hall where it would seem that Nell had never moved from the foot of the stairs, because she was still standing there and alone, as if waiting. And when Fiona whispered, 'A tray of tea, Nell. A tray of tea. I . . . I can't believe it.' Nell shook her head from side to side and said, 'Nor me,' then hurried away.

Fiona remained standing for a moment with her hand tightly on her throat as she muttered to herself, 'What have we done?'

When she returned to the room the woman was saying, 'From what she's told us in bits, it's as if she's still frightened to say anything.' She was looking towards Mamie who was now sitting with her head deep on her chest, and she went on, 'One thing was sure, she was scared to death of Owen. I think it's him that's knocked her partly out of her wits. And whatever happened, it's made her afraid of men, 'cos she wouldn't let you near her, would she?' She again turned to her husband as if for confirmation, and he said, 'No. No, not even to take her hand, and help her out of the car.'

'Anyway,' the woman went on, 'these last few weeks things have begun to happen. When Mam said to me the solicitor man had been next door, 'cos there's nothing escapes my mam—' She smiled here and nodded her head before going on, 'When I said to her, "How d'you know it's a solicitor, Mam?" she said that it was the same one she had gone to ten years ago when she was protesting about the playing fields. Well, there wasn't only her then, there was a group of them. But she remembered him well: as she said, he had an extra large nose and he wore sideburns, and there were the sideburns still. She came on him by accident, she said, as she was coming back from the shop. He was stepping out of his car and she said it was his nose she noticed first; the only difference was, it had got redder.'

There hadn't been a smile on her face as she related this. And now she went on, 'Anyway, Mam said there was a lot of hustle and bustle in the house after that, and what should happen but the doctor was sent for again. The old 'un had had a seizure. Perhaps the solicitor had brought it on, some said, because there was something fishy. They had known before the girl came to the house that the old man was guardian of her money, and that she couldn't touch a penny of it until she was sixteen. Yet, as my mam said, the Pearsons' life-style, you know, as it's called, changed after their son was killed. The old girl would go tripping out into Cardiff like she had never done in her life before, and come back loaded with parcels. The village had been good enough for her before.

'Well, anyway, when, a fortnight gone Sunday, not one of them entered the chapel all day, the pastor arrived to enquire if they had all caught the rash from the girl, and there was Mary Pearson, tearful, saying that Owen and his Betty had gone away for a time, but they'd be back. Yes, they'd be back. Then the next thing my mam sees is the young thing there' – she pointed to Mamie – 'in the garden emptying a bucket of ashes. And she said, she had never got such a surprise in her life, for it was about a year since she had last clapped eyes on her. She said she walked like a ghost. And when the girl saw her, she dropped the bucket and came running to the gate, and there she began to gabble, and my mam couldn't make sense of it at first. She said she put her arm around her and told her to talk slowly, and what she was saying was, would my mam write to her uncle and aunt and ask if she could come back; she would do anything if she could come back, and that she was frightened. When my mam asked her what she was frightened of, she did what she's doing now, drooped her head on to her chest and wouldn't say. Mam then told her that she would write to you, or better still she would phone. But the girl couldn't remember your number. Well, it's another long story after that. Oh!' She looked towards the door where Nell was coming in, pushing a trolley on which there were not only five cups of tea, but, on the lower shelf, a plate of some buttered scones and a cake.

'This is Mrs Ormesby,' Fiona said, 'a friend of mine.' And at this they both answered simultaneously, 'Please to meet you.'

And now speaking for the first time, Bill asked, 'Have you come all the way from Wales today?'

The man nodded, saying, 'Yes, we left Cardiff this morning.'

'By, that's a long drive! Did you have many stops?'

'No, only one.'

'You must be pretty tired.'

The man smiled, then wagged his head a little before he said, 'We're not so tired as stiff. But it's no distance to Morpeth now, and we should be there before dark.' He looked at his wife and she nodded at him. Then, turning to Bill, she said, 'Yes, we would like to be there before dark. They're expecting us, you see.'

'Oh yes. Yes.'

They both said, 'Thank you. Thank you,' to the cup of tea that Nell handed to each of them. And when she asked, 'Would you like a scone or a piece of cake?' they both answered, 'No, thank you. No, thank you.'

Nell was standing in front of the girl, whose head was up now, and she was looking at Nell who said quietly, 'Hello, Mamie.'

'Hello, M . . . M . . . Mrs Nell.'

'Drink this tea . . . Would you like a scone?'

The girl glanced quickly at the woman as if asking permission. Then again looking up at Nell, she said, 'Yes, please. Oh, yes, please.'

Nell brought her a buttered scone and a piece of cake, and when she laid a napkin over the girl's knee, the girl took hold of it and fingered it as if it were something strange, which prompted Nell to turn quickly away.

When the man looked at his watch, the woman said, 'We'll have to be away. But I can tell you this: my mam went to old Mrs Pearson and she put it to her straight that, if she didn't let the girl come back here and see if she could stay, she would go to see the solicitor man in Cardiff and tell him what had been happening to her, and it would be a court case. The girl was nearly out of her mind. So, here she is.' She put out her hand towards the couch, and Mamie, who was chewing on her last bite of cake, swallowed quickly and coughed as if she were going to choke. Then her hands were gripping each side of the empty plate and she was looking from Bill to Fiona, and her voice seemed to be a whimper as she said, 'If . . . if you don't have me to stay, I . . . I won't go back there; I'll go some place.'

'It's all right. It's all right.' Fiona went to the couch and sat down and, loosening one hand from its grip on the plate, she repeated, 'It's all right, Mamie, it's all right. You may stay.'

They watched the girl close her eyes tightly, open her mouth wide as if she were about to yell, then close it as tight as her eyes were. Then dropping back in her seat she sat gasping for some seconds, until Fiona said again, 'Now don't worry. Don't worry. It's going to be all right.' And her own voice was breaking now, for her mind was in a turmoil, denying the guilt, saying, don't forget what she was like, and she wanted to go. She wouldn't stay with us. She wouldn't have stayed with us in any case, if we would have had her. But we couldn't, not after that, could we? No. And she could have been the death of Sammy. But . . . but look at her. She seemed to be still a child then, but this person is no longer a child . . . she's no longer a girl. Her face looks old, as if through age. Dear God! What has she gone through to appear like this?

She turned her head quickly to hear the man, who had now risen to his feet, saying to Bill, 'Could I have a private word with you, sir?'

'Yes. Yes, of course. Will you come this way?'

Bill walked towards the door, and the man followed him along to Bill's study; where Bill pointed to a chair, and said, 'Sit down.'

'Time's getting on,' the man said, his head bobbing now, 'and I just want to say a few words. It's this: I think you should have a doctor to her straightaway. Between you and me something happened to that girl and it was to do with that upstart, Owen. He's neither worked nor wanted in his life. And . . . and as I understand it, she's to come into money in a very short time, and from what she let drop to my mother-in-law, things would happen to her if she didn't sign papers. Then she was supposed to have fits and to have fallen downstairs, and apparently she was kept on bread and water for days. But then it seems they stopped asking her to sign papers. But she said she became more frightened still. One thing at least is certain; that fellow Owen did something to her that has put the fear of men into her, not of God as they had intended, but the fear of men. Well, you saw what happened when you put your hand on her shoulder. So, as I said, sir, I would have her examined. You know what I mean?'

'Yes. Yes, indeed, I know what you mean. And I thank you for bringing her. She left here in very difficult circumstances. I suppose you know why.'

'No; we never got to the bottom of it.'

'Oh, well, you might as well know. She got into some very bad company and was shoplifting and taking drugs. And when my adopted son followed her, he surprised a gang of drug distributors and they overpowered him and drugged him and bundled him up, and threw him into a lot of coal slack, expecting the tide to either take him out or bury him further.'

'Dear Lord! Dear Lord! Was that it?'

'Yes, that was it. So, you can understand why I insisted on the grandfather taking her away from here. It was either that or she would have gone into a reform home, or wherever it is they send the young offenders. And if Sammy, my boy, had died, then I don't know what we would have done with her. So that is why I insisted the grandfather should take her. Legally I was responsible for her, but I had never touched a penny of her money.'

'You hadn't?'

'No. No.'

'Dear, dear!' The man shook his head. 'Well, it wasn't said openly, but it was suggested that she had been paid for to be brought up by you all those years.'

'The old devil!' Bill bridled now, and the man said, 'Another thing, sir, the solicitor has made a number of visits to the house during the last two weeks, and has been accompanied by another man. We feel it can only be to do with the girl's money. So, if I were you, sir, well, I needn't tell you, a businessman, what you should do. But on her behalf, I think it should be looked into.'

'Indeed it should. Indeed it should. And it will be. Take my word for it. And thank you very much indeed for taking this trouble over her.'

'Oh—' The man now looked down towards the

floor as he said, 'If I'd had my way, I would have probed sooner than this. But not living in the village any more and no longer a member of the chapel, I had little say. However, although I prompted my mother-in-law, and she, I know, opened her mouth as she is apt to do, to the minister, I got the impression that she was told not to interfere with people's private business. In fact, it was I who went to the old woman and told her what we were going to do. And, you know, she didn't protest. This was yesterday. But she said a strange thing. She said, "I knew it would come to an end sometime. And God will judge and He knows I did try." So, what can you make of that, sir?'

They stood looking at each other and Bill said, 'Well, if I have my way, somebody will judge her before God, and the other two when they are found. As for her grandfather, if he's had a stroke, his deserts are starting now.'

'That indeed could be true. That indeed could be true.'

The man now turned towards the door, saying again, 'Well, I must be off, sir.'

In the hall the woman was waiting for them. 'It'll be dark before we get there,' she said, 'and you know I don't like driving in the dark.'

'We are going now. We are going now. Have you said goodbye to her?'

'I have. I have, and I have leave from Mrs Bailey to come and see her on our way back.'

Bill saw them to their car and he thanked them

again for what they had done. And the woman murmured, 'Well, thank you for receiving us so civilly. Many a one wouldn't. And it's the most beautiful place you've got here, if I may say so.'

Bill nodded at her and smiled, then watched the car drive slowly away.

When he returned to the hall, Fiona was waiting for him, together with Nell, Sammy, Willie, and Katie. It was Katie who said, 'What's it all about?'

'We'll tell you later, all of you. Where's Daisy and Sep?'

'They're at the table, playing ping-pong.'

'Well, don't you think you should join them? Except you, Katie. You come in with your mother, and talk to Mamie; but you two,' – he now looked at Sammy and Willie – 'don't go near her. There's a reason.'

'A reason?' Willie screwed up his face.

'Yes, there's a reason, a good reason. But she can't stand . . . well, oh dear God! I'll tell you all about it later. Get yourselves away. Nell, she'll have to go into one of the guest rooms tonight. Can you see to it?'

'Leave it to me.'

When they entered the drawing-room Mamie was sitting on the edge of the couch, her hands gripped between her knees, her tension expressed in the whole of her body.

Fiona straightaway took a seat beside her and said, 'You . . . you remember Katie? She's grown a lot since you last saw her.'

'Hello, Mamie. Nice seeing you again.'

The girl stared hard at Katie, then drooped her head slightly, and Katie and Fiona exchanged a look.

On a high note, Katie said, 'Well, take your coat off.' And at this Fiona exclaimed, 'Oh, my, my! Of course. What am I thinking of? Take your coat off, dear.'

Mamie stood up and slowly unbuttoned the four buttons of her coat. As she took it off, Katie took it from her, then stood staring at her, as did Fiona. The coat had been drab-looking, but the dress that was hanging on the girl's thin body like a brown sack was more so, for it was shapeless and the material looked rough. Again Fiona and Katie looked at each other. Then Mamie dropped back on the couch and covered her face with her hands, and as she began to sob she whimpered, 'I won't do anything bad. I promise. I promise. And I won't go out. I won't! I don't want to! I don't want to go out. No, never! Never!'

'It's all right, dear. It's all right.' When Fiona put her arms around her, the girl turned and pressed herself so tightly against her that Fiona almost overbalanced. And now she stroked Mamie's hair, saying, 'It's all right now. It's all right; you're home, and quite safe.' As she said the word she glanced up at Katie who was biting hard on her lower lip.

When the sobbing gradually subsided and the girl leant limply against her, Fiona found that she, too, was unable to speak for a moment. It was Katie who said, 'Come on upstairs, Mamie. Would you like a bath after that long journey? And look, as you haven't brought any things with you, one of my shorties will likely fit you.'

The girl now brought herself from Fiona's arms, and when she rubbed her wet face with her hands, Fiona said, 'Here, dear,' and handed her a handkerchief. Then Mamie, turning to Katie, said, 'Thank you,' and slowly she pulled herself to her feet; then, about to walk down the room at Katie's side, she suddenly turned and, going back to Fiona, who was sitting as if still unable to take all this in, she said, 'I . . . I can . . . can stay then? I can st . . . stay for good?'

'Yes, dear. Yes, you may stay; you're back home.'

'Oh.'

Fiona watched the girl, this strange girl who carried no semblance of the Mamie she remembered, draw in a long breath before saying, 'I . . . I can help, m . . . m . . . make myself useful.'

'Go along, dear, and don't worry any more. Go along.'

When the door closed on them, Fiona brought her hands together and pressed them against her lips, and again she wondered what they had done. What had she done? Because she had been adamant that she couldn't and wouldn't stand that girl any longer, that not one of the family could stand her. But what had happened to her in those short two years? She had the appearance of a frightened animal. The door opened again and when Bill reached the couch and sat down beside her, he did not speak for a moment, nor did she; and when he said, 'My God! Did you ever see such a change in a human being like there is in that child?' she immediately said, 'She's been badly treated.'

'Badly treated! Not only has her brain been washed, but her body's been mauled.'

'No!'

'Yes. And I mean to get to the bottom of it, after the doctor's had a look at her. And by what that couple said, I shouldn't be surprised if her money's nearly all gone. Why did those two abscond of a sudden?'

'Will you go down to see?'

'I can't. I can't at the moment, but what I shall do is get my solicitor to write to hers. And another thing: I'm sending my accountant down there for a couple of days. Gerry's a very astute fella. If there's anything fishy, he'll dig it out. But first things first, I'm ringing Dr Pringle. I know it's Sunday, but I'll put him in the picture and he'll likely come in first thing tomorrow morning, if not tonight. If she's so afraid of men as not to let them near her, well . . .' He nodded at her and left the sentence unfinished. But Fiona ended it for him, saying, 'Oh, dear Lord! I hope not that. I feel bad enough as it is.'

He now took Fiona's hand, saying, 'Look, dear, I know you are feeling just the same as I am at the moment; part of you is riddled with guilt, but we've got to look at it this way. What we did was necessary at that time. Anyway, dear, her presence won't spoil your plans, will it?'

She stared at him for a moment. She would have wanted to answer, definitely no, dear. Neither she nor anything else will spoil my plans. But now she wasn't so sure. And that is what she said, 'I'm not so sure, dear. Just let things hang; we'll see how she behaves.' Then she added, 'Have you put the others in the picture?'

'Yes, as much as I can. I related what that garrulous lady told me. But garrulous or not, it was good of her, and the mother, to take all this trouble. And I must write to her. Anyway, we'll wait a bit and see how things turn out.'

'Her clothes are dreadful. That dress she had on looked as if it had been made out of brown sacks. She's having a bath and Katie's trying to fit her up now. Then I think she should come down into the recreation room and see how she reacts.'

'Yes. Yes.' And he nodded at her. 'And anyway, we must stay for a while and watch Sep doing his stuff. And, of course, Willie showing off his prowess too. Presentable young fella, that Sep, isn't he?'

'Yes. Surprising: and in a way he was as entertaining as Daisy. It's odd, isn't it, that you should have three of her family working for you now?'

'And you know what she said to me the other day . . . Daisy? She said, "Life's funny, isn't it? If I hadn't met Willie, we'd all be still living on short commons in our house." And I haven't heard that expression for years. But there she came out with it; short commons.' They were moving towards the door now when he stopped and, putting his hand on her shoulder, he said, 'I wish you liked her.'

'I do. I do,' she was quick to protest.

'Aye, you do, but you wouldn't like her in the family, would you?'

'Oh, Bill, that's another subject.'

'Yes, it's another subject, dear. But you've got a tenacious son, and you wouldn't want to lose him, would you?'

'Bill!'

'I'm stating a fact, Mrs Bailey. He'll go where his heart beckons. It might tear him apart, but he's set on her. If anybody was ever set on a lass, he's set on her. The same as he was on Sammy; clings like a limpet. And in the last year I've noticed that she's somehow changed her opinion about him being just a young kid; and from what he's let drop to me he makes himself quite at home in her house, and he seems to have been accepted. Although he's burning the midnight oil here working for his A levels he still spends time, I hear, helping the twin with his homework. And he's a very bright boy, I'm given to understand. Well, he proved that, didn't he? With our Sammy's business. Anyway, how have we got on to this subject? Let's get along and see what's happening at the far end.'

They had entered the corridor when Katie's running steps down the stairs halted them. And she, leaning over the bottom of the banister, said, 'I've left her . . . she's had a bath . . . I've left her in my room, trying things on. Mam,' – she shook her head – 'she's all marked, on her back and her thighs, and she's as thin as a rake. But . . . but I really do think the doctor should see her.'

413

'He's going to, dear. Yes, your father's going to phone him.'

'And . . . and she's got bruises on her arms. You remember, she was plump and white.'

'I'll be up in a minute.'

'No. No, I'll see to her. She's nervous. All the time she's nervous. There's something wrong with her, Mam.'

'Yes, we know, dear. Anyway, once she's dressed bring her down into the recreation room and see how she reacts.' . . .

Sep and Willie were in the midst of a game and they did not turn to look at Fiona and Bill as they entered the room. But both Sammy and Daisy came up to them, and it was Sammy who asked, 'Is she all right? Is there anything wrong with her?'

'She isn't well, dear, that's evident. Anyway, she'll be down in a minute. But Willie, don't touch her. If you talk to her, just don't touch her.'

'No. No, I won't.' He shook his head.

Fiona closed her eyes for a moment, saying, 'It's . . . it's because something has happened that we don't know about.'

'Well, is it she doesn't want any male to touch her, Mam? It seems pretty evident.'

Fiona looked at her son, thinking, Willie would speak his thoughts, wouldn't he?

Daisy now said, 'I've never seen her before today. How old is she?'

Fiona and Bill exchanged glances as if asking a question of each other, then Bill said, 'Just on sixteen.'

'Well, she looks older in one way, yet younger in another.'

'Who's winning?' put in Bill, looking towards the table where Bert was standing at the far side, umpiring. 'Willie's one up,' Sammy answered, 'but I think Sep's going easy with him.'

'He's not! He's not! Not that our Sep wouldn't, but Willie's playing brilliantly.'

'All right, all right, if you say so.' Sammy laughed at her. Then they all went back to the table to watch the game in progress.

Fifteen minutes later, after Willie had, in fact, been allowed to win the game, the recreation room door was thrust open, and Katie entered, calling behind her, 'Come on. Come along in, dear, it's all right.'

When she drew Mamie into the room, the transformation in the girl surprised them all. She was wearing one of Katie's dresses, held up round the waist with a belt so that the bodice part appeared like a blouse. Her hair was combed out from the tight bun at the back and hanging loose on her shoulders. And on her feet were a pair of open sandals.

'Oh! well.' It was Bill who broke the silence. 'Oh, now you look more like yourself.'

As he made to go towards her, Fiona gently restrained him, and it was she who advanced half-way down the room to where Mamie was now standing close to Katie; and smiling at her, she said, 'Oh, you do look nice, Mamie . . . like your old self.' And without hesitation, she indicated Daisy, saying, 'This is Daisy, Katie's friend, and that young man,' she pointed to Sep, 'is Daisy's brother Sep. Now let's all sit down and watch the champions.'

And so it was that Sammy and Willie took up the game, and the rest sat round watching them, making favourable and unfavourable comments on their actions.

It was as if they all knew now that everybody was in a game, and the game was to put this strange girl at her ease.

It was leaving time. They were all in the hall, and it should happen that Willie was standing next to Bert Ormesby, when Bert, his head lowered, said under his breath, 'When you get to Daisy's, don't keep bragging about winning, because Sep let up on you.'

Willie's head jerked and he stared at Bert for a moment before saying, 'He didn't! Did he?'

'Oh, yes, he did. He's a good fellow, is Sep.' Then nudging Willie with his elbow, he said, 'But you're not bad yourself, you know.'

Willie's voice was very low as he muttered, 'I feel an idiot, and that's what I am most of the time.'

'Well,' – and Bert was also whispering now – 'God has a special place for idiots of your type.'

Willie glanced sideways at this good man who rarely pushed his religious belief and he grinned at him now as he whispered, 'You'll be there ushering us specials in.'

'I hope so. I hope so.'

'What d'you hope?' Bill demanded loudly. 'Oh,' – Bert laughed – 'I was just saying that I hope the council grant you the building licence for the fields tomorrow; with one exception, of course, they'll cut out the cemetery.'

'So do I,' Daisy called back from the step, 'those poor souls shouldn't be turfed out of their basement flats. They likely had enough of that when they were alive.'

'Get on with you.' Bill pushed Daisy forward. 'No cemetery, no work for your three brothers. Just think of that, madam.'

'Aw, you!'

'And you, miss! And you.'

And on this note they drove away. But the door had hardly closed on them when Nell said, 'We too will have to be on our way; Andrew is getting whingy.'

'He's always whingy, because he's spoilt.'

Nell rounded on Bill now, 'He's not spoilt, and he's not always whingy. Anyway, if he was spoilt, I haven't very far to look for the cause of it, have I? Give him this; let him have that; leave the child alone.' She turned now to where Mamie was standing next to Fiona, and she said, 'He's ruined Andrew. D'you remember Andrew?'

Mamie nodded, and Nell went on, 'Every time he comes here, all the good we do at home is undone.'

Fiona laughed and said, 'Well, not quite. Remember Bill taught him a grace before meals.'

'Yes,' put in Bert, 'but one that shouldn't be heard.'

'Oh, you're a couple of old fogies,' said Bill as he turned now and made for the drawing-room; and Bert, winking at Fiona, said quietly, 'But we must be off. I'll go and bring the car round.' And Nell said, 'Do that and we'll go upstairs and get the children ready. Will you come and help us?' She looked at Mamie; and Mamie turned quickly towards Fiona as if she were asking permission, and Fiona said, 'Yes, let's all go up. It's far past Angela's bedtime,' and to Mamie she added, 'You'll be surprised how she's grown.'

Mamie said nothing, but just walked with them up the broad stairs and into the nursery. But there, she didn't speak to the children or take any part in their dressing; and Fiona was reminded of the defiant silence Bill had encountered; and yet this wasn't of the same kind, she was sure; this was a fearful silence, and it was frightening in itself.

Willie's room lay at the end of the long corridor from which a shorter one went off at right angles and in which were the three guest-rooms. It was in one of these, and next to the one known as her room that Nell had made up the bed for Mamie.

Later in the evening, after Willie and Bill had gone to their rooms, Fiona took Mamie up to hers. She had one of Katie's shorty nightdresses with her and, handing it to Mamie, she said, 'This will certainly fit you.'

She stood aside and watched the girl take off

Katie's dress, fold it and lay it over a chair. Then what followed next caused her eyes to widen and her mouth to gape; first, the girl brought her arms out of the taped shoulder straps of what looked like a rough linen petticoat; then picking up the nightie from the bed, she pulled it over her head and began to wriggle out of her underclothes. But then she stopped and said, 'I needn't, need I?'

'You needn't what, dear?'

'Undress under my nightie,' and with a swift movement she pulled the nightdress back from her head and almost savagely now she tore off the knickers which were apparently of the same material as the petticoat. And she stood for a moment looking down at her thin body before again picking up the nightdress, when Fiona gasped, 'Oh, my dear, wait! Wait a minute,' and she gently turned Mamie about, only to mutter, 'Oh no! No! Oh, my dear! Who did this to you?'

Now she recognised the old Mamie, for the girl bowed her head and remained mute; and it came to Fiona that the action was the only characteristic she had brought over from her childhood.

After Mamie had put on the nightdress, Fiona sat down on the side of the bed with her and put her arm around her shoulders before drawing her gently to her, saying, 'We'll get to the bottom of this.'

The head came up quickly now as Mamie muttered, 'No, no! He may come.'

'You were going to say that somebody might come back? Well, you're not going back there, so you need not fear. You're back home; you're safe here,' and she was about to add, 'You'll soon get back into your old life,' but, oh no, she wouldn't want her to do that. Oh, no. So she added, 'And we all want you and are glad you are home again.'

The head was lifted now, the deep fear-filled eyes holding a question, and Fiona answered it by saying, 'No, you've got to believe this, never again will anyone harm you. You must try to forget what has happened. And those who have done this to you will be punished.'

She felt the thin body shiver now, and she thought she heard Mamie mutter, 'Punished. Punished.' But when the word wasn't spoken aloud, she said, 'Now come on, get into bed. Nell has put hot-water bottles in. Let me feel. Oh, yes, it's lovely and warm, you'll soon be asleep. And tomorrow we must think about getting you some new clothes, pretty clothes, like you used to have. Eh?'

There was no answering smile, just that stare. And again the words, oh, dear Lord, passed through Fiona's head. When the girl lay down on to her pillow, Fiona bent over her but found that she couldn't kiss her . . . well, not as yet. But she put her hand on her face and stroked it gently; and as she did so the girl closed her eyes as if she were already asleep. 'Good night, dear.'

'Good night.' Mamie did not add "Auntie Fi," but Fiona hadn't reached the door when she turned quickly to see the girl sitting upright and saying on a gasp, 'You . . . you won't lock me in?'

'Oh, no, my dear.'

'Can . . . can I have it open?'

'Yes. Yes, of course. And if you want anything in the night, well, you know where our room is, just round the corner. Now lie down. Lie down and go to sleep. We'll see you in the morning.'

In their room, Fiona said two words in answer to Bill's, 'How is she?'

'I'm devastated.'

Willie was the first to be woken by the scream. It brought him upright in the bed, blinking and gasping as if he were going to choke. He had been dreaming about something, but there had been no screaming in the dream.

Or perhaps there had.

When it came again, and a voice shouting, he sprang out of bed and pulled on his dressing-gown. On opening his door it was to see his mother running up the corridor towards him with Bill behind her, the while dragging on his dressing-gown. And he was about to speak when the scream came again.

As Mamie had requested, her door had been left open, and when Fiona switched on the light, it was to see Mamie rolling about in the bed, her arms and legs flailing. The bedclothes had piled up at the bottom of the bed, and when Bill, gripping her arms, went to lift her back on to the pillow, his head jerked backwards as she let out another scream. 'It's all right, Mamie,' he shouted. 'It's all right. Wake up! Wake up! It's all right.'

Of a sudden she collapsed back on to her pillows, muttering, 'Don't! Don't! I . . . I'll do it. I'll do it. Don't, Owen! Don't!' The last word came out as a wail and Bill, who was still holding her arms, cast his glance towards Fiona and the knowledge it conveyed was repeated in her own.

Gently she pulled the clothes over the now limp form, and as she did so Willie said in an awe-filled whisper, 'Somebody must have been at her. She's terrified out of her life.'

'Shh!' Bill's warning came as Mamie slowly lifted her lids and, peering up at the group standing to the side of her, she whimpered, 'I . . . I'll sign, I will.'

Fiona pressed Bill to one side now and stroked the girl's hair back from her wet forehead, and her eyes, opened wide now, looked into Fiona's face and she said, 'Oh! Oh! I . . . I've been dreaming.'

'Yes, dear. Yes. But go to sleep now. You're all right.'

'I'm . . . I'm here?'

'Yes, you're here. You're back home. You'll be all right.'

She watched the small breasts rise upwards; then on a sound like a long, drawn out sigh Mamie said, 'Will you leave the light on?'

'Of course, dear. Of course. And I'll push the door wide, so don't worry. Now go to sleep.'

They were making for the door when a small voice came to them, whispering, 'Auntie Fi?'

When Fiona stood by the bed again, Mamie raised herself from her pillow and in a whisper she said, 'I . . . I did see Sammy last night, didn't I?'

'Yes. Yes, of course you did, dear. He's not dead.'

'No, of course not. I thought I had dreamed that I saw him, but he was there, wasn't he?'

'Of course, my dear, he was. You mustn't trouble your head any more about Sammy.'

The girl now lay back on her pillows and she whimpered, 'They said he had died, and all through me, and that unless I stayed with grandpa I'd go to prison. But . . . but he was downstairs?'

'Yes. Yes, of course, my dear, he was downstairs. And now you must try and forget everything but that you are back home. And you'll never be hurt again.'

When the girl's head turned on the pillow and two round eyes were directed at her, Fiona found the expression in them unbearable, and quickly she said, 'There now. There now. Go to sleep, dear. You're home. Nothing can happen to you here. You'll never be hurt again.' And this time she did not pat Mamie's face but bent over her and kissed her gently on the cheek, and at this Mamie closed her eyes . . .

Down in the kitchen, it was Bill who put the kettle on and mashed the tea. Fiona sat at the table, one hand covering her face, and she repeated for the third time since sitting down, 'You'll never be hurt again.' Then, looking up at Bill, she added, 'Her look seemed to say, I've no need to be hurt again; I've suffered enough to last me a lifetime.'

'Oh, that's in your mind, woman.'

'No, it isn't in my mind, Bill; you didn't see what was in her eyes. They looked old. She'll never be a girl again; and yet, in some ways, she's returned to childhood.'

'I know what you mean, Mam,' Willie put in. 'I sat looking at her last night and seeing her when she was about seven or eight. She seemed like that one minute and then a stranger the next. And I thought a lot about it before I went to sleep, and it's this. We're all in this, you know about having sent her away. I couldn't stand the sight of her – well, I fought with her when she was young – she was such a little upstart, and always on about her grandfather's money. And as she grew she seemed to get worse. And then the whole thing came to light, and we nearly lost Sammy. We mustn't forget that, Mam; she had been shoplifting and lying to you in a clever way. And when she took whiffs of drugs she must have known what she was doing. True, she might have just started on them, but she would have gone ahead. So we mustn't blame ourselves for not wanting her back here. But . . . but whatever they've done to her at that end has had a terrible effect. At times last night she looked like an old woman.'

'Willie's right.' Bill now sat down opposite Fiona, then added, 'You mustn't be like that. If it were to happen again I would act as I did then, definitely, for all our sakes. And we mustn't forget Sammy could have died through her. But at the same time, as Willie said, we mustn't forget that she has been treated in the most terrible way, and it's my guess, and a strong one, that she's been interfered with and bodily abused, besides being starved. So, somebody's going to pay for this, and I'm going to see to it. I'll have those two hunted down, because the old 'un couldn't have done all this on his own.' He took a drink from his cup, then said, 'Well, Dr Pringle will be here in the morning and one thing I'm going to get him to do straightaway is to get in touch with her doctor at that end. What was that fellow up to, not to know what was happening to her? There's something fishy somewhere. Well, this time next week we should know a great deal more. But in the meantime, life has to be lived. There's work to do for all of us. And you, my dear, are going to have your hands full for some time, because it's on you she is going to rely.'

As Fiona rose from her seat, she said, 'Strangely, I don't mind. My only hope is that we can get her back to normal, because, as she is now, she is far from it.'

3

It was a week later and Bill, Fiona and Nell knew most of what there was to know about Mamie's stay with her grandfather, but not all.

Before the doctor's visit on the Monday morning, it had taken some time for Fiona and Nell to convince Mamie that all he would do was examine her bruises, and that they would be with her all the time. After his examination he had sat on the side of the bed and patted the young girl's hand, saying, 'Now, what you must do, my dear, is to eat big meals, really big meals,' – he had nodded at her, emphasising the 'really big' – 'because you need a lot more flesh on this long frame of yours. And when your cheeks puff out, we'll have a very, very pretty young woman.'

Mamie made no reply to this, but just stared at the grizzled man.

But once out of the room, the doctor's note had changed. He had walked smartly down the stairs and into the drawing-room, where coffee was awaiting him, before he said, 'Bad business that. Very bad. Oh, yes,' he nodded at Fiona, 'she's been interfered with, and roughly. The scars on her back are old, but not those on her thighs. And they weren't made with the strap. I fear that whatever has happened to her has affected her mind in some way. I don't know who her doctor was, but I mean to find out, and this very day. I shall come back to you with what he has to tell me. And if what I have to tell him doesn't come as a surprise to him, then there has been great negligence on somebody's part. Oh, yes. Oh, yes.'

After he had gone, the two women had looked at each other, and it was Nell who said, 'God in heaven!' She added, 'Well, we half expected it, didn't we? But, you know, Fiona, I feel sick.'

Fiona had said nothing. Sick could not have described her own emotions at this moment.

Again guilt was sweeping through her. Yet she reminded herself of what Willie had said last night and of what Bill had said before that, and of what she had told herself. But all this didn't help much when your imagination gave you a picture of what the doctor had described.

On Tuesday, Bill had sent his accountant off to Wales, and on Wednesday afternoon Fiona had a phone call from Dr Pringle. He had been in touch with the doctor, who was apparently attending the old man Pearson, and the story he had to tell was that he had first been called to the house when the girl was covered with a rash. This would have been about six months after Mamie's arrival. In his opinion the rash wasn't contagious, but the cousin could not be convinced other than it was. And they kept her away from the school and the chapel for some long while.

The next time he was called to the house to attend the girl was when she was supposed to have fallen down the stairs and was badly bruised and concussed. It was following this that she had what he termed slight epileptic fits, and also that her personality seemed to have changed. They had pooh-poohed the idea of another opinion, impressing on him that they were quite capable of seeing to her themselves.

Dr Pringle had said that the doctor had intimated that he hadn't been happy about the girl. But what could he have done? She was under her grand-father's care and she definitely needed looking after. At this point Fiona had put in, of course she did, but had he had no inkling that she was being interfered with?

And to this, Dr Pringle had replied that the man had been astounded to hear it, but that the girl had given him no inkling. Anyway, it was emphasised that the old woman and the younger one were always in the room when he attended her. But he did admit that they were a very odd and secretive family and, in a way, were religious fanatics.

Dr Pringle had then asked, 'Has she talked to you at all about her life there?' To which Fiona had replied, 'No, and she can't be drawn either. She seems afraid to speak about it.'

'Well, in that case,' he had replied, 'she definitely does need treatment, because she is carrying a heavy load, and she'll be no better until she gets rid of it. I think we'll have to have a psychiatrist to see her. I'll pop in at the weekend and we'll talk about it.'

As a result of this phone call, Fiona had felt that no new light had been thrown on the subject, and any news Bill's accountant would bring back with him, would be mainly about money. In a way, this seemed of little importance now, for money wasn't going to help that girl who at the moment was sitting upstairs playing with Angela. It was only when she was with the child that there was a semblance of a smile on her face, and a slight lightness in her tone. Outside, it was as much as Fiona could do to get her to take a short walk in the garden. But she wouldn't go out alone, it had to be with either her or her mother or Nell.

So she agreed with the doctor; a psychiatrist was indeed needed.

On the Friday afternoon Bill almost bounced into the house. His accountant had returned from Wales, and with such a story to tell.

The capital of Mamie's inheritance was intact. The £100,000 paid by the insurance company following the death of her parents and brother, and the £60,000 from the selling of the house, together with £2,100 from the sale of furniture and effects, was intact, but not a penny of what would have been interest was left, the accumulation of which over the past twelve to thirteen years, when compounded, should have amounted to well over £200,000.

This sum had been drawn on before Mamie's arrival, presumably for her upkeep with her adoptive parents and her allowance. Bill ground his teeth as he said, 'I could go through there and murder that fella, I really could. But he's on the point of snuffing it; the other two, though, if they hadn't flitted, God knows what I would have done to them. He was down with the old man as a trustee and every year they've picked up the interest. As it is, she now has only what was left to her in the beginning. Although it is quite a bit, it isn't worth half as much as it was thirteen years ago.'

'But what would they have done with it, living in that village?'

'I don't know what the old fella's got stacked away, but I bet that that young nephew of his and his missis, who is as bad as he is, have lived it up over the years. But the money business is secondary in their case. Oh, yes! It's rape and the result of it, and whatever else the beast put her through that have turned her mind. As Dr Pringle has said, all the peace, quiet and good feeling in the world is not going to help much, till she gets rid of this fear. And she won't get rid of it unless she's able to speak about it. And I doubt, dear, whether she'll ever open up to us, so I too think we must follow his advice and get her to a psychiatrist.'

'Well, if she's afraid of the males in this house, you, Willie, Bert, and there was Sammy and Sep on Sunday, if she's afraid of us then we're not going to get her to lie on a couch and talk to a strange man, are we?'

'No, but she could lie on a couch and talk to a strange woman. There are women psychiatrists too, and undoubtedly, in many cases they'll be better than men.'

'Because they talk more?'

Fiona sighed, saying, 'Yes, you're right. Of course, you're right. But it's getting her there. D'you know that when she walks in the garden with us she hates to cross the drive, because the gate's at the end of it, and she can see it. Twice she's attempted to come straight back indoors, when I've said, "Let's go into the wood. Nothing but the birds and rabbits, and there's a fox's hole there." I took her and showed her the fox's hole, but she just stared at it as if she weren't interested. And yet you can never tell by her expression because she suddenly said, "Has it got young?" This flummoxed me for a moment, but I said, "No, not now; it had a litter in the spring. At least they used to run around here just as it was getting dark. You'll see them next year." And she nodded but said nothing. But this morning you know what she did? She went into the kitchen and asked Mrs Watson if she could do the vegetables. At the time, I was in the pantry and she hadn't seen me. And Mrs Watson said, "Well, lass, yes. Yes, you can do the vegetables. There are not so many to do now, with three of them away, but we've still got to eat, haven't we? And the master likes his taties, mashed or roasted. Yes, you may do the taties; and there's parsnips there, too. Yes, I'll be glad of a hand."

'When I emerged from the pantry, Mamie looked at me and said, "You . . . you don't mind?" And I said, "No, my dear; I certainly don't mind. I would be glad of a hand at any time. And Mrs Watson hates scraping carrots. Don't you, Mrs Watson?"

'"Yes, ma'am," said Mrs Watson, "one thing I can't abide and that's scraping carrots; I'll peel them. You'll lose half the goodness, but scraping, no."'

'Well,' Bill now asked Fiona, 'did she do them all right?'

'Perfectly. She did carrots, she did the potatoes and the parsnips, then she peeled the apples for a pie.'

'Well, she must have been made to work at that end, 'cos she never did it when she was here, did she?'

'No, oh, no.'

'I'll tell you what I'll do,' said Bill, springing up from the chair. 'I'll phone that doctor who saw to her when she was in the hospital here. I'll put him in the picture.' . . .

Fifteen minutes later Bill came back into the room, saying, 'Well, that's fixed. He put me on to a Dr Sheila Smith, a common name but an uncommon woman, or so he said. She's also a hypnotist and very good with disturbed children. She said she would come out, but she hasn't a vacancy until next Tuesday, three o'clock next

432

Tuesday afternoon. Well, now,' – he nodded towards her, smiling now – 'I feel we're on our way. But to tell you the truth, dear, I won't feel right until I see that girl smile and laugh and stand near something male without flinching.'

4

It was the week before Christmas and Dr Smith was paying her fifth visit to the subject, as she called Mamie. She was a small woman, in her forties. She had a bright face, the prominent feature of it being the eyes, which were grey and, at times, looked colourless. There was nothing about her to suggest a forceful personality, except when she was talking, and then her manner only suggested a quiet pressure.

'Give me your coat,' said Fiona. 'What a day!'

'You can say that again. I skidded twice on the main road, the second time near a lorry. Do you know, lorry drivers have the greatest command of words in the English language. Some, as yet, I don't understand, although I've heard them a number of times. Apparently not one of them thinks I'm a good driver.'

Fiona laughed as she said, 'Come into the drawing-room first and have a cup of tea. It's all ready or nearly so. Mrs Watson was just about to bring me a tray.'

'Oh, this is a lovely room.' The small woman walked smartly up to the blazing fire; then turning her back to it, as a man would, she lifted her longish skirt well up past the back of her knees and let out a slow, 'Ooh! That's lovely. The heating system in my car has gone haywire and the seats are leather.'

She looked now to where Mrs Watson was entering with a tea tray, no smile of welcome on her face, for, in her estimation, psychiatrists came under the heading of dim-wit diggers . . .

'Well, any progress?' Dr Smith asked Fiona, as she gulped at the hot tea, and Fiona, shaking her head, said rather ruefully, 'Not noticeably. Although on Sunday she did play a game of table tennis with Katie, so, I suppose, that is something. However, she still veers away from my husband and Willie and, indeed from any other male person coming into the house. The sight of them seems to make her dumb. But the other day she said rather a strange thing when we were walking in the wood. She stopped suddenly and looked up into the big oak that we have down there and she said, "I like trees, especially when they're bare; you can see them better then . . . the shape and the pattern on the bark." Don't you think that was a little unusual for her to say?'

'Yes, I do, I do. But it means that her mind is moving away from the grim depths that she's lived in for so long. Yet so far, I have been unable to draw from her what happened in that house. It's been either yes or no, or I don't remember. So, I propose today, with your permission, to use hypnotism. I've spoken to Dr Pringle about it and he agrees with me that he thinks the time has

435

come when the treatment should be changed. If, as is often the case, I had progressed as far as to get her to talk a little about herself and why she is so fearful, then I would not have suggested this. I'm afraid you will have to sit in with me again, for she becomes very uneasy out of your presence.'

'Oh, I don't mind, and although I know nothing about hypnosis, may I ask if it can have any detrimental effects?'

'No, not in this case it won't. I think it can do only good, because if this fear remains with her it won't lessen, it will deepen. The memory of whatever has happened has almost become engrained in her, and I am positive it is a fear that is making her remain in this childlike form. Although I must say, I can't promise that hypnotism will make her absolutely . . . well, say, be her age. In my estimation, she is not what you would call deranged, but there is something wrong there, and whatever it is it will keep her in this state for the rest of her life if we don't drag it out of her. And they are the words: it will have to be dragged out of her.'

'I'll call her. She's in the recreation-room with my mother and Angela. You'll want to see her in the little sitting-room again, I suppose?'

'Yes, that's as good a place as any.' . . .

They were seated in the little sitting-room and Dr Smith was saying to Mamie, 'What kind of a week have you had?'

'All right.'

'Have you been for walks?'

'Yes, in the wood.'

The doctor now turned to Fiona and said, 'There's a very funny pantomime on at the Royal. Do you like pantomimes?'

Fiona smiled as she answered, 'Yes, we generally all go together as a family. The only trouble is, we've got to stop Angela from screaming her delight when she sees the horse or the cow, or any supposed animal come on the stage.'

Turning now to Mamie, the doctor said, 'Do you like pantomimes, Mamie?'

Mamie stared at her for a moment. Her brow was furrowed and her lids blinking as if she were trying to recall something, and then she said, 'Yes. Yes, I like . . .' She broke off here and showed slight agitation before she ended, 'I . . . I don't want to go.'

'All right, my dear, you needn't.' Then, moving her chair closer to Mamie, Dr Smith said in a soft, low voice, 'In a minute or so you're going to feel very sleepy . . . would you like to lie on the couch?'

'No!'

'You'll feel more comfortable on the couch, Mamie,' said Fiona gently. 'But please yourself.'

Mamie turned to Fiona and looked at her steadily for a moment; then rising slowly from the chair, she lay on the couch.

Dr Smith sat down by the couch and, taking Mamie's hand, she said, 'Relax, dear. In a minute you are going to sleep.' Now she held up one hand in front of Mamie's face and, moving one digit after the other, she said in a rhythmic tone,

'Five . . . four . . . three . . . two . . . one . . . Now you are nicely asleep.'

She waited a moment, the while she kept her eyes on Mamie's closed lids, and then she said, 'I want you to imagine you have reached your grandfather's house and describe what happened from then on.'

Mamie's eyeballs now began to move rapidly under the closed lids, and her voice, beginning as a whimper, said, 'Awful . . . nasty,' and she now leaned forward and gripped her knees, saying, 'Sore. Sore . . . always praying . . . I hate you, Grandfather. I hate you! I'm itchy all over . . . itchy.' And she rubbed her arms, then her stomach.

Lying back now, she muttered, 'I'm hungry. I want a drink . . . You're cruel! All of you. I won't sign your papers, I won't! I want to go home, I want to go back . . . Prison. All right, prison . . . My back is so itchy . . . I can put it on myself. Owen . . . Don't! Don't do that. I'll tell.' Her arms were now flailing the air and she was crying, 'Please! Please. Owen!' Her hands came forward like claws, her head jerked back as if it had been struck and her knees came up and she was yelling now, 'Oh please! Please! No, don't do that. You're hurting. Oh, no! No!'

Her body was now twisted into a heap, and she groaned before suddenly falling back on to the couch, her head and every part of her, limp.

There was a long silence; her eyeballs were moving slowly now from side to side; then the words came, low and clear, 'I'm going mad. I hope they take me away.'

There was another silence, before a whimper came from her, 'Oh, if only . . . if only . . .'

The doctor looked at Fiona, whose face was streaming with tears, and she said softly, 'Very good. Let's hope it's done it. It must have done something, but just what, remains to be seen. Now, if I were you, I would go and make a cup of tea.'

After the door closed softly on Fiona, Dr Smith spread a hand in front of Mamie's face and said, 'When you wake up you'll feel so relaxed and you'll welcome a cup of tea.' And she snapped her fingers.

'Where's Auntie Fi?'

'She's gone to make that cup of tea, dear.'

'Oh, that's nice. I'd like a cup of tea.'

5

The kitchen looked bright: the wallpaper had a yellow base, the floor was newly covered with modern linoleum in a warm brown colour and it had the appearance of being tiled. The long table was covered with a chenille cloth; the old couch was enhanced by a chintz cover; and on the floor in front of the hearth was a multi-coloured rug. Overall, the kitchen had a new look. And Len Gallagher was wearing a light coloured cardigan. The expression on his face, too, was light as he looked at Willie who was sitting to the side of him. Annie was busying herself at the side table, and she made no comment as she listened to her husband saying, 'You know, lad, the world's changed since our day. There's that one upstairs, packing what she calls her weekend case. Can you imagine it? And as for changes, just look what's happened in this house within the last three years. And, you know, lad,' he now stabbed his finger towards Willie, 'all through your family. Oh, yes, all through your family.'

Willie could say nothing to this; he just smiled at the man he had come to know so well and whom he liked more than a little. And when Mr Gallagher said, 'And you're sitting there, lad, telling me you're goin' to marry me daughter. Eeh! Lad, we can't believe it. Can we, Annie?' He looked over his shoulder; but when his wife made no answer, Willie put in, 'Well, as I said, Len, it won't be for some long time, but we want to announce our engagement today. I have a long trek before me, possibly five years, and Daisy herself is going to be busy, so she tells me.'

Len's voice was low now when he said, 'How are your people goin' to take this, eh? Have they any inkling?'

'Oh . . . oh, I think so.' He gave a short laugh as he added, 'More than an inkling.'

When he didn't go on any further, Len said, 'Well, I can see your dad accepting her, and I'm speaking plainly now, lad, but what about your mam, eh?'

Willie did not speak for a moment, but he thought, Mam. She welcomed Daisy to the house, she was nice to her, but, yes, there was still a barrier there, for she never brought up the subject now of how he felt about her. And so it was in a rather lame tone that he said, 'Oh, Mam likes her.'

Letting this pass, Len said, 'As her ma there' – he jerked his head towards Annie – 'told her some long time ago . . . well, since she came out of that mad gear and began to dress like a woman, or a young lass, which she still is; well, Annie told her that she should mind her manners and alter her ways. But no, she wasn't going to change for anybody. And yet, there's been a difference of late, hasn't there, Annie? We've noticed it, haven't we?'

'Yes. Yes, we've noticed it,' Annie said. Then, as she sat down on the bench at the end of the table, and looked towards Willie, she added quietly, 'Your mother won't like it; I mean, your news, will she, lad?' she said.

'Oh. Oh.' Stumped by the question, Willie shook his head before saying, 'She likes Daisy, she does. She does. And more so lately. I mean, she couldn't help but like her, because she's really beautiful now, the way she dresses, and . . .'

'Yes, lad,' Annie cut in, 'she has changed in that way, and she has quietened down a lot, I must say that. But still, there's a big void, isn't there, twixt your family and us? And don't come back, lad, and say, oh, today there's no class business any longer. Well, that's just wishful thinking by kindly people: you know and I know there's still them and us. And being human beings there always will be. It makes me sick to hear some of them yarping on. We're all equals, they say, but they live up Brampton Hill and around the better quarters and in the houses that your da has been building. Oh, they are packed with them.' Annie smiled now. 'And what gets up my nose, there's a lot of Labourites among them, pushing education for the working classes. I thought that was already there, if they wanted it, in these comprehensive schools. Why then do they send their bairns to private schools? But there, God provides but the devil decides where to divide. Still, as has been proved and in this house an' all,' she now smiled at Willie, 'it's up to the individual. In all ways it's up to the individual. But one thing I'm going to tell you, Willie, no matter how my Daisy dresses, or what extra she puts into her head, and let me tell you she's put in a lot lately, as you'll find out, don't think it's going to change her character. She's too strong that way. She'll always remain herself. And it's a pity in some ways, because she'll say what she means and upset people. But then you know all about her. Oh, yes, you know all about her by now. So, I've said me piece. It isn't often I get a chance.' She now nodded towards her husband, then added, 'But I'll say this one thing: I don't blame them who've gone to live in your da's fine houses, no, not if they have the money, because,' she laughed now, 'I wouldn't mind going to live in one meself.'

At this Len said, 'Talking about those fine houses, it's a pity they're just on finished. But what a stroke of luck, for this family anyway, that not many will be stood off now that your da's got those fields at Grey's Farm.'

Willie nodded from one to the other, saying, 'Oh, yes, he is pleased. It was a long fight, but what pleases him most is, as you say, that he'll be able to keep on most of his men. It always worries him when he's got to stand anybody off.'

'Well, he's keeping our three on, and I thank God and him for it. I do really,' said Len, 'especially Harry, for he must have been the last employed there, and it's generally last in first out. Anyway, lad, I can tell you he's made a difference to this family. Our lives have changed and, I've got to say it, for the better. Oh, aye, for the better. And there's our Mike, I never thought he'd fall for a lass, or a woman in this case, for there she is, nearly five years older than him. But he's clean gone on her. Now he'll be the next one to move out. But strange, of all of them, it's him that wants to do it properly and get married. And what d'you think? Our Danny's wanting to stay on. He wants to go to the technical college and be an engineer. Well, I say, good luck to him. But just a few years ago that wouldn't have happened, simply because we couldn't have afforded to keep him there in clothes and things. And you know something, Willie, lad?' Len bent towards Willie now and in a conspiratorial whisper said, 'It was our Daisy who put that into his head, and she said she herself would see to whatever had to be spent on him, you know, in clothes and things. Thick as thieves those two. Our Sep would have been the same, but he didn't have the chance. Sep's a bright fella and—'

His voice was cut off now by Annie, saying to Willie, 'How is the young lady getting on? Sep doesn't say much, but now and again he speaks of her.'

'Oh, she's getting on splendidly. Well, I say splendidly: in one way she's almost back to her old self, yet in another, she never wants to leave the house. It's a form of agoraphobia, and she always wants to be near my mother or my grandmother, or with the children; that is, our friends' two children and my sister Angela. At these times she seems entirely happy. Again, I just say not quite, because, although she now can suffer being near a male, she's still not quite at ease with us, although she doesn't shudder when we go near her. But, you know, Sep was the first to play table tennis with her. I was very peeved about that.' He smiled deprecatingly. 'I thought I would be the one to get her to play. But no. Then one evening . . . well, Sep got up and handed her a bat and said, "I've got no need to show you how to play, have I?" She didn't answer but she went to the table and she played with him. And we all sat there amazed. And she's even played tennis outside a number of times with him.'

'Oh, aye. Oh, aye.' Len threw his head back now and laughed loudly. 'He had a job to hide that racket. He brought it in in brown paper, and all kinds of things. But the lads chipped his ears off. Still, he took it in good part. But just think; one of my crowd playing tennis. Well, that's another thing I've got your father to thank for. Oh, aye. 'Cos Sep's got a different outlook on life . . . well, he's more like Mike, thoughtful like. He's the kind of fella who won't talk unless there's something worth talking about. You know what I mean? But, oh, I'm glad to hear the lass is improving. Does she never leave the grounds?'

'Oh, yes. Yes. We got her to the pantomime earlier in the year. And she'll go for drives in the car. But my mother or grandmother have to be with her. And you know, she never laughed, well, she didn't even smile for months. And then,' he nodded, 'it was one Sunday tea and Daisy was at her best. I can't remember what she said, but it caused Mamie to splutter into her tea. And then the whole family was laughing with surprise, and relief, in a way, because there she was, smiling, the while she looked at my mother saying, "Sorry. I've spilt my tea." And when Dad said, "Well, let's all spill our tea," she then started to laugh again. It was a queer sensation to hear her, like someone coming back from the dead. And last weekend she spoke to Dad. She opened up a short conversation with him. It was while they were in the nursery and it was about Angela's modelling. You know, she's very good at modelling animals. And I understand, she talks to Sep quite a bit. But she doesn't to me and I get peeved about that too.'

Annie laughed as she said, 'Oh my! Willie, I couldn't imagine you getting peeved or losing your temper.'

'Oh my! Mrs Gallagher, I'm noted in the family for flying off the handle. You ask Katie.'

'Well, in that case, laddie, Daisy'd better look out, hadn't she?'

'She had, Len, she had.'

'What had she better do?' The door from the passage had opened and there appeared a tall young woman, with no vestige of the punk remaining. Her dress matched her coat, which was of a soft grey material.

The sight of her made Willie draw in a sharp breath before he exclaimed, 'Oh! That's lovely. When did you get that?'

'Oh, a week or so ago.'

'And you never said!'

'Why should I?' There was a vestige of the old Daisy in her manner and tone. 'Look at this inside.' And when she opened the front of the coat Willie said, 'Good gracious! It's a soft gold colour. It's most unusual.'

'Of course it is. Of course it is.' She now spread her arms wide and turned slowly about, saying as she did so, 'It was a Paris model.' She stopped. 'Look!' She now pulled the neck of the coat back, saying, 'Read that.'

When he read the tag, he said, 'My, my! Did she keep this to one side for you?'

'Of course she did. And, as she said, this suit would turn a weed into a flower . . .'

'What's she talking about? You've never been a weed.'

'Oh, I was, Da. Oh, I was. A colourful one, but nevertheless, a weed. Well, that's how she saw me; and not only her.' Now she turned to Willie and repeated, 'And not only her, sir. Am I right?'

'No, you're not right. It was a poor simile, she should have said—' He paused now and his head bowed slightly to the side and towards her as he said, 'She should have described you as a daisy being turned into an orchid.'

'Go on with you!' She pushed at him, and he caught her hand, and as he held it he looked into her face and said flatly, 'You've got too much make-up on.'

'What!' She tugged her hand from his. 'I haven't got too much make-up on. Now you stop it!'

'I'm not going to stop it; you've got too much make-up on. Hasn't she, Len?'

Len put his elbow on the table and rested his head in it, his hand smothering his laughter. He muttered, 'Now, don't bring me into it. I lost that war years ago. There's no fight left in me.'

'Well, there is in me.' Willie was nodding at Daisy now. 'You have no need to emphasise your eyes with that black muck. You've got long lashes to begin with. As for the marks in the corners, you don't want to look Chinese, do you? You've got round eye sockets, not oval ones. And your pink lipstick would go with your suit, but not that red.'

Her pale creamy skin was now flushed and her voice was the old Daisy's as she said, 'Why I don't slap you across the mouth, Willie Bailey, I just don't know. But I will one of these days.'

'Daisy!' Her mother's voice was harsh, and Daisy turned on her, crying, 'Well, Ma! I haven't got half as much on as I used to.'

'Well, that's still twice as much as you should have. And Mr Willie is right.'

'Oh Ma! And another thing when I'm on, stop calling him Mr Willie; he hasn't got a title.'

'Well, in my eyes, he has, lass. He'll always be Mr Willie to me.'

Daisy now turned on Willie, crying, 'You cause trouble in this house, you know. You have for a long time. I've kept it to myself, but you've caused trouble.'

There was a serious expression on Willie's face as he turned from her and looked, first at her mother, then at her father; and Len, still laughing, shook his head and said, 'The only trouble you've caused in this house, lad, is in improving her. And if anybody on God's earth wanted improving, it was her. Not so much on the inside, no, but definitely . . . what am I talking about? Yes, she wanted improving on the inside, and it's taking place if she'd only let it.'

'I'm going to get out of here.'

'Well, I'm not.' Willie now sat down on the chair Daisy had vacated; then, looking up to her, he said, 'Not until you take some of that coal dust off.'

As she stared down at him, her face crumpled and then it looked as if she were about to cry, and he jumped up and took her by the shoulders as he exclaimed softly, 'Oh, love, love! It's mostly in fun.'

'No, it isn't. You mean it, don't you?' Her voice was soft and had a break in it. And she was talking as if her parents weren't standing viewing her. And after a moment, he said, 'Yes. Yes, I do, because you're so beautiful without it . . . well, just a little. And you are beautiful.'

There was dead silence in the kitchen for a moment, and then there was a quick movement that could have been the outcome of ju-jitsu practice: Daisy released herself from his hold and stalked out, and presently her high heels could be heard clicking up the stairs. And Willie, consternation on his face and in his voice, said, 'I shouldn't have gone for her like that.'

'Yes, you should, Mr Willie. Yes, you should. You did right; and to be truthful, her face did spoil that lovely outfit. It is a beautiful outfit, isn't it? I've never seen anything like it in my life.'

'Yes, it is. And' – Willie sighed – 'she doesn't need make-up, does she? Not a lot, just a touch here and there. She's got a lovely skin and lovely eyes, and . . . well, all you can see is . . .' he sighed.

As Len looked at Willie he recalled the day that this wild daughter of his had come home one dinner-time and asked them for advice on her first, second and third choices. Thank God she had come to her senses and had picked on this young fella, who, socially was as far above her as was a star, and yet there was no-one more down to earth than him. She was lucky, and he knew that at bottom she was aware of it, and, if he knew anything more, she was very much in love with him.

As Annie was saying to Willie, 'She fell on her feet when she found that shop,' the door opened and there stood Daisy.

Her face looked clean as if she had just washed it: her lips were a pale pink, and there was a thin brown line pencilling her eyebrows; there were no black marks at the end of her eyes and just the ends of her lashes were touched with mascara.

Willie immediately went to her, but he didn't speak, he bent towards her and kissed her gently on the lips. And it was a matter of seconds before she pushed him away, saying, 'You do the daftest and most embarrassing things, Willie Bailey.'

'Yes, I know I do, Daisy Gallagher. And that makes a pair of us.'

'Well, now we must be off else we'll miss that bus again.'

Daisy now moved towards her father and, touching his cheek with her finger, she said, 'Bye-bye, Da. See you the morrow night.'

'Bye, lass. Have a good time. Well, you always do.'

Her mother was standing near the front door. She did not touch her cheek, they just looked at each other. Then Annie said almost in a whisper, 'Don't let your suit down, dear.' And Daisy's voice was as low as her mother's as she answered, 'Don't worry, Ma. I'll live up to me suit the day, and more. You don't know the half of it. You will the morrow night.'

For a moment Annie looked puzzled before she said, 'Go on with you. Go on with you.'

It was a five-minute walk from the bus to the beginning of the drive. And once inside the gates, he stopped her and, pulling her into his arms, he said, 'You know something, Daisy? I'm bursting out all over with love for you. I want to shout, yell, dance, play a tom-tom.'

'Oh, Willie. You know, you are daft. I'm not worth all that. I really am not; I know myself, and I'm not worth all that.'

'Leave it to me to gauge what you are worth. I've had long enough practice, haven't I, during all your stages? From your colourful roots stage, through the transition period when your upper half was spoilt by your lower half, with woolly stockings and shoes like clogs, then into your dressy stage. And the only thing that spoilt that was your face, your beautiful, beautiful face,' – he now cupped her cheeks in his hands – 'ruined with make-up. But now you are as I've always known you could be, complete.'

'Ladylike, is that what you mean? Because if you do, you've put your money on the wrong filly, Willie.' She laughed here, then repeated, 'Wrong filly, Willie.'

They stared at each other in the dim light coming through the sun-dappled trees of the avenue, and when he asked softly and simply, 'Do you really love me?' she put her arms around his neck. She didn't fall against him, but leant back from him, saying 'When you know what I'm doing for you, that'll be your answer.'

'You've got something up your sleeve, haven't you? You've been hinting at it for days.'

'Weeks, months.'

'Weeks, months? What d'you mean?'

'Oh, you won't be kept in the dark much longer.'

'I shouldn't be kept in the dark at all. Now come on.'

'Look,' she took her arms from his neck and drew herself from his embrace, saying, 'we are going to drop a bombshell in that house at the top of the drive. Oh,' – she shook her head – 'they know what you think about me, and they guess what I think about you. But they also know, at least some of them do, that these things fizzle out. We are young, foolish, we don't know our own minds. Oh yes, some couples of our age have got three bairns now and a fourth browning off in the oven. But as for engagement or marriage between . . .'

He thrust her from him, then pulled her quickly into his embrace again, and his body was shaking with laughter as he said, 'I'll remind you of that some day when our fourth is browning off in the oven.' And at this her own body shook now and she leant against him, and then she muttered, 'Oh, Willie, Willie,' his mouth sought hers and he kissed her long and hard. And now he whispered, 'And I can't see us waiting for the next five years. Can you?'

'Yes. Yes, I can.' Her voice was a hissing whisper now. 'For who's going to keep us in the way you have been accustomed to? My stipend,' she stressed the word, 'won't do much towards it, and we're not living on your folks. Get that into your head. Anyway, come on. I'm dying to get to the house.'

His face came close to hers again and he said, 'Dying to get to the house? What for?'

'You'll see, you'll see.' And now she hurried away leaving him to pick up her case again and to hurry after her, the while muttering, 'There are times when I could shake you.' She answered, 'Yes, and there are times when I could put you on your back, and not in fun either.'

'I'd like to see you doing that, Daisy Gallagher.'

'You will one day, Willie Bailey.'

And then they were on the open drive before the house. And there was Fiona standing at the top of the steps and Bill was about to get into his car; but seeing them, he called, 'Oh, you've got here then.

Good! Good!' He slammed the car door before adding, 'Come on! I've got something to show you.' And he began to walk towards the courtyard and the garages.

Willie looked up at his mother, who was standing smiling at him, shrugged his shoulders and said, 'The lord commands, so we'd better obey.' And he grabbed hold of Daisy's hand again, but she pulled away and said, 'Go on. Go on. I know all about it. I'm going indoors.' And she ran towards the steps and up them, and into the hall where Fiona was now standing looking at her in real amazement.

When Daisy said, 'Well?' Fiona replied, 'Oh! What a beautiful outfit. It's lovely. Where did you? Oh, I forgot, you didn't get it at the shop.'

'I did. I did. It was put to one side for me. My lady friend thought of me the minute she saw it. When I went into the shop, a number of people were there and she took me aside and told me to wait, because she had a piece, she said, a French piece that was really elegant. Would I mind waiting! And you won't believe it, but there's a hat goes with it and gloves.'

'No!'

'Yes. It really is a French rig-out.'

'It's lovely.' Fiona was fingering the material now as she added, 'Good gracious! Dare I ask what you paid for it?'

'Oh, a pretty packet, for me. The suit, hat, gloves, three pieces of silk underwear, two pair of shoes – it's a pity the shoes pinch – twelve pounds fifty.'

'Never!'

'Sure thing, twelve pounds fifty. That's a lot for me.'

'Have you any idea what that suit would cost if you bought it in London?'

'Well, I would have thought it would have been in the two hundred region.'

'My dear, double that and add a bit more.'

'No!'

'Oh, yes. Yes. Let me look at the make?'

She helped Daisy off with the coat, and when she saw the tag, and not only the tag but also the inserted piece below the armhole, describing in French how this garment had to be cleaned, she said, 'You'll never get another bargain like this. And it suits you. It's as if it were made for you. Oh, you do look nice . . . no, not nice, lovely.' She stared at Daisy. Then she said, 'Come along in, dear. I'm expecting the others at any minute, I mean Katie and Sammy. And Bill has a surprise for Willie. You'll hear about it in a minute.'

'Fiona.'

Her name drew Fiona to a stop at the foot of the stairs, and she looked at the young woman who was staring fixedly at her. A different young woman from what she used to be, at least outwardly, for she still wasn't sure that Daisy would ever be any other than Daisy. But she had called her Fiona, not Mrs B, as Sammy did.

'Willie and I,' she didn't say 'me', 'have something to tell you. But I'm going to pave the way first by explaining how I have prepared myself for it, in the hope that, well, you might see me in a different light for, from where I stand now, at least how you see me now, you're certainly not going to welcome me into the family with open arms. Oh, it's all right, it's all right.' She put up her hand to check what Fiona seemed about to say. 'Just wait a minute. Wait a minute. First of all I'll tell you, I've been going to a night school at the polytechnic for the last year or so. That's why I couldn't see, I wouldn't see, Willie on Mondays, Tuesdays or Thursdays. And now I have three O levels, English, History and Social Studies.'

As Daisy watched Fiona's face stretch and her hand go to her chin, she again put up a hand and said, 'That's nothing. That was just preparation. Wait for it. What d'you think? I've been picked, I mean I've been accepted for a degree course at the Open University. I wrote last year but I had to wait, and then, just this morning, I heard I had been accepted.'

It was now Daisy's turn to be amazed to see Fiona's mouth open wide, her head go back and a great burst of laughter come forth from her, which caused her to say tartly, 'It wasn't meant to be funny.'

'Funny! Funny! Oh, Daisy! It is, it is funny! You see, I too received a letter this morning. I too am starting at the Open University, for a degree in English. Oh, Daisy! Daisy!'

Who put her arms around the other first won't ever be known; but there they were, hugging each other like long-lost friends. And their loud laughter, interspersed with the exchange of comments of amazement and surprise, brought Bill and Willie to a standstill in the hall doorway. And their expressions could only be described as incredulous and neither of them could conjure up any far-fetched reason to explain what they were seeing. These two, this woman and this young girl who, they both knew, were at opposite poles in their thinking and attitudes with regard to life and how it should be lived, were embracing each other and crying with their laughter.

'What on earth! What's this? What's this? Am I seeing aright?' Bill's voice was a boom; and when they both turned towards him, their arms still about each other, Fiona almost spluttered as she said, 'You . . . you won't believe it.'

When their laughter was rising again, Bill called impatiently, 'Stop it! Stop it! Both of you. Believe what?'

It was Daisy now, her head bobbing she looked towards Willie and gulped, 'I've got three O levels and . . . and I was telling Fiona, and something better still.' She turned now and looked at Fiona, and again they were laughing as she added, 'And . . . and when I told her I'd applied to . . .' – she gulped for breath – 'the Open University and that I heard just today that I was in' – she again flapped her free hand towards Fiona – 'she said that she too had received one this morning. And we're both going in for the . . . same thing.'

'Open University?' Willie's voice was high. 'You! You! And to have kept it dark. Oh, what I could

457

do to you.' He had hold of her now, pulling her from Fiona and saying, 'How did you manage the O levels?'

'The polytechnic.'

'The polytechnic?' Willie now turned and looked at Bill, but Bill was staring at Fiona. She had stopped laughing and was looking back at him, and her voice was quiet now as she said, 'Yes, dear. Yes. I . . . I got it this morning.' When he continued to stare at her, she said, 'Well, aren't you going to say something?'

His head jerked to the side and his voice, without enthusiasm, said, 'Good for you. Oh, aye, good for you.' Then, looking at Daisy, he shook his head, and now he did smile as he said, 'Dark horse, aren't you? A dark horse. But what's going to happen to Minnehaha? I suppose you'll bury her under your degree, eh?'

'No, I couldn't bury her if I tried. But I have no intention of burying her . . . she's going places.' She laughed again. 'But don't you think it's funny that we both' – she now put her hand out to Fiona – 'have been doing the same thing and have kept it a secret?'

'Not funny,' – Bill shook his head – 'devious, I would say.'

'Oh, go on with you!' Daisy flapped her hand towards Bill. 'There's nothing devious about either of us. Is there, Fiona?'

Fiona smiled at her but made no answer.

There was something about his father's face and his mother's attitude to cause Willie to say loudly,

'Well, now it's my turn to throw surprises. What d'you think?' He poked his head towards Daisy. 'Dad's bought me a car.'

'Really? Oh, that's wonderful.' And she glanced towards Bill and, in her old manner, she said, 'Aw, that's marvellous of you, Big Chief House-builder. What is it, a BMW?'

'No, nor a Jaguar! It's a second-hand Morris Minor.'

'Well, I wouldn't mind if it was, as long as it goes.'

'It's a Rover,' Willie said, 'and it's lovely. Come on, have a look at it.' As he went to pull her away, she turned and said, 'You coming, Fiona?'

'I've seen it, dear. I've seen it.'

'Of course. Of course.' Daisy looked from one to the other, then allowed Willie to pull her from the hall and down to the drive. But before they reached the courtyard they stopped their running and she said to him, 'He's not pleased, is he? I mean, with Fiona.'

'No, not over much; but I had thought they had this all out some time ago. Still.' He pulled her to a stop just within the courtyard and, looking into her eyes, he said, 'I didn't think I could love you one ounce more than I did, but at this moment I could say, Daisy Gallagher, I adore you. And you've done all this to get on the right side of Mam?'

There was indeed a sober look on her face now as she said, 'Yes, mainly I suppose; but then it's something I've always wanted to do; I mean, to learn English, the grammar and all that. I don't suppose you believe me.'

'Oh, I believe you, dear. I believe you. But whatever made you do it has proved you to be a very exceptional human being. And I'm so proud of you this minute I could . . . bust.'

'Burst, Mr Bailey. B-U-R-S-T.'

'B-U-S-T, Miss Gallagher. Bust.'

They were again enfolded for a moment, and then they were running towards the end garage. And when she saw the car, she said, 'Oh, I want to throw myself on the bonnet and hug it. But I'm wearing this very expensive dress.'

When he said, 'Let me take you for a run. I've driven Sammy's and Katie's, and you know I passed my test last year in . . . antici . . . pation' – he spread out the word – 'for I knew it was coming some time.' She said, 'No, let's get back to the house; we must tell them the real news.'

'Yes. Yes. Good Lord! We came full of it, didn't we? And we've never mentioned it.'

'I . . . I don't think I need to, not to your mam, now.'

'No. No, I don't think you need to, darling. No.'

When again he went to take her into his arms, she said, 'No! let's get back. I'm dying to tell somebody, anybody.' And at this, joining hands, they ran from the courtyard to the house. But as they entered the hall they heard Bill's voice coming from the drawing-room, and the sound of it stopped Willie in his tracks. 'Oh, dear me,' he said. 'Let's go up and tell Grandma?'

'They can't be quarrelling.'

Willie's voice was low as he said, 'No, not quarrelling, just discussing something, I should imagine, very deeply. I'll explain it all to you later.'

They were on the first landing when he stopped her again and, still quietly, he said, 'Never let me possess you wholly, Daisy. Always keep a bit of yourself for yourself. You know what I mean?' She stared at him, her face equally straight now, and then she nodded, saying, 'Yes, Willie, I know what you mean. And thank you for looking at things in this way.' And with this she took his face between her hands and, putting her lips on his, she kissed him gently. Then they went up the remainder of the stairs and into the nursery.

Downstairs Bill and Fiona were facing each other across the width of the open fireplace, which left a good five feet between them, and Fiona's voice was loud as she cried, 'Yes, I know. I know all credit is due to her, and I think she's marvellous. And I know that she's done this so that I would accept her, as you have so forcibly said. In any case I would have had to accept her, because Willie being Willie, he would have gone his own way in the end. But yes, as you have also said, she was wise and she's prepared herself to come up to my level so that I can't look down on her. But you're wrong there. I would never have looked down on her, not in the way you mean. And I know their intention today was to tell us they were engaged. I guessed as soon as I saw them on the drive. So, I know all this and it doesn't need to be repeated again and again. You said it all. And I'm glad she has found such favour in your eyes; but then she always did. And I'm in no way belittling her efforts because they've been double those of my own as she's been attending nightschool for over a year and has got three O levels. But our efforts, in one way, remained the same: we are both going in for the Open University course, and in English. So, would you mind, Mr Bailey, making some remark about,' her voice broke slightly here, and she gulped before she finished, 'my efforts. For, you know, you agreed to my going in for it.'

'I did nothing of the damn well sort.'

Her mouth was in wide gape as she said, 'Then you forget the night when you went on your knees . . .'

'No, I don't forget anything about that night. But what I did say was, if you wanted to go ahead with it, you could go ahead. And you gave me the impression that you were going to drop it. Yes, you did. You did.'

'I did nothing of the sort.' Her voice was deep and quiet now. 'I remember, because you were in such a dreadful state; and I remember saying that I wouldn't go ahead with it and you insisted that I should, because if I didn't you would feel more guilty still. And not only guilty, but inferior. You forget.'

'I forget nothing, woman. Nothing! Nothing! Only, when Mamie came on the scene shortly afterwards and you had your hands full with her, and still have, because she depends wholly on you, that your highfalutin ideas about further education were knocked on the head. But what did you do? You applied to the Open University straightaway. And oh, I know quite a bit about it. For instance, they get so many applicants for doing English, because it's the easiest of the lot and they've got a waiting list.'

There was silence for a full minute before she said, 'Well, if you've been informed that it's the easiest of the lot, then you have been informed wrongly. And there's nothing easy when you have to work mentally, do you hear? Mentally, for five years at least. Then your *mental* ability has to be such that your work is of the standard that will enable you to have earned a degree.'

Again there was silence between them, and she knew that if she didn't get out of the room quickly she would burst into tears. She had the weekend before her and all her children home; even Mark would be here tomorrow with his friend, Roland Featherstone, and she'd be expected to lay on a special table for an engagement party. So, she must control herself. She must get away from him.

So that she shouldn't pass him, she went round the head of the couch and behind it, and when she was half-way down the room, her way was blocked.

'Come and sit down. We must talk.'

'I think we've done all the talking necessary for one day.'

Again she went to move past him, when he said, 'You go out that door and you'll have a cold bed for many a night ahead.'

She lifted her head sharply and stared at him, then marched towards the door. It was something he had never expected her to do. But once again he was ahead of her with his back tight against the door, and, his voice different and his manner almost one of bewilderment, he said, 'What's come over us? What's the matter? Why are we like this?'

She looked straight up into his face as she said, 'Ask yourself. You'll find the answers there. Let me out!'

'Oh no! Oh no!'

He actually took her by the shoulders now and forced her back up the room and onto the couch, and, although he didn't throw her, she fell with a plump into the corner. And then he was sitting beside her, gripping her hands, and again he said, 'What's come over us?'

She turned her head fully to him; her glance was not only cool, but cold. And as he looked back into her face, he cursed himself for the domination that ruled him, at least with regard to her. When his head dropped before her gaze, his hand loosened on her arm and he turned from her and leaned forward, his head in the palms of his hands, his elbows on his knees. And like this they sat for some minutes before he said quietly, 'If you want to go, go.'

Again there was silence between them. Then he startled her by flinging round and gathering her to him.

'Why does this happen to us?' he cried. 'Why?' Then without waiting for an answer he went on, 'Oh, I know, I know. It's me. But . . . but, as I told you before, there's something in me where you're concerned. It is because you're all I have and ever want to have, and I can't share you. And yet it isn't only that; it's that I can't bear you to think of anyone but me.'

'But this isn't a person, it's a thing.'

'Yes. I know, dear, but it doesn't seem to make any difference. You see, it's as I said, it's something that moves you away from me.' He turned from her, saying, 'It's no good. I've tried. I've tried. And, oh God! The things it makes me say to you.' He swung round again and pulled her into his embrace. 'I never thought in my whole life I would ever say you'd have a cold bed to come to. Where do such thoughts come from? I think, you know, love, I'm a little insane. Yes, I mean this, at least, about you. Everything else I have to deal with, work, people, those high up and those low down, every facet of business, they're all in order in different pockets in my mind, so to speak. But when I think of you, it's as if my whole being was a pocket and full of love. But the love is mixed up with jealousy and domination and everything that I would condemn in anyone else.'

'Oh, Bill! Bill!' And when he muttered, 'It's like a disease and I know I'll never be cured of it,' she thought, yes, it is a disease, and it wasn't right, for her life was contaminated by it now. But what was the solution? Give in to him? Let him have all his own way? Let him possess her as he wanted to? And what about her and her feelings for him? Would this deep love which, in a way, consumed her, would it last? No. No, it wouldn't. Not under those conditions.

When he said, 'Everybody except me has known what you were doing,' she pulled away from him, saying, 'No! No, Bill. Nobody knew. I was going to tell you myself, but . . . but Daisy sprang her surprise on me. Nobody, no-one else knew.'

'Not Nell?'

'No. Well, she knew I had had it in mind a couple of years ago, but she thought I had dropped it, especially with all the business after Mamie came back.'

'But Katie knew.'

'No. No more than Nell. I've told no-one. This was between you and me.'

From the look on his face she felt that his self-esteem was being eased just the slightest, and when he said, 'Not your mother, even?' she replied, 'No. No. Of course not.'

He pulled her gently towards him and dropped his head onto her shoulder and he muttered, 'Of all the maniacs in this world, I'm one. And it's like being mad, I suppose. It's worse when you're aware of being mad.'

When there came the sound of a car-horn hooting, they both looked upwards.

'That'll be Sammy and Katie,' she whispered. When she added, as if in a plea, 'Oh! Bill,' he said, 'Don't worry. Now, don't worry. I'm all right. It's something to know, like a salve on a sore, that this is just between you and me, that the whole house-hold hasn't been aware of it.'

'Bill,' – her voice was very low – 'there'll always be just you and me. Can't you believe that? Everybody else is secondary, all of them. There'll always be just you and me.'

As a loud exchange of hooting and laughter came from the hall, he kissed her hard on the lips, then held her back from getting up and said, 'We'll just sit here, the old couple waiting for the family to descend on them.'

Fiona smiled, took his hand, and leant back in the corner of the couch.

When the door burst open and they came in amidst laughter, high chatting, and pushing one another, but all in the direction of the couch, Bill cried at them, 'Stop making that racket.' Then, putting his hand out to Katie, he said, 'Hello, love,' and she answered, 'Hello, Mr Bill.' Then she bent and kissed Fiona. But as she straightened up, she said, 'You all right, Mam?'

'Fine. Fine.'

'What d'you think about these two?'

'Not much, never have.' And to this there was hooting and cries of 'Many a true word spoken in jest.'

Willie and Daisy were standing before them now, he in front of Fiona and Daisy in front of Bill. When, nodding from one to the other, Daisy had got as far as saying, 'Our main purpose for . . . I mean, my main purpose for coming here today all dressed up and my face naked—', she couldn't go on for the laughter and jibes, Sammy crying, 'You look barefaced,' and Katie cried, 'You look lovely, Daisy. Lovely.'

Willie shouted, 'Shut up, you lot!' Then looking at his mother, he said, 'We came to tell you we were engaged.' And, turning his look on Bill, he said, 'I wanted to tell you outside, Dad, but the car—' He now tossed his head from side to side, as he added, 'Well, the car was more important at that moment,' which brought him such a push from Daisy that it was only Fiona's arm going out that stopped him toppling on to the nearest chair.

Daisy was again looking at Bill and saying, 'But it's a lovely car. Beautiful. And you're kind, as ever. I've got to give you that.' She was bobbing her head at him now. 'You may be . . . no, you are a great Big Bawling Chief, but' – her voice dropped – 'you're a very kind Bawling Chief, and it's our house that knows it.' And with this she leaned forward, and when she went to kiss him, he put his arms around her and she fell onto his knee amid more laughter.

On her feet once more, she said, 'And, you know, you're going to be my father-in-law. Coo! Lord! Anyway, you'll have plenty of time to get used to it before Christmas and the big event.'

'What!' The 'what' came both from Katie and Sammy and Katie yelled, 'You're not, are you? You're not?'

'No, I'm not,' said Daisy. Now she was pushing at Katie. 'Of course, I'm not. It's like you two;

it'll be years. But I wanted to put the fear of God into him.'

After she had kissed him, Bill had sat back and just looked at this young girl. If ever there had been a rough diamond in this world, it had been her. Look what she had done to turn into this beautiful butterfly on the outside, the while inside she had been preparing herself to come up to Willie's standard of upbringing. And he would like to bet, ten to one, she would outdo him in brains before very long. And how would he like that? He looked at Willie, who was now standing with his arm around Daisy's waist, and he thought ruefully, he won't mind. He'll just be proud of her. In fact, he could see him helping her along that mental road, for Willie too had a good brain on him. Acknowledgement of this fact made him more aware of his own deficiencies, and he asked himself, why he couldn't be happy for this lovely being at his side wanting to improve her mind? Oh, he didn't want to go into it all again. It was the way he was made. But he would have to do something about it, for were he to bring his real feeling out into the open concerning her, they would all hate his guts. Look how Katie had turned on him that day.

IF YOU CAN'T BEAT 'EM, JOIN THEM.

The words ran like an illuminated advert through his mind, and he repeated them to himself, 'If you can't beat 'em, join them.' It was an idea. But what would he take up? What could he take up? Good God! There was plenty to choose from.

And he was no dullard; he had a brain all right, and with a little effort he could turn it into any channel he liked. Oh dear! Here he was, thinking big again. Well, why not? In this case, why not? And there was no need for him to come home and work at nights like he often did. At the moment it was like keeping dogs and barking yourself; there were others on the site to do what he did now. So an hour or so a night could be given over to . . .

There was the sound of a commotion in the hall and Sammy cried, 'It's Nell.' And when he hurried down the room and opened the door, Nell was about to push it from the other side. When she saw them all together in the room, she said, 'What's this? Having a party already?'

Bert, coming in behind her, called, 'Hello, there, Sammy. Hello, there, Katie.'

Then Nell, who had stared at Daisy for a moment, exclaimed, 'Why! Daisy, you look . . .'

'Don't say it, Mrs Nell. I'm respectably dressed. I'm barefaced, but that's the only change in me; inside I'm just the same. My mouth will tell you that.'

'She's not just the same, Nell,' Willie was crying now. 'She never will be again. We are engaged.'

'Eng . . . engaged? Oh! Lovely! Lovely! Congratulations, dear!' Nell was kissing Daisy and Bert was shaking Willie's hand; and then Nell said to Fiona, 'What d'you think of this, eh?' Although, in her own heart and soul she was thinking, oh, dear me! Oh, dear me! Another trial.

Bill was now asking Bert where the children

were, and Nell answered for him, saying, 'Well, where they always are, upstairs in the nursery.' Then looking over the back of the couch to where Katie and Sammy were standing, she called, 'Now, you're all set. That's the pair of you.' Only for Bill to pull himself to the edge of the couch and say 'You don't know the half of it, nosey. Look, Willie, run upstairs and bring Gran and Mamie down, and the children. This event, and others to be revealed to you, Mr and Mrs Ormesby, deserve a toast. And you, Sammy and Katie, go and bring in some sherry and glasses and a tray of lemonade for the children.'

When Mrs Vidler entered the room with Mamie and the three children, followed by Willie, she hesitated for a moment while looking up the room to where Daisy was standing. Then she exclaimed, 'Good gracious! Daisy. I . . .' She stopped. And Daisy, walking towards her, said, 'I know what you're going to say, Mrs Vidler; you hardly knew me. And it's me, all right. You've only got to listen to me, haven't you?'

'Oh, my dear girl—' but what she would have added was interrupted by the clinking of glasses on the tray Sammy was carrying into the room. But she wasn't to be denied. 'Are we going to have a party?' she called out to her daughter.

'Not quite, Mother,' said Fiona, and something in her voice made Mrs Vidler walk over to her and ask, 'Are you all right, dear?'

'Yes, Mother, perfectly all right. Come and sit down here.'

When Mrs Vidler sat down, she glanced about her as she said, 'All the family's here except Mark. That's nice, isn't it? It isn't often we're all together now.'

The next five minutes was taken up with the clatter of glasses and settling the children with their mugs of lemonade.

Mamie was seated beside Angela and in the process of pushing the end of her handkerchief into the top of the child's dress and saying, 'You don't want your frock splashed, do you? because this is the one you like.'

Daisy stopped in front of her, saying, 'Still busy at your nursing, Mamie?'

'I . . . I wouldn't call it nursing, Daisy, not real nursing.' The words came slow but clear.

'Oh, I don't know,' said Daisy. 'I'm told that children's nursing is more trying than looking after adults.'

Mamie looked up into Daisy's face as she said, 'I'm so glad you're going to marry Willie, because Willie's nice. He's like Sep, isn't he?'

For a moment Daisy couldn't find an answer to this, until a quick thought flashed through her mind, and she said, 'Yes, they both have many of the same qualities, the main one being that they're kind.'

Then she was given another question before she had time to remark on the previous statement.

'Will Sep be coming today?'

'Oh, not today, I don't think. He's . . .' She couldn't say that Sep was going to a disco tonight, but she also knew that if he had been invited up here he would have jumped at the chance. She saw the disappointment plain on the girl's face and she heard herself saying, 'He'll likely be over tomorrow; that's if you would like him to come and give him a game.'

'Oh; oh, yes, I would like that. Yes.'

'Well . . . well, I'll tell him.'

'Thank you. Thank you, Daisy.'

What she must do is tell Willie, and get him to ask Sep over. She'd have to have a talk with their Sep. He was very fond of Mamie, she knew that, but fond wasn't enough. And the girl was quite normal now. Quiet, yes, but quite normal. At times she talked very sensibly and thoughtfully. And what was more, she was quite rich in her own way. But Sep wasn't the mercenary type and he had taken to her from the first time he saw her, and she certainly hadn't been very attractive-looking then, and had been petrified of Sep. It would be odd, wouldn't it, if . . . 'Oh, all right! All right! I can hear you.' She was answering Bill, and he countered with, 'Well, if you can hear me, come over here and stand near this bloke that you've inveigled into giving you a ring . . . By the way, where's your ring?'

'I haven't got one.'

This brought remarks from all around the room, 'You haven't got a ring?'

'No. I wouldn't have one. Willie wanted me to have one; in fact, he had it picked out for me, but I wouldn't have it.'

Bill's words came slowly now as he said, 'Would you mind telling me your reason for not having a ring, when you tell me you're engaged to be married? It's usually done with a ring.'

'Well, I'm not a usual human being, as you know. So I said, no ring until I know how . . .' She stopped and glanced at Willie, and they exchanged a smile before she turned to where Fiona was now sitting on the edge of the couch, and her voice was soft as she said, 'I wanted to know how I was going to be received first; or if I *would* be received. I wasn't going to put myself where I wasn't wanted.' This caused the concerted response, 'Oh, Daisy!' And Bill exclaiming, 'Did you ever hear anything like it in your life? She's got a nerve, you know, when you think of it.'

'Dad! Get on with it, will you?' And to this Bill answered, 'I can't get on with it until I'm offered a glass; until we're all offered a glass.'

There was a scramble now to bring the tray of glasses round, and when everyone had a glass in his hand, Bill looked at the pair in front of him, and began, 'Willie is my son,' then paused, and in the pause Willie bit tight on his lower lip because he really felt that this man was his father, not the man he had never known and whom, by all accounts, he wouldn't have liked. This man, he could say, he loved.

Bill had resumed his toast, 'And if I'd had to choose a wife for him from all the smart, beautiful and clever girls in this town . . . in this county, I

474

would have picked on Daisy Gallagher. So, let's drink to them both.'

As the glasses were raised and voices mingled, crying, 'To Daisy and Willie. To Daisy and Willie.' Bill said, 'Just stand where you are and hold on to your hats, so to speak. And Mrs Vidler, would you mind moving your carcass from the couch for a minute and standing by me?'

'Not at all, sir. Not at all. How could anyone resist such a polite invitation?'

Bill now shouted to Katie and Nell, 'Stop your giggling, you two! And listen. But first, I want you, miss.' He now tugged Daisy from Willie's hold and pushed her towards the couch, saying, 'Take your seat next to your marra.' And when Daisy was plopped down beside Fiona, they looked at each other, then laughing, they turned back to Bill who was pointing towards them as he cried, 'There sit the two most devious people I've ever come across.'

'We're not!' Fiona and Daisy's voices were mingled in protest, and to this he answered, 'Shut up!' Then, looking at the others about him, he said, 'Minnehaha, there, has, for your information, been attending the polytechnic for the last year or so, and she has gained three O levels, one in English, one in Social Studies and one in History.' Exclamations of well done and good show came in high tones from the others and again Bill cried, 'Shut up, will you! You haven't heard it all. Moreover, some time ago, she applied to the Open

University. Do you hear? The Open University. But that's not all. She didn't know, nor did anybody else, that my wife had secretly applied at the same time and was also preparing herself to take up a degree course in English. And this day as ever was, this very morning, they both received letters of acceptance.'

'Well I never!'

'Good for you!'

'I can't believe it.'

'And you've kept this to yourself all this time?' This was Nell's voice above the rest. And now she was stabbing her finger into Fiona's chest, saying, 'I thought you and I were as close as sisters?'

And Bill now shouted back at her, 'Now you know, don't you? If her husband didn't know, why should you?'

'Because, Bill, women talk to each other; they can't get through the stupidity of men!'

'Quiet, all of you!' said Bill. 'Let's drink again to two wonderful people and the Open University.'

When glasses were again raised and there was about to be more chatter, he said, 'Just one minute. There is enough deviousness about when it is practised by two individuals, and I'm not going to add to it, so, I will come into the open. There's a saying, "If you can't beat 'em, join them." And so I have decided after deliberation that I might have a shot at this Open University lark myself. There are two subjects I've always been interested in, one is maths – I was pretty good at maths at school, up to a certain level, of course – the other is geography. Even as a boy I could tell you the produce of most countries and their capitals and a river here and there. I loved maps. You see, and you must know that with my set-up, I can't see me going into old age sitting watching her expanding her mind while I'm going into my dotage and spluttering over my porridge.'

The laughter became mixed with high-voiced comments of 'Oh, we can all see that,' and, 'Well, you're near that stage now. Don't you think it's too late to be trying a different tack?' And from Sammy, 'You know, Bill, maths is not just figures; it's mainly ideas.'

'Well, sir, I've got the idea that I'll put you in your place one of these days.'

As the back-chat and laughter went on, Fiona looked at this man whom she loved so dearly, who was big in all ways, but who had a flaw in him that touched on her life and could wipe out all his good points; and he knew this.

If you can't beat 'em, join them.

And he would do what he said. He would take up something. It would have been quick thinking to choose maths and geography. Even if he could take those, what good would this boastful attempt do him in the end? In her case, she had seen the course at the Open University as a sort of fulfilment, and at the same time as a freeing of some part of her shackled mind. And it had been shackled by her love for him: everything had revolved around him, because he had demanded that it should.

And so it would go on.

If you can't beat 'em, join them.

Oh, Bill Bailey! Bill Bailey!

THE END

BILL BAILEY: AN OMNIBUS
by Catherine Cookson

Bill Bailey came into the life of young widow Fiona Nelson and her three children as a lodger. He appeared to be ordinary enough but behind his rough charm lay some remarkable qualities, which were to have a great and lasting effect on the future lives of Fiona and the children.

Before long Fiona and Bill are married and they embark on a life together. They adopt a child and have one of their own. But their path is never smooth, and fluctuating fortunes take them from success to failure and back again . . .

Collected together in one volume for the first time, Catherine Cookson's first three Bill Bailey novels are richly entertaining tales of family life and relationships which touch the heart and offer much shrewd observation of the human condition.

Three magnificent novels in one volume:

BILL BAILEY
BILL BAILEY'S LOT
BILL BAILEY'S DAUGHTER

0 552 14624 2

A SELECTION OF OTHER
CATHERINE COOKSON TITLES
AVAILABLE FROM CORGI BOOKS

14624 2	BILL BAILEY: AN OMNIBUS	£7.99
13576 3	THE BLACK CANDLE	£5.99
12473 7	THE BLACK VELVET GOWN	£5.99
14063 5	COLOUR BLIND	£4.99
12551 2	A DINNER OF HERBS	£5.99
14066 X	THE DWELLING PLACE	£5.99
14068 6	FEATHERS IN THE FIRE	£5.99
14089 9	THE FEN TIGER	£4.99
14069 4	FENWICK HOUSES	£4.99
14050 7	THE GAMBLING MAN	£4.99
13716 2	THE GARMENT	£4.99
13621 2	THE GILLYVORS	£5.99
10916 9	THE GIRL	£5.99
14071 6	THE GLASS VIRGIN	£4.99
13685 9	THE GOLDEN STRAW	£5.99
13300 0	THE HARROGATE SECRET	£5.99
14087 2	HERITAGE OF FOLLY	£4.99
13303 5	THE HOUSE OF WOMEN	£4.99
10780 8	THE IRON FAÇADE	£4.99
13622 0	JUSTICE IS A WOMAN	£5.99
14091 0	KATE HANNIGAN	£4.99
14092 0	KATIE MULHOLLAND	£5.99
14081 3	MAGGIE ROWAN	£4.99
13684 0	THE MALTESE ANGEL	£5.99
10321 7	MISS MARTHA MARY CRAWFORD	£5.99
12524 5	THE MOTH	£5.99
13302 7	MY BELOVED SON	£5.99
13088 5	THE PARSON'S DAUGHTER	£5.99
14073 2	PURE AS THE LILY	£5.99
13683 2	THE RAG NYMPH	£5.99
14075 9	THE ROUND TOWER	£5.99
13714 6	SLINKY JANE	£4.99
10541 4	THE SLOW AWAKENING	£4.99
10630 0	THE TIDE OF LIFE	£5.99
14038 4	THE TINKER'S GIRL	£4.99
12368 4	THE WHIP	£5.99
13577 1	THE WINGLESS BIRD	£5.99
13247 0	THE YEAR OF THE VIRGINS	£5.99